SPECTACULAR
SILVER EARTHLING

SPECTACULAR
SILVER EARTHLING

Reality Collision Publishing

ALSO BY

MARA LYNN JOHNSTONE

Sweeping Changes

(fantasy novel)

We're the Weird Aliens

(science fiction anthology)

(edited and contributed)

Dedicated to the many helpful people on the internet, both friends
and strangers, who have been eager to help out a fellow writer.
I couldn't have done it alone. Thanks, everybody.

Chapter 1

"But I love terrible ideas!" Hubcap insisted. "And so do the viewers! More importantly, it's a terrible idea that's safer than it looks!" The robot waved a silver arm toward the massive purple jetpod behind him. Workers were strapping a saddle onto it, pretending to ignore the conversation. Still attached to its tree, the alien seedpod rested atop the aircar that the group had flown there in. Soon the pod would be ready. Then the safety railing would be swung open, the stem would be cut, and the jetpod would blast forward in a spray of seeds and glory.

Assuming, of course, that Hubcap could convince his director that this was just what the show needed.

"A seatbelt and handlebars don't make it safe," she said, crossing muscular arms and frowning. Taller than Hubcap and most other humans, with the tan skin and strength of her islander ancestors, Victoria Paewai could sway most people's opinions with a scowl.

Hubcap wasn't even close to being most people. "It's like riding a hoverbike," he insisted, metal eyebrows tracking upward in innocence. "Just way the heck up in the sky. But the safety guy will be right behind me!" He pointed at the burly worker wearing day-glow orange among the others in beige and gray. When Hubcap had introduced himself to the man before takeoff, he'd learned that the position of safety guy traded off on a weekly basis. Probably for the best in terms of getting the crew used to being safety-conscious, but probably also best not to mention that to Vic now.

"If the pod spins out of control badly enough, I doubt he'll be able to catch you," Vic said. She jerked her head towards the railing and the skyscraper-sized distance to the ground. Other purple-green trees stretched taller than any Earth redwood, with their branches far above. There wasn't much to break a fall into the very distant alien shrubbery.

Hubcap waved a hand. "Eh, I'll be fine. I've survived long drops before. Do I look like someone who would lie to you?"

Vic held her silence and a skeptical expression while she looked him up and down, from the pointy feet that could grip a seaside cliff, to the leg compartments that had once held bandages and now held cameras, to the arms that could rip a door off a crashed car, to the angular jaw and after-market eyebrows. Hubcap tried to look trustworthy.

She knew him too well. "You would absolutely lie to me, in the sneakiest of ways," Vic declared. "This is a much longer drop than you're made for."

Someone cleared his throat. "If it helps," said Anrik Tate, the crew chief of the jetpod harvesters, "This is something we do on literally every tree, one way or another. This tree has already been tested and everything. It's pretty darn safe."

Hubcap nodded vigorously as Vic regarded the shorter man. Anrik's tan was of the sun-worn variety, and he bore the calluses of much experience in wrangling. Despite the easy smile, Hubcap was sure that the man was impatient to get on with it.

Before Vic could decide on an answer, Hubcap's human co-host strolled past with a machete over his shoulder. "We do need a good intro to the episode," Elliot said. His red hair shone in the sun and his eyes twinkled with mischief that was a reflection of Hubcap's own.

Vic threw her hands into the air. "All right," she said. "Just don't break yourself on our first day here, okay? Of all trips, be careful!"

Hubcap clicked his heels and saluted. "Yessir, ma'am sir. I will wait until we have footage that will double our ratings before breaking myself."

"You do that," Vic said. She shook her head and crossed the deck to where the three camera people waited against the tree trunk, their pale work clothes stark against the deep purple bark. Hubcap opened his mouth in a mechanical grin, then scampered after Elliot.

He knew that Vic was concerned for a good reason. If the filming on this uninhabited world didn't work out, they were sunk. But as always in this job, the answer was to make good television.

The workers helped Hubcap into the saddle and fastened his safety harness with care. The camera crew got into position while Vic chose the best camera angles. Elliot waited with the machete.

When all was ready, the only thing left was to try several versions of their usual opening lines. Hubcap liked the last one best.

"I'm Hubcap!" he said from atop the pod.

"And I'm Elliot McElmore," said the human beside him.

"Did you know you can get paid to do this?" Hubcap asked. He leaned over to thump the side of the jetpod like it was a trusty steed, mindful of the spiral ridges that would help it fly straight. Elliot sidestepped and made a sharp motion with the blade. When they'd filmed this part to Vic's satisfaction, the cameras switched position and they were ready for Elliot to finish the slice.

Hubcap grasped the handlebars and waited, picturesque in his shiny silver magnificence (not too shiny for the cameras, but only just), while Elliot reared back and swung the machete through the stem of the jetpod.

Hubcap rocketed away from the tree with a comical yelp that he knew would make the harvesters laugh. Only half his mind was on the people behind him. The rest was busy piloting the insane piece of vegetation, which had looked much easier when the experts did it.

"C'mon, you plant," he muttered while he tugged on the handlebar. "Left! Go left!" The jetpod kept up its blistering pace forward, spinning madly beneath the saddle. Hubcap thanked the tiny stabilizers on the sides keeping him upright.

Finally the pod obeyed him by angling to the left — and about time, because the other trees were getting awfully close. Shouts from the crew filtered into his awareness. Turning his head out of the wind, he magnified his hearing.

"Look out!" he heard. "There's teeth! Teeth!"

A glance up showed a predator of considerable size swooping down at him.

He shrieked and yanked on the handlebar, slewing the pod aside just as the mass of wings and fur whooshed past. Hubcap leaned, making the stabilizers whine, and tracked the patch of black among the greenery. The creature looked much like a giant bat with stronger back legs and extra claws and— Hubcap didn't have time to stare. It was already flapping into position for another dive. He sped for the trees.

It's one of those omnivores they told me about, he thought. *It's after the jetpod, not me. Maybe I confused it by swerving.*

The wingspan longer than an aircar folded into diving position.

That's not confused enough!

The trees were too far away. He wouldn't make it, and another dodge might not help. Hubcap skimmed over his stored information about the local animals. It wasn't much, but...

He turned in his seat and roared: a high-def recording of an angry treehorn.

The creature pulled up sharply. Hubcap put his head down and powered for safety while the enormous flying thing decided that a seed pod that made that kind of noise wasn't worth it.

Hubcap continued into the dense grove just in case. Massive trunks closed around him, their purple bark and wrinkled texture making for many shadows that could hide smaller predators. He sampled the air for danger. None of the smells of this alien world were in his scent bank, so it did little good. He tried not to waste too much processor speed on the possibilities. Only when he was certain that the creature was long gone did he wrestle the jetpod around to head back the way he had come.

And I did NOT run into a tree, he thought. *Thank you — yes, I'm amazing.*

He breathed out a recorded sigh of relief as he piloted the unwieldy rocket-plant toward the big tree covered in similar pods. The crew on the platform cheered and waved when they saw him.

As if to make up for his tardiness, the safety guy met him halfway across the open space and showered him with praise.

"Well done!" the beefy human shouted as he pulled alongside on his own pod, having to yell over the sound of both pods jetting steam. He steered with the confidence of long practice, as if he rode reliable technology instead of an alien plant that would run out of steam in a few minutes. "That was the perfect thing to do," the man said. "Those guys hate treehorns! The only prey animal around here that really makes them keep their distance. Like cranky mountain goats crossed with flying squirrels; they'll charge you into thin air and keep coming. Anyway, that dodge at the last minute was downright professional. You could ride circles around anyone."

"Thanks," Hubcap said drily. "If I was one of you fleshy types, I probably would have wet myself. Now how do I land this thing without an explosion?"

The human pointed out the part of the aircar platform to aim for, and reminded him that the brakes on his jetpod had snapped into place as soon as it had spun away from the tree. Hubcap pretended that he'd known all along that he could slow down the feral thing, and managed to dock the jetpod with only minor bumps against the railing. With a thought for impressionable audience members back on Earth, he resisted the impulse to scramble free of the harness before anyone got there to help him.

"Hooray, you're alive!" Elliot greeted him, flanked by cameras and grinning like a gatorcat. "Way to surprise us all!"

"Yes, well, I just live to do that," Hubcap said as he accepted a hand down. He flashed his biggest robotic smile. "Your turn!"

But it was not to be. They needed to film other things now, which would surely be safer.

"I imagine you all want some variety anyway," Anrik said, squinting at the angle of the sun. The cameras filmed the conversation. "Can't have folks thinking that there's just a single odd job to be had here!"

Elliot spread his hands as if visualizing it. "We'll rebrand the show," he announced. "*Odd Job Off-World: Just The One*."

Anrik chuckled. "Sounds like a winner. I'd watch that."

"Have you seen any of the show?" Elliot asked.

Anrik shook his head. "We don't get any broadcasts this far into the fringes. I may have to look it up after this, though. Gotta see our moment of fame!"

"It will be glorious!" Hubcap assured him, waving Tarja the camerawoman forward for a closeup of Anrik. "That confident posture, the chiseled jaw — this is a boss who knows what he's doing. He's not held back by the fact that he's a meaty fleshling."

"Mostly," Anrik added, stroking his chin with metal fingers.

"Mostly!" Hubcap agreed. He inspected the cybernetic hand. "I almost forgot. It's very dashing."

"It's very useful." Anrik pulled up his sleeve to show an arm that shone gunmetal gray to the elbow. "Much tougher than the one I lost. Fair warning to your viewers: we get hazard pay for a reason here, and it's not just the risk of space frenzy. Though that's a big part of it too. If anyone's found a cure yet, it hasn't reached us."

"Don't forget the wildlife that wants to eat you," Hubcap said. "So what happened, did you crash into a tree?"

Elliot tried to steer the conversation in a lighter direction, but Hubcap insisted on a full rundown. It would be up to the editing department back on Earth whether the footage would be used.

"At any rate, that was in the early days before we had a full grasp of how powerful the pods are," Anrik said. "We could have used some sturdy metal folk like yourself to help us out, but at that point they were expensive things to buy, not people to hire, so the beancounters wouldn't have it." He shrugged and pulled his sleeve back down. "You'd think things would be different now, but change is slow around here. Anyways, we should get moving. This was a good spot for a test flight, but the real action is up at the big cluster."

An explosive hiss made Hubcap whirl, his arms out to shield the humans. Workers looked up at him, nonplussed, while the jetpod that had just been freed of its saddle rocketed away into the forest.

Hubcap was glad he couldn't blush. He'd seen Elliot do it, and it seemed to make embarrassment extra humiliating. He straightened up and turned back to the conversation like nothing had happened.

Anrik thankfully played along. He directed the workers to stow the saddle below deck and get ready to move up the tree. "Take your places," he said to the TV crew. "Check your safety clips and don't drop those cameras when we lift free."

They did as he suggested, turning off the cameras for the time being and trooping over to line up against the railing. There they tugged on their harnesses and made sure the cables were securely fastened to the hooks. Hubcap also took the precaution of casually grasping the railing in case the ride was bumpy. Elliot did the same, scolding the cameraman next to him for being slow to check his own safety gear.

Hubcap could hear the workers snickering at all the precautions. Experts that they were, no one was making them wear safety clips. Hubcap pretended not to notice. Instead he watched as they shut the hatch to the aircar's cabin, then took their own positions and waited while the engines roared to life.

"Heave-ho!" someone shouted from below deck, moments before the platform jolted and pulled away from the tree. Hubcap simply clamped down on the railing more firmly, noticing that Elliot flinched in a dramatic human fashion. The robot opened his jaw in a smile and tilted his head so his co-host could see it.

"Silence, toaster oven," the human said with dignity.

"Whatever you say, meatbag."

The rough tree bark was moving past them more quickly now, and in no time they had reached the most expansive cluster of jetpods. The TV crew held onto the railing while the aircar maneuvered up close to the trunk, coming to rest with a thud. Something underneath them whirred to clamp the rig in place.

"Nets!" Anrik called, heaving a pile of black cord up onto the platform. While the workers converged, he closed the hatch and told the newcomers to just watch for now. Hubcap and Elliot stayed put. Vic and the three videographers took the chance to edge along the railings for a better view of the workers strapping pods down tight.

Vic used her own camera as well, for maximum coverage.

Hubcap waved over the eldest cameraman and pointed at the straps. "That's so the pod doesn't escape if they cut the stem too short," he narrated.

"Or fly in an unplanned trajectory," Elliot added in his deadpan announcer's voice. "And kill someone."

"Right," Hubcap said, turning to look in a different direction. "With that in mind, who can tell me what Dale is doing wrong?" He gestured toward the young cameraman who had stationed himself directly in front of a pod for better viewing.

"Hey, greenhorn!" Anrik called. "Move your fool ass outta the line of fire!"

Dale realized that someone was talking to him, and raised his head from the camera to blush at the number of people waving for him to move. He scrambled to the side with a lack of grace that left Hubcap shaking his head.

"What *are* we going to do with him?" the robot asked as the workers continued and Vic had a quiet word with Dale.

"Remind him until he starts to notice his surroundings," Elliot said. "Either that or smack him with something next time."

"I like this plan." Hubcap pointed to his co-host.

"Cutting!" a worker announced. All the cameras turned to watch a sturdy fellow hold clippers far away from his body to sever the stem of the jetpod, much closer to the tree than the one Elliot had cut. That should have been a guarantee that the thing wouldn't erupt in a geyser of seeds, but the man jumped back anyway. The pod fell tamely into the net with a thump. The workers were already in motion, unlatching its restraints and hauling it toward the aircar.

"Cutting!" called another voice. The camera crew edged in a different direction to observe. This pod behaved as well, and so did the next.

"We are O-for-three on the explosion-versus-nothing score," Hubcap said into a camera, sportscaster-style. "But stem lengths vary. It's a tense atmosphere, and things could change at any moment."

"And that will probably be when a cameraman is standing in just the wrong place," Elliot added.

Hubcap sighed. "Dale! *Behind* you, meathead!" He pointed down at the deck by his side. "C'mere; you're assigned to railing duty until further notice." The young human kept his mouth shut and hurried to the patch of deck that Hubcap was still pointing at.

He said nothing, but the pink flush of embarrassment reached his ears. "Good boy. Now watch the dance of caution." The robot gestured toward the workers, who were keeping up a steady pace while staying out of each other's way. They hauled the pods to Anrik, who levered each one over the side with a hydraulic jack and fastened them to carrying hooks.

Elliot moved to narrate into a different camera, studying how the pods would be held in place for the ride home. Hubcap stayed where he was.

Soon enough Anrik announced that they were moving up the tree for another load. "Just a few more, then we'll be ready to empty the car," he said. "Take us up, pilot!" He shouted this last to the woman driving the aircar, giving the rookies time to gather at the railing.

"Wheeeeee!" Hubcap squealed as the platform rose again. Elliot said nothing, serene and unflappable this time. "Wooo — Aw, we're there."

"If you want to put that enthusiasm to work, boyo, I might let you have a shot at harvesting some of these," Anrik said as the platform docked. Once everything was stable, he brought out the next pile of nets and ushered Hubcap forward. When Anrik looked away, Hubcap gave the nearest camera a thumbs-up and Fist Pump Of Joy. Then he strode forward radiating calm. Elliot snorted at the theatrics.

"The first thing I want you to do — you too, Coppertop," Anrik said with a wave to Elliot, "Is to choose a pod. These should all be ripe, so pick any one you like."

Hubcap flipped his safety line forward and moved to inspect the nearest jetpods. Elliot did the same, though with far less elegance in minimizing the tripping hazard. He was efficient though, wasting no time in untangling a net to fling over a pod while Hubcap was still feeling ridges and rapping on pods with his metal knuckles. Hubcap saw, and hurried to join him.

"Faster, new kids!" Anrik laughed. "You'll never meet quota at that speed!"

The duo sped up their efforts at pulling the net into place. They eventually got all of the hooks fastened, and stepped back for Anrik's inspection.

He tugged on the straps and shoved the pod with a shoulder, then nodded his approval. "Good enough. Now who wants to cut the stem?"

"Ooh! Pick me!" Hubcap hopped in place.

Elliot pointed at him.

"All right, then." Anrik waved for everyone else to get out of the way, then produced a pair of long-handled gardening shears. "You wait for my go, okay?"

"Yes sir!" Hubcap accepted the tool with glee.

Anrik pointed to a place on the stem well away from the pod. "Cut *here*. Or better yet—" as Hubcap nodded eagerly, he tugged a pen from his pocket and marked a fat black line on the stem. "Here. Got it?"

Hubcap saluted. "Got it!"

Anrik snorted and walked to the far side of the deck. "Everybody ready?" At the affirmatives, he nodded to the robot. "Cut it clean, then jump back."

"Right!" Hubcap lined up the shears with Anrik's mark, ignoring the ominous melody that his co-host was humming. "Cutting!" he announced, then sliced and leapt back like it had bitten him.

The pod thumped to the deck, swaddled in netting.

"Woo!" Hubcap said.

"Aw, no explosion," Elliot said. "I mean, good job."

"Let's get it in place, boys," Anrik hurried them on. Hubcap set down the shears and joined Elliot in wrestling their catch toward the rail. The ridges made this more than a little challenging. Workers and camera crew moved around them, doing their best not to bump into each other. They were mostly successful.

When the pod rolled farther than expected, causing a worker to jump back, he collided with Graham the cameraman.

"Whoa, sorry!" Graham said, regaining his balance.

"Watch where you're standing!" the local snapped. "You're in my way!"

"I said sorry," the elder cameraman repeated, eyeing the younger man and stepping back, lowering his camera. Hubcap swore internally and tried to edge closer without letting go of the pod. Heads popped up all across the platform and Vic hurried forward.

He's a bigot, he hates robots, he thinks I'm going to send others to take his job and now he's taking it out on Graham—

But the man was too furious for that. Face red and veins bulging, he barked "Not good enough!" His hands curled into fists and his eyes looked wild.

Graham dove to the side and rolled as the man swung at him. Someone yelled "That's frenzy!" and all of the workers rushed their comrade.

The grayhaired cameraman scrambled clear while the other newcomers stared, cameras riveted on the scene. Thoughts of *Not again* and *Not already* chased each other through Hubcap's head. He kept clear of the scuffle. They had it handled.

"Got him!" called Anrik's voice from the middle of the dogpile. "Power down!" The wordless yelling of the pinned man trailed off, and the pile of humans stilled. It looked to Hubcap like they were deliberately breathing in unison. After a long minute, Anrik gave the cue to get up carefully.

The workers disentangled themselves, each holding something small and round ready in one hand. Hubcap didn't recognize the brand, but these were obviously stunners of some kind. The man at the bottom of the pile was breathing evenly with his eyes open.

Anrik felt his pulse and exchanged looks with the safety guy. "Leaving early," Anrik announced. The workers rushed to haul in the rest of the pods, while the camera crew filmed it all.

Hubcap showed his best concerned face to the nearest camera while Elliot approached Anrik and the fallen man.

"Keep your distance, friend," Anrik told him. "No use chancing anything." He waggled the round item in his hand, which was set lightly against his own leg.

"I will," Elliot said. "I was just wondering about your type of sedative." He held up a pen-shaped object that Hubcap recognized as the match to the one he carried in his own leg compartment. "It looks more effective on frenzy than ours is." Hubcap had noticed the same thing. He listened intently now.

"I'll give you the rundown when the danger's over," Anrik said tersely. "Just keep an eye on your own for any emotion they're not prone to."

Elliot nodded, and rejoined the crew. "Everybody feeling okay?" The humans all sounded off as unsettled, but not frenzied.

"Good, cuz I'm watching you fleshy types," Hubcap said. "And any camera you break comes right out of your salary." What went unsaid was *Don't break yourselves.*

Not again.

"Careful now," Anrik was saying to his team as they opened the trapdoor hatch that led down to the cabin. "Put him in the back seat. It's farther from the door, but it has the good harness." The camera crew turned to see the deck clear of jetpods, and the fallen worker being carried toward the hatch. Anrik looked at them. "Hurry up."

They hurried, still filming. Elliot followed Vic while Hubcap took up a position beside the ladder with his own syringe of sedative at the ready. All of the camerapeople passed under his watchful eye, and he shut the hatch after himself. The aircar roared to life. It separated from the tree slowly, then gathered speed and flew back toward the base like all the predators on the continent were behind it with mouths open wide.

Chapter 2

"So Anrik," Hubcap said, "What can you tell our viewers about this 'space frenzy' business?" His footsteps echoed down the hall outside the medical wing, and the camera crew adjusted volume controls to compensate. The air here was full of familiar human scents: body odor, perfume, soap. Hubcap had added Anrik's individual odor to his scent bank earlier, and now the man glowed on his mental map the same green as the TV crew around him. None of the unknowns in the building were close enough to be a concern at the moment.

Hubcap tilted his head at Anrik while they walked, waiting for an answer and hoping that it would be one the editors would like. Frenzy was common knowledge, but the editors always wanted people to over-explain things just in case. They could edit it down.

"Well, it's terrible stuff," Anrik replied. "We still don't know why it happens. People suddenly get stuck on an emotion and work themselves into a froth. If the emotion's an angry one, it can get dangerous for everybody. We get a lot of it here, but it's worth it for the exports we're harvesting. Jet pods are in high demand, and more importantly, some of the native creatures make venom that can be scienced into the best sedative for frenzy yet. In fact—"

Vic interrupted. "Sorry, looks like the lead microphone cut out. Can you try that again? Short and punchy for the TV?"

Anrik huffed and adjusted his posture, looking from Graham's camera to Tarja's. Both videographers — tan graybeard and tawny brunette — gave him the silent thumbs-up while the others trailed farther down the narrow hallway. Elliot walked on Anrik's other side, the picture of calm patience while Hubcap nodded eagerly at the crew chief to continue.

"Frenzy can be terrifying," Anrik said. "We're lucky not to have it on Earth. Back home, when someone is really happy or angry or sad, we don't expect them to die of it. But out here, we have to keep an eye on each other, and keep a sedative handy." He pulled something fist-sized from his pocket and held it up for the cameras. "This is our latest and greatest. We call it a SedEgg." The silvery thing reflected the overhead lights, with a sparkling golden band and an odd tapering shape.

"Pretty," Hubcap said. "Why's it shaped like it came from a constipated duck?"

Anrik smiled. "That's so it doesn't get away if you drop it. Look." He bent to set the thing down, and there was a brief shuffling of camera angles. When everyone settled, Anrik aimed down the hall and let it roll. The SedEgg wobbled in a tight circle. "Clever, yeah? No losing the things when you need them most." He stood back up, and the camera crew followed. "Lemme show you how it works. Come close now."

Tarja moved her camera forward while Anrik demonstrated. He squeezed the gold band and pressed a finger against the small end, which made the wide base snap open to show a field of hypodermic needles.

"Galloping gearshafts, man," Hubcap exclaimed. "Overkill much?"

Elliot murmured agreement.

"When the frenzy takes a body, you've got to be sure that you tag 'em the first time," Anrik said. "This mess of spikes will go through a decent layer of clothes, and the sedative doesn't cause problems with overdosing."

"That's impressive. Humans are notoriously vulnerable to extra chemicals in their bloodstreams."

"I know, right?" Anrik laughed and put the thing away. "I don't pretend to understand how it works on a scientific level, but I can tell you that it *does*. We harvest the ingredients locally, and that's the main reason we're here. My crew's jetpod harvest is a nice gig for the extreme sports market, but saving folks from the frenzy is where it's at. When the jetpods aren't in season, I'll be harvesting venom with the rest."

"Would you say that's more or less fraught with danger?" Hubcap asked.

"Oh more, for certain," Anrik said. "Jetpods don't fight back. Well, not much. And there's been more frenzy than usual lately too."

"Is it a different prospect," Elliot asked, "Handling frenzy attacks that high up? I noticed you folks don't wear harnesses."

Anrik shrugged one shoulder. "We just have to be quick to react, and tackle the person to the deck before sedating them.

Otherwise somebody might take a header."

Hubcap nodded. "I'm sure it helps to have sedatives that don't waste time. And I assume that those needles have an antibacterial coating of some sort, to prevent other problems?"

"Of course. Don't want an infection from the life-saving tool."

"Good." Hubcap nodded again in satisfaction. "We newbies would do well to get SedEggs of our own, yes? They look a little more effective than our best model." The robot pulled a small hypospray from his leg compartment.

"That looks like a decent one-shot," Anrik said. "Assuming the patient holds still for you."

Hubcap flexed a metal hand theatrically and intoned, "I can make them hold still." He relaxed. "But yes, it's a bit annoying. Where might we find these?"

Anrik led the way. The hall opened up to where they could walk more easily without bumping shoulders, with the camera crew soft-shoeing it backwards ahead of the group. Anrik did a fine job of pretending this was a normal stroll through the compound. He only glanced up a couple of times when Vic silently guided the other three around trash cans and passersby.

"So what do you well-travelled TV types think of our operation so far?" Anrik asked, turning the conversation around.

Hubcap held up a finger. "It is full of danger and excitement. I look forward to learning more."

"This is a fascinating place," Elliot said. "One of the nicer-looking Earthlike worlds we've seen in a while. What's that travel slogan? *Pretty to look at and alien enough to look at twice*? And the air is even breathable, if a little funny-smelling."

"Yes, may your fleshy gods forbid you ever have to wear a gas mask and cover up your boyish good looks."

"Hey now," Elliot objected in his deepest voice. "I have *manly* good looks, thank you very much. And rugged charm."

"Nope, definitely boyish," the robot insisted. "You need a few more wrinkles to have rugged charm. Or a scar."

"Anyways," Elliot said to Anrik, "It's a nice location. We're lucky no other intelligent race called dibs first. Something to be said for exploring the outskirts of the galaxy, I guess."

"Yep," Anrik agreed. "This may be the boonies, but it's human-claimed boonies."

Hubcap made a throat-clearing noise. "Earth-claimed, if you please."

"Right; sorry. Earthlings all around."

Hubcap inclined his head in a gracious nod, accepting the human's apology.

Elliot kept talking. "At any rate, I'm glad we're here. Everything we've seen so far is fascinating. I understand tomorrow we'll go out on a science expedition with the biologist contingent. It should be interesting to see how their role here differs from the jetpod harvesting."

Anrik nodded. "That lot gets up early. They were already out in the field by the time you arrived today. Make sure you get plenty of sleep tonight."

"Will it be challenging?" Hubcap asked. "Difficult for the squishy humans?"

"Difficult for you too, I'll wager. The beasties don't take kindly to people harvesting their venom."

"I would hardly expect otherwise."

They arrived at the stockroom where SedEggs were kept. Anrik opened the door and directed attention to the one-button vending machine that kept track of distribution. Tarja filmed over Anrik's shoulder while he pressed his hand to the identity scanner. When it lit up green, he spoke into the microphone port: "For the newly-arrived TV folk." Then he hit the button six times and retrieved shiny new SedEggs from the tray.

The camera crew filmed Hubcap and Elliot accepting the devices, then shut off the cameras to properly stow their own. At the insistence of both Vic and Anrik, they made sure to put them within easy reach.

"Are these all for restocking the vending machine?" Elliot asked about the boxes piled against the far wall.

The cameras were still turned off, so Anrik answered candidly "And for when it breaks." He opened a box to show half of its contents gone. "When lives are on the line, there's no time to be messing around with proper procedure." He opened a different one. "The refills are over here, which the machine doesn't dispense. Not the easiest thing to install, but it makes for less of a pile of empty eggs to deal with. We make the sedation, but a factory somewhere makes the SedEggs themselves, and ships them back to us complete. Usually too many. But I'm not complaining."

"I see why you directed our cameras away from that side of the room," Dale said with a smirk. "Are you supposed to use the machine every time?"

"That is the official way, yes," Anrik said. "But the Earthbound beancounters who make those rules have never dealt with frenzy."

"Just how common is it here?" Dale asked, fidgeting with his camera strap. "Are there some areas that get it more, or…?"

Anrik clapped a heavy hand on his shoulder. "It's pretty common; I won't lie. But we know how to deal with it. Just keep a calm lookout. A level head is the best defense, along with your trusty SedEgg."

"And your trusty robot," Hubcap put in. "Honestly, I'm surprised I don't see others. I'd think you'd want people who are immune working here."

"We do!" Anrik said. "But the law is new enough that there hasn't been much of a chance to hire any. We only get a certain number of passenger ships per year, and well, they need to apply for the job first."

"They haven't?" Hubcap asked. "I am disappointed. Both in my fellow bots and in your marketing people. You're obviously not advertising in the right place. When the ruling first came down and I was wandering around free, I was certain that I'd end up picking trash for lack of anything better to do. Something like this would have been great."

"Maybe we can help get the word out," Elliot suggested with a glance at Vic. "Put a little segment at the end of the first episode about the need for robots specifically. I know that a lot of them watch the show for ideas."

Vic nodded. "That could increase our viewer base too. I'm sure the producers would be on board."

"I should think so," Anrik said. "I'll tell you: the first thing I thought when I heard there was a show called '*Odd Jobs Off-World*' was that it sounded like a fine source of potential careers. Your own marketing people didn't miss a trick. And thank you, that would make things better for us." He lowered his voice, eyes flicking down the hall. "It's a pretty tight balance at times, proving to the moneygrubbers that the whole operation is worth what they spend on it. Our company basically rents space here from the Earth government, and that rent is high."

"Even with the miraculous fantastical SedEggs?" Hubcap wanted to know. "If you harvest the ingredients for them here, and they're the best, you should be rolling in money."

Anrik shook his head. "This place takes a lot to keep running. And there's hazard pay for a reason, not to mention more safety inspections than you'd expect for someplace this far from Earth."

Vic frowned. "Is it because of the frenzy, or other dangers?"

"Probably both, though the inspectors really only got interested when they started getting higher-than-average reports of frenzy here. Never mind the fact that we're handling it just fine. They're still poking their noses in to make sure we do things by the book!" He sighed in exasperation. "I shouldn't complain. They're just following the rules like the rest of us. But it gets a little irritating."

Vic glanced at the inert cameras. "We understand. There's been more attention than usual thrown our way since a frenzy incident last season. If our next few episodes don't make enough profit to pay off the fines, we'll be shut down. But that's strictly off record."

Anrik nodded and touched a finger to his lips. "Not a word."

Elliot sighed. "Add that to the usual pressures to get more people watching with each episode," he said. "They're not making it easy on us. Never mind how many people are helped and entertained, or how many businesses get showcased, it's all about the ratings and viewcounts."

Hubcap nodded with vigor. "There is rampant asshattery in the command structure. That's off record too."

Anrik draped a companionable arm across the shoulders of each co-host and spoke to Vic. "My friends, I think we can help each other out. Let's see what kind of TV-worthy excitement we can rustle up in the remainder of the day to encourage some of your metal viewers to come join the fun."

Chapter 3

Elliot looked from the one-gallon bucket in his hands to the growth of alien popperweed in the emptied storage closet. The bucket was much too small to cover it. Ventilated air breezed past, carrying the smell of cleaning chemicals and the sound of Hubcap chattering on about his plan for tackling the rogue weed. The robot was the picture of confidence. Elliot, however, had done a stint of professional yard work between auditions, along with tending a garden or two of his own, and he had significant doubts.

The plant was enormous and volatile. Its leaves spread like an extra-feathery fern colored in anemic yellows, and the long stems held poppers in the final stages of ripening: rust-red seeds peeked through the seams of the long fruits. This thing had grown remarkably well for something hidden in the back of a closet.

Hubcap held out a hand. "Gimme the bucket. I've got this."

"If you say so," Elliot said, passing it over. "Did I tell you about the time I fell into a Peruvian pricker bush? And how many prickers I had to get off my clothes, skin, and hair?"

"Nope!" Hubcap said cheerfully. He brandished a pair of wire-cutting shears. "I have none of those things. Shoo."

"On your head be it," Elliot announced. "I'll be out here with the door closed."

Anrik chuckled from the doorway. "I'm sure you can handle it just fine," he said to Hubcap. "Your reflexes are bound to be better than ours. And yeah, no clothes to get the bits caught in! I tell you, nothing's more annoying than getting stuck with popperweed duty only to track the things into your own living quarters. They're ungodly sticky."

Elliot edged past Anrik to join the camera crew in the hall, where they were monitoring the screens of two remote-control rigs.

Before Anrik closed the door, Hubcap spoke up. "I have only one question."

"What's that?" Anrik asked.

"Is *every* plant on this world explosive?"

"Nope, just the fun ones." Anrik backed out the door with a smile. "Good luck!"

The door clicked shut, echoing from the two viewscreens. Elliot took a position at Vic's elbow to watch as Hubcap turned to regard his adversary. The robot angled his metal eyebrows into his best determined scowl and approached the popperweed.

Anrik had described the complicated steps that the workers usually took to remove the weeds, using tarps, tape, and several people. Elliot would have liked to use the trusted methods, but he'd been outvoted. Hubcap had made a convincing case that this way made better television. Surely he could snip the stems without setting the poppers off, and pin everything between the bucket and the floor rather than the corner that the plant was smugly occupying at the moment. Surely.

Elliot knew full well that the robot had never trimmed a plant before, but it was Vic's choice as director, and the tall woman had been grinning when she gave him the go-ahead. The people in charge of casting hadn't shared their reasons, but Elliot was fairly sure that this sort of shenanigans was what they'd had in mind when hiring the two co-hosts. Elliot had the levelheaded demeanor and the TV experience, while Hubcap had the enthusiasm.

It's a good thing we emptied the closet first, Elliot thought. *Just in case those phenomenal robotic skills aren't up to doing this without a mess.*

He watched as Hubcap settled on a line of attack. The robot knelt on one knee with the bucket clamped in place with his other leg (something that Elliot winced at on behalf of his own knees), then positioned the bucket as best he could. It was still far too small, but it would catch some of the seedsplosion. With all the care of a surgeon, Hubcap lined up the shears and closed his metal fingers around the bundle of stems.

Elliot stifled a laugh as red seeds exploded in all directions. The first popper set off the others in a rolling cacophony of tiny impacts, thundering into the bucket and peppering the robot as well as the walls. The camera crew managed to keep their reactions to a professional volume. Anrik brayed with amusement.

On the viewscreen, Hubcap held his position until all the popping was done. Then he snipped through the stem bundle and trapped the spent weeds under the bucket.

"I got it!" he called through the door.

Elliot swung the door open with cameras behind him, and he burst into laughter as he surveyed the scene. "You sure did!" he said.

"You got it right in the face. Can you even see?"

Red seeds covered the robot's eye sensors along with the rest of him. Hubcap turned his head toward the wall. "Who said that?"

Anrik appeared at the door with a wet cloth, saying nothing but grinning widely. Hubcap accepted this and wiped his face with dignity. Anrik produced more wet cloths and a pair of squeegees.

Elliot joined him in tackling the walls. "So, Peruvian pricker bushes," Elliot said. The cameras filmed from the corners and the doorway. His voice was calm, measured, and full of amusement. "They're an accidental success of a hedge, cultivated for their berries and kept as an effective deterrent to trespassers. Depending on the season, a plunge into one of those might land you in the hospital. I was lucky, and only got the small prickers."

Elliot and Anrik traded anecdotes about disobedient plant life while they cleaned the closet and Hubcap cleaned himself. This sort of talk made for more interesting footage, a better rapport with the show's guest stars, and it made the experience more enjoyable for everyone.

Plus it made Hubcap roll his eyes each time Elliot came out with yet another story about things he had done or seen. "You did not have seeds sprout in your shoes," the robot said. "You made that up."

"They really did!" Elliot insisted. "I'd walked through newly-seeded soil and got a bunch jammed in the treads, then left the boots outside in what turned out to be a really damp area. I forgot where I'd put the boots, and by the time I found them, there was a tiny crop of sprouts growing from the bottom. They were lying on their sides, see, and got just enough sun."

"Sure they did."

All told, the adventure took less than an hour, which left them with more free time before dinner. Anrik had another idea. Once the weedy mess was bundled away into the trash and the brooms and whatnot were put back in the closet, Anrik led the way eagerly toward a different part of the compound.

There was something else just perfect to throw a robot at.

"So, how alien would you say these creatures look?" Elliot asked as they walked, with cameras trained on the conversation. These hallways were color-coded differently from the last, but were otherwise identical. "On a scale of 'cutesy puppy' to 'tentacle horror'?"

"Eh, tentacle frog?" Anrik replied. "They're weird looking, but not too bad. Just don't touch 'em without gloves."

"That toxic?" Elliot asked.

"I'll say yes, shockingly toxic," Anrik said. "I wasn't around for the initial discovery of the little critters, but I would bet you money that there were fatalities. And they're not even aggressive; you just can't touch them."

"Until you need to, for science." Elliot looked over his shoulder. "You ready to wash some tentacle frogs, Invulnerable One?"

But Hubcap wasn't there.

A confused moment later, his voice could be heard down an adjoining hallway, with the distinct tone of taking someone to task. "Prop that up this instant; it's about to fall over. And who decided to store this medicine on its side? The sediment will clog the applicator. Do you lack the strength to lift — here, let me do it. Honestly. Humans."

Vic and Elliot spun to follow the sound.

Anrik smothered a curse. "What is he doing?" he demanded. "He's not allowed in there. *I'm* not allowed in there!" He pointed at the orange stripe on the wall. "I only took us around the back as a shortcut!"

Elliot let Vic handle Anrik's questions, tuning them both out. He'd reached a door that was just swinging shut, with an indignant robot and confused humans on the other side. He didn't bother to read the sign over it. "I'll get him," he said to Vic. "You guys stay out here. Let's not make it worse." He slipped inside to a well-lit room that smelled of antiseptic.

Hubcap was fastening tongue depressors to an IV hose with medical tape, while chastising the medical professionals for not fixing the kink in the line earlier. "Using partially-activated cooling gel is one thing, but there is no excuse for this. The patient is unconscious and would not notice that the medicine isn't reaching her, and I will NOT have that on my conscience."

A man standing behind him was insisting that he'd been about to fix the problem himself, but Hubcap wasn't convinced.

"Hubcap," Elliot said from the doorway. "This isn't your job."

The robot pointed a tongue depressor at him. "It still needs to be done."

"I think they can handle it now." Elliot looked from Hubcap to the woman on a gurney with bandages on her arms, to the half dozen people in medical scrubs wearing expressions that ranged from confusion to suppressed anger.

"Will you get him out of here?" exploded a man with his arms full of medicine bottles. "He just waltzed in and—"

An older woman with an air of authority made calming gestures and the man shut his mouth with a click of teeth. "Your expertise is appreciated," the woman said to Hubcap. "We have things under control. You may go back to your previous task with a clear conscience."

Hubcap muttered and strapped more tape in place, then set the supplies on a desk and moved toward the door. He turned back to push the tongue depressors farther from the edge, and left with his head held high. "Do your best, humans. I'll be around if you need me."

Elliot held the door open for him. While Hubcap fended off attention from the camera crew and a distraught Anrik, Elliot waved apologetically and whispered "Sorry."

Before he could leave, the older woman pulled him aside. "I've trained with rescue bots," she said in an undertone. "I always figured they'd be opinionated when off the clock. See if you can keep an eye on him, all right?"

"Yes ma'am," Elliot agreed. "He's been retired for longer than I've known him, but that doesn't stop him butting in. And opinionated doesn't begin to cover it."

"I can see that. If I'd put in as much time as he probably has in getting humans out of self-inflicted predicaments, I'd be opinionated too."

Elliot nodded. With another wave, he stepped outside and closed the door.

* * *

Hubcap didn't need protective gear for safety's sake, but he'd learned long ago that it was easier to remove the gear than to wash his various seams and joints to perfection. So when the TV crew was barred entry to the new filming location unless they suited up with gloves, aprons, and long-sleeved plasticky clothes, he went along with it. Not without critiquing the fashion, of course.

"This is lovely," Hubcap said. "Marshmallow mystique. Or Trashcan Liner Lifestyle." He posed, modeling the white clothes under the room's multicolored lighting: clear from the ceiling, blue and green from the various fish tanks that lined the walls. "This will be all the rage once our viewers catch sight of it, I'm sure."

He hoped for witty banter from Elliot, since the cameras were coming online, but Elliot was deep in conversation with Vic and the local authority figure. A glance toward that side of the room showed a tall thin person of indeterminate gender but very stubborn body language. Apparently there was some convincing to be done if the duo were allowed to handle things they shouldn't.

A sound of disgust pulled Hubcap's attention back to the camera crew. Dale was coughing about a sudden smell, while Graham waved a hand in front of his face and Tarja tried to pin the blame on something in the tanks.

Hubcap blinked over to heat vision long enough to spot a warm patch of air, then shared his findings. "Let the evidence show," he declared, "That there is a cloud of gas the exact temperature of a human's insides following Tarja." He pointed with a flourish.

The woman gave him a withering look while her coworkers exclaimed in amusement and Anrik chuckled from his seat next to a table full of more tanks.

"Thanks a lot, Hubcap," Tarja said.

"You're very welcome! Just putting my abilities to their intended use."

She busied herself aiming her camera at the nearest blue tank. "Keep it up, and I am going to unscrew your feet."

Hubcap barked a laugh and spun on his heel, striding over to thump down into a chair next to Anrik.

"I need my feet," Hubcap told him.

"I'm sure you do!" Anrik said with a grin.

While the camera crew got to work filming background footage, a door opened with a clang, admitting a delicate twig of a human. Her hair was a pale green that certainly wasn't factory standard. She wore gloves that reached her armpits, and she carried a sealed bucket that sloshed as she hauled it up onto the table by Hubcap and Anrik.

She gave them a nod of greeting. "'Scuse me," she said. "Food for these guys."

Hubcap rotated in his chair. "Feeding time? Let's get the cameras over here!"

The woman shook her head as Hubcap waved at the crew. "Not yet, just putting it here for later."

"Oh. Pity." Hubcap lowered his arm. "What do they eat?" He glanced at the pale blobby things in the tank while the woman wrenched open the bucket to show him.

"It's a variety of plants," she said, fishing out a handful of stringy seaweed. "This tank is all new captures, and we're trying to find something they like."

"Looks tasty," Hubcap said. He peered into the bucket. "Leaves and stems and slimy, slimy water plants. Is that one tied in knots?"

The woman looked where he pointed and pulled up a tangled mess of waterweeds. She frowned. "That could explain why Ilsa didn't get much gathered this morning. What a waste of time." She tried to untangle the clump, only succeeding in freeing a couple strands that were studded with complicated knots. "Excuse me," she said. "I need to have words with someone." She gathered the dripping bundle and left with another curt nod.

"Well," Hubcap said. "Guess we didn't need to film that. Getting people in trouble isn't good TV."

"Not unless it turns out that the animals did it instead of the human!" Anrik said, spreading his fingers. "Big exposé: Scientist Blamed For Slacking Off, Discovers Knot-tying Talent In Wildlife!"

Hubcap pointed at the tank. "That wildlife?"

Anrik shrugged. "Eh, probably not."

"Yeah, these barely have heads, much less hands." Hubcap gave the slow-moving creatures inside the tank some proper scrutiny. They oozed through puffs of algae like apathetic snot balls — shapeless, yellow-white, and underwhelming. "These look nothing like frogs. Anrik, your eyes are broken."

Anrik shrugged, adjusting the glove on his metal hand. "More like frogs than puppies."

"So's your mother," Hubcap replied.

Anrik laughed at that. "Man, it must be a long time since I've talked with a robot if that surprised me. I would expect a 'So is your maternal unit,'" he said, affecting an electronic voice.

Hubcap looked away from the heavily-reinforced glass tank to regard Anrik. "I've got to ask, are you sure there aren't any other reasons why there are no robots here?"

"No, it really is just a matter of hiring new people," Anrik said. "There's pretty high turnover, with a ship every three months. That's for supplies and passengers both, which is why things tend to break and stay broken." He gave Hubcap a sidelong look. "Like medical equipment. Folks get creative with temporary fixes."

"Hmf. I would have brought more duct tape if I'd known."

"You lot aren't staying the whole three months though, are you?" Anrik asked. "Don't you have a special ship coming sooner than that?"

Hubcap nodded. "We've got two weeks. That should be enough to film material for several episodes, then we're off to the next place while they edit the footage. I hear the next one's an asteroid mining colony."

"Is that the kind of thing you usually film? I haven't even seen an ad for the show. Sorry. I'm sure it's good."

Hubcap waved a hand, turning back to stare into the tank. "We do whatever we can find that makes good TV, with people who will let us film there. Speaking of which, is that critter … no, it stopped. I thought it was going to do something interesting."

"I don't think these do much at all," Anrik said. "I'm mainly on jetpod duty, but I think they're always pretty calm."

"Yes, you get the glamorous job, wrangling dangerous things! You must be highly respected by the more sedentary types."

Anrik shrugged. "Everything's dangerous here, one way or another. We're all just doing our jobs. Maybe the stories will be good for impressing folks Earthside, but I don't see myself leaving anytime soon. It suits me. Your job though, is this your long-term plan? How did you end up with this gig?"

"I'm sticking with this as long as they'll have me," Hubcap said. He held a hand to his chest. "I was selected for my riveting personality and superior build. They wanted two co-hosts, so they settled on Elliot who is a calm and collected meatbag to balance out my excitement. And he used to be in professional sports, so he can keep up with me better than most."

"Really? What sport?" Anrik gave Elliot an appraising glance. Hubcap followed his gaze. Clothed in badly-fitting protective wear, the wiry redhead didn't look exceptionally athletic.

"Scatterball," Hubcap said. "Gave it up when he hurt his knee or something. I think he planned to be a sportscaster first; he dabbled in a lot of things. But he's still fast on his feet, which is good. And he's never caught frenzy, which is more impressive given the places we've gone. There was one space station in particular that was downright deadly. They were running out of sedative, and you could see the panic in people's eyes."

"That sounds pretty terrible," Anrik said. "We're lucky here. Frenzy is a fact of life, but we make the dang sedatives, and they work well. Can't remember the last time someone actually died."

Hubcap nodded. "You are definitely lucky." They were quiet for a moment, watching the blobby creatures ooze about their tank.

Anrik glanced at the robot beside him. "So," he said. "I wouldn't have guessed you had a background in rescue. Didn't see a halo on you." He gestured toward Hubcap's chest plate, which was free of symbols.

An electronic snort was his reply. "I had *that* removed a long time ago. People came up to me with the stupidest problems." He rapped knuckles on his chest. "Got a duct tape dispenser there now. And pockets for my own stuff, not just tools for fixing injured humans."

"Must be nice."

"So nice! I can even make expressions I wasn't able to before. Got my eyebrows fixed." He demonstrated by scowling fiercely, the brows rotating in place. His angular mouth gaped in a grin. "I can swear too. I usually don't, 'cuz I get yelled at if they have to censor me too much, but it's nice to have the option now. You have no idea how much I wanted to on some of those rescues."

"I bet!" Anrik said. "You probably didn't mind leaving that behind, did you? How did you go from rescue to television, though?" he pressed. "Sorry if you'd rather not talk about it. I'm just curious."

Hubcap shrugged. "Someone talked me into an audition. Thought I had TV potential after a video went viral of me being theatrically glad to be free."

"'Theatrically glad?'" Anrik's eyes lit up. "Wait, you're CurseBot 9000!"

"Oh, so you've seen it?"

"Ages ago! That was hilarious! I kept expecting you to run out of insults, but you kept on going. Makes sense that you'd been waiting years to say all that. So were you actually called 'CurseBot,' or—"

Hubcap shook his head. "No no, that was just the title that the enterprising meathead with the camera gave the video. And I wasn't yelling at a specific person, mind you, just yelling in general. Getting it out of my system, you might say."

"Because you finally could. Right." Anrik leaned back with a smile. "Man, if I wasn't allowed to complain at all, I'd do some yelling myself. People can be really stupid."

"That they can! Especially when it comes to their own safety."

Anrik smiled. "Kinda makes you want to shake 'em like a

bobblehead doll sometimes."

Hubcap agreed heartily. "While asking the tough questions! Like 'Why are you so dumb?'"

"'Hey idiot, why'd you stick your head through a fence'?"

"And 'Just because sledding off the roof didn't kill you last time, it doesn't mean you should do it again!' And '*Why would you light a match to clear the smell of gasoline?*'"

As they shared stories of boneheaded accidents, Elliot came over to join them. "Looks like we don't get to handle the critters after all," he said. "No one is surprised. But we can film a 'Hey robots' segment here."

"Sure, let's do it." Hubcap stood tall and yodeled unnecessarily loudly to gather the camera crew.

Anrik rubbed his ears. "Hey, can you do that again? I think I can still hear a little on this side."

"Don't tempt him," Elliot said while Hubcap smiled and arranged the shot.

"Maybe he can put that volume to use tomorrow on the big beasties," Anrik suggested. "That ought to get their attention."

"Will we need to attract them?" Elliot asked. Hubcap listened for the answer too.

Anrik shrugged, stepping out of camera range. "Maybe while they're chewing on him, you can tackle them from behind."

Chapter 4

Elliot had hoped that they would find more to film that day, but no luck. Dinner came and went, and soon he was in a communication booth with Vic, preparing to report back to the showrunner on Earth. He tried not to fidget.

"I hope today's footage is good enough," he said to her while the call connected. The spinning symbol on the screen felt a lot like his life at the moment: in limbo. No one could say whether the show would be on the air much longer.

Well, maybe the showrunner could say.

Vic faced the screen squarely. "Confidence is everything," she told him. "We'll make this work."

Elliot stilled his hands and adjusted his posture, following the director's lead. If he wanted to direct someday, he had to learn as much as possible at times like these. He was glad that Vic had let him be in on the conversation.

The screen beeped, and bloomed into a larger-than-life image of the lead executive producer. She was dressed for battle. A tailored black suit coat spoke of money and power, while an artfully arranged headscarf turned her steel-gray hair the red of fresh blood. Being face to face with Ms. Salma Kaleel usually made Elliot feel like he was staring down a hawk, and today was no exception. She was an excellent boss, but more than a little terrifying.

"Hello Paewai, McElmore," she said crisply. "Tell me you have promising material for me."

Vic nodded, pressing a memory stick into a port. "Transmitting now. Today held rocket plants, an encounter with a predator, poisonous animals, and miscellanea."

"I'll have a look," said Ms. Kaleel. "You should know of an unpleasant development. There is an up-and-coming bit of drivel called 'Space Fashion' that is gunning for our sponsorship slot." She wrinkled her nose in disdain. "They're more popular than they deserve. If we can't pull in exceptional numbers soon, they just might get it."

Elliot felt weak. "But people need our show!" he blurted.

"And yet people will watch this for the hair- and tendril-pulling," the showrunner replied.

"But—"

Ms. Kaleel waved a hand. "Let's not fool ourselves. People stop watching us when they get their jobs. They keep watching this garbage in the hopes of a wardrobe malfunction."

Vic spoke up. "Do we have hard numbers to meet?"

"I'm working on it. I'm also putting out feelers for our next step if worse comes to worst. Elliot, I may be able to get you a position in broadcasting. There's an opening for a Scatterball commentator along with Chad Bachman."

"Chad? He's—" Elliot held his tongue about the old teammate with the cruel streak. "Thank you for looking out for me," he said instead.

"I've got to keep my stars gainfully employed, don't I?" She smiled briefly. "Hubcap will be more of a challenge. So far all I've found is a job as the on-site medic for a celebrity stunt show. He has all the qualifications."

Elliot winced.

Vic laughed humorlessly. "Just not the patience. Or the appropriately-sized ego."

Ms. Kaleel nodded. "It's not the best fit. I'll let you know if I find anything better. But in the meantime, let's all do our best to blow those fashionistas out of the water!"

Elliot and Vic readily agreed. The showrunner continued.

"Your focus should be on the eye-catching, as well as the educational," she said. "Get our media team something they can use to draw in casual viewers who don't need to find jobs. Unique things. They've already seen standard offworld stuff. Space is in danger of becoming mundane. You have to show us the vibrant excitement that you and I know it holds."

"Yes ma'am!" Vic said. "Tomorrow we have an expedition lined up for wrangling dangerous alien lifeforms. It ought to make for dramatic media spots."

Ms. Kaleel nodded and leaned back. "Good. Call me again tomorrow and we'll go over the highlights of your riveting television."

Vic said that they would. She and Elliot bid the showrunner goodbye. The screen went blank, leaving the small room very quiet indeed.

Elliot slouched in his chair and let out a breath. "What are we going to do?" he asked. Visions of an unpleasant future paraded through his head. Faking a smile at someone he hated each day sounded like his version of hell. As challenging as his current job was, losing Hubcap and the others would be like splitting up a family.

Vic removed the memory stick and stood, shoulders back. "Our best," she said. "Come on. Tomorrow starts early."

Chapter 5

Elliot blew into his hands and rubbed them together for warmth, stamping his feet on the concrete floor of the hangar. It didn't help. Getting up before dawn was old hat by now, but no amount of early mornings would make him enjoy being cold. Even the air smelled icy. Elliot tried to focus on that instead of the high expectations for today.

The rest of the camera crew huddled together while they waited for their guide. Thuds and clanks echoed as workers of various sorts hurried around loading gear into trucks and aircars, lit up by technology while the sun got its act together outside. The distant mountain range delayed sunrise here. This didn't help the temperature situation.

Hubcap joined the group slightly tardy, in a chipper mood that told Elliot he wasn't planning on bringing up the bad news either. "I've scouted out some interesting restrooms for you biological types!" Hubcap announced. "There's one on every floor next to the main elevators, but also several in high-traffic locations." He pointed. "The one by the break room has fake plants all along the ceiling. It must be horrendous to dust. I was hoping for another of those fish tank tunnel extravaganzas, but no luck." He took in the silent and coat-swaddled forms of his coworkers. "You lot look cold," he exclaimed, spreading his metal arms. "Who needs a warm hug?"

"Don't you dare," Elliot said as Hubcap moved closer with a threatening grin. "I know perfectly well that you don't have any heating coils."

"Ah, you're no fun," the robot said. "You're lucky I'm not made for cold-weather rescue; those guys are bulky and inelegant. Got compartments for blankets and everything. A far cry from my svelte splendor."

He posed with one arm upraised until Elliot told him he looked like a teapot.

"Well you look like a tofu hot dog," Hubcap retorted, dropping the pose. "Did you remember sunscreen? The weather will warm up later, and we don't want your delicate skin to suffer damage."

Elliot rolled his eyes while the camera crew snickered. "Yes, I remembered sunscreen. I've only had pale skin my whole life."

"Did you cover your ears?" Hubcap pressed the redhead.

"Yes."

"And the back of your neck?"

"Yes."

"And the—"

"Hubcap," Elliot said. "I even got my shoulders in case I need to take my shirt off. I'm good."

"Okay fine, but did you—"

"Say, is that coffee?" Elliot said, turning to address the local man walking over with a tray of mugs. The other humans hurried to meet him halfway. Elliot walked away from the conversation that he'd had many times, in many different forms, which got a bit tiresome. He knew that Hubcap couldn't help being a little mother-hen towards people that he cared about, and also that Hubcap would have scoffed loudly at being accused of caring for the fragile meat creatures that he worked with. Elliot didn't hold it against him. The robot had been a regular citizen for years now, but he was still finding his way. And Elliot knew that he cared, despite the way he would have loudly enjoyed making fun of Elliot for getting sunburned.

The coffee cups were disappearing quickly as Elliot approached.

"Are there any options?" he asked. "Or all standard brew?"

"Your options are 'Yes' and 'No,'" the man told him, holding out a cup picked at random.

"Then thank you very much," Elliot said as he took the cup. He kept his preference for hot chocolate to himself. His silent crewmates collected their own warm drinks, becoming more animated as they did.

"Mm, alien coffee," murmured Tarja, holding the mug in both hands.

"Alien, nothing; this stuff's Brazilian." The employee with the tray of cups leveled a stern glare at the TV people. "You guys better not be the type to call everything 'space food' and 'space clothes' and 'space forks.'"

"Don't forget the space toilets," said Graham, looking around. "Speaking of which, Hubcap, where'd you say the nearest was?"

34

The local muttered about tourists and simply pointed, beating Hubcap to it. Graham downed the rest of his coffee and hurried away with a nod of thanks. The other camera jockeys sipped their warm drinks while the man took the tray away and the locals continued bustling around them.

"Strong stuff," Tarja said. "Is it hot enough to be proper coffee, Vic?"

Vic swallowed a mouthful and breathed steam. She gazed down at the smaller woman. "Almost. Proper coffee should hurt."

"I'll take your word for it," Tarja said. "As long as it's warm and caffeinated, it's proper enough for me."

Elliot muttered into his mug, gripping it with both hands and feeling his fingertips thaw. "Yes. Warm good. Caffeine nice too."

"Especially today," Dale put in, looking nervous. "Today sounds dangerous."

"With precautions, that's a good thing!" Vic said, raising her coffee. "Here's to a fine day of filming, and an episode that will put us at the top of the ratings chart."

"Cheers," Tarja agreed, clinking cups.

Elliot nodded. He waited to see if Dale would argue about the danger, but the younger man focused instead on his drink, making a visible effort to ignore Hubcap's comments. The robot was casting pointed looks in Dale's direction while speculating about the alien creatures they would be facing off with soon.

Elliot was glad that his co-host was pestering someone else for the moment. He sipped his own coffee and thought for the umpteenth time that it was a pity no one ever served hot chocolate at these work sites. Graham rejoined them moments before the crew chief made an appearance.

"Step lively, kids!" exclaimed the thin blond man who looked a bit young to use such a greeting. He was dressed in khakis, and almost as pale as Elliot. "We're off in five. I'm Owen Cosgrove." He stopped in front of the newcomers for handshakes all around. "Nice to meetcha. How was the harvesting yesterday?"

"Full of excitement," Vic told him.

"Good, good. Ready for a day of wrangling venomous beasties?"

"Why, that is our favorite thing," Hubcap declared with an arm around Elliot's shoulders.

"You bet," Elliot agreed, his fingers tightening on the coffee cup of their own accord.

"Great." Owen grinned. "Today should be a lot of fun! Let's find you some armor, then we can get going."

*****

The gray, full-body armor was not comfortable to ride in, but at least Elliot could appreciate the scenery. The rattletrap aircar was an open-top model that made for an unobstructed view. He changed position in his seat, wind whistling over his helmet as he tried to focus on the piercing sunrise over the mountains rather than the way the metal plates dug into his legs. When the ocean came into sight in the other direction, he was struck with an odd feeling of relief at its similarity to the ones he knew on Earth.

Elliot gave the ocean his full attention. The colors of the wind-smoothed rocks behind him felt slightly wrong somehow, too dark or too mismatched next to the purple-tinged plantlife. But the water was blue with little white-tipped waves, just as it should be. Today promised to be full of dangerous things that were entirely new to him, but that was the name of the game in this job. It helped to find touchstones of familiarity.

Across the aisle, Hubcap was pointing out an unsteady-looking rock formation and talking about a rescue that it reminded him of. Hubcap always talked, and that was familiar too. The day he sat quietly for more than a minute would be the day that something was really wrong.

The camera crew were largely ignoring the robot, focused on getting background footage with the audio turned off. All that wind played hell with the microphones. Vic had suggested filming Owen during the ride, getting a rundown on the animals they would be dealing with, but it was too much for even their best tech to filter out.

The aircar came in for a landing on a rocky hilltop with a view of the shore. The dozen locals and half dozen rookies all piled out, everyone stomping to settle their armor back into place except for Hubcap. He had laughed at the idea of armor, and was laughing again now.

"Oh, it looks even better in the sunlight!" the robot exclaimed. "Tarja, you've got to get a shot from this angle. Hold still, Elliot. Strike a pose. Your helmet has a glitter finish; did you know that?"

Elliot sighed and modeled for the camera. The viewers would find it funny.

Owen hopped onto a rock and called for everyone's attention, his own helmet off for better communication. "All right! Everybody still have their SedEgg in reach?" he asked the crowd. There were murmurs of assent as everyone double-checked their special hip pockets. "Armor secure? Good. TV people, your job for now is to keep yourselves safe, and to sing out if you spot anything dangerous or useful. I'll give you a quick rundown in a minute. Larry and Jerry, you ready to scout?"

A pair of workers nodded, identical in their armor except for vastly different heights. They took off on silent feet. At Owen's behest, the rest of the locals prepared tools of the trade: bags, ropes, and odd-shaped items with no clear function.

Elliot stood aside with Hubcap while the camera crew filmed the goings-on. He wondered if Vic had told Owen about the urgency of their agenda, or if the crew chief thought today was business as usual for the TV show. Elliot vowed to keep an eye out for opportunities that would otherwise be missed.

Beside him, Hubcap narrated to the nearest camera a made-up list of explanations for the tools as the workers unpacked them. Elliot couldn't decide whether to contribute believable uses or more outlandish ones, so he kept silent. It wouldn't do to muddy the audio with unnecessary dialogue.

Owen hopped down and addressed the co-hosts. "I was going to tell you before about the animals here," he said with an eye for the cameras. "We're looking for anything poisonous, since most of the poison in this area can be used to make frenzy sedative. Of course, most of the toxic creatures here live in the water, so catching them can be tricky. The easiest way is to let the local predators do it, then steal from them. Not very sporting, but effective. Yes, a question in the front row?" He pointed to Hubcap, who had his hand in the air.

"Will we be tackling alien sharks and gutting them, or sneaking dead fish from bird nests? Comparatively speaking."

Owen thought about it. "Neither," he said. "More something in the middle. If you've ever tackled an ostrich and made it throw up, then you're partway there."

"That sounds awesome," Hubcap said. "Bring on the ostriches!"

"Really, they look more like featherless pelicans," Owen said. "Or pterodactyls. At any rate, they eat out of the sea and the tide pools, and at this time of day, they're far ashore with bellies full of seafood. Much easier to catch." He glanced up as a worker pointed out the stealthy return of the scouts. "Ah. One moment." He went over to confer, leaving the camera crew to themselves.

Elliot straightened to attention when Vic took the opportunity to remind the others of the safety rules. Buddy system; watch each other as much as the camera screens; speak up about dangers. Elliot knew the rules well — they all did, but no one objected. Elliot was aware that if anything went wrong because of the crew's negligence, it would be Vic who was blamed for it. Something else to remember for later, if/when he got to be a director someday.

When, he told himself. *Not if.*

"Let's go, folks!" Owen called, dashing back to the aircar and grabbing a bag of supplies. "Big spear birds over the rocks there!" He waved toward the south.

Elliot looked southward while the locals grabbed their things, but he didn't see much past the pale sandstone boulders. When the whole group moved out, he kept close to the camera crew and hurried in the direction that the scouts had gone. Despite shouting moments earlier, Owen urged everyone to be as quiet as possible in their approach.

This proved to be a challenge on the rough terrain. Dale and Tarja tried at first to film the running, but gave up in short order when Dale nearly pitched over a rock. Graham caught him, having never turned on his own camera.

"Sorry," Dale muttered with a glance at Vic, his face a bright red behind his visor. The director just urged him onward, then moved to catch up with the rest.

Elliot kept quiet, but Hubcap wasn't so reticent. "Good catch, Graham!" he congratulated the older man with a pat on the armored shoulder. "Way to save the young'un from denting the camera! His face would probably be fine, what with the classy robo-skin, but we don't want to wreck any equipment right out of the gate! At least wait until a monster chews on it first!"

Elliot called back for the robot to keep up. Hubcap scoffed, then shut his mouth and outpaced him. Elliot smiled inside his helmet at the show of spite.

A red-striped sandstone cliff hid the locals from view as the TV crew approached. Hubcap took the lead, waving the others into silence as he peered over the edge. Elliot joined him to see a landscape punctuated with boulders that were distractingly full of holes. The locals were doing their best to hide behind these as they crept toward the several large animals that strode around the tide pools at the far end of the beach.

Elliot decided that they did look like big featherless pelicans, with long legs to let them walk through deep water. Their beaky faces held jaws full of teeth, which seemed more dangerous than actual beaks would have. As the humans eased forward, it became obvious that the spear birds were easily twice as tall as anyone there.

Owen was still at the back, whispering strategy with a pair of muscular workers. He waved for the camera crew to hurry and join him, pointing out the easiest way down the slope. Hubcap scurried down first, then waited with arms outstretched in case any of the humans slipped on the way down. None did.

Elliot was aware of the cameras filming when Owen gave him and Hubcap the rundown of the plan. He could almost hear the background music amping up.

"We're going to move closer," Owen said. "You guys meet at that big rock, and try to keep out of the way. We'll be tackling the closest one. C'mon." He broke cover and made a soft-footed dash for the next boulder. Elliot followed, senses alert. The air through his helmet vent smelled of tidepool salt, sand shifted under his boots, and his pulse was loud in his ears.

The closest spear bird was an elegant thing, colored in palest brown with delicate patterns along its back, and eyes of piercing blue — at least four of them. Weirdly beautiful. Very dangerous. Elliot shot admiring glances as he ran, watching the creature stride around the tide pools with repeated stabbing motions down at something that eluded it.

Elliot sank into a crouch behind the rock that Owen had indicated. He was glad that Owen wasn't asking them to get involved just yet. It was becoming obvious that the plan of attack for stealing this thing's lunch was a very low-tech approach.

"Are they seriously going to lasso it?" Hubcap asked as he slid down beside him. "Fantastic. Here, can you see?" He ducked lower so Tarja could film over his head. "I can't wait. Cowboys never go out of style. Let's do this."

They did. The locals spread out and approached the preoccupied creature, all holding coils of rope in their heavily gloved hands. When they were as close as they could get without being spotted, Owen shouted and lassos sprang into the air.

The spear bird raised its head as the shadows twined around it, but this only served to put it in perfect position for at least three lassos to catch around its neck.

Elliot exclaimed as the calm scene exploded into thrashing spear bird and straining humans. Hubcap added a "Whoa, broncho!" while the other enormous birds took to the air in a tornado of wingbeats. The wranglers leaned into the wind. Several looped their ropes around boulders while some edged closer in hand-over-hand fashion, and others added more lassos to the mix. They had obviously done this before.

It didn't take as long as Elliot had expected for the crew to get the spear bird pinned on the ground. They held its limbs down while Owen and two others straddled the neck. That was when Owen waved the TV crew forward.

Hubcap whispered, "Showtime," and scampered ahead. Elliot followed at a cautious jog with his heart in his mouth and the cameras behind him. He kept an eye out in case the creature decided to throw everyone off with mayhem on its mind.

"I need one of you to get the facejack," Owen said as Elliot approached, nodding towards the bag on his own back. His hands were occupied with holding the toothy maw shut against the ground.

"Facejack?" Elliot asked, eyes trained on the sharp teeth very close to his legs. Hubcap ignored the predator and unzipped the bag to pull out a strange metal contraption.

"To jack its mouth open," Owen told him. "Now I've got him pinned; you go ahead and slide it onto his head from the front. No, the other way around."

Elliot helped Hubcap get the thing oriented correctly, doing his best to ignore the very real threat to life and limb that kept trying to buck free. By the time they got the metal frame in place around its head, the spear bird wasn't the only one breathing hard. Elliot had a fleeting thought that Hubcap was likely the only person present who wasn't.

"Why aren't we just sedating it?" Elliot asked as he followed Owen's instructions to crank the jack open, baring the sharp teeth.

Owen shook his head. "Can't. The sedatives that work on us don't do much to them. Different physiology and all that. And no one's fronted the money yet to make one that does work. So we do it the hard way; we just have to be quick. A little bit farther — there, that's good enough. Now if you can get the barf bag out of my pocket here, and tent it over his face, we'll be set."

Hubcap did that part, opening the wire-rimmed plastic bag

and placing it to catch anything that might be forthcoming.

"Perfect," said Owen. "Now flip over that bit on the side there, and press it against the roof of his mouth. Push it a little farther, and..."

"*Huerkk!*"

Splat, splash.

"Ewwww." Hubcap said it, but Elliot was thinking it. He was glad to let Hubcap handle the messy work.

"Well done! Now grab up the bag, careful not to spill — yes, twist it — and there's just one thing left to do before we undo the jack. Elliot, if you can grab my chalker out of my other pocket here..."

Elliot followed the nod and elbow waggle to find a pocket with an oversized stick of kid's chalk in it. "This?"

"Wow," Hubcap said. "That there is some stylish day-glow."

"Make a quick line across this guy's face," Owen instructed, gesturing with his head. "Across the snout, from teeth to teeth."

"This way?" Elliot mimed the motion, and at Owen's nod, he drew a bright orange stripe across the twitching jaw.

"Good. That will mark him for now as someone we've already pestered, then it'll wash off by tomorrow. Let's get the facejack off and leave this guy be."

Elliot worked with Hubcap to quickly close and remove the jack. Hubcap stuffed it into Owen's bag while Elliot returned the chalk, then the two co-hosts followed the example of the camera crew by retreating up the shore. Elliot ducked behind a rock.

The workers had managed to remove the lassos without freeing the creature yet. As soon as they were all at a safe distance, Owen called "Now!" He and the others leapt free, dashing for safety while the spear bird sat up and shook its head, flapping its wings and looking irritated but not overly hostile. It launched itself into the air while the humans gathered at the cliff and congratulated each other.

"Flawless performance, all!" Owen said. He took off his helmet and approached the rolling cameras. "Let's see what we got for our troubles."

Elliot joined the group as Hubcap held up the barf bag. Elliot removed his own helmet, anticipating seaside breeze, only to get treated to the stink of alien bile. He squinted and made a show for the cameras of waving away the smell.

Owen took the bag and untwisted it, looking inside with an exclamation of delight. He crumpled the bag to raise its contents without touching them. "Look at these fine specimens!"

The cameras gathered closer while jaded workers chatted in the background, having seen all this before. The pile of electric blue squishiness in Owen's hands turned out to be a dozen different creatures, all with vibrant coloring and odd shapes. He managed to separate one from the rest by poking at it through the bag. Even sitting by itself, the thing was hard to make sense of.

"It looks like a salamander that wants to be a featherduster," Hubcap said, inspecting the fluffy appendages.

"It's a nudibranch," Owen told him with a grin. "They're actually very like the sea slugs at home on Earth."

"Doesn't look like any slug I've ever seen," Elliot said. "No touching, right?"

"Right! They're exceptionally poisonous to humans. Useful, but not something you want to touch. It's surprising how similar they are to Earth creatures, which are fascinating in their own right. Marine biology is a subject full of bizarre creatures and odd beauty. Did you know—"

Elliot felt someone elbowing him in the side. He looked to see a brown-haired local man smirking with a nod toward Owen.

"Best never to get him started on the similarities between alien critters and Earth ones," the man said. "Our boy here has the fanciest of credentials on the stuff, and can't wait to share it."

"Good tip," Elliot murmured back. "Thank you." He stepped forward to rescue the camera crew from an enthusiastic lecture about the habits of sea slugs. "So how many of those squishies should we aim to catch today?" Elliot asked.

"Oh, as many as we can," Owen told him. "This is a pretty good haul for one spear bird, though we'll want to get a few more, and see if there are some springmouth snakes to vomit as well."

Hubcap straightened up. "Those sound fun!"

"Oh, you don't know the half of it," Owen said. "They can get big enough to swallow any of us here. Though they'd probably spit *you* back out. Anyways, let's get this puke stowed..." He wrapped the bag tightly and stuffed it into a container in his backpack, which locked shut with an audible click. "...And find us some more spear birds! You boys ready to take part in the alien bird rodeo?"

"Me first!" Hubcap exclaimed.

"By all means," Elliot agreed. "Him first."

"Sounds good," Owen laughed. "This way!" The cameras followed him like hungry ducklings.

Chapter 6

Hubcap held his lasso at the ready, just waiting for the signal. This was infinitely more fun than throwing life preservers on ropes, which was the bulk of his experience. He knew how to do a proper lasso, and he considered it a pity that he'd only ever needed to do it once, during a flood. He'd done himself proud that time, lassoing the leg of an upturned table that a semiconscious human had clung to. While that was undeniably grand, this promised to be better. Dinosaur-looking alien beasties beat table legs any day.

And it would make for excellent television if he had anything to say about it. There was no way he'd spend the rest of his career pandering to big-headed humans who did stupid things for money.

"All right," Owen whispered, "Wait for it, just until Fern gets up to that ridge." He peered around a boulder next to Hubcap and Elliot, with one camera behind them and others stationed at different rocks.

Hubcap looked to see who he meant, and spotted a tall figure with armor painted in brown camouflage moving in a flurry of quiet footsteps across the sandstone. When the woman got into position, Owen began twirling his lasso.

Hubcap wasted no time in stepping to the side and spinning his own rope into the air. Elliot had to back away from the both of them for his own attempt. The human's result was of course lackluster at best, but Hubcap wouldn't hold it against him. Other lassos were whirling, and the spear bird was just raising its head to notice.

Owen yelled "Go!"

Hubcap flung the lasso with all his concentration. It landed with the other professional efforts around the spear bird's neck. Then his attention turned to bracing his feet on the sandy rocks and hauling on the rope while the gigantic animal protested its capture. Wingbeats blew sand everywhere, making Hubcap regret not taking a helmet. He blinked his wiper panels down to shield his eye sensors from the worst of the grit, still able to make out basic shapes through their translucency. Then human workers piled on to the spear bird's wings and the air stilled.

Hubcap opened his eyes to see the creature struggling mightily against the humans. Owen hauled on his own rope and yelled commands. Elliot tossed aside the lasso that had missed its target, and cautiously joined the workers in attempting to pin the wings down. Hubcap held his rope taut as the spear bird tossed its head. He let out a cowboy whoop and edged closer.

Other workers jumped on, with someone brave closing in on the head. Owen yelled more directions while the muscular local looped the rope under his foot and put all his weight on it, driving the beast's head down. The man slid closer, keeping carefully out of reach while pulling the rope further under his foot, then the bird lunged and the rope pulled free.

The armored man didn't have time to react as the long neck snapped forward and the toothy maw bit down on his helmeted face.

Hubcap's thoughts flew to damage control as he leapt to yank on the rope. He hadn't heard the helmet crack yet. Other workers yelled and dogpiled the spear bird, driving it to the ground while it worked its jaws against the helmet, teeth grating. As its legs were knocked out from under it, the bird whipped its powerful neck to smash the captive human against the ground in a move that would have crushed the skull of many a prey animal.

Hubcap abandoned his rope and dove for the creature's head, prying apart the jaws with metal fingers impervious to the teeth.

The human was already struggling free. "I'm okay!" he said, twisting to throw himself across the spear bird's beak. Other armored figures joined him, and in moments the creature was pinned. A facejack and bag were deployed with impressive speed. Hubcap grabbed onto a rope where it looped around the neck and held on while the spear bird retched.

As one worker whipped off the facejack and bag, another appeared at Hubcap's elbow to tug the lassos forward. Hubcap released his hold and lay across the neck while the armored figure worked the ropes free.

"It's chalked and done!" someone yelled. "Ready, set, OFF!"

Hubcap sprang to his feet, waiting to see that the injured worker was running easily before sprinting to safety himself. He bolted for the nearest sandstone ridge with an eye on the spear bird. The creature shook itself and launched into the sky.

Hubcap scanned the area with a glance: all the humans were standing, none looked hurt, and the cameras were rolling. Success.

"Woo!" he cheered, hiding his relief. "Good job, team! And way to take it in the face, Nameless Guy! What is your name, anyway?"

The group converged on the man with the vicious scrapes across his armor. He tugged his helmet off with a rueful grin and a wince, proclaiming himself a bit shaken with a sore neck, but otherwise none the worse for the wear. The armor had good shock absorption and neck support.

Owen called for someone to bring out a medical kit anyway. Elliot and the camera crew gathered close.

"I'm Sanjay," the man said as he applied a cold compress to his neck. The medic gave him a once-over with a handheld scanner and nodded at the results.

"Well done, Sanjay," Hubcap told him. He put an arm around the man's shoulders and posed for the camera, taking care not to jostle his injuries while singing his praises. "Putting your body on the line for the good of all! Did that helmet take any honorable war wounds for you? Oh my, yes." He plucked the helmet from Sanjay's hand to show the cameras. It was clear where his face had hit the rough ground.

Elliot whistled. "The visor might need a little polish."

Sanjay shrugged. "Maybe a little."

"At least it wasn't your skin!" Hubcap exclaimed. "That doesn't polish well at all!"

The other workers chuckled and congratulated the man on his successful survival. Hubcap saw Owen looking around at the empty beach, and wasn't surprised when the crew chief suggested that they move on. Daylight was a-wasting.

When Owen asked the scouts to take a look, Vic spoke up. "I saw something big from up on the rocks," she said, pointing further south. "What do those springmouth snakes look like exactly?"

Owen said, "They're huge and black-with-gray, slimy looking. With weird jaws. Was that them? How far away?"

"A few minutes walk, assuming the commotion didn't scare them away. We can probably still see from here." She pointed toward the high rocky area that she had been filming from earlier.

"Race you to the top!" Hubcap said to no one in particular. He darted forward while Owen cautioned him to stay out of sight. Several people followed.

Hubcap scrambled atop the highest boulder. All those holes made for good handholds. Owen and Elliot were hot on his heels while Hubcap peered over the edge in search of alien monsters.

Laid out before him was empty landscape, with weird rocks close to the sea and plains covered in purple grass up above. Wind pulled at him. In the distance, dark snaky shapes writhed.

"They're moving away," Owen said, taking a position beside Hubcap and shading his eyes. "Probably to the sunning area over the next ridge. It's a big patch of dark rocks that will be getting warm before too long. Let's be off!" He started scrambling down. "The aircar is too loud, so we'll have to hoof it. The mud flats will be faster than all those boulders, though not by much."

"Mud flats, you say." Hubcap followed him down.

Owen was still talking. "Unless I miss my guess, those looked like adolescent males. Just small enough to handle, while just big enough to be a challenge! You should like this part," he said to Hubcap. He clapped his hands at the crowd. "To the mud flats!" More than a few groans sounded, but the workers dutifully gathered their things and moved out.

Hubcap walked alongside Elliot. The camera crew stowed their equipment in the triple-strap backpacks they wore just for uncertain footing like this, freeing their hands. Hubcap nodded in silent approval and turned his attention to the path that ran along the sandstone ridge toward its lowest end. It was there that the mud came into view. Rocky ground tapered off into a spill of dirt from the grasslands above, which appeared to have mixed with the puddled seawater to produce mud that was the perfect consistency to suck boots off of feet. Soupy brown goo awaited them, with occasional rocks sticking up like ineffective handholds. Owen was already striding gamely forward.

"Ah," Hubcap said. "Those mud flats."

A couple of the cameras started rolling again while the workers plodded into the muck. Their footsteps made noises that were sure to entertain more than a few viewers back home.

Hubcap clapped Elliot on the back. "Well, I hope you laced your robo-skin shoes tight," he said. "Don't be losing one, now." He hopped over a rock and tested the slipperiness of the mud.

"They don't have laces," Elliot said. "These things have some very high-tech buckles, I'll have you know."

"I'm happy for you, fleshface!" Hubcap strutted ahead with confidence. "Hurry up!"

"You're going the right way for a mudball to the back of the head, you know," Elliot admonished.

Hubcap flashed him a grin, saying nothing. He waited for his co-host to join him.

Elliot spoke into Dale's camera. "Watch him carefully. If he falls in the mud before I do, I get to laugh at him." He switched to Tarja's camera. "A lot. With maniacal glee. Don't let me down, now." With that, he turned and continued forward.

Hubcap chuckled and caught up with the experts.

The experts, as it turned out, didn't have a much better time of it than the newcomers. The depth of the mud varied without warning, going from ankle-deep to thigh-deep between one step and the next. Progress was slow, with everyone having to feel their way along, and even then there were more than a few stumbles. Great care was given not to drop the supplies.

This was of special concern to the camera crew, who gave up on filming with the big cameras right away. The few seconds of unfortunate nosedives would have to do. The cameras were packed away in favor of several hands-free headcams.

Hubcap, of course, took no tumbles into the mud. He showed appropriate humility about his superior balance, pointing and laughing from a shallow patch when yet another human made a spectacular pratfall. Mud painted his legs brown, but it would dry up and flake away soon enough.

Elliot waded over to where Hubcap was slapping his metal knees in laughter. "If you're quite done," the human said with dignity. "We have a show to film." He walked past, deliberately high-stepping to free his feet.

Hubcap just laughed more, pointing in another direction. "This is good TV right here. I don't know what you're talking abou — Augh!" He was interrupted as Elliot shoved him from behind, lifting with his knees to counteract the robot's superhuman balance.

It was just barely enough. The mud caught at Hubcap's feet, and he went sprawling into a deep puddle. His face clanked against a rock, but he got up laughing like everyone else.

"Am I missing an eyebrow?" he asked, holding a muddy hand away from his face.

"Actually yeah, I think it snapped off," Elliot told him.

Hubcap stopped laughing. "What?" He cast about in rising panic for the missing eyebrow until Elliot admitted that he was joking.

"I got you good!" Elliot said, edging away. "You deserved that."

"All right then, if that's how you want to play it," Hubcap said with an ominous smile. He bent and flung a spray of mud at the cackling human. Elliot managed to dodge the worst of it, though his side was splattered brown.

"Come on kids, you can make mud pies after work," Owen called with a smile in his voice. "Besides, you'll scare off the snakes."

Hubcap made a half-lunge toward Elliot just to see him flinch, then pointed in silent laughter and made childish taunting gestures as the human shook a fist at him. Behind the pair, Dale squelched down into the mud.

Instead of getting up, he flailed wildly.

"Ahh! Get it off!"

Hubcap whirled and saw tentacles.

Chapter 7

Elliot yelled for Owen. He struggled in the mud toward the young cameraman, his head full of recent trauma and childhood nightmares about being unable to outrun something. The mud pulling at his feet felt more malevolent than it had moments before. Dale thrashed. He'd only been with the show a few months. Elliot strained toward him.

"Get it off, get — Ah!" Dale's frantic movements flung something into the air: a head-sized mass of red tentacles that pinwheeled, grabbing wildly. Elliot thought for one sick moment that it was red with blood, but he didn't see any on Dale. The thing splashed into the mud and disappeared.

Hubcap made a bigger splash as he landed by Dale's side, having leapt from a rock. "Where are you hurt?"

"I, uh," Dale stuttered, scrambling to his feet and running muddy hands over his helmet. "I think I'm okay."

"Are you sure? Hold still."

Elliot got there just after Owen, and the three of them made certain that Dale hadn't been injured. Owen was less concerned.

"It was a mudsucker," Owen said, glancing at the undisturbed surface of the mud. "They're not all that dangerous, though they do look it."

A local waded over and plunged her arms into the muck. She felt about, emerging moments later with a double handful of squirming tentacles.

Elliot felt Dale shudder beside him. Graham's camera quietly clicked on.

"Woah, tentacles!" exclaimed Hubcap. "Nothing more alien than that!" He made an exaggerated display of covering his mouth, eyes on Owen. "Shouldn't have said that, should I? Now's where you tell us more than we ever wanted to know about squids and octopus."

Elliot kept an eye on Dale while Owen rose to the challenge. Dale shook himself and found stable footing, then belatedly started wiping mud off his camera case. The case had been shut tight, so no harm was done there either. Elliot breathed a quiet sigh of relief.

"Technically, a tentacle has suction cups only at the end," Owen was saying. "Squid have two tentacles and eight arms, while octopuses have only the eight arms."

Elliot joined the conversation. "Isn't it octopi, not octopuses?"

Hubcap pointed at him in delight. "You'd think so, wouldn't you? But it turns out that the root of the word is Greek, not Latin, so 'octopus' is the proper plural as well." He paused. "Or maybe it's Latin and not Greek. But anyway, that's right."

"And you're sure of this?" asked Elliot with a faint smile.

"No!" Hubcap said in delight. "But that's beside the point!"

Owen waved the woman forward who held the thrashing mudsucker at arm's length. "We would also be correct to say 'octopodes,' but who can remember that?" He used both gloved hands to brush back the wiggly limbs and display the creature's mouth. It was round and full of teeth.

"Ooh, creepy," Hubcap said. Elliot stepped aside so the camera crew could get a close-up. He hoped the headcams had gotten a good view of the scare. Unpleasant as it had been, he knew the media people could craft a fine hook out of the footage.

"It works a lot like a lamprey," Owen said, pointing to the creature's teeth. "With a serrated jaw for digging into flesh. From what we've seen, these guys latch onto live creatures as well as dead ones; they're probably one of the biggest parts of this ecosystem's cleanup force."

"Fascinating," Hubcap said. "How hard can they chew?"

The woman suggested, "Why don't you put your finger in there and find out?" She smiled behind her visor.

Elliot could tell Hubcap was considering it when someone further south relayed the suggestion to "Hurry the hell up, and don't scare away the snakes."

Owen pointed south. "The scouts have spoken. Let's be off."

The local tossed the mudsucker away from the crowd and started walking before it landed. Elliot watched it fly, glad that she hadn't simply dropped it at her feet. The thing flopped into the mud and quickly burrowed out of sight. Dale muttered and trudged away at his best speed while Hubcap followed Owen southward, peppering him with questions about the springmouth snakes.

Elliot stared at the mud, trying not to think of the last time a cameraman had screamed.

* * *

They had been filming alongside a space station's cleanup crew, emptying the force field capture bins and sorting the trash after the bioscanners had filtered out anything organic. This particular day had yielded a wide range of space junk intercepted on its way to the station, from micrometeors to empty fuel canisters to the wreckage of a rich person's shuttle when it crashed drunkenly before docking. The exciting portion of the day's filming had been taken care of on the spacewalk. Sorting was the part that came afterward.

Elliot and Hubcap stood with the trio of local professionals, all wearing heavy gloves and poking fun at what they found. Tarja and Graham filmed from close up, while Vic covered everyone from the doorway, and Kareem got wide-angle shots from the crane above.

It had seemed safe at the time. Kareem had proven time and again that his climbing skills were excellent, and no one doubted his ability to keep track of both handholds and camera. He'd done this many times before.

He'd never caught frenzy when high up.

No one noticed at first. Elliot was finding signs that the rich individual had brought an automobile to the space station, and the locals were telling stories about the unnecessary things they'd seen people bring. Then Elliot adopted a serious expression and said, "Oh no. Hubcap, I've found your people."

The robot appeared alarmed for the split second before Elliot held up a chrome hubcap. Then he burst into laughter with the rest of them.

"That was a good one," Hubcap admitted, shaking a finger at Elliot. "You might have a future in television after all."

The camera crew tried to stifle their chuckles, so it wouldn't have to be filtered out. They were all successful except for Kareem. He guffawed loudly from above, his laughter echoing through the sorting bay.

When he didn't stop, Elliot put hands to hips and looked sternly upward, expecting the cameraman to pull himself together at any moment. Frenzy was far from his mind. They had been told that it was almost a zero risk at this location. But as the laughing fit continued and Kareem's grip loosened, Elliot realized the truth with dawning horror.

The others saw too. They scrambled in circles — to climb after him, to calm him down, to call for a medic — but he was already sliding off the crane.

Hubcap leapt to catch him, too late. Kareem hit the rubble with a crunch that broke several bones and shattered his camera.

He kept laughing. But it was higher pitched now, screeching and desperate. Turning into one long note.

Elliot rushed forward helplessly while the other humans moved to assess, to sedate, to call for help. Cameras were forgotten. No one had a sedative on them, since it had been unthinkable that they would need it here. They wouldn't make that mistake again. Hubcap was the first to reach the frenzy kit on the wall, ripping it free with little regard for the stiff latches. He bounded over and skidded to a stop, pulling out an inhalant in very old packaging.

A puff of air escaped as he opened it. Elliot's worry level ratcheted up when Hubcap confirmed that the sedative was expired.

As Hubcap out-shouted Kareem in telling the locals just what their negligence had done, Elliot heard Vic dash away through the mess. He turned to see her dig into a camera bag and come up with the medical kit that the TV crew always carried. Hubcap met her halfway, still yelling. Elliot got out of the way as the robot returned with a fresh injection stick.

One jab to the thigh, then the waiting period. It wasn't instant. As far as Elliot was concerned, it really should have been. By the time Kareem's spasmodic giggles finally lapsed into unconsciousness, the sound of approaching sirens could be heard. Elliot thought numbly that it was a good thing they had already docked with the main station. He didn't want to think what a long wait would do to Kareem's injuries. Or how bad they were already.

When the medical professionals arrived, they took care of everything. Kareem was stabilized and whisked off to a lengthy hospital stay with a broken pelvis and collarbone, plus various contusions. To everyone's relief, the quick action with the sedation had prevented any damage from the frenzy itself.

Legal action, on the other hand, was another story.

Elliot wasn't kept privy to all the details, but he knew that the space station's crew faced some harsh penalties, and the entire command chain of the TV show landed in hot water. The team's reaction to the frenzy was beyond reproach, but according to the overly-strict guidelines for space travel in frenzy-positive areas, mistakes had been made. Never mind the fact that there hadn't been another case in that region for years. And the fact that operating in handholding pairs, even in the bathroom, with sedatives ready in every room, was infeasible for just about everyone. Those were the rules for places where frenzy was known, and those were the rules that were brought to the table when the government fines were getting laid down.

They almost lost the show right there. They did lose Kareem, who had a long road of physical therapy ahead of him. He wished them well, and they told him the same, then the producers started looking for a replacement cameraman who could travel into space immediately.

The only hirable candidate turnout out to be more inexperienced than anyone was fully comfortable with.

* * *

Elliot snapped out of his reverie as someone called his name. The sucking footsteps were growing distant. He hurried after his coworkers through the thick mud, his eyes seeking out Dale just to make sure he really was okay. Every time Elliot's feet slid, he expected to feel something wriggly under his boots. But nothing else surfaced, no one cried out or fell over, and the rest of the slog was blessedly without incident.

Elliot breathed easier when the mire trailed off into muddy sandstone. A glance around showed most of the camera crew looking winded, though the local workers were apparently conditioned to walking through deep mud. Either that or they hid it better. They probably didn't want to get made fun of by Hubcap.

The robot vaulted up onto a rock with all the energy in the world. "Ooh, those are big 'uns!"

"Get down, y'idiot!" a local smacked his foot while keeping his own head down below the level of the rock.

"Why?" Hubcap asked, scrambling down. "Surely they can't bite us from here."

"You'll scare 'em away," came the answer. "They're too fast to catch on foot."

"How many were there?" Owen asked, materializing out of nowhere.

"Three," said the local.

"Good," Owen said, waving everyone closer. Elliot shook mud off his feet and took a position next to Hubcap. The film crew was close on his heels, cameras at the ready.

Elliot risked a peek over the rock while Owen talked. There were, as promised, three large snaky shapes colored in dark grays, sunning themselves on an equally dark rock slab. Elliot decided to focus more on the old volcanic patterns in the rocks than on the alarming size of these "juveniles." The waves lapping at the bottom of the sunning area made for the kind of calming white noise that people Earthside paid good money for.

Owen outlined the new plan, which sounded to Elliot remarkably similar to the old plan. The only difference was the tools.

…Which really didn't look strong enough for wrangling creatures made of solid muscle that couldn't be sedated. Elliot resolved to stay to the rear and let the professionals handle it.

"Let's move out!" Owen said. He led the way, creeping low around the boulders. The rocks were especially rough here, and Elliot found that everything he brushed against either scraped loudly on his armor plates or caught at the duracloth in between. He was so preoccupied with this — and with the awareness that there were cameras filming his every stumble — that he was surprised to look up and see Owen signaling a halt with the ocean just yards away.

The waves were loud. The snakes hadn't heard them yet. But the creatures appeared to be getting restless, or maybe hungry. One was starting to slither away while another raised its head to watch the first. Elliot was pretty sure he could hear the scrape of scales across rock. Or maybe it was Hubcap's hands on the boulder he was peering over like an excitable kid.

Owen whispered commands for a pincer movement, then disappeared with a pair of workers holding capture poles. Other workers scurried off in the opposite direction while one stayed put with the TV crew.

"Are these things territorial?" Elliot asked. "Or pack mentality? If we tackle one, will the others go for us?"

"No, they tend to scatter well enough," the man told him through a mud-smeared face mask. "They mostly seem to hang together because they scare up more food as a group."

"Okay, good. I don't want any of them mad at me, much less all of them."

A grin flashed behind the muddy mask. "No, you don't!"

A scuffle erupted up ahead, and the local leapt to his feet. It looked to Elliot's startled eyes like the attack had begun before everyone was in position. The man he'd been talking to vaulted over the rock and dashed to join the two who were hanging on to a capture pole looped around the neck of a thrashing black monstrosity. The other two snakes were speeding away while the rest of the humans scrambled to get their own nooses around the massive neck. The snake kept ducking. Then it dove for its captors.

Elliot yelped at the sight of the springmouth's jaws unfolding, but the workers kept their cool. The two maintained their grip on the pole, holding the horror away from them by a rapidly shortening distance. The snake was squirming its way up through the noose, and the pole was starting to bend. People were shouting everywhere.

Then two more nooses made it into place, cinching between vertebrae as the snake strained toward its prey. That extra-hinged mouth was terrifying from where Elliot stood. He could only imagine what it must look like up close, with most of the view eclipsed by folded out flesh and teeth. The mouth was more than capable of swallowing anyone present.

But the humans were hauling away at the ropes with all their might — Elliot was startled to see Hubcap up there with them — and the nightmarish jaw soon inched backward, then fell to the side as the creature tried another route of escape.

Elliot glanced around to see only the camera crew keeping out of the action, and even they were easing past the rocks to get a better look.

The creature was trying to wriggle away. Elliot hurried to his feet and raced forward, hoping he'd figure out what to do when he got there.

The thrashing snake figured it out for him. The tail hit him in the hip, sending him sliding off-balance to carom off a spiky rock. He recovered, grateful for the armor, and launched himself back at the tail, determined to pin it down.

The ride that ensued was part rodeo and part wrestling match, and by the time someone else jumped on with him, he'd completely lost track of which way was up. The tail finally settled to "twitchy" status. Elliot maintained his death grip, breathing hard inside his helmet and listening for cues on what to do.

A detached part of his mind wondered briefly whether the new brown streaks across his viewplate were in fact mud. Then he firmly told himself that he didn't need to think about where the alien snake pooped from. He really didn't.

"I've got the jaws shut," someone was saying. "Go ahead with the jack."

The disjointed conversation sounded to Elliot like another contraption was being put into place with some difficulty. Under other circumstances, he would have wanted to be up there in the action, but right now he was content to lie on the rough ground, hugging the gigantic snake's tail. The world had stopped moving dizzily around him. That was enough.

He couldn't tell, moments later, if the workers had finished yet when something snapped free and the tail flashed into the air.

Elliot yelped in alarm as he spun skyward for the briefest of moments, then came to rest against a *very* solid rock.

He lay there with a ringing head while the snake thrashed and spun and hissed, no doubt snapping at all of the little intruders.

Elliot wondered if it could bite through armor.

Then he wondered if his aching head was making him imagine things, since the world was moving again. The rock he lay against seemed to be standing up and poking his chest. He couldn't tell through his blurred sight and muddy visor if he was seeing a gigantic crab, a turtle, or some bizarre alien monster that had no name. He supposed fuzzily that the camera crew would be able to tell him later.

Something appeared over his shoulder to whack at the turtle-crab-rock-thing, and he figured out that it was one of the capture poles. Other poles joined in, causing the whatsit to retreat back out of his field of vision. He felt hands grab him and pull him to safety, then a stronger pair lifted him like a baby and ran with a familiar stride to a flat spot up the shoreline.

Chapter 8

Hubcap looked down at the human's face, and didn't like what he saw. With the visor opened, he could see that Elliot's eyes were open and tracking, but not well, and the pupils were far too dilated.

"Medic!" he called over his shoulder, bellowing in the face of the local who was coming up behind him. "Oh, there you are. He hit hard. What have you got?"

The man opened a large medical kit. He wasn't swayed by Hubcap's reaching and pointing, and a glance at his own visor showed Asian features set in a professional level of calm. "I got this," he said. "Scoot." He gestured for the concerned robot to move aside.

Hubcap did, but he stayed hovering over the proceedings just to make sure it all went well. And he completely ignored the quaint human signs that he was standing too close. Sighs and eye-rolling he could handle.

"There," the medic said, packing up his gear but leaving the neck brace and pillow. "He's asleep and he'll stay that way for at least six hours, and I've got the internal bleeding stopped with the tissue on the mend." He looked up at Hubcap, and Vic who stood behind him. "The scan shows relatively slight damage, especially since we caught it so soon. He should be fine with further treatments."

"Right, scan sessions an hour apart and all that. Good." Hubcap nodded and noticed with some surprise that the entire crew was huddled around them, with the cameras filming away.

A lesser individual might be compelled to feel embarrassment at this juncture, Hubcap thought, *But not I.*

"Well that was exciting!" he said to the nearest camera in his best upbeat tone. "Good ol' Elliot has demonstrated not only the best way to flush out the local wildlife and the worst way to hold on to a snake's tail, but he has also sampled the medical abilities of the local field doc." He clapped the man on the shoulder. "What was your name again?"

"Xian."

"Right, Xian, good man. I can see you know your stuff. Now let's get our adventurous friend here back to base, shall we?"

Xian agreed, and so did Owen, who showed up with a stretcher made from capture poles and tough cloth. The locals got Elliot into it with practiced ease, and carried him in a fast and sure-footed manner toward the parked aircar. Hubcap was glad to see that they were charting a course around the mud flats, and sending a pair of runners ahead to bring the car to them.

Looks like they know what they're doing, he decided. But he was still going to keep a careful eye on everything just in case. Humans broke far too easily, and he wasn't about to lose a friend to something as piddling as a crack against a rock.

Not again.

Despite the armor, Elliot's scent trail was clear on the sea breeze. Hubcap jogged after the stretcher. The cameras were still watching, so he did his best to pretend he wasn't listening for breathing problems from here.

Chapter 9

Peering out from between two rocks, something watched the activity with interest. Something unfamiliar with Earthlings. Something taking in every detail with the intense curiosity of a scientist discovering new life.

Someone.

She observed the tall figures moving back the way they had come, and she did her level best to capture the important facts in writing. Her hands moved with all the speed of a deep current, but they weren't fast enough to record everything she saw. They couldn't be. She silently railed against the impossibility of writing with the eloquence of speech. Also against her limited time, and limited resources, and the fact that she would never get to share her findings in person.

She put it from her mind and focused on the details. The creatures were shaped like trees, wearing armor that she had taken for scales at first. They appeared to be unsuccessfully hunting the large bodiless tails — that term was particularly hard to write at this speed, nearly causing her to fumble and start fresh. When one of the creatures was injured, she realized several things: they were social animals who cared for each other's welfare; they had helmets that could be removed; and the one with the shiniest armor was exceptionally strong.

She stared as the strange beings cared for their comrade, many questions swimming past her mind. What was their relation to each other? Were they all siblings of a hive mother, or did they all hatch from a communal clutch with many parents, or did they have insulated family units? Did they make that armor themselves? Were they as civilized as they seemed? Could they be communicated with? How might they react if she approached them?

Probably not well at the moment, given their concern over the injured one. They might reasonably think her a threat. As much as she wanted to try, interaction would surely end badly. And they certainly wouldn't understand her speech. But what if they did?

As she agonized over the thought, fingers still dancing, the choice was taken from her. A roaring sound filled the air, and something shocking floated into view.

She didn't know how to describe it. A flying rock, with windows. Large, angular, loud. The creatures hurried forward to meet it, pulling open its side when it landed. That was a door. They were climbing into a moving building. How did they make a building fly?

The creatures all settled inside. The last one shut the door, and the building lifted into the air, moving on wings of sound alone. It disappeared over the hill while she wrote furiously, futilely, forlornly. No one would ever read this. But she had to record it anyway. On the sliver of hope that her words would find their way home somehow. And as someone who had spent a lifetime studying every form of life within reach, she could do nothing else.

When she was done, she spread the journal entry against the rock in front of her, looking for errors. There were none. Her knotwork was tidy and precise, with no stray loops. The waterweed hadn't torn. The braided spine-strand was sturdy, and the sentences that hung from it were a masterwork of intricately knotted words. Something to take pride in, given the speed of her writing, but it brought her little joy now.

How many of her predecessors had done the same? She hadn't spotted any signs of intelligence once she left the river, but that didn't mean much. How many other curious souls had made it to this shoreline? How long had these intelligent animals been here?

And what would they do next?

Chapter 10

Hubcap balanced a cue stick on his palm, heavy end up, watching with surgical focus and trying to figure out which ceiling vent was making the troublesome breeze while he did his level best not to think about his partner convalescing in the medical ward. There were precious few distractions here in the common room. Hubcap would have liked to be doing something worthwhile, but Vic had told him and the camera crew to stay put for now.

Vic herself was in a side room making a report to headquarters, something that Hubcap did not envy her. The authority figures back Earthside would be worried — about Elliot's well-being, about time lost in filming, and about the medical costs. Hubcap was happy to steer far away from that little room and the video screen full of unhappy faces.

It was much better to practice his balancing tricks and watch the camera crew take turns at being horrible shots at the antigravity billiards table.

"I'm gonna get the blue one," Graham promised. "Easy pickings." He lined up his cue stick like a rifle, much to the amusement of a pair of locals following the action from a nearby table. They laughed when he missed the ball he was aiming for, and knocked Dale's away from the target as well.

"Oh, come on!" Dale said. "Now I have to go for the one hiding way over there."

"After my turn," Tarja reminded him. She aligned her own cue and made a passable shot, one of the first that hadn't prompted at least a snort from the peanut gallery.

Then her follow-up landed only the cue ball in the tiny gravity well that passed for a corner pocket. Other balls clacked against each other and bounced silently off the force field at the table edges, coming to rest in a very different arrangement. Dale crowed in delight and stepped up to take his turn.

Hubcap put down the cue stick he'd been playing with, considering showing up the humans, then a dark-skinned man approached him with concern for Elliot. This wasn't the first local to do so. They all showed a gratifying level of worry as far as Hubcap was concerned, though he hoped this wouldn't hamper their filming efforts later. Apparently there was an official memo posted that the guests would not be allowed to do anything that dangerous again, never mind the insurance coverage.

"I heard what happened," the man said. "Is he gonna be okay?"

"Yeah, he will." While Hubcap assured him that the lesser star of the show would be fine, several other worker types entered the room and joined the conversation. Hubcap made sure to learn all their names before steering the conversation elsewhere. Other ways to get hurt was always a fun topic. The locals gladly obliged.

"One of the little predators tried to set up camp in the main hangar last year," said the man who'd introduced himself as Booker. "A hopscotch burrower. I thought I got it pinned with a tarp, but the thing turned its head sharp like, and tore out a chunk of my leg." He lifted a pant leg to show where a pale gouge marred his shin. "I squealed like a dying rabbit and bled all over the floor, and couldn't walk right for the longest time."

"Hey, at least you didn't lose anything important," said Salome, making a rude gesture with one of her silver fingers.

"Oh, tell him that story!" Booker urged. Salome needed little encouraging. Her story included machinery in the wrong place, and uneven footing.

"Now wait a moment, go back a bit," Hubcap said. "You were out killing *what* in the garden?"

"Oh, did nobody tell you about the supergophers?" Salome asked with a grin. "You'll love these guys. They eat our crops, and small animals besides, so they've been known to attack people's feet. You usually have to kill them with a shovel," she said matter-of-factly.

"A shovel," Hubcap repeated while the others chuckled. "A regular shovel, or some scary razor-sharp space shovel of death and destruction?"

"While one of those would be nice, I'm afraid that all we have is the regular kind," Salome told him. "Though we have been known to sharpen the edges of them, just in case. You just have to be careful not to hit anybody with the sharp edge."

"Yeah," chimed in another voice pointedly. "It kind of hurts."

"Ha, yeah Ramón, show him your scar."

The young man did, though claiming that a bite from one of the creatures would have been worse. Others agreed. The conversation and show-and-tell continued, gaining Hubcap both ideas for things to film later, and credibility with the rough-and-tumble workers when he finally began matching their stories with anecdotes of his own.

"You know, that reminds me of an encounter I had with a hippo about nine years ago," he said casually. "People tend to underestimate them, but those buggers can run like horses, and they have teeth like rebar. One tore this leg clean off once…"

By the time the camera crew finished with billiards and moved on to magnetic darts, Hubcap had cemented his reputation as a past master of dangerous situations. It wasn't surprising, then, that when someone called from a doorway that the last opportunity for "skeet-boom" was happening, the group hustled Hubcap along with them.

"You've got to see this," Salome told him. "You did jetpods yesterday, right?"

"Yes," Hubcap said, dragging his feet. "Are they going to go boom now?"

"Only once they're launched far away," she said. "Totally safe. Ish. Anyway, this is the last of the extra pods for a while, and lunch break only goes so long. C'mon, the side hangar's not far."

Hubcap did a quick danger assessment, then glanced at the door to the communication room. It was still closed on Vic's conversation with the bosses. The game of darts was in full swing. Experience had taught Hubcap that he didn't want to be anywhere near magnetic things designed to be thrown, even if he did have an insulation layer to protect from magnet damage.

He knew his coworkers. He would absolutely get a dart to the head the moment his back was turned.

"Hey guys, I'll be in the side hangar if you need me!" he called. Graham gave him a thumbs-up. Hubcap opened a leg compartment, pulled out a small headcam, and snapped it to his forehead. "Lead the way," he said to Salome.

She fairly ran down the hallway on the heels of Booker and the others, urging Hubcap to keep up. He did, narrating as he went for the benefit of the camera. Just in case this little adventure was TV-worthy without getting anyone in trouble. It did sound like the kind of thing done on lunch break because the workplace safety rules weren't enforced when the workers were off the clock.

He asked about that, and got an "Oh it's fine," that didn't do much to convince him that skeet-boom was officially permitted. He made a mental note to find out for certain before submitting the footage.

Then they arrived, trotting out into a hanger with space for only a few vehicles, none of which were anywhere in sight. Instead, several deep purple jetpods were gathered by the door, along with a dozen people and supplies that didn't make sense yet. Hubcap's nostril sensors alerted him to the scent of combustible fuel.

As Booker loudly greeted the others, Hubcap started to piece it together. The mangled trash can strapped to a stack of tires was a launch platform. The length of pipe with one end capped was a firearm of the potato launcher variety. The box of pottery shards was ammunition. And the colorful stuff — was that fireworks?

"Just in time!" said a beefy man of the sandy-blonde variety. "You can help us load up!" He stepped forward and held out a hand to Hubcap. "I'm Zack. Sorry about your friend. He'll be all right, yeah?"

"Yeah." Hubcap shook his hand. "In good care, and only slightly dented. Now what sort of ill-advised shenanigans do we have going on here?"

Minutes later, when a jetpod was rocketing into the sky in a deafening blast of steam, and Hubcap was helping aim the potato launcher full of sharp things, he was reasonably sure that he was filming something worth putting in the show. If this sort of tomfoolery wouldn't draw in more viewers, then he would eat Elliot's hat.

At any rate, it kept his mind off worrying about his wounded friend. And that was just as important.

Chapter 11

Elliot spooned eggs into his mouth, and found himself preferring to think about what kind of animal had laid them instead of focusing on the robot who hovered with a concerned air across the table. The cafeteria wasn't loud enough to be a distraction.

"Does your brain hurt?" Hubcap asked. "I can get the medics back in here if you still have swelling."

"I'm fine, Hubcap." He took a drink of green juice that tasted unpleasantly tart. "Their scanners are new and functional, and I have every confidence that they fixed each broken blood vessel there was to find."

"The tech isn't all that new," the robot protested. "Pseudo-new at best."

"Not the point," Elliot said around another mouthful of eggs. "No medical supplies are up to your standards unless they came straight from the factory. These people have equipment that's perfectly good."

The robot scowled, deliberately looking away with his chin on one fist and the fingers of his other hand tapping on the table. Elliot focused on his food.

"The only thing I will grant them," Hubcap said. "Is that they have a very effective sedative for the frenzy. It sounds like the death rate here is negligible, and that's mostly due to the SedEggs. But that does not make this planet safe!" he hurried to point out.

Elliot just nodded, chewing.

"Until someone figures out what actually causes the frenzy and how to stop it for good, sedatives are a temporary fix," Hubcap concluded.

"I thought they decided it was brought on by psychological trauma from leaving our mother world," Elliot said mildly.

Hubcap gave him a look. "You know better than that," he said. "Humans first left Earth in the 1900's. The frenzy has only been popping up for what, a decade?"

Elliot shrugged. "Something like that." He polished off the

weird juice and searched for a new topic. "Ooh, I smell fresh cookies!" A glance at the buffet table showed him a kitchen worker bringing out a plate of breakfast pastries that were turning heads with their newly-baked goodness.

Hubcap shrugged. "If you say so."

Elliot gazed at him in amusement. "You can sniff out a lost hiker using nothing but an old sock, but you can't smell cookies right out of the oven? And you make fun of me for inferior senses!"

The robot pointed a finger at his grinning face. "Yes, I do. When you show me a cookie that I can use for more than an inefficient paperweight, then I might be interested in detecting their scent."

Elliot eyed the pastries, still smiling. "I dunno, man. You're missing out."

"And you don't have heat vision at all. I can tell you which of those cookies is still warm, as well as which plate is too hot to touch and which coffee has gone cold. I win."

Elliot tilted his head. "I suppose that's fair." He looked at his watch. "On another note, we're behind schedule, and that's a problem. Has Vic said what we'll be doing today? It looks like the locals are already out and about."

Hubcap leaned both elbows on the table. "No, but someone from the office of Lord-Lee The Overboss stopped by while you were still resting your squishy brain, and he sent some ideas for low-impact work."

"Lord-Lee?"

"I hear that's his preferred nickname these days. Or Righteous-Lee, or Majestic-Lee, or Triumphant-Lee. You know, the nice complimentary stuff."

"Uh-huh," Elliot said.

"Sometimes he goes by more specific names, like Speedi-Lee when he gets things done fast, or Unexpected-Lee when he sneaks up on somebody."

"I do believe you're making that up," Elliot said, tossing his napkin onto his plate.

"Me?" Hubcap asked. "Would I behave so false-lee? Underhanded-lee?"

"Only on days that end in a Y," Elliot said. He leaned back in his chair.

"You wound me!" Hubcap exclaimed. "So deep-lee and mortal-lee!"

"I'm sure you'll get over it. You might say you recover quick—"

"Lee!" Hubcap finished.

"Look at that, you're better already!" Elliot pushed back from the table and picked up his tray. "Let's go find the others, shall we? I'm more than ready for some low-impact adventures."

"Yes, I will take any impacts for you!" Hubcap said, bounding to his feet. "And today is all about SCIENCE!"

Elliot hazarded a guess. "Is this the kind of science that will leave me wishing I hadn't eaten so many eggs?"

"Probably!" Hubcap said with delight.

"I *will* puke on you, given a chance," Elliot said.

The robot clapped him on the back. "Just be sure to tell me, in the name of scientific curiosity, how they taste on the way back up."

"Oh, I'll make sure you know."

***

Half an hour later, Elliot regarded Hubcap through the viewplate of a full-body biohazard suit. "I have detected a flaw. I can't throw up in this."

"Well, technically you *can*..." the robot said with a grin, encased in his own suit. "But I wouldn't recommend it."

Elliot shook a fist at his friend, making the sleeve crinkle. It smelled like plastic inside the suit. At least the thing appeared to be a new one, not gear that got washed once a month. Resigned, Elliot turned to watch the camera crew getting into their own suits. Local scientist types were moving around the cleanroom, helping to make sure everything was zipped and sealed in the safest manner possible. Soon the team had passed inspection and the camera crew were picking up their carefully-wrapped video equipment. When Vic was satisfied that the cameras would still work through the wrapping, she set up the filming angles for Elliot and Hubcap's exit from the room.

The large scanning arch looming in the doorway made Elliot a little worried about contagion, but no lights lit up in alarm as a local led the way through. Elliot followed her. He breathed easier when he was on the other side. It occurred to him that the scan on the way back would be more important, but he was still glad that things were going smoothly now. The clean room was so white and sterile, he felt like any sign of untidiness on his part would reflect badly on the team as a whole.

The room on the other side of the scanner was painted in a

calmer off-white, but it was still very clean. And this one held their new boss for the day. Elliot squared his shoulders and greeted her with Hubcap at his side and cameras all around.

"Hi there," said the stocky and cheerful woman in another biohazard suit, offering a hand to shake. She was a study in contrasts, with dark skin showing through the viewplate in the white suit, and a bright smile competing for attention with the fringe of blue hair — not the only person here with dyed hair, but the most vibrant Elliot had seen. "Welcome to the lab," she said. "I'm Sera Jones." She had just finished the sentence when someone called for her attention from a different doorway, addressing her as "Dippy."

"...Serendipity, that is," she amended, turning to give instructions on where to put a certain box of supplies. The other suit-wearing scientist left with a nod, and the boss turned back to her guests. "As I was saying, you can call me Sera. Nice to meet all of you."

She shook hands with Hubcap too, and introductions were made. Sera was especially curious about Hubcap's name. "Did you start out in the auto industry?"

"That's a common misconception," Hubcap said, raising a suit-covered finger. "Actually, I narrowly avoided being melted down to make car parts, back in the old days before I was legally a person." He shrugged. "I chose the name as a reminder not to get complacent."

Sera nodded slowly. "Well, all right then," she said. "So it's not your original title."

"No, the factory designated 'name' will not be uttered, and should die in a particularly hot fire."

"Oh, now I have to know!" she said with a smile. "I won't tell."

Hubcap gestured to the cameras. "This is all being filmed for posterity. So … no."

Sera continued trying to wheedle it out of him. Elliot would never betray his friend's trust by sharing that particular secret, but he wasn't above leaning over and pretending to whisper it. Hubcap whacked him on the arm.

"Hey," he said with a glare. "I will shave you in your sleep."

Elliot just grinned, and Sera changed the subject by ushering them on to do some actual work. Elliot followed eagerly.

But first, they would need to take a cart ride to the far end of the science wing. These carts turned out to be simple hover platforms with seats, railings, and an odd amount of floor space in the front. When everyone climbed onto two of the carts, and not a single local touched the seatbelts despite the cameras, Elliot privately decided that the belts and the floor space were both in case of frenzy. Unconscious people would need to be restrained or laid flat.

"Can I drive?" Hubcap asked. "I have a permit!"

Despite his assertions of expertise, Sera did not allow the robot to drive. Instead she piloted the lead cart down a long hallway that had only every third light turned on, while a solemn local man drove the other.

Elliot talked to the man about saving electricity while they rode. They both ignored Hubcap being a chatterbox and rocking the lead cart. Elliot knew that Vic could handle Hubcap's shenanigans just fine. And the cameras were off now, so it wouldn't be giving any young viewers bad ideas about vehicle safety.

Soon enough, the carts arrived at their destination: a brightly lit chamber with parked carts and doors lining the walls. While Elliot disembarked and the cameras got back into position, Hubcap was already guessing which door they would be headed through.

"Ooh, they're even color-coded," the robot said. "Will it be the green door, cryptically marked "Wash"? Or the black door, ominously labeled "Purifying?""

"We'll be taking the red door," Sera told him as Elliot walked up. "Where we finalize the ingredients into a product we can use and sell."

Hubcap sidled up to a camera to mutter. "I never would have guessed that's what happens here." He pointed up to the label over the door, which read "Finalizing."

Elliot nodded. "A shocker, to be sure."

"This way," the boss said, waving the duo forward. "Mind you don't bump into anything. Glass vials full of poison are the name of the game."

"Duly noted," Elliot said. "So what will we be doing to finalize things?" Dale's camera filmed over his shoulder as he followed Sera through the red door into a room full of tables and equipment, with scientists in biohazard suits doing various things to the promised glass vials. A faint chemical smell drifted through his suit's filter.

"Mostly adding ingredients and some diluting agents to the concentrated toxins that come from the purifying room," the short woman told him. She stepped aside as the camera crew slid past, still filming. "And we'll have to test to make sure it's the right ratio for the best effects."

Hubcap stuck his head around the door frame. "What do you test it on? Human subjects, perhaps?"

"No," Sera laughed. "Nothing like that. We just analyze it with machinery to see the chemical composition, then run virtual tests."

"Bah, that's no fun," the robot said.

"Neither is an overdose of poison, funnily enough," the scientist replied. "A lot of the steps to this are incredibly delicate, but there are a few things that we can let you guys help us with."

"Such as?" Elliot asked.

"Mostly measuring out the ingredients and putting the little containers into the machines. Things like that."

"Sounds fascinating!" Hubcap declared. "On with the science!"

Elliot glanced at Vic, privately hoping that the science would be more interesting than he feared it might be.

* * *

"So I was wondering," Hubcap said as he watched the test tubes spin with his head on the counter. "Can somebody frenzy on boredom? I mean, it is an emotion, right?"

"Hush," Elliot said, keeping an eye on the digital readout that kept track of how many times the rack had spun.

"It's a legitimate question!" Hubcap protested. "I know the frenzy is all mysterious and unexplainable, but surely someone here has enough experience with it to say. Who can I ask?" He raised his head and looked around eagerly, but Elliot shushed him.

"I'm sure they all find their jobs to be full of fascinating scientific interest," the human said.

"Ha, only on the good days," offered a passing scientist with an armload of empty test tubes. His breath fogged the inside of his mask. "The rest of the time, it's just about playing music and trying to stay sane."

"Music!" Hubcap exclaimed. "That's what we need! Where is it, man? Turn it on!"

"Well, the speakers are a little tetchy," the man said, setting down his armload. "I can give it a try, but it may not work. It takes a while to get new supplies here, at least for things that aren't classified as important."

"Music is always important," Hubcap declared. "Go on and give it a whirl."

The man did, making his way to the other side of the crowded room to fiddle with a bit of machinery that had been hidden by a stack of boxes. After a few silent moments, static blasted the air for a startling split-second, making all the humans flinch and the man apologize. Then he twisted more knobs and dials, and only then did the music pour forth.

It was a merry little ditty about snowballs and cooking pies and family togetherness. One that Hubcap knew Elliot hated with a passion.

"A little out of season, don't you think?" Hubcap asked mildly while his co-host tried to cover his ears through his suit.

"Yeah, sorry; we had it on random shuffle last," the man said as he hurried to press another button. The holiday cheer was replaced by peppy, wordless piano. "How's that?" the man asked.

"That will do just fine," Elliot said. "Thank you."

"No problem." The man gathered up his test tubes and wove his way to the door, past the beige worktables staffed by scientists in white suits. Some of the vials were brightly colored, but otherwise the room was dull to look at. Nothing even smelled interesting; Hubcap knew that every vial was likely the strongest of poison, but none set off warning bells for him. This was disappointing to say the least.

Hubcap turned his attention back to the still-spinning test tube rack. The numbers were getting higher, but not there yet. He waggled his gloved hands in mock-excitement. Elliot set a finger on the Stop button, and moments later, pressed it.

Hubcap dinged like a cooking timer. "Poison's done!" he declared, turning to look for the overseer and bonking his head on a camera instead. "Ow! Use the zoom function, Dale! You don't have to stand that close!"

The chastised cameraman stepped back as Elliot mused aloud. "Y'know, I often wonder why you say 'ow,' when we both know that didn't hurt."

"Many reasons!" Hubcap ticked off points on his fingers while the test tube rack spun to a tinkling halt. "It's part of fitting in with you fleshy types, and not making anyone jealous of my supreme durability. It shows impressionable human larvae watching our show an accurate representation of the reaction they could expect to have. It's programmed habit. I find it funny. It's more TV-acceptible than saying -*bleep*-." In place of a word, he mimicked the TV censor noise. Elliot just shook his head. Hubcap was about to go on when

Sera appeared from behind the cameras and asked about the state of the test tubes.

"Just finished," Elliot told her. "Now what?"

"Now we carefully put them into one of these lovely padded boxes, and bring them to that station over there." The short woman set the box on the counter and waved to a table at the other end of the room. She began to demonstrate the proper packing procedure, then stopped when Hubcap pointed to her hands.

"Hang on a moment. *How* many fingers do you have?" he asked.

Sera laughed and held up her hands, and it was obvious that her suit must have been custom made. "Six on each hand," she admitted with a grin. "They tell me it's really rare for the extra finger to be functional."

"You don't say!" Hubcap gave one hand an exploratory poke.

The cameras zoomed in, and Elliot also got a look. "I thought people usually had that sort of thing removed as infants," he said. "I always thought it kind of a shame; as a kid I wanted extra fingers. I was convinced that I could do much more with them."

"Normally people do get them removed," Sera said. "Mostly to keep the kids from getting picked on later, but my parents were big believers in random chance happening for a reason." She bobbed her head. "Thus the name."

Hubcap looked up from his inspection. "What name? Oh right, Serendipity. Happy chance indeed. Well, I am impressed with your fleshy digits."

Elliot stage-whispered. "That's high praise coming from him."

Hubcap flicked his helmet in reply.

"Ow," Elliot said, while Sera laughed.

Hubcap was still curious. "So was child-Elliot right? Does this allow you to play instruments in mindblowing fashions, undreamt-of by lesser mortals?"

"It might if I played any," the scientist replied. "As it is, I couldn't tell you. But I'm told I handle syringes and test tubes with an especially steady hand."

"Two steady hands!" interjected a passing hazard suit with a female voice.

"Yes, two hands." Sera said. "Thank you so much, Jaya, for helping me count."

The younger woman paused long enough to give the group a thumbs up, then move on to the other end of the room.

Hubcap and Elliot asked a few more questions about the boss's extra fingers, then reluctantly got back to work. As they did, Elliot talked about someone he'd known as a child with an extra toe. Hubcap packed test tubes while the human jawed away.

"He got the impression from science class that one of his parents had to have an extra one too, and since they didn't, he went home and asked when they were planning to tell him he was adopted." Elliot gave the cameras a concerned look while he picked up a test tube.

Hubcap blinked his wiper panels. "And they said?"

"They got in a fight, because he wasn't adopted. Then the kid brought it up when all the relatives were visiting, and the grandma said 'Oh, your father used to have an extra toe! We got it removed when he was a baby.'"

Hubcap picked up the container of vials. "That sounds like an unfortunate family dinner."

"You would be correct!" Elliot stood aside. The anecdote was clearly concluded, recorded for the editors to keep or toss, like many of the human's stories. Hubcap nodded and ceremoniously set off with the container toward the table across the room, where new suit-clad scientists promptly took the tubes out again.

"Hello again, Mister Test Tube!" Hubcap greeted one vial of yellow liquid. "Why I haven't seen your face in, oh, three seconds!" The technicians around him chuckled, and Elliot objected that it had been at least twenty seconds. "Oh, glory be, could it be true?" Hubcap pressed both hands to his facemask. "That's nigh unto an eternity!"

The younger scientists laughed again, and Elliot said. "That only encourages him, you know."

This of course prompted Hubcap to begin enacting conversations between two different test tubes, which he kept up until Sera told him sternly to quit fooling about.

"Yes'm," he said, placing the test tubes back in the box and bowing his head. "I will not risk breakage of the horrible toxic bad-stuff-which-will-be-good-stuff." He stepped back a pace with his hands up, bumping into Dale and stepping down on the cameraman's foot.

The robot turned with superhuman reflexes, but Dale was already on his way to the floor. Hubcap snatched the camera from his hands, leaving the human to tumble into a pile of knees and elbows. The two nearest technicians jumped back, first surprised, then bursting into laughter when Hubcap posed with his save.

"I got it!" he said. "Eh? Eh? Oh, good landing, Dale," he said as an aside. "But you should really consider rolling when you fall; it's much easier on the joints."

The cameraman got to his feet while Sera asked if he was hurt, and one of the technicians kept laughing.

"No, I'm fine," Dale said uncomfortably, adjusting his suit and taking the camera back. He glanced at the cackling woman next to him, who was starting to wheeze from laughter.

"Jaya," the boss said sharply. When only laughing greeted her, she grabbed the young woman's shoulder and shook her hard enough to make her head bob. But the technician laughed louder, eyes staring. Sera swore. "Give me space!" she shouted, turning the other woman to face away from her, then pulling at the safety tab on the laughing scientist's suit.

"It's frenzy," Hubcap exclaimed as he hovered about the two. "What can I do?" He set down the camera as heads popped up all around the room and Vic hurried over.

"Stay back," Sera instructed. She pulled back the covering over the tiny hypospray built into the suit, and lined it up with the back of Jaya's neck.

But Jaya was doubling over in convulsions that were barely recognizable as laughter any more, and her neck wasn't holding still. Sera muttered about puncturing the suit with a SedEgg if she needed to.

Ignoring the directions to keep his distance, Hubcap grabbed the young scientist's shoulders to hold her in place. He tried not to leave bruises. Then Jaya's knees buckled and she collapsed to the floor, taking Hubcap and Sera with her.

"Oh my god, just put her in a headlock!" a man exclaimed. Gloved hands appeared to wrench Jaya's head downward, baring her neck. Sera aimed the hypospray while Hubcap leveled a stern glance at the man yelling directions.

"Nobody here knows the first thing about subduing a frenzier!" the man said. "We should all be taking judo classes, but no! Meditative breathing, my ass!" His face was reddening inside the suit. He held his coworker's head down like he had a grudge, and he shouted far louder than necessary. Hubcap tried to free a hand to reach his SedEgg.

Another man crept up behind the first and pulled the tab at his neck. But the angry scientist whirled to yell at the new target.

Hubcap felt Jaya go limp as Sera fired the sedative. He looked away from the impending fight for just long enough to make sure Jaya didn't bump her head during the boneless slide to the floor. Then a foot hit his shoulder and knocked him aside.

The two men were a vicious whirlwind of limbs, their shouts turned into a wordless harmony of rage. Scientists were leaping out of the way, some focused on getting to safety while others tried to find an opening with a SedEgg. One dragged a table covered in vials to the far side of the room. Another hid under it.

Hubcap was getting his feet under him to leap into the fray when a tall woman landed a SedEgg on one combatant, then two more got the other. Both men collapsed. Sera got to her feet and shot a hand in to the air.

"Clear!" she called. "Who's okay?"

Hands raised around the room in a chorus of clears. The shivering figure under the table didn't answer. Someone else crawled under with comforting words and a SedEgg, then crawled out dragging a sedated form. Everyone was accounted for.

Hubcap found Elliot and the others gathered against the wall, as far out of the way as possible. Every face was wide-eyed and every camera was filming. They still filmed now, as Hubcap joined them in watching the scientists nervously clean up the mess.

Sera set the speakers to playing some babbling-brook nature sounds while foldable gurneys were brought out of closet storage and the four unconscious people were loaded onto them. No one spoke. Within seconds, the gurneys were wheeling away with extra escorts, and the other scientists were leaving the room in unseemly haste.

The camera crew hurried to join them. Hubcap kept a close eye on his humans, SedEgg ready and his other hand free to grab.

Dale seemed the most anxious. "Four people!" the cameraman whispered loudly. "Four at once! And just two days after the last attack!"

Elliot agreed, following him out the door. "Yeah, that's a lot. And intense."

Hubcap looked at Vic, who was frowning down at her camera as she walked. "Do we want to ask how many times we're likely to go through this while we're here?"

Vic nodded. "I'm starting to think certain details were left out of the briefing about this place. I need to talk to Mr. Lee."

A voice rose in panic ahead of them. Heads snapped up.

Hubcap shoved past his coworkers to get a clear view, and saw one white-suited form clinging to the bars of a cart and wailing that there weren't enough seats to get everyone to safety. Other scientists swarmed to hold the man in place while someone pressed the hypospray. He fell limply onto the cart. Two others lifted his feet and piled onboard, sending the cart rocketing down the hall. One drove while the other held a SedEgg aloft. Hubcap hoped that they would make it.

At the rising murmur of worry, Sera calmed the mad rush to the remaining carts. She reminded her subordinates that they were levelheaded professionals who had weathered this storm many times before. Then she commanded them to sing.

That same obnoxious holiday song filled the cavernous room, accompanied by exasperated looks and resignation. Hubcap snuck a look at Elliot.

His incredulous expression was quite the sight. Hubcap snickered.

Sera waved them forward. "Proven technique for calming a group," she said over the chorus. "Works for us. Now up you go! Visiting celebrities get first priority. Nina, Will, drive safe and come right back."

Two scientists stopped singing and hopped into the drivers' seats. Elliot thanked Sera for everything. The camera crew climbed on and held tight when the carts took off.

Hubcap watched the cluster of scientists recede into the distance, their song echoing through the building while they waited for their ride into the sunlight.

The boring science had turned interesting, but not in a good way. Not unless the editors wanted to completely change the tone of the show. Hubcap set his jaw and faced forward, keeping an eye on the humans around him.

Chapter 12

"So now what do we do?" Elliot asked Vic, raising his voice over the hubbub of the decontamination room. The crew had left their biohazard suits behind and been cleared to leave. Dozens of other people were going through the process now, and it was a wash of noise. No one stepped forward to chaperone the TV crew.

"We're going to find Mr. Lee," Vic said. She strode to the door. "Waiting here is no good. Let's get some fresh air."

"Yes, please!" Elliot agreed. He followed her into the welcome daylight outside the science wing, with the rest of the team close behind. Hubcap brought up the rear. Elliot noted that the robot had one hand hovering near his hip like a gunfighter, with the SedEgg in his leg compartment in easy reach. This was both a comfort and a reminder of the danger that could strike at any time. Elliot was glad that Hubcap was guarding their backs.

Once outside, Vic paused to take stock of the several pathways leading to the main compound. To Elliot's eyes, they all looked the same: concrete weaving toward airlock doorways, with a local or two walking to and fro. The low grass was closer to an Earthlike green here, though faded-looking and stubby. Nothing overgrew the pathways. Elliot didn't know which path led to Mr. Lee.

And as it turned out, neither did Vic. "They never said where his office is," Vic said, hands on her hips. "I could have asked, but it never seemed important. Guess we'll have to ask around." She strode down the pathway with the closest local: a stocky tan woman with safety gear slung over one shoulder.

Hubcap spoke up from the back. "I'd offer to track him, but I don't know his scent. The meathead really should have met with us by now. Shoddy leadership."

Vic talked over her shoulder. "The majordomo told me yesterday that he's ailing somehow." She glanced at Elliot. "We talked while you were in the med ward. He was supposed to be catching up with us today." She frowned and faced forward. "Well it's today. Let's get some answers."

The woman with the safety gear didn't know where Mr. Lee was at that moment, but she did know where the office was. Vic thanked her for the directions and led the way toward the tallest building in the compound.

Elliot cast an appreciative glance at the scenery while he hurried along. He wasn't all that eager to go back inside where frenzy was a higher risk, statistically speaking. Staying outside where there was alien scrubland up close and bizarre trees in the distance sounded much more appealing. He could have spent a long, pleasant time studying the differences between the twisty bushes with mint-green leaves and their Earth analogues, or trying to come up with some excuse to visit the pyramid-shaped things that passed for tree trunks off to the east. He only had a brief look now, and it wasn't enough.

The air-conditioned coolness that breathed over him when he entered the building made him shiver. Everything smelled stark and sanitized compared to the alien world outside. Familiar, but unwelcome.

Vic made a beeline for the elevators. Elliot said nothing during the ride up, leaving it to Hubcap to fill the air with chatter about an elevator shaft rescue he'd done once.

"The thing was stuck between floors, so getting folks out through the top hatch was the way to go," the robot said. "Humans in the hallway were going on about getting a ladder down there, but no need. Dispatch had sent three of us, after all. So we just jumped down and did it. Thankfully I got to be the standing part of the ladder, not the kneeling footstool. I would have liked to be the one on top of the car boosting people up to safety and gratitude, but... no seniority."

The door dinged and opened, punctuating his story. Vic led the way across the hall to a spacious waiting room and a receptionist's desk. She told Elliot and the others to stay put while she had words with the man who had convinced the producers to film here.

Elliot was happy to do so. "We'll be over there," he told her, wandering over toward the arrangement of cushy chairs, panoramic windows, and a table with bagels and coffee.

"Good. I may call Earth afterward," Vic said before turning to address the receptionist, who Elliot recognized as the liaison who had met them when they first got off the shuttle. She was a sturdy gray-haired woman with eyes that missed nothing. Elliot would have looked right past her in a crowd, but he got the impression that this woman ran the place, and ran it well.

He left Vic to the conversation while the camera crew made themselves comfortable. Elliot peered over Graham's shoulder at the stale bagels and decided against them. Hubcap was moving chairs aside with the announcement that he would be practicing his handstands and fancy dance moves.

"You do that," Elliot said. "Just don't break stuff."

"I promise nothing."

Elliot walked over to the windows. This third-floor vantage point had a stunning view of the alien landscape, much better than what he'd been able to see from the ground on the other side of the building. There were even different plants on this side. Like the coast, the area looked familiar at a glance: mossy soil rose and fell, marked by tall feathery things that put Earth ferns to shame. But the waving fields of green grass below them were migrating as he watched.

Elliot blinked and looked closer. It was the grass itself moving; he hadn't imagined it. Then a section of turf raised its head briefly, and he remembered something Owen had said. *Grassback flatworms,* he thought. *That's nice and weird. Might make some good scene-setting footage.*

Elliot was about to suggest it to the camera crew when something closer to the building caught his eye: a man walking with a shovel held like a broadsword. He was treading a concrete path toward a good-sized garden, where Elliot thought he saw dirt moving. His boots shone with armor plating.

"Hey Hubcap," Elliot said. "What did you say those supergophers look like?"

He was greeted by an excited whoop and a thud. "Do you see one?" the robot demanded, springing to his feet and leaping over chairs to get to the window.

"Not yet, but I'd hazard a guess that they live there," Elliot said, pointing.

"That's the garden, all right! We've got to go film it. Come on, we can leave a note for Vic. She'll probably be talking to Unhealthi-Lee for ages."

Elliot was reluctant to go off without the director. But at Hubcap's insistence, he let himself be convinced. He hoped privately that it wouldn't be a mark against him in getting recommendations to direct his own show later. But this show came first, and they needed good material.

"We won't be far," Hubcap told him. "The outside is safer anyway, right? That guy isn't even following the buddy system. And this should definitely be interesting footage!"

"Okay, as long as we're careful. I'll tell the receptionist."

"All right!" Hubcap exclaimed. "Come meatheads, eat your fuel later!" He clapped metal hands at the three at the snack table. "If we get out there fast, there's a good chance we'll get to see an epic fight against an ankle-biting beastie, and maybe even a decapitation with a shovel. C'mon!"

Elliot had a brief conversation with the sharp-eyed woman, who said she'd pass on the message, then he rejoined his team. As he arrived, Hubcap insisted that the stairs were faster than the elevator, and led the charge downward. Elliot and the others followed at a reasonable pace. Soon they were trotting along the path outside with Hubcap narrating to the cameras.

"...Maybe even a decapitation with a shovel," the robot was saying. "It should be great. Extreme gardening! Oh look, there it is!"

The garden patch came into view, looking innocent enough. It was one of several, Elliot saw, reaching around the building with greenhouses and other structures for food cultivation. People moved in the distance, but up close there were just the many rows of leafy things, and the one man digging at the end of a row. His shovel sent the smell of spicy alien dirt drifting their way while the TV crew hurried to get closer. Elliot watched the ground for motion.

"Hello there!" Hubcap called out as they approached. "Mind if we join you?"

The solidly-built fellow looked up, flicking black hair out of his eyes. "Sure thing, just watch your feet," he said. He lifted up one heavily armored boot by way of demonstration. "There's biting creatures underground."

"So we've heard!" Hubcap looked around eagerly. "How often do the toothy little bastards show up? I'm Hubcap, by the way."

Elliot introduced himself and the others while the cameras got into position as best they could while staying on the walkway. The man said they could call him Ted, and told them that the alien gophers were never far from the surface. He spoke in a remarkably offhand manner, continuing to shovel as he did. Elliot wasn't sure if he was putting on a show for the cameras or if he was confident that his shovel-fighting skills could handle a creature leaping out of the ground.

"No wire mesh underground, I take it?" Elliot asked. "That

works pretty well on Earth gophers."

"Oh, we tried it," the man said, stepping down on the shovel edge. "These guys just force their way through. But they don't take enough of the crops to be what we call a 'budget priority.'" He unearthed a pair of root vegetables the same dark brown as the dirt. "Oh good, no bite marks."

"Is this one of the gophers' favorite foods?" Elliot asked.

"Anything we plant is their favorite food," the man said, tucking the round things into a bag at his hip. "These grow really well here, so we eat a lot of them. They have to be cooked hard though, cuz they can kind of poison you if they're raw."

Elliot glanced in the direction of the science wing. "Yes, there seems to be a lot of that going around," he said. "What kind of poison would this one be?"

"The pooping your guts out kind," the man said, digging up another tuber and brushing dirt off it. "Depends on how much you eat and how raw it is, of course, but yeah, it can be pretty bad."

Hubcap put a hand on his partner's shoulder. "Enjoy your dinner tonight, meatling!"

"Some day I will find a way to give you the robot equivalent of diarrhea," Elliot said. "And I will laugh."

Hubcap just patted his shoulder and smiled.

"Hold it," the local said, raising a hand. "Everybody shut up for a second." The offworlders went silent, with the cameras searching the ground for any sign of motion. Dale shuffled nervously. After a long few seconds, Ted shrugged. "Never mind. Keep an eye out, though. They can sneak up on you."

"So what do they actually look like?" Elliot asked. "Are they furry like Earth gophers? Large snaky things?"

Ted shook his head, getting back to shoveling. "Naw, nothing like that. They're built more like big drills with feet." He stood up and gestured about his head. "They've got this pointy horn thing going on that lets 'em break through the hardest dirt, and there's lots of feet with digging claws. I forget how many feet exactly."

Elliot nodded while Hubcap stared at the ground. "Now I really want to see one," the robot said. "Is there a way of attracting them? Any sounds they like?"

"Not that I know of," Ted said. "They usually *don't* like loud noises, but I haven't seen anything in particular that could be said to draw 'em in closer."

"That's a pity," Hubcap said, still scanning the dirt. "Maybe if we squeak like little defenseless eatable creatures? What do they eat aside from plants and ankles? What sounds do those make?"

Ted described it as best he could, and Hubcap made an experimental squeal. Ted shifted his grip on the shovel. "Yeah, it's a lot like that, except with more interruptions, not so much one long sound, if you know what I mean."

"I think so," the robot said, then repeated the note with some chattering thrown in.

Elliot made a show of wincing and covering his ears.

"Like that?" Hubcap asked.

"Yeah, that's a lot closer," Ted said. "If you can make it sound smaller and weaker, then I'd say you've got it."

Hubcap gave it his best, squeaking away while the cameras panned across the garden and everyone listened for digging. Nothing happened.

"Hey Ted," Elliot said. "When they do jump out at someone, do they do it from the side or from below? Can you see them coming?"

"They're pretty stealthy," Ted said. "Sometimes you see 'em try for something in a different place first, but a lot of the time they just appear from underneath you."

"Seems like they would just end up biting the soles of people's shoes," Elliot said.

"Well, their mouths aren't at the tip of their heads," Ted explained. "So they have to kind of lunge out sideways." He gestured with his hands, pantomiming something like a whale breaching. "They're pretty fast, so they usually don't miss. And they can bite through boot leather."

"But not metal," Hubcap added pointing to the man's armored shoes. "Right?"

Ted nodded. "Right."

"So I'm safe," the robot announced. "You lot, not so much. What's that?" He pointed at the other end of the garden.

Everyone whirled to look, and Dale yelped suddenly.

"What? What?"

"Something bit me!" The cameraman hopped on one leg, then looked down to see nothing more ominous than Hubcap's foot where he had been standing. Dale swore. The robot whistled innocently and pulled his foot back.

"Hubcap!" Elliot admonished, smiling despite himself. "That was a little heartless."

The robot rapped his chest with metal knuckles, making a hollow sound. "Yeah, well, that's just me all over, isn't it?" he said lightly. "I'm lacking many of your squishy organs. And you can't tell me that wasn't funny."

Ted snickered, leaning on his shovel. "That was a cute little yelp you made, son," he said to Dale with a grin. "Sounded almost like a little prey animal yourself there."

Dale harrumphed and readjusted his camera while the others hid their smiles.

"Anyway," Elliot said, getting the conversation back on track. "How many of those plants do you need to get today, Ted?"

"Oh, not too many more," the man said. "Just enough to go in tonight's casserole. There'll be plenty of other ingredients, especially with the haul of edible water plants that we just got in." He dug up a few roots in quick succession.

"Would that be Earth waterweeds, or native plantlife that's safe for human consumption?" Elliot asked.

"Ooh, who was the first to test it?" Hubcap wanted to know. "What daring soul risked death by intestinal misadventure for the sake of food?"

"Honestly, it was probably tested by computer scan," Ted said. "No messing about when it comes to unknowns like alien food."

"Wise choice," Elliot said.

"How boring," Hubcap said at the same time. "Messing about is half the fun. At least that one scientist made some knot-tying artwork with the other seaweed. That's some fine messing about."

"Knot-tying?" Ted asked, standing up from shoveling. "Which scientist?"

Elliot was curious too. This was the first he'd heard of it.

"Ilsa something," Hubcap said. "But if she gets in trouble for it, you didn't hear that from me."

"That's weird," Ted said. "The guys were talking about some other waterweeds they found tied in knots." He shook dirt off his shovel. "Must be the new craze in slacking. Couldn't have been the same person; there's no Ilsa on their team."

Elliot glanced at a camera. "Is there a chance the native life is doing it?"

Ted looked into the distance. "Hm. Doubt it. I haven't heard of anything with fingers dexterous enough for that. And it sounds like some complicated knots. Anyway," he said, rooting around in his bag. "I've probably got enough for the casserole. Should be heading back now."

"Aw, we didn't see a supergopher," Hubcap pouted. "Maybe if we squeak some more." He let fly with a series of high-pitched chirrups that made all of the humans cover their ears. Elliot winced as Hubcap held a pose with one hand cocked to the side of his head, listening with a hopeful expression. When only silence greeted him, he dropped his hand. "Well, poop."

"We can always check back later," Elliot told him.

"Yeah, we should go hurry up and wait," Hubcap said with a look at the third-floor windows.

Elliot thanked Ted for the education on the gardens and dangers therein, offering to help carry the bag of tubers. Ted politely declined and led the way back along the concrete pathway. As they walked, Elliot pointed out the grassback flatworms for some long-range footage, but otherwise the cameras stayed off.

He was talking about a friend's escape-prone pet ferret with a talent at hiding in tall grass when Hubcap jumped and pointed back at the garden.

"That plant just moved!" he said. "Come on!" Hubcap sprinted away. Ted dropped his bag on the concrete and raced after him with the shovel at the ready. Elliot and the others hurried, cameras clicking on.

"There!" Hubcap said, pointing to a jiggling plant at the end of a row. "It was just sitting in a burrow waiting for us to leave!" He dashed forward and leapt with a yell to land heavily next to the plant. "Missed it!" He began leaping around with both feet, apparently trying to stomp on either side of the animal and trap it.

"It'll be gone by now," Ted told him, jogging to a halt. "Just dug straight down."

"Crapdoodle," the robot said, ending his hopping dance and regarding the many footprints he'd left. "Should we dig this plant up and see what's left of it?"

"Naw," Ted said. "If it's dead, we'll know next time we're out here, but if it's good, it'll keep growing. Let's be off, then."

"Oh, fine."

The group moved out again, but this time they didn't get far before Hubcap yelled. "Wait!"

"What now?" Elliot asked as his co-host sprinted away in a different direction, this time launching himself toward a half-buried boulder at the far edge of the garden. The robot plunged his hands deep into the soil.

"Ha!" he exclaimed, rearing back and pulling free a wriggling shape that flung dirt everywhere.

"Wow, nice catch!" Elliot said in surprise while the camera crew spread around to get better shots. The creature was roughly the size of a house cat, with a horn-covered head that tapered into a point, and multiple feet with long claws doing their best to maul the impervious robot who held it.

"Hold him still!" Ted instructed, taking a stance with his bladed shovel.

Hubcap started to object, but the animal squirmed violently sideways. Ted's shovel clanged harmlessly off its drillbit head. The impact was enough to jolt it loose from Hubcap's grasp, and despite the robot's quick reflexes, the creature kicked free and dove for the ground where it vanished with impressive speed.

Hubcap dug after it, but the thing was gone. He finally sat back and exclaimed in good-natured frustration. "Dang. At least I caught one!" he said to the others. "And no killing defenseless beasties on camera," he told Ted sternly.

Ted shrugged. "Got to protect our food somehow. Good catch, though. That's the first time I've seen anybody pull one out of the ground like that."

Hubcap bowed while Elliot speculated whether the squeaky animal impressions had really attracted the creature.

"Could be," Ted said, swinging his shovel back onto his shoulder. "We can play with it another time. But fun as this is, I really need to get those roots to the kitchen. There's a lot of chopping and washing to do."

"Well, thank you for talking with us," Elliot said with a handshake. "We'd love to do this again another time."

"And I will show off my critter-catching prowess!" Hubcap said, getting up.

They walked back at a brisk pace, with Elliot asking Ted about nonlethal pest deterrents and Tarja pointing out halfway there that Vic was in the window waving for their attention. The TV crew said goodbye to Ted and ran for the stairs. Elliot hoped desperately that Vic had some good news.

Chapter 13

Vic certainly had news, though Elliot wouldn't call it good. She met the group outside the office with an explanation for why Mr. Lee hadn't met with them yet. "He had a frenzy attack right before we arrived," she said, gesturing helplessly.

Elliot nodded but didn't interrupt. It must have been some frenzy to keep the man bedridden for two days.

"It began with stress over us, actually," Vic continued. "Worry about getting everything arranged, while oh by the way the frenzy is much *worse* now than when he invited us here. Then he worked himself into a tizzy getting ready to meet us, and other people didn't notice until he almost passed out."

Elliot winced. "So has he been comatose for the past two days?"

"No, but the doctors have been very concerned. He's an older gentleman, and they don't want a relapse."

"Ah. Right."

Vic addressed the group. "Mr. Lee is very apologetic, both for being unable to meet us and for the unexpected rate of frenzy attacks lately. He insists that it wasn't this bad when he first contacted us." She coughed. "I did call Ms. Kaleel to see what she had to say. It was less than encouraging."

There was an electronic snort from Hubcap. "Surprise surprise."

"She thanked me for the update, but said there will be no change of plans. No early shuttle home for anything less than an outbreak threatening everyone's life." Vic's expression turned sour. "It's just as well. We need those new episodes to carry the show. Leaving early would mean handing over our sponsorship to the competition. Plus we're contracted to get footage for a half dozen episodes. So we're stuck."

Elliot wasn't sure whether to feel glad for the chance to save their show, or to worry about their safety. His emotions settled on "distressed" and refused to budge.

"What does she suggest that we do," Hubcap asked slowly, "To minimize risk to ourselves? Please don't say 'be careful.'"

Vic wore a wry smile. "That's a given. No, we're encouraged to film things that are safe, outdoors if possible, and also the most captivating television we can manage."

"How helpful," Elliot said. "Safe and captivating both, huh?"

Hubcap craned his neck in a full-body eye roll. "This wisdom knows no bounds."

"Mr. Lee said he would find something for us," Vic said. "He's looking into a couple possibilities now. And he is very sorry for downplaying the level of frenzy here. It wasn't bad at all before, and they really do need both employees and funding. They're hoping for good press from our show."

Hubcap straightened up and crossed his arms. "Well, that depends on whether or not their lovely planet kills one of us, doesn't it?" He looked at the others. "One of you, I mean. I'll have to deal with it afterward."

Elliot huffed a silent laugh. "Yes, thank you for clarifying."

Graham spoke up. "What's our next move, then? Wait until Mr. Lee gets back to us with options?"

Vic shook her head. "We should use our time productively. He'll find us. Did you see anything else out in that garden?"

Elliot thought hard. "Nothing we didn't already film. We could wander around looking for more workers, but that's probably a waste of time."

"Ooh!" Hubcap said. "Let's find Ted in the kitchen! It's not outdoors, but I'll keep an eye on everybody. Kitchens are a universal human experience, but this one's exotic. It could be good to show that even on an alien world, people still have to chop vegetables. Maybe we'll get lucky and find one of those chefs who do tricks flipping dough and shrimps and whatnot. Or weird alien food that *does stuff* when you cook it! We've just got to see the alien food, you guys."

Elliot looked to Vic for a decision.

She shrugged. "Worth a try. Mr. Lee should have a new location for us soon anyway." She went to tell the receptionist where Mr. Lee could find them while Hubcap waxed poetic about the many possibilities.

"We can have the Hubcap & Elliot Cooking Show!" he said. "With those silly white aprons that highlight every bit of dirt except for white flour. They will be cooking some bizarre plant that people on Earth will want to try, and we'll start a new trend. It'll be great."

Vic returned to lead the way while Hubcap continued to talk. Elliot was feeling almost optimistic until the robot gave them all a reminder.

"Just try your best not to frenzy in the kitchen," he said. "There's knives there."

Everyone except for Hubcap was quiet for the rest of the walk. He didn't seem to notice, taking over from Vic in leading the way, since he'd memorized a map of the complex at some point.

Elliot was no longer surprised at Hubcap's preparations. Evacuation routes, fire extinguishers, restrooms and water fountains were important. Terrible artwork was less important in emergencies, but the robot tended to memorize the locations of that too. It was Elliot's theory that he liked to have a ready stock of things to make fun of. This might have been a remnant of his rescue programming to help him lighten the mood on a tense mission. Or it might have been Hubcap's delight in poking fun at anything he could feel superior to.

If I didn't know his background, Elliot thought, *I might think he was built to be egotistical.* But knowing that the robot had spent most of his life not allowed to speak badly of anyone made Elliot more understanding of his loud opinions now. Like the running commentary he was currently doing on the hallway's decorations.

"This painting!" Hubcap pointed with glee. "Did you guys see this yet? It's amazingly bad! I mean the color choice is reasonable and the detail work is flawless, but you'd think it would be obvious somewhere in the early stages that human spines don't bend like that. Seriously, try to hit that pose. You would sever a nerve. And the hands are too big. The artist should have done the hand-in-front-of-the-face trick." Hubcap held his own hand up, fingers splayed. "Although there is that one genetic condition. Hey Dale, is your hand bigger than your face? Hold it up and see."

"No, I will not," Dale said, walking stubbornly past. "I went to public school. I know that joke."

"Aw," Hubcap complained. "Dang larval humans, ruining my best jokes."

Graham looked quietly confused. Elliot caught his eye and explained that it was a prank to slap a person's palm into their own face. "And then he could say 'Quit hitting yourself,' which is peak humor for most ten-year-olds I've known," Elliot said.

Graham laughed. "Of course."

Hubcap pointed at them with a smile, walking backward. "I am nothing if not peak humor!"

Elliot smiled back. "I'd say that's debatable."

"I will debate you any time."

Vic spoke up. "The only debating that will happen in the next few minutes is us versus a busy kitchen crew with no space for visitors to be getting in their way with cameras. Let's be on our best behavior."

"We will surely win that debate," Hubcap said. "We have stickycam rigs, and dainty individuals like Dale and Tarja who can fit up on a shelf somewhere." He looked up at Vic. "You'll get a good view from a doorway, I'm sure."

"Or I could use that little thing called a zoom function," the towering woman said. "No use blocking the door."

Hubcap patted her on the arm. "Lesser mortals shall pass beneath you like monkeys beneath a great tree," he declared.

Vic snorted. "Monkeys climb trees. You can think up a better analogy than that."

"Like … rabbits beneath a national monument?"

"That doesn't even make sense."

"Should have stuck with the tree," Graham said

"Scurrying ants below a towering boulder!"

"Now I'm a rock, thanks." Vic smirked. "Something tells me you're not trying too hard."

"There's nothing wrong with rocks!" the robot protested. "I've always admired them. The way they just sit there, unperturbed by the goings-on around them, undamaged by the ravages of time … they're a lot like meditative proto-robots in a way."

Vic stared at him while Elliot stifled a chuckle. "Meditative proto-robots," she repeated.

Hubcap threw his hands into the air. "What?"

"Nothing. Nothing at all."

The kitchen entrance appeared around the corner before Hubcap could marshal a proper response. He shook off the conversation with the air of a cat that had just slipped off a couch and wanted to pretend it meant to do that. Elliot just grinned.

"Ah, there's the kitchen!" Hubcap exclaimed. "Right where it should be. Show us your mysteries, kitchen."

* * *

The kitchen wasn't all that mysterious, as it turned out, but the TV crew was welcomed with no debate. The various camera jockeys found positions that wouldn't be in the way, and Ted happily put Elliot and Hubcap to work. Elliot thought privately that the white apron was a distinct improvement over the white biohazard suits they'd worn earlier. He put his own worries aside with the ease of long practice, and did his best to make captivating banter with Hubcap.

"Are you setting a new landspeed record for chopping?" he asked over a stack of bowls. "I'm going to finish the dishes before you're done."

"Nonsense!" Hubcap replied. "Behold, I have vanquished the entire bucketload of — oh, there's more." His glee subsided as the tub of cubed potatoes was swapped out for a tub of freshly scrubbed carrots. "Well, all right, then."

Ted grinned. "These ones should be cut into coins instead of cubes. Thanks for making my job easier."

"That is my purpose in life, my good meatsack," the robot said with dignity as he picked up the first carrot. "So how thick should the coins be?"

Ted demonstrated, then left Hubcap with the rest and checked on Elliot's progress in loading the industrial dishwasher. "You don't have to scrub off everything," he said. "But these ones will need to soak a while before you put them in. Put that one upside down, otherwise you'll get scalding water on your hands when you open the door. Got it? Okay, I'll be right back."

Ted left, and Elliot immediately asked if Hubcap wanted to trade.

"No thank you," the robot said, merrily attacking a carrot.

"Oh come on, you know you want a chance to make fun of the gross squishy things that the humans eat."

"I can do that from here," the robot declared. He held up a large carrot and pointed at it with his other hand. "Ha!"

It was while Elliot was still trying to convince him that Mr. Lee arrived. Elliot heard Vic calling from the doorway, and looked to see her waving everyone over to meet someone significantly shorter than herself.

The TV crew extricated themselves from their positions. While they did, the kitchen workers greeted the man with a degree of concerned affection that said volumes about his leadership. Elliot and the others circled up in the cafeteria outside the kitchen for proper introductions.

"Hello everyone," Mr. Lee said with a warm smile and a surprisingly deep voice for someone so delicately built. He seemed healthy enough, despite a fair share of wrinkles and gray hairs, and he moved slowly. Elliot spent a moment debating with himself whether the man looked more Japanese or Chinese, but he gave up, not being much of an expert. "I apologize for not making an appearance sooner," Mr. Lee continued. "I am Hikaru Lee. Pleased to meet you."

They all took turns shaking his hand gently, and he apologized on behalf of the station for the crew's misadventures so far. "I feel terrible for what you've gone through," he said. "I want to make sure that nothing else is liable to happen. Elliot, have you fully recovered from your injury?"

Elliot assured him that he had, not wanting anyone in the room to be worried. A full half of the circle currently staring at him was likely to break out in overprotective concern.

"I'm glad to hear it," Mr. Lee said. "With that in mind, I have a filming opportunity for you. Some interesting shells have washed up at the river, and we would like to find more of them. They're both durable and aesthetically pleasing. If there's a sustainable source, we could find a market for exporting them. I understand they have already been used as backup tools here. I'm told they make fine shovels."

Elliot watched Hubcap open his mouth to say something that was almost certainly about the gophers, but he showed admirable restraint and kept silent.

"This should be a very low-risk trip," Mr. Lee continued. "Just searching and gathering. I will tell you that we aren't certain what type of animal sheds these, but we're sure that it's at least partially aquatic, and unlikely to pose any danger to an aircar at a safe height." He spread his hands. "We will take every precaution. Is this something you'd like to film?"

Vic nodded decisively and said that it was. She and Mr. Lee talked scheduling while the camera crew consulted about waterproof gear.

Hubcap sidled up to Elliot. Expecting a new "Lee" joke, Elliot was surprised to hear Hubcap mutter, "Alien clams. Or mermaids."

"What?"

"That's my bet. It could be fish scales, or chicken feet or something actually alien looking, but I'm thinking clams are more likely. They're shovel-shaped."

"And mermaids?"

"I've got to make the wager interesting, don't I?"

Chapter 14

"That is all kinds of nifty," Hubcap said, flipping over the colorful scale and holding it up for the cameras with a hangar wall as backdrop. "It looks like it's made of fire." It also seemed to have come from something shaped like neither a clam nor a mermaid, but Hubcap was ignoring that fact. He'd privately revised his guess to "alien lobster." Time would tell. He'd noted its scent, and looked forward to searching. The mood was optimistic.

Elliot had watched him take a good sniff in the cold morning air, and was making a point now of discussing the detailed texture of the one he held. The human knew full well that Hubcap's fingertips weren't calibrated to that degree.

"It feels like a topographical map of the desert," Elliot said to Dale. "This part has sand dunes, and these edges have rock formations like the ones in Utah. What do you think, Hubcap?"

With hands pressed together in front of his closed mouth, Hubcap regarded his grinning co-host. "I think," he said, "That I will find it first, no matter what it feels like."

"Okay," Elliot said, grin still in place. "You do have the superior robot senses, after all."

"That's right."

"So, Owen!" Elliot turned to address the slender biologist who was once again the crew chief. "Do you think the bright colors are a sign that the creature is poisonous?"

Owen stowed the last of the gear they would need in the aircar, breath puffing in the cold. "It certainly could be," he said. "As far as we've been able to tell, the same principles apply here as on Earth — tasty edible creatures try to blend in while the deadly ones make clear warnings. Of course, with armor like this, it's hard to imagine an animal needing poison. But it could either be mimicking the coloration of a legitimately poisonous animal, or it becomes poisonous if it eats the right diet. Lots of possibilities; science is fun that way!"

Hubcap blinked his wiper panels. "Thank you for that

rundown. So, do we know what the thingies look like?" He tapped a metal finger on the plate-sized piece he held.

"Nope!" Owen said cheerfully. "This is all we know about them." He waved to the half dozen other scales distributed through the group. They ranged in color from Hubcap's fiery red to Elliot's purple/black to those that the half dozen biologists held that were everything in between. Each piece was curved into either a dome or a cylinder, adorned with small ridges and dull spikes, and they were very, very tough. Owen had demonstrated this right off the bat by flinging one like a discus against the wall.

It had rebounded and nearly hit Hubcap, who had to be convinced not to start a frisbee war. He was still looking for an excuse to throw the one he held now.

"Well, let's go learn some more!" Elliot said. He handed his piece to Owen, who collected the others and led the way into the aircar. Hubcap hurried to get a good seat. This might just be an exciting trip.

Minutes later, the vehicle was speeding over the landscape at hovering height. Hubcap knew they would be going higher soon, since mountains were approaching fast and there were no good routes straight through. He would have asked about their flight path if it wasn't a struggle to be heard. This aircar was a bigger enclosed model, but it was no quieter than the first.

That didn't stop Owen. "Did anyone tell you about these mountains?" he called back from the copilot's seat, shouting over the thunder of the engines. "They're called the Razor Range!"

Hubcap raised his own volume. "Yes, because they're sharp enough to make the sky bleed. We heard about the rainstorms." An official on the shuttle ride from the space station had gone into detail in describing the local environment. Hubcap hoped that Owen wasn't about to repeat the lecture.

"That's right; they're like one long bladed mountain," Owen said with all the delight of a science geek who gets to explain something. If the cameras had been filming anything other than silent background shots right now, it could have been useful footage. But with the engines this loud, it was just conversation. "The seasonal rainstorms tend to run up against them before reaching us out here." Owen continued, pointing down at the temperate land speeding past. "This would look very different if those mountains weren't there."

"So does that mean there's rainforest on the other side?" Elliot asked, prompting an avalanche of data. Hubcap didn't bother interrupting.

"It's not a rainforest like the kind you're probably thinking of," Owen replied. "Most of the year is dry, so the trees have to be able to withstand drought. But all that rain does make things interesting this time of year. There's widespread flooding that's still at its peak now, even though the rains have cut back to a storm every few days instead of each morning."

Hubcap found a few things in the lecture interesting despite himself, and when the river at the foot of the mountains appeared with muddy glory, he leaned forward in his harness for a better look.

"Which way is the waterfall?" he asked, searching for the landmark Owen had described. "Oh wait; I see it!" Owen pointed it out anyway, talking about how the flow of water from the flooded area above widened the existing river.

The camera crew aimed downward, doing their best to focus on the distant scenery. Hubcap watched with interest as the aircar rose to follow the waterfall. This was at the southern tip of the Razor Range, where a crack in the sharp wall dipped just low enough for dark water to pour over. "That must be some massive flooding," Hubcap said.

He felt Elliot tap his side. "What did you say about encouraging him?" the human asked.

"You hush while I'm being hypocritical."

Then the roaring engines raised them up to the break in the mountainside, and the car darted into the shadowy chasm just above the water.

Hubcap threw his hands into the air as rock walls sped by on either side, and he made happy roller coaster yells.

"Wooooo, yeah!"

Beside him, Elliot was shaking his head. Then the scene brightened as the other side raced toward them with a splash of brilliant blue sky.

When the little aircar shot out of the rift, it suddenly seemed tiny indeed as it hovered over a vast green forest with muddy water glinting between the trees.

"Will you look at that," Elliot said.

"Oh, I'm looking!" Hubcap answered. "I've always wanted to swim through a jungle!"

"It's not really a jungle," Owen said. "It's a forest, but..."

"Curses, I set him off again," Hubcap said, glancing at a

muted camera. He sat back to withstand more lecturing, and watched out the windows with interest. Vic had said that the showrunner was looking for eye-catching footage. This looked pretty eye-catching to Hubcap.

It soon became obvious that the whole forest wasn't flooded, only the area surrounding the river. The aircar slowed to follow the curves of the original riverbed, which was visible only because there were no trees there. Owen urged the pilot to go lower, while the biologists peered intently out the windows.

"Keep your eyes open for flashes of color!" Owen yelled. "They'll probably be washed up against rocks and fallen trees. That's how we found the other ones."

The aircar traced the path of the river, finding nothing more than water, weird trees, and colorful flying creatures that looked like bats who wanted to be parrots when they grew up. Hubcap pointed out a couple for Graham to film.

"There! Set down there!" Owen said, pointing, and the pilot angled the car downward. The river was still wide here, but it bent sharply, with a gravelly beach on the inside of the curve and a herd of large gray boulders on the outside. Owen was talking about the mechanics of the water flow in relation to digging canyons and pushing big rocks about, but Hubcap's attention was on the flight path of the aircar.

For a moment he thought the car would be landing on the beach, but he was wrong. Instead, Owen directed it to hover over the rocks. The noisy flight engines turned off with alarming suddenness, to be replaced by the quiet hum of the hover engine and a chorus of what passed for native birdsong. Hubcap tried to locate whatever was making the chirps and squeaks, but had no luck. Apparently they weren't scared into silence by aircar engines. They were staying hidden, though.

Hubcap saw the camera jockeys turn their volume on. He started to narrate for the nearest two, but he was interrupted by a worker spotting color among the dark rocks. The pilot didn't need Owen's urging to float over in the right direction. Once, the sighting was confirmed, the biologists started getting out of their seats. Hubcap did the same. They weren't about to make fascinating discoveries without him.

"We're not going to land?" Elliot asked, unbuckling his harness.

"Nope!" Owen told him cheerfully. "There's nowhere flat

enough. We'll stick with a getaway landing. Those come in handy when the wildlife gets restive!"

"Oh goody," Hubcap said, heading for the door. "Restive wildlife makes for great TV!"

He was caught before he could throw the door open and make a wild dive into the muddy depths. Apparently there were ladders for this sort of thing. How boring.

"Everybody watch your step on the way down," Owen said. "And be careful of slippery rocks — things still look wet from the rain. Make sure you can get back to the rock we're setting down on." He kept up the advice as the biologists opened the door and set up the ladder, which was made from metal cable and steps. A few of the local experts went down first to demonstrate the safest technique, then it was the newbies' turn. "Make sure each handhold and foothold is secure before moving on to the next," Owen advised, gesturing toward the open door.

"Got it," Hubcap said with a salute. He turned to the rest of his crew. "Come, meatbags; there is exploratory science to be done!" With that, he swung over the side of the aircar with what he knew looked like careless abandon, but was really a move that he had perfected over years of water rescues. He led the way down the swaying ladder with Elliot explaining to Owen that the robot really did know what he was doing.

He made landfall easily on the largest rock. The humans took their sweet time behind him. He sniffed about while they dithered over whether or not to leave the puffy jackets behind since the morning was heating up. Nothing smelled like the shell he'd held earlier — or rather everything did, since it had stunk of algae and mud. Hubcap peered between boulders.

Jacket-less, Elliot made his way to the ground with the camera crew moving slowly behind him. A glance showed that Graham had chosen to stay in the aircar and film from above.

A reasonable idea, Hubcap admitted as he stepped out of the way of several locals climbing down. *We may want a view from up there, and I suppose Graham is a little old for the acrobatics.* A brief flailing of arms on ground level reminded him that it could be worse. Two biologists were giving Dale a hand before he could lose his balance or his camera. No one had frenzied. Good enough.

Soon everyone was down on the rocks who was going to be. The aircar left its ladder ready, hovering in place with Graham filming from the open door in the company of locals who pointed things out to him.

"They were over that way," someone was saying. Hubcap focused his attention back on the task at hand, and hopped merrily over the damp rocks in the search for colorful mystery shells. The sun was bright and the air was full of alien birdsong. With less frenzy to worry about outdoors, he found himself looking forward to filming with more optimism than the day before.

There would be interesting things here; he just knew it.

There had better be.

***

Elliot picked up a domed shell fragment that reminded him of a Scatterball kneepad: smooth and white on the inside. He flipped it over to find the outside covered in spikes like something from the more violent street leagues. The white color turned yellow at the edges, then swiftly changed to dark purple across the craggy outer surface. Sky blue spikes poked out everywhere. Elliot compared its shape to the others scattered about, and he wondered what kind of body part it had fit over.

The smell of it reached his nose, making him exhale forcefully. *Whoo, ripe seafood,* he thought. *With water moss and mildew. I hope somebody packed hand sanitizer.*

As he thought it, he heard Hubcap call out, "Look at me, I have red hair!"

Elliot looked up to see the robot capering about on a flat rock with an orange-red scale on his head.

Elliot wrinkled his nose. "Careful, you'll get alien algae on you," he said.

Hubcap didn't let that deter him. He left the scummy helmet in place, and took off bounding from rock to rock with a disregard for the deep, dark river that lurked below. Elliot shook his head, thinking that if it had been a human jumping around like that, he would have called him careless. But this was Hubcap, and he always moved like that. He had a surprisingly good safety record to back it up.

"Sign of life!" crowed Owen. Elliot turned to see everyone converging on the crew chief, who was pointing towards the water and leaping boulders much like Hubcap had. He stopped on a low rock in the shade of several trees that drooped like yellow celery. Vic and Tarja were right behind him, aiming cameras.

"What? What did you see?" Elliot called, setting the shell down and making his hasty way over.

"Something fast and pale, down there," the biologist said in excitement. "It looked massive!"

Everyone peered into the depths, but try as they might, no one could make out anything farther than a foot or so. Hubcap started looking around for a "pokin' stick," while Owen described what he'd seen. Elliot listened carefully.

"It was kind of drifting at first," Owen said. "Moving slowly like it didn't want to get our attention, then I guess it saw me, because it sort of jerked sideways and disappeared. I think it kicked off the rock to go deeper."

"What was it shaped like?" Elliot prompted.

Owen made vague hand gestures. "Blurry. Big, definitely — longer than I am tall — and I got the distinct impression that there were lots of legs. Stiff ones, not flippers or tentacles. I suppose it could be something crustacean in phenotype." He chattered away in a cloud of scientific excitement.

Hubcap trotted over with a hefty tree branch that looked like it had been moldering under the water for a long time. Eliot and the other humans gave him a wide berth.

"Heeeere fishy fishy fishy," the robot chanted happily. He thrust the slimy branch into the water, poking about for all he was worth, but nothing surfaced. The branch was only visible for a short distance before the end disappeared into the murky green-brown. The robot soon gave up and tossed the branch out into the river, where it sank without a trace. "No fishy. I am made sad."

Elliot patted his shoulder. "You tried. We'd need a high-powered searchlight to find anything in this water."

The robot shook his head. "I was hoping it was just hiding, and would show up on heat vision with a little persuading. But no luck." He blinked, adjusting his eyes, and looked up like he'd had a good idea. "I could jump in and swim around—"

"Nope," Elliot said.

Owen chimed in. "No, let's look for more shells, shall we?" he suggested. He ushered the robot away from the edge, distracting him by pointing out that there was a boulder to look behind that only he could reach. Moments later, Hubcap was leaping across open water to land like a gecko on the side of a large sloping rock. Elliot watched him scramble over to the other side, and complimented Owen on his Hubcap-handling technique.

"Well, he does remind me of my young cousins," Owen admitted. "There's no way to convince them not to do something they've set their minds to, except by giving them something else to do instead."

Elliot nodded. "That about covers it," he said.

"Jaaaaaackpot!" the robot yelled from the top of the boulder. "I found stuff!" He ducked back down out of sight.

"What kind of stuff?" Owen wanted to know. "Is it portable?" He edged along the boulder he stood on, visibly looking for a way across that wouldn't leave him swimming. Elliot made sure the cameras were pointed in that direction. Vic was already on it.

"Yeah, lemme move some plants first," said Hubcap, followed by splashing and scraping sounds. Moments later the robot reappeared with an armload of colorful things. "They're kind of beat up, but here you go!" He made another dramatic leap across the water and landed awkwardly, barely managing not to drop anything.

The biologists all got grabby with the pile. Elliot let them have first dibs on the interesting pieces, then picked up a yellow shard. He held it up for Tarja's camera while Dale and Vic covered the rest. It looked like lemon rind crossed with a crab shell.

"This is fascinating," Owen said. "These cracks could be from an impact with a rock, or the jaw of a predator — while these holes and cuts appear to have been ground out."

"Maybe a burrowing parasite?" suggested a woman whose hair was an explosion of blonde ringlets, as she held a shell above her head to look through the hole.

"That's possible," Owen agreed. "They're definitely not made by impact. See there's no sign of cracking, and these hairline scratches around the holes indicate repeated circular motions." He held up a purple fragment with one perfectly round hole bored through the edge of it. As he kept talking, fellow biologists crowded around to inspect it and offer their own theories.

Elliot regarded the piece that he held, finding nothing more significant than a missing chunk that appeared to have been broken off. There were no marks that he could find — well, no big ones, anyway. He squinted closer, second-guessing himself while the others talked.

"This one seems to have been broken by the grinding action," said a black woman with a short fuzz of hair. "See the scrapes at the edge of the crack here?"

"And this one has an abortive attempt!" added a white man with similar hair. "Look, there are swirling scrape marks, but it doesn't make it all the way through."

"Oh, maybe the parasite was scraped off before it got that far," the woman said.

"I wonder if these are predatory parasites, or just barnacle-style hitchhikers that dig too deep?" suggested the blonde woman.

"I'd bet on predatory," Owen said. "There's no reason why something would need to keep digging like that just to stay in place. Look, the marks would be right under where it sat. No, this has to be some sort of rasping tongue, or similar action."

Elliot didn't have much to add to the conversation. When he was sure that the cameras had recorded enough of him standing there looking thoughtful, he crouched to join Hubcap in playing jigsaw puzzle with some of the shells. Tarja filmed from the edge of the huddle. The robot still had the red shell dripping down his neck. He looked to Elliot like a particularly unhinged conspiracy theorist as he studied the colorful pieces before him.

Elliot cocked his head. "You know there's a good chance that these all came from different animals, right?"

"Oh, sure. But this is fun."

Elliot nodded. "True enough. Hey, this one's different," he said, picking up a dark blue scale with a much bigger area ground down to a pale blue-white. He ignored Hubcap's noises of irritation and waved it above his head. "Owen! Here's another clue."

The head biologist snatched it up with an exclamation of great interest, and the cameras followed him intently. "Oh wow, this is huge!" Owen said. "Imagine the size of the parasite that could do this!" He and the others were off again, chattering away about the possibilities. Elliot waited for a moment then went back to the puzzle. Hubcap was arranging the pieces in a new way, and Elliot wanted to see if he'd figured out anything important.

He had not. "As best I can tell," the robot said, "This beast was a large segmented snake, with many heads. Yep, that's got to be it."

"I see."

"My work here is done!" Hubcap said. "I shall now climb more rocks and attempt to spot one of the things, thus proving my theory."

"You do that," Elliot said. He glanced at the huddle while the robot once again leapt into space. The thump of his landing on another boulder was pretty quiet for someone with metal feet.

Elliot got up and found a different vantage point to climb: a cluster of rocks farther from the water. He set his feet with care on the damp surface. Slipping now would be both dangerous and humiliating, especially since Tarja was still tracking him with the camera.

The biologists sounded like they'd be at it for some time. Normally Elliot would be down there with them, in front of all the cameras asking questions, but today he just couldn't. Not when he stood a chance of spotting something "riveting and eye-catching" to film instead.

He saw Tarja elbow Vic to point out the absence of both co-hosts. While Elliot chose his next step and pretended not to watch, Vic sent Tarja and Dale to follow them. She also had a quiet word with Owen, who had to be pried away from the shells. By the looks of it, the head biologist was briefly concerned about the guests he was supposed to be keeping an eye on. But Vic calmed him down.

Probably pointing out that we're not that far away, Elliot thought. *And if we spot something good from up here, they can all scramble to join us.* Whatever she'd said, Owen turned his attention back to the shell he was holding.

Elliot made sure to stay in view as he set his feet on the top of the first rock. Shading his eyes, he peered around dramatically for the sake of the cameras. Nothing moved aside from the water. Determined, he sought handholds and climbed higher.

Motion caught his eye as he reached the top, but it turned out to be a leafy frond dipping in the breeze. Branches and other debris were caught between boulders, a sign of higher floodwaters in the past. Elliot moved to address the cameras at the foot of the boulder, keeping his balance with one hand on a straight branch that was wedged between the rocks. Something small bounced off his head.

"Ow." He looked around to find Hubcap holding a handful of nuts or pebbles or something, and wearing a wide grin.

"Two points for me!" the robot exclaimed, tossing another.

Elliot dodged that one, bumping against the branch and knocking it loose from its perch. Hubcap kept up his cheerful barrage. Elliot decided that enough was enough.

"All right, you varlet!" he exclaimed, hopping to his feet and grasping the end of the branch. "Now you face the wrath of Excalibur!" With a mighty wrench, he pulled it free and aimed it at Hubcap's startled face. "En garde!"

At Hubcap's look, Elliot froze. The stick of wood ended in a very sharp splash of red. He stared down at the pointed shard of red shell that was tied to the pole with some sort of sinew.

Hubcap said it first. "That's a spear."

"Yes," Elliot said, his pulse speeding up. "Yes it is." He brought the point close to his face, reaching out a cautious fingertip to test its sharpness. It was very sharp.

"The question now is…" Hubcap began.

"…Who made it, when there's not supposed to be intelligent life on this planet?" Elliot finished. He held the spear aloft, in full view of the cameras. "Hey Owen!"

Chapter 15

The discovery of the spear changed everything. All the cameras were focused with intent, filming the alien-made weapon from every angle and getting Owen's in-depth analysis. Elliot re-enacted his discovery of the spear, minimizing the horseplay with the full knowledge that this could be history in the making. The biologists speculated madly and Hubcap helped them tear up the area looking for more signs of intelligent life. There were none, but the shell fragments with holes were evaluated in a different light.

"It's the same exact scrape markings on the blade of this spear," one of the biologists was arguing. "This has to be intentional carving!" He held up the most intact shell fragment, a blue-black dome with a crack in one side and two holes on another. It reminded Elliot of a bowl designed to leak.

"It certainly could be the same marks," Owen admitted. "But we shouldn't jump to conclusions. What would the purpose be for holes like this?"

The scientists all began suggesting ideas. Then one smart fellow looked from the shell in his coworker's hand to the one on Hubcap's head, and came to a conclusion of his own. He plucked the discussion piece out of the man's hand and swapped it with Hubcap's hat.

The robot stared out through what were now obviously eye holes in a helmet.

Elliot made appreciative noises and complimented the stylish algae. Hubcap posed as cameras circled.

"Well, all right then," Owen said. "It's not a perfect fit, but it would be a bit much to expect any sentient alien to be built like a human, much less a robot."

"I feel vaguely insulted," Hubcap said.

Owen ignored him and focused the conversation on this new revelation. The group came to the quick conclusion that these were armor pieces of various types, though it was next to impossible to reconstruct how they might fit together without knowing the body shape of the people who had carved them.

"This is big," Owen said, hand over his mouth. "We'll need to start searching the area for more signs. I can't believe they missed this in the original explorations."

"How much detail did they go into back then, anyway?" Elliot asked. "The planet is pretty huge. Surely that would be a massive undertaking to do it right."

"Well, that's assuming they were interested in doing it right," the crew chief whispered. He glanced at the nearest camera. "But you didn't hear that from me." He spoke in a normal volume. "The people who do the scans of a new planet are highly trained, with some impressive technology. When they get the time and money to scan a planet in the way they're trained to, it is unlikely that they are going to miss anything. But then, the universe is a big place, and intelligence can take any number of forms. If this is something we haven't encountered before, then it's possible that the scanners just aren't capable of detecting them."

Hubcap looked at the primitive spear. "And what if they just missed something? What is this going to mean for the whole operation here?"

Owen raised his hands in an exaggerated shrug. "It depends entirely on the aliens. Our setup is funded on the promise that we avoid significant damage to the native ecosystem, and if we find out that we have ruined some intelligent being's way of life, then we're probably going to have to pack up and go home. But if there's any way of coexisting with whatever natives there may be, then that will be our only option."

"Wow, alien intelligence," said a tall man with dusty lavender hair. "I never expected to meet any here."

"I know!" agreed the man beside him, who was shorter with dark skin and hair the same lavender. "This is gonna be amazing!"

Elliot nodded and agreed with the duo, recognizing them as the runners Larry and Jerry from the beach the other day. Without their body armor, they were easier to pick out of a crowd. Anodized purple wedding rings glinted while they gestured excitedly.

"I've never been part of a First Contact," the shorter Larry was saying. "We're going to be famous!"

"Yeah! And just imagine: what kind of bizarre creature did the probe teams miss?" Jerry enthused. "We could learn mindblowing things from them!" He beamed, as excited as a kid entering a theme park. "We'll get to *name* stuff!"

Owen laughed. "Yes, well, somebody will. I'm sure a lot of that will be right place, right time..."

"Oh man, I can't wait to be in the right place!" Jerry danced on the rock, his motions speeding up.

Owen began to look concerned. "Well, we'll just have to take it one step at a time," he said, his hand creeping towards his SedEgg pocket as Jerry refused to settle down. Larry glanced up in obvious worry.

"Oh, this is gonna be great!" Jerry exclaimed, hopping in place and waving his arms. "I'm gonna get a personal headcam to wear all the time, and maybe I'll be there when we first meet them — Wow, this will be fantastic!"

"Jer," Larry said, reaching for his arm, but missing it as the tall man jittered about. Other workers edged toward him too, and he didn't seem to notice.

"Oh, I wonder if they'll have a sense of humor," Jerry said to no one in particular. "And pets! Do they have alien pets? Who knows?" He grinned and flung his arms in the air, accidentally whacking Larry. "Oh, I can't *wait!*" With that, he leaned back and deliberately tipped into the water.

Owen grabbed for him and missed. "Jerry!"

The biologist happily splashed about in the murky river, sending waves of spray toward the rocks. Larry dove after him. The slow-moving water tugged them both downstream as half of the crew poured in as well, stamping Jerry's chest with SedEggs and supporting him when he collapsed. Hubcap stood sentinal on the rock with his knees bents and his vision undoubtedly scanning the water in ways human eyes couldn't.

Elliot joined the line of people helping to haul Jerry's limp body back onto the rock, with Larry at the front. He was glad to see that everyone made it up without either frenzying or being eaten by mysterious river creatures.

The science team worked in concert to bring down a collapsible stretcher that would allow the crew in the aircar to haul Jerry up to safety. Xian the medic applied extra antiseptic to the SedEgg puncture wounds, in case of river contamination, then helped strap him in. Hubcap watched the procedure with as much hawklike intensity as Larry did, while Elliot kept out of the way alongside the cameras. Soon the patient was up in the car and the rest of the team were taking their turns climbing the ladder. Owen sent up the spear and shell fragments tied in a bundle on their own line. The workers scrambled after. Elliot hurried to keep up.

When he reached the top of the ladder, Graham offered him a hand. The senior cameraman helped him out of the way of the next person, then spoke in a low voice. "Congrats on the discovery. Hey, the guys tell me there's been a lot more outbreaks of frenzy lately. Maybe even more than Mr. Lee let on." He glanced around. "Everybody's expecting someone else to flip out any second now, so keep your eyes open."

Elliot agreed quietly that he would, and he moved to pass the word on to Hubcap, who was stepping off the ladder behind him. If the frenzy swept through the car, then the robot would be the only person left with the ability to sedate the others.

"Hey Hubcap," he said with deceptive casualness. "How well can you fly an aircar?"

Chapter 16

Dr. Paul Rhodes got the news as he was finishing a routine psych evaluation. The mechanic he was evaluating was rambling on about an old breakup, his clothes more memorable than his words. The rust-covered blue uniform was the most striking thing in the room, which had been decorated in neutral tans and golds, and Dr. Rhodes was certain that there would be red dust to brush off of the chair when the man left.

Then the door flew open to admit a woman tracking mud on his floor. "Aliens!" the woman exclaimed, apologizing to the mechanic she had interrupted. "Sorry. Doc, we need you. It looks like there's something here after all."

"I'm sorry, something where?" the psychologist asked, setting his notepad down to regard the woman in damp clothes and muddy boots, with a biology-branch symbol on her shoulder and a wild expression.

"Something intelligent, on the other side of the mountains!" the biologist said with exaggerated waves of her arms. "We haven't found them yet, but we did find a weapon and armor, and somebody made those!"

Dr. Rhodes suddenly understood what his patients meant when they described the feeling of the floor dropping out from beneath them. His stomach clenched and he found himself starting to sweat. "Are you telling me that I will be needed for a First Contact?" he asked, struggling to maintain his professional calm.

"Yes, and soon!" she said. "Come on — there's a meeting in the big conference room!" She waved an arm for the titular diplomat to follow. It was clear that she had faith in his ability to mediate between species, which was something he'd been assured he'd never have to actually do.

Dr. Rhodes tried to collect his scattered thoughts. "I — yes, I will be right there. You can tell them I'm on my way." He gave the woman a confident nod of dismissal, and was grateful to see her leave with the same speed she had arrived.

"Was she serious?" the mechanic wanted to know.

"It certainly appears that way," the doctor said. He closed his notebook and stood to place it in his desk. "I'm sorry, but it looks like we'll have to cut our session short. Would you like to reschedule?"

"No thanks, I don't really have anything else to talk about." The mechanic levered himself out of his chair and stepped around the muddy footprints. "See you next time. Good luck with the whole alien thing! Keep us posted, yeah?"

Dr. Rhodes nodded and said his goodbyes, mechanically writing end-of-meeting notes in his planner instead of his notebook. He barely heard the door close.

First Contact, he thought in shock. *They told me it would never happen here, that the place was nothing but animals. "The title's just a formality," they said. "Something to make the legal types at home happy. And it will look good on your resume." And I believed them.* He shook his head, not managing to move toward the door just yet. Then something occurred to him. *I hope the translator still works!*

He tore open the nearest cabinet, trying desperately to remember where he had put it the last time he'd organized the office. He finally found it, in the second-to-last possible place it could have been: one of his lower desk drawers, way in the back. He had to blow dust off of the screen and search for the manual. But it worked, lighting up when he pressed the button. The list of possible languages scrolling down the viewscreen was just as long as he remembered, and the instructions seemed simple. He resolved to figure it out posthaste.

But for now, I'll have to settle for looking like I know what I'm doing, he thought, shutting the machine off and hooking the strap over his shoulder. He glanced about the office out of habit, not even seeing it, then left with a slam of the door. He forgot about checking for rust. *So help me, I really hope this is a false alarm.*

* * *

One meeting later, Dr. Rhodes the Official Diplomat found himself in an aircar speeding across the uncultured landscape. He had at least been given the chance to change into some less stainable clothes, but that didn't do much to make him feel at ease.

I can't let on that this is at all worrisome, he thought to himself, taking a deep breath and letting it out. *I need to be the reliable authority figure here.* He had been telling himself this ever since he'd heard about the discovery, but he still didn't believe it.

It had been hard enough getting the older employees to treat him with authority when he was doing a job he had spent over a decade at. This diplomat business was something he had never done, and had barely trained for, and he was pretty sure they all knew it.

The problem was, no one here was really trained for it. The planet had been classified as uninhabited. There was no need to have an actual expert on staff. *I'll just have to fake it,* he thought. *Lord, I hate faking it.*

He clutched the translator in his lap, hearing nothing over the roar of the aircar's engines. He felt like the roaring would continue when the car set down.

To distract himself, he undid the neck strap of the translator and turned it over to read the instructions one more time. The thing was plain enough at a glance: just a flat touchscreen with a microphone and several other sensors on the back. He'd tested it in the hangar, but there had been only humans there.

He wondered if the aliens would be violent. He tried not to think about it.

"To operate," he read. *"Aim microphone toward subject. Select language or 'unknown,' then..."* The instructions were enough to occupy himself for the rest of the ride. He switched the machine on to see what it would make of the engine sounds. He was impressed when it processed for a moment, then picked out the inaudible sound of two people talking at the front of the car.

As prepared as he could be, he shut it off and watched the mountains pass by. Sunlight reflecting off the flooded river hurt his eyes, and he turned away for a moment. When he looked back, the waterbound trees were getting bigger as the aircar descended. He tried to will the car back into the sky and toward the base. It didn't listen. Soon it was landing on a rocky beach, and the engines were turning off.

He had been right; he did still hear a faint roaring in his ears. Maybe it was the river.

"Come on, everybody out!" someone said with an easy authority that he envied, and he hastened to undo his seat harness. The doors opened. The flooded river was quieter than he'd expected it to be. Dr. Rhodes clenched his jaw and stepped out onto the crunching gravel.

The speaker turned out to be Owen Cosgrove, head of the biology team. He seemed to have the situation well in hand. "All right," Cosgrove was saying. "We found the spear and armor wedged in those rocks over there." He pointed at a cluster of boulders at the far side of the river. "They appear to have been washed downstream, so logic dictates that the sentients who made them should be this way." He pointed upriver. "Let's give the area a thorough scanning, then move upstream. We can take the car when we run out of ground, though we won't be as effective from high above." His eyes darted to Dr. Rhodes. "Does that meet with your approval, sir?"

Dr. Rhodes blinked in surprise, then nodded and did his best to appear calm and unflappable. "Sounds good," he said.

"Then let's move out!" Cosgrove directed. "Find them, but don't scare them!" The workers scattered in pairs with their hand-held scanners, which Dr. Rhodes hoped were more modern than his translator. They appeared to be models designed for finding people trapped under rubble.

Cosgrove made an "after you" gesture, then fell into step beside him as the two strolled toward where the trees began: sagging things that could almost pass for weeping willows with some sort of lichen infestation. Dr. Rhodes tried to think of something to say, but Cosgrove beat him to it.

"If there's anything you need us to do, let me know," he said. "Otherwise I'll be happy to call the shots for my crew. I know how they work."

Dr. Rhodes agreed readily. He would be the first person to speak with the aliens if Cosgrove would orchestrate the operation. Whoever had decided that putting the diplomat in charge of the whole search effort had been more than a little shortsighted. He didn't know the first thing about this kind of field work.

A worker called them from the river's edge. Cosgrove sprinted off. Dr. Rhodes followed with the translator bumping against his side, his heart in his mouth.

Chapter 17

As far as Owen was concerned, this mission had gone badly from the beginning. It was rushed. Gear had been forgotten and packed wrong; that one scanner had been crushed by medpacks falling on it; and to top it off, the head of the whole affair was not a natural leader.

The doctor who walked nervously beside him now was a fine therapist, and Owen had no complaints with him in general. But it was obvious that when the man had been chosen for this position, no one had expected him to ever need to do the job. It looked like he hadn't even used the translator before. Owen was just glad that Dr. Rhodes had agreed to let him lead the expedition. It would be easier for everyone this way.

A voice called for attention, and turned out to belong to eagle-eyed Namina, who met them halfway with her search partner and an intriguing new piece of shell. Her dark face was lit with excitement, and it was easy to see why.

"Ooh, that's a good one," Owen said, accepting the eight-inch hollow spike that was held out to him. "It was all by itself?" He flipped the pale orange thing over in his hands, marveling at its similarity to Earth crustaceans.

"Yeah, right here between the rocks," Namina said, pointing at nearby chunks of gray river stone, turned brown with dried mud. "It was wedged in there pretty tight."

"We're guessing it got stuck during higher water than this," chimed in Namina's partner Joey. The short white man puffed with pride, though his eyes darted nervously. "Looks like it came from something pretty big, huh?"

Owen inspected the piece further while the psychologist shifted uneasily on the gravel. "Could be," he said. "Keep an eye out, and make sure everybody stays in pairs."

"Yessir!" the two workers chorused.

"Do you want us to go put this in the car?" Joey asked.

Owen handed it back. "Sure thing. Have Walt add it to the list

I left for him."

The pair hurried off, and Owen was just turning to say something to Dr. Rhodes when he heard the unmistakable sound of someone falling down.

"Sorry!" Joey was saying when he turned back to look. "That rock slipped under my foot!"

"I'm fine, I'm fine," Namina grumbled, getting her feet under herself. She rubbed a hip. "Man, this is not the best ground to take a fall on."

"I am so sorry!" Joey insisted, grabbing an arm and hauling her upright. "I didn't push you on purpose, I swear! I wouldn't do that to you! Are you sure you're okay? You could have a hairline fracture!"

Owen was already getting out his SedEgg and striding forward before Dr. Rhodes said anything.

"He's not usually—" the doctor said.

"I'm on it."

Namina was trying to reach her own SedEgg while also trying to calm the inconsolable teammate who had hold of her right arm.

"Are you bleeding anywhere? You could get an infection! Do you want me to get a first aid kit? We need to make sure you're not bleeding internally!"

"No, I'm fine, I'm sure it's just a bruise. It's okay."

"But you can't know that for sure!" Joey continued, eyes wide. "Stay here! I'll be right back with the medkit!" With that he took off sprinting for the aircar, leaving the others swearing behind him.

"Joey!" Namina yelled, scrambling after him. "Come back!"

"Or better yet, sit down!" Owen added as he raced after.

Closer to the aircar, Walt and Diana were just looking up from their guard duty and noticing the commotion. Owen yelled at them to meet Joey with SedEggs out. They didn't need to be told twice.

"I need the medkit, fast!" the panicking man was saying as he ran. "Namina might be hurt!"

The duo met him at the door with spread arms. He managed to dodge Walt in a lunge for the open door of the aircar, but Diana stamped the back of his neck as he passed.

"Medkit… it's right there…" Joey trailed off as he collapsed on the doorstep. "Somebody get it to her… Sorry…" And with that he was out.

Owen came sliding to a stop moments after Namina, and he thanked the two guards for acting quickly.

"No problem," Diana said as they moved the unconscious man onto the level floor of the aircar. She flicked a black braid out of her way and straightened up. "Do you want us to fly him back to base, or keep watch on him here?"

"I've already lit up the medic light," Walt added. His own gray hair was tied back in a braid longer than Diana's, but tucked into his shirt. "Xian should be back here any second."

Owen thought about it. "Normally I'd say to take him back and not risk anything, but we have a lot of other people out here today, and it's an important trip. So let's just keep an eye on him for now. He wasn't frenzying for long, even though he did get a running start." He clapped the victim's partner on the shoulder. "Keep an eye on him, all right?"

Namina nodded. "Of course."

Owen looked around, just now remembering the hollow shell fragment and the psychologist. "Now where did—" He spotted both the shell and the doctor lying on the gravel far from the car. "Crap."

A quick jog later, he found Dr. Rhodes staring skyward and muttering about the futility of it all. He sighed and dug out his SedEgg again.

"…Can't even run very fast, and I have no idea how to fight if the natives are violent, and what if the translator doesn't know their language?" Dr. Rhodes clutched the machine and didn't even notice when Owen pressed the needles against his arm. "What am I supposed to do while the machine figures it out…" He lapsed into silent breathing, though much faster than usual.

Owen called for the guards to bring him a stretcher, wondering as they did whether Dr. Rhodes was out of breath simply from frenzy, or also from trying to keep up with the running. Not a great sign if the man was so out of shape that such a short jog could make him pant.

He made sure that the doctor was in a comfortable position while he waited for the stretcher, securing the shell while he was at it. Other workers were noticing the continued commotion and heading toward him, but he waved them back to their tasks. Further anxiety wouldn't do any good at this point.

When the stretcher arrived, Owen made sure the doctor was carried safely into the aircar, then he headed back out in the company of a different pair of explorers who had come bearing a few more shell fragments.

But the day didn't improve from there. Not ten minutes later he heard a yell and a scuffle, followed by the shout of "Frenzy down! Stretcher and an ice pack, please!"

Other incidents sprang up all along the riverside, making Owen start to worry that they wouldn't have enough space in the aircar. He clamped down on the emotion, and didn't let himself think about what would happen if they ran out of people to pilot the car.

"All right, game's over for today!" he called from the door of the aircar. "Everybody out of the pool, and back onboard in an orderly fashion!" He spoke quietly to the driver. "Call base to expect us. And to come find us if we don't show."

The driver kept her calm, for which Owen was grateful, but there were two more frenzies and one mundane panic attack by the time the engines started.

"We need to leave right now," someone was saying as Owen shut the door and did a quick head count. "Before it spreads farther!"

Owen didn't look for the speaker, still counting. "Everyone think about breathing evenly," he said when he had finished. "Anybody who can't handle a nice quiet ride home can do so unconscious."

The same voice spoke up again, only to trail off as the speaker was sedated by a neighbor.

"Good move," Owen said, giving the go-ahead to the driver and strapping himself in. "Make sure his head is secure, will you? Everybody breathe with me, and we'll be home soon."

The car lifted off with a thunder of engines. Owen was glad to see that the slumbering victims were all properly strapped in place while the rest of the crew appeared to be keeping their cool. Now that they were moving, the air of panic should subside.

Still, he thought as the river receded in the distance, *This has got to be the worst expedition I've seen in quite a while.*

Chapter 18

Elliot sat cross-legged on a metal plate in the garden, with the lowering sun warming his shoulders and the smell of spicy herbs perfuming the air. Four cameras peered over his head at the plastic box with the alien gopher in it.

The cameras were recording, but the gopher did nothing.

"Well, this bites," Hubcap said from his position on the ground next to the box. "And not in the fun way. After the fight that other one put up, I expected some action! I got dirt in my seams for this?" He brushed off his arms and addressed the animal wedged into a corner, studiously ignoring him. "Shame on you. So boring, while other people are out looking for real aliens. And not letting us come along, so they can hog the glory for themselves. Don't you know we're depending on you to entertain Earthlings you've never met?"

"Try squeaking again," Elliot suggested. "This guy's just not motivated." Hubcap obliged by making prey noises, but the horn-headed creature didn't budge. Even a whack on the box from Ted's trusty bladed shovel did nothing.

"Yeah, he's gonna stay like that until we leave," Ted said, leaning on the shovel next to Hubcap. "Probably hoping we don't see him there."

"Harrumph," Hubcap declared. He put a hand on the dirt, fingers splayed. "None of the others are moving around anywhere nearby, not while we're here being loud and scary. Bah."

Elliot slumped back. "Well at any rate, I'm pretty sure this guy can't climb the sides when they're this slick, but I don't know about jumping. Is he likely to get out, Ted? Or is a barrier this size tall enough to protect the whole garden from above-ground pests?"

"Couldn't tell you," Ted said. "I've never seen 'em with a reason to jump. They always come from below."

"Right. Still, I think you might be able to wall them out of the area," Elliot insisted. "You'd need industrial wire mesh underneath, of course..."

"Only problem would be funding," Ted said.

"Dun dun dun," Hubcap sang. "Funnndinnng!"

"Yes," Elliot sighed. "I suppose it wouldn't be a high enough priority to order enough plastic or metal to wall in the entire garden. Maybe just the most important parts?"

"Probably not," Ted said, spinning his shovel. "Not when we get enough food as it is, fighting the little bastards off by hand."

Elliot grumbled, frustrated at the lack of better options. Hubcap patted him on the head. "Poor sentimental human," the robot lamented. "So sad about the plight of the supergophers."

Elliot brushed the hand away, turning to deliver a retort. But he stopped, looking past Hubcap. "Aircar!" he exclaimed, jumping to his feet.

"With aliens?" Hubcap asked, whirling to look.

Tarja and Dale turned as well, cameras ready, while Vic and Graham watched the co-hosts for reaction shots. Elliot squinted into the distance, deciding that the incoming vehicle was big enough to house all of the explorers, and it was heading for the hangar. He held a hand out to the gardener. "Ted, it's been fascinating, but we may need to finish this later," he said.

"Good for you; I wanna see if they found any aliens!" Ted exclaimed, striding toward the building.

Elliot glanced at Vic before following. She gave him the thumbs-up and kept filming. Behind her, Hubcap picked up the plant that the gopher had been eating when they caught it, and dropped it into the box.

"Here you go, Pointy," he said. "We'll be back for you later." With that he burst into a run past Elliot. "Last one there doesn't get to meet the aliens!" he called over his shoulder.

Elliot sighed into Vic's camera, and followed in a dignified trot. He heard the sounds a moment later of the camera crew switching off their cameras and running as well.

When Elliot jogged around the outside of the building, he met Hubcap waiting at the door to the hangar. Elliot peered inside, hoping for a scene full of scientific delight, but instead he got a panicky medical drama. People were pouring out of the aircar with a herd of gurneys wheeling to meet them.

"What happened?" Hubcap asked the first human to run past. "Were the aliens dangerous?"

The woman shook her head. "No sign of 'em," she said, looking slightly haunted. "But frenzy was everywhere." She hurried away into the growing crowd of people.

120

Owen's pale hair was easy to spot leaving the aircar. Vic handed her camera to Tarja and told the crew to stay put. "I'll be right back," she said. "No wandering off." That last was aimed at Hubcap, who managed to look innocent as she shook a finger at him before hurrying away.

Elliot stepped to the side and watched the gurneys roll towards the medical wing. "Looks like they barely made it out of there," he said. "At least they all had good sedatives."

Hubcap made a mechanical snort. "What they needed was some robots. All of this emotional fiddle-faddle could have been easily avoided."

"Yep. Too bad none are applying to work here."

"Yeah. Well, no more." He spoke into Graham's camera, which was filming again. "All of you robotic citizens looking for work, you are needed here. Planet IGN-47. Look it up. Next time they have a shuttle ready for new employees, I want to see a load of you on it." He pointed a finger at the lens and gave the camera a stern look, then turned away.

"I wonder how long before that next shuttle," Elliot said, looking around. "Ted's gone, but I'm sure somebody knows."

"We can find out later," Hubcap said with folded arms. "It'll be a while before the message gets out in my lovely clear tones, but anyone with brains on their hard drive will have figured out the need by their first look at this location. Here's hoping they act on it." Hubcap began walking in the direction Vic had taken.

"Where are you going?" Elliot asked.

"To make sure they don't leave us behind tomorrow," Hubcap told him. "They had their chance to handle the situation without cameras making them look bad."

* * *

"I'm glad you insisted," Elliot said over the roar of the engines.

"Me too," Hubcap said. "This is what we're here for! To show people at home the kind of stuff they do! And there isn't much that's more important on an alien planet than finding intelligent life. Plus, y'know, our ratings will be bananas. That's kind of important."

Elliot nodded. "The locals should be grateful we're here to film it," he said. "This is a big deal."

Hubcap scoffed. "The only way it could *not* be big is if some of the off-duty workers made the spear as a prank."

"That doesn't bear thinking about." Elliot fought off a moment of panic. Vic had already told Ms. Kaleel about the spear, and Elliot was certain that the showrunner was putting things into place with the hopes of a historical discovery. If the alien artifact turned out to be human-made, then it would be a massive upset, to say the least. *Heck, I'll bet the locals told their own higher-ups,* he thought. *I hope nobody's contacted the news media yet. We don't need pressure from them to search any harder than we already are.* He leaned his head against the window. *This is going to be huge.*

Suitably worried now, Elliot did his best to think of best-case scenarios for the rest of the flight.

Soon the aircar was dropping to hover near the water, where the air smelled of mud and warm plants. The driver switched off the flight engines, leaving things quiet enough for Owen to address the troops. He rose from the copilot's seat with a comradely pat on the shoulder of the nervous-looking psychologist who was supposed to be translating for the aliens, then he addressed the rows of people before him.

"All right, crew," he said. "Today will be different from yesterday. We'll save the handheld scanners for later; we're starting from the air. The dashboard scanner should be just powerful enough to reach the ground from this height, especially if we put it on disaster rescue settings. Your job for now is to keep an eye out for anything interesting. Anything at all that could be a sign of intelligence out here. Questions? No? Good. Let's get going." With that, he sat down and began messing with controls as the aircar eased forward.

Elliot could barely see Owen's viewscreen from where he sat, so he urged Dale in the seat next to him to raise his camera for a better look. Dale did, and Elliot was reduced to waiting. He was glad when the first shout of discovery sounded.

"Back there, hidden by the plants," a woman was saying, pointing out the window. "Pretty sure it was a living creature with those scales."

Owen nodded. "The scanner doesn't register anything intelligent, but that's still a fine place to start! Maybe our intelligent aliens keep these as livestock to harvest their scales. Carla, about face!"

The driver sent the aircar into a sharp turn back toward the way it had come, following the biologist's directions. No animals were visible from the air, and Owen soon had the team gearing up for a trip to the ground. He gave special attention to everyone's frenzy precautions.

The aircar landed on a strip of rocky beach lined with more of those wilted-celery trees, and the door flew open to the sound of rushing water. The river moved faster here. As soon as the crew started pouring out of the car, someone pointed out the creature with a shout. This sent it scuttling away into the green-blue bushes before the camera crew could get outside.

"You know better than that!" Owen admonished one of his louder subordinates with a good-natured smack on the back of the head. "Indoor voices, kids!"

"I love how he calls everyone 'kids,' Hubcap said to Elliot in front of a camera. "My sense of age in regards to you fleshy types might be out of calibration, but he seems like he may be younger than you."

Elliot nodded. "I'm pretty sure he is. But as they say, it's not the years; it's the mileage."

Hubcap pondered. "Humans say that? Really?"

"Really."

Then the crowd was haring off after the thing, and the TV crew had to scramble to catch up, their footing uncertain on all the fist-sized rocks. From what Elliot could gather from the back of the herd, this creature was fast, brightly colored, and the handheld scanners didn't recognize as intelligent either. But it was covered in those scales.

He caught a glimpse as the group got closer. The thing dashed from one bush to another, looking like a monstrous lobster-crab hybrid. Elliot saw spidery legs and a long torso covered in overlapping blue scales with yellow edges. It moved too fast to see anything more detailed than that.

"It's heading for the water!" someone yelled.

"Try to cut it off!" Owen replied.

"Almost — Aw, no!"

Sploosh.

The river's surface rippled and wavered. The creature was gone. People grumbled and swore, censoring themselves mid-word with a glance at the cameras.

"All right, huddle up," Owen said, waving everyone closer. "What have we learned about it?"

The biologists all talked at once while the TV crew observed.

"Those scales definitely grew on it," said a dark-skinned man almost as tall as Vic. "Attached, not clothes."

"It looked awfully hard to kill," said a pale woman whose skin was mostly freckles. "I wonder if our sentients have them domesticated."

"They could gather the scales after the things have died naturally," suggested an Asian woman with freckles of her own.

"That's hardly a reliable source," said the pale woman.

"But what do we know about how often they shed?" Owen pointed out.

"True…" she admitted.

Elliot could see that Hubcap was bored already, watching the river instead of the conversation. Suddenly Hubcap jumped and pointed with no small amount of delight.

"Look! Little ones!"

The biologists whirled as one, and followed his pointing arm. There were indeed small colorful things further up the riverside. Elliot had half expected a prank.

"See if you can net one!" Owen said. "Careful now!"

They were off. Elliot and the others ran after them.

* * *

When it became obvious to Hubcap that the humans weren't about to do anything more interesting than huddle around the slow-moving pools of water at the river's edge, he decided to kick-start things again. "The view will be better from up there," he announced, pointing at a looming cliffside. "We could get back in the aircar to look from above, but there's probably nowhere for it to land if we find excitement among those trees." He strode toward the best route up. "Go ahead and finish what you're doing; I'll scout."

This of course prompted Owen to leave the puddles and make sure his TV star guests weren't getting into danger. Hubcap let Vic handle the conversation behind him. He heard Elliot talking to one camera or other; as long as neither of those humans thought he needed to stay on solid ground, then he was cleared to climb as far as he was concerned.

And anyway, they all followed him.

The climb up was easy enough, even for those carrying cameras or scanners, and even considering the rain-wet rocks. As fun as it would have been to take a challenging route up, Hubcap was a professional. He led the humans up to the flat clifftop without incident. The plateau made a good viewpoint, with more large rocks keeping the forest at bay. Hubcap eyed the treeline with interest while the various humans got settled behind him. Elliot was complaining about mud from the climb.

Hubcap regarded him with amusement. "Poor human, your clothes are a slightly different color about the knees."

"And damp," Elliot retorted. "You're one to talk; you hate getting dirty. Be grateful you don't have clothes that stay wet."

"Yup!" Hubcap agreed easily. "But look at this view! Surely it is scenic enough to distract your delicate sensibilities from damp knees?"

"It is pretty nice," Elliot agreed.

Laid out below them, the muddy river snaked off for quite a ways until it dropped to lower ground and spread between the trees. Everything was lush foliage and dampness, with a variety of native animals visible. The biologists were already at work scanning the area for intelligence. They weren't finding anything other that the two humans they'd left watching the aircar, but that didn't blunt their excitement.

"Look look look!" Owen said, "Two of the crustaceans over there! What are they doing?"

Elliot dutifully stepped in front of the cameras to join the speculation about whether the pair were building a nest or looking for food.

Hubcap did the same, though his interest didn't last long. This was not riveting television. He cast about around for anything better. A fluttering motion near the boulders caught his attention.

"Behold!" Hubcap exclaimed, "An alien butterfly! Is it a clue?"

"A what now?" Elliot looked up. "Oh. Yeah, that's not a butterfly. That's one of the mini-winged-whatchacallems. It was in the briefing."

"Whatever. Watch me catch it."

"I don't need to warn you about venomous bites, so go ahead. Just try not to bring down a hive on our heads."

"I promise nothing!" Hubcap said, leaping for it. The creature flitted away, looking to his eyes like a tiny green bat. But then, feathers didn't seem to exist on this world, so most of the flying animals he'd seen reminded him of bats.

This one was a master of evasion. It fluttered and dodged, causing Hubcap to lunge about like a madman and the camera crew to object while they tried to film his antics without getting stepped on. Hubcap apologized halfheartedly and continued leaping about. Riveting or not, at least this was fun. Then the animal made an adorable little chirrup, and he forgot about his frustration.

"*Chirpy-tweet?*" he replied, clambering up the rocks.

"There he goes," he heard Elliot say.

"Up we go," Vic replied. "Hubcap, walk slowly please."

"Sure thing, boss. As slow as a butterfly." Hubcap followed the chirping creature while the various humans trailed after him. There were purple-green shrubs and orange trees on the other side of the rocks. The cliff opened up on a thriving alien forest, full of dripping water and animal noises.

"*Chirrrrr, throot, pir-tweet?*" Hubcap spared a moment to congratulate himself for getting the sound bite module installed years ago. It had brought him much joy in poking fun at his friends, and it was pulling its weight again now. Hubcap made his stealthy way into the plantlife, recording and repeating every sound he heard. Except, that is, for those made by the decidedly un-stealthy humans behind him.

"Shush, you," he said over his shoulder. They managed to shush a little, and he went back to exploring. He crouched to sneak through the bushes, emerging into a clearing with Elliot's cautionary words not to stray too far echoing in his ear sensors.

"Killjoy," he hissed. "Now hush. Ahem. *Chirp!*"

None of the animals up in the sturdy orange trees were answering back, but then, none of them seemed scared of him either. He walked out onto the purple grass, marveling at the fact that none of the creatures had learned to fear two-leggers. He caught glimpses of them up on the golden-brown branches, scurrying from place to place and chattering at each other. They were little stripy things, though he couldn't be sure if they had fur or bare skin. Switching over to heat vision showed that they were warm, but that was about it: red shapes on a dark branch, with varying shades of sunny-day warmth around them. He switched back to normal sight and appreciated the colors.

The things were still chirping away. He did the same, wandering across the small meadow to sit down on a log. This was a massive thing of dark orange that had probably created the clearing when it fell. Plenty of colorful undergrowth had sprung up in the sunlight since then. Hubcap made himself comfortable as he repeated back the animal calls, ignoring the camera crew who were filming from the cover of the bushes. Hubcap expected Vic to decide as soon as the biologists joined them that that was enough meandering. She would usher them all back down to the aircar to fly off to some other patch of wilderness in the search of noteworthy things to film.

In the meantime, Hubcap craned his neck back, watching the treetops. The plantlife next to him rustled, and the humans made surprised noises.

He looked down and stared into alien eyes.

Chapter 19

When Shortclaw ran ahead of the nearest not-me, she didn't know what she expected to find among the straightweeds and mindbogglingly tall trees. Maybe there would be more of the air-swimmers, certainly more eatables in types that didn't grow near the water. Maybe something she couldn't even imagine. She was out of breath from the running, but didn't care.

Then she heard the air-swimmers calling louder than before, with some of the sounds coming from the dirt level, instead of the sky. She hurried forward, dimming her colors from excited gold tones into deep greens to blend in with the trees, and she searched for the air-swimmer that must be close enough to see in detail.

Her colors flared yellow again when she saw the bizarre creature moving through the spikyweeds. It had only one color, but this was a color she *had never seen before*. She tried to place it, and nearly could, but no. It looked almost like the shine of light across the water, almost like the polished inside of certain shells. But that wasn't it. This thing seemed made of light, and reflections, and — gray. Nearly gray. That was the best she could come up with. Amazed, she crept further forward.

The sound of crunching leaves behind Shortclaw told her that a not-me was catching up. She flashed bright red patterns along her tail in warning. The footsteps slowed, and she knew that she had been heard.

The not-me drew level with her, crouching down next to where she hid; it was a male she thought she had seen once before. He saw what she was watching, and flared his own swirling golds.

=*What is it?*= his colors asked her.

=*I do not know!*= she replied, brown circles chasing each other across her face in delighted confusion. =*But listen to it — it sounds like the air-swimmers!*=

The pair listened intently, and she had been right; the strange creature with the uncolored flesh was making the exact same sounds as the animals above. And it did so after each animal called. Like it was answering them.

=*Is it … talking?*= the not-me asked in amazement. =*It seems to repeat their sounds, like a Greeting of Us, only with noises!*=

=*I think it is!*= Shortclaw said, speckling with delight. =*This is amazing!*=

She heard another not-me approaching, and another behind that. The sound-talker was standing on two feet, moving slowly and looking upwards. And still it called back in what must be the language of the animals above.

Something dawned on Shortclaw. =*This isn't an animal,*= she said to the not-me beside her, =*This is a not-us!*=

=*Are you sure?*= he asked.

=*It must be!*= she replied as the others came up behind them. She directed their attention with one brightly-colored arm. =*Look!*=

The others understood immediately, and they shared her excitement.

=*Look at its color!*=

=*Are all those noises coming from one creature?*=

=*Not just a creature,*= she insisted, =*A not-us!*=

The others were astonished, and not sure how to proceed. They all knew how to greet a not-me, but no one had ever met a not-us.

Shortclaw stepped forward. =*I will. You stay here, so we don't scare it away.*=

The others colored in muted tones of agreement, sinking back into the sheltering green fluffweeds. Shortclaw moved on alone.

The not-us was sitting on a fallen tree, still looking up at the air-swimmers and repeating back everything they said. She hoped that she wasn't about to interrupt an important conversation.

Then something else occurred to her: she didn't know if she could properly mimic its strange color. A botched Greeting of Us would be a horrible way to meet the only not-us she had ever seen.

Well, she'd have to do her best.

Quietly, she crept out into the open and toward the fallen tree. Only now did it occur to her that this not-us could be dangerous, and she hadn't bothered to put on armor when she had left the river. Buckling it into place would have taken too much time.

Nothing to be done about it now.

The not-us was still looking up at the sky when she placed her hands on the tree and raised her head to its eye level.

She adopted what she sincerely hoped was a good enough

approximation of the strange not-color. Then when the not-us looked down to see her, she changed her colors into the accepted greeting.

=*Hello. I feel as you do. Will you be friendly?*=

Chapter 20

The eyes were a shock, and the whirling colors around them were more so. Hubcap jerked back in surprise. The alien flinched as well. He held his pose, staring at the strange creature that had crawled out of the woods.

It was roughly the size of a large dog, but there the similarities ended. While its body was long and sinuous, its legs were short, its face tapered into a triangular beak. Its colors were constantly changing. Hubcap could swear that a moment ago the entire creature had been silvery, but now it was a complicated mix of pinks and greens and grays, with patterns that changed almost too fast to see. The colors seemed to come from the skin underneath clear scales, shining with impressive clarity. The alien stared at him unblinking.

He heard the human camera crew whispering excitedly in the bushes, and it occurred to him that no one had scanned for intelligence here. He regarded the creature anew. "Um, hello there," he said to it. "I'm Hubcap. What's your name?" He put a hand to his chest then pointed toward the alien, in his best Tarzan-and-Jane fashion.

The creature looked at the outstretched hand, then back up at his face.

"Do you have a name?" he persisted.

Instead of answering, the alien sat on its haunches and imitated his gestures. It was suddenly wearing his colors again; he hadn't been imagining that. The reflections weren't quite right, but it was definitely silvery.

And it was trying to communicate.

I hope the meatheads are thinking, he thought to himself. *We could really use a translator up here.*

The alien's hand was still waiting in the air, with its stubby claws and a blush of purple. Hubcap moved to grasp the hand and introduce the alien to the fine art of handshakes, but the alien moved first. With catlike grace, it twined around him where he sat, returning to its place and leaving Hubcap wondering if he'd just been scent-marked. He didn't smell anything new, but he was designed to sniff out humans, not whatever this was.

The whatever-it-was stared at him with its head cocked, looking like a dog expecting him to throw a stick. His turn.

"Wow, okay, so I'm not as graceful as all that," Hubcap said, listening with half of his attention for the sounds of the humans. He thought one of the crew had been sent back to summon the others. "Um. Okay, well, when on Mars…" Hubcap stood up and did his level best to repeat the motion. He wobbled a bit as he padded around the alien on all fours — it was with no small amount of relief that he sat down on the log again, having completed the maneuver without falling over.

Darn embarrassing, though. He was pretty sure he heard snickering in the bushes.

Then louder noises sounded as the rest of the humans started pushing through the plantlife. They were probably trying to be quiet, but they sure sucked at it.

The alien flattened to the ground in fear as Owen and that nervous-looking diplomat appeared. The camera crew followed right behind, causing the creature to scuttle behind the log.

"Hey, careful, guys!" Hubcap chided the crew. "You're scaring Rainbow here!"

"Oh, that is amazing," Owen breathed. "Sit down, everyone; body language is important." He got the growing crowd to settle onto the wet grass, and Hubcap looked back to the alien while they fiddled with scanners and the translator.

"Hey there, it's okay," the robot said at his most gentle. "They're just noisy."

The multicolored creature regained its confidence now that the sound and surprises were done with, and it sat back up with regained brilliance.

"Ohh, that's just beautiful!" exclaimed a biologist.

"Look at the speed of the color change!" added another.

"That's like an octopus, only better!"

Hubcap let Owen rein in the chattering. He kept his attention on the alien, who had apparently gotten over its startlement. Now that everyone was sitting — and thus shorter than it was — the alien flowed over the log and trotted up to inspect the newcomers.

"Hold still, guys," Hubcap cautioned. "You may get an alien handshake. Be cool."

The alien sat down in front of Owen and easily adopted his colors. There was impressive attention to detail; Hubcap moved closer and noticed patterns for pockets and even seams where the human's clothing had them. Then the alien rubbed its head against his shoulder and moved on to the next person.

Owen was smiling like all of his childhood dreams were coming true at once. He elbowed the doctor next to him to have the translator ready in case it spoke.

Hubcap looked back to the alien and found it nose-to-nose with Elliot, who was grinning like an idiot at the sight of his own bright orange hair color on the top of the dragony creature's head.

"Look, it's even got my freckles!" He pointed in delight. "Do you see?"

Hubcap did see. He saw more than the human did; not only were the freckles the right color, but they were even in the right arrangement. The constellation that was stretched across the long face was a very familiar one.

"That *is* impressive," Hubcap said. "So Owen, is this our sentient?"

"Oh, without a doubt!" the biologist said, reaching out a hand but stopping short of touching the alien. "This is remarkab— What's that? Oh my." He broke off at the sound of more rustling behind Hubcap, who turned to find three more of the creatures making their cautious way into the clearing. One was even wearing some of the bright scales like armor.

"Hey there!" Hubcap greeted them. "Can you guys grow freckles too?"

They could. These three went into the same routine as the first alien had, copying the colors of the person they were greeting, then rubbing their heads against elbows and shoulders. Hubcap considered this far cuter than he would admit. And they seemed to find him the most interesting.

"They know a superior being when they see one," he taunted Elliot when the first alien returned to stare at him again.

"They probably think you're a rock or something," Elliot said. "And they're wondering how you manage to move."

"You can kiss my -*bleep*-," the robot said, censoring himself and slapping his hind end with a clank.

Beside him, the alien he'd dubbed "Rainbow" imitated the gesture.

Hubcap guffawed. "I like this one!" he said, pointing and

resisting the urge to pat it on the head. "Anybody have some alien doggy treats? Or some fish?"

No one did, but the nervous doctor had an announcement.

"The translator doesn't work on them," he said, more loudly than was necessary, dropping it on the grass. "It's on and functioning, but it can't read them at all."

"Well, they haven't said anything…" Elliot tried to explain.

"Yes they have," the doc grumbled, jerking a thumb at Owen. "Ask the animal expert; he knows."

"…They do seem to communicate by color," Owen said. "That translator only works on spoken language, doesn't it?"

The psychologist gestured at the machine on the ground. "Of course it does! Every race I've ever heard of speaks with words!"

Owen frowned. "Of course."

"This is pointless! How do they expect us to talk with something that doesn't talk out loud? It's impossible!" The good doctor was working himself into an ominous froth.

Without even looking at the man, Owen slapped him on the back, and Hubcap heard the telltale click of a SedEgg. The psychologist sagged downward, falling into someone's lap. Hubcap looked to make sure the aliens hadn't been disturbed.

They hadn't, but when he turned back, the man who held the doctor's head off the ground was starting to hyperventilate.

"He's the one who's supposed to be in charge here!" the man said. "We're supposed to let him do the talking! Now wh—" Another slap with the SedEgg, and he was slumping over the doctor.

But that wasn't the end of it; people at the edges of the crowd were starting to panic for no reason, and someone in the middle started yelling that they all needed to shut up and appreciate how awesome the moment was.

Owen swore and shouted commands, and the orderly cross-legged crowd devolved into a bedlam of frenzy and attempts to sedate. Hubcap had never seen so many attacks at once.

The aliens apparently hadn't either, and they didn't like it. The brilliantly colored creatures scattered to the edges of the meadow, pausing there to look back at the chaos before vanishing completely.

"No, come back!" Hubcap exclaimed. "It's okay, or it will be in a minute!" The last face to disappear was the first he had seen. "Rainbow, come back! Aww…"

The bushes were empty.

Hubcap turned back to face the struggling crowd. He pulled

out his own SedEgg and waded into the mob. "Shame on you!" he said, stamping the first flailing human he came across. "And on you! You made them leave, with your fleshy weaknesses! Shake it off!"

They didn't shake it off, and he had to help sedate over half of the crowd and three camera folk before the frenzy was gone. Under other circumstances, this would have been nearly panic-inducing, rather than the height of frustration.

Hubcap stood next to Elliot, looking past the sprawled humans toward the empty plantlife. He searched for an appropriate swear.

"Bleeping bleepmonkeys?" Elliot asked, guessing his train of thought.

"No, this is a family show," Hubcap said with a wave to Tarja's camera, which was the only remaining one. He voiced his favorite electronic sigh. "Let's get the slumbering meatwads down the cliff. Or get the aircar into the clearing here. Or turn this thing into a teleporter." He kicked the translator. "You know, something constructive."

"Good idea," Elliot said.

They joined Owen and the remaining crew in checking the fallen workers for injuries. But Hubcap couldn't help looking back at the trees one more time.

Chapter 21

It was probably his levelheadedness, Elliot reflected, that kept saving him from the frenzy. He wasn't prone to emotional outbursts at the best of times, and as far as he could tell, that left little for the mysterious ailment to capitalize on. This gave him no small measure of comfort as he helped lift and carry all of the unconscious people. He took extra care with those he knew well.

He tried not to dwell on how much worse this disaster could have been.

The aircar managed to fit down into the clearing with a minimum of destruction to the plants, and it was a short walk there with each victim. But strapping them into their chair harnesses took time, and he was glad that others were handling that part. Everyone's clothes were damp with former rainwater and sweat.

Finally every Earthling was on board, awake and otherwise, and they were ready to take off. Elliot looked over at Hubcap, who was staring forlornly out the window.

"We'll come back," he told the robot. "Probably right away."

Hubcap shook his head. "But we scared them. They might not come back to us now."

Elliot didn't have anything good to say to that. "We'll just have to see," he said. "We'll do our best."

Then the engines came on, and there was no further talking.

One long, tense ride later, the aircar was nosing into the hangar as the more lightly sedated victims were starting to wake up.

"Ugh, what happened?" asked Dr. Rhodes, raising his head wearily a few seats over.

"You went nuts and ruined everything," Hubcap replied, waving an arm through his harness. "Now keep your head down or I'll stamp you again."

With a wordless mutter, the psychologist lapsed back into unconsciousness.

"That would be impressive, to stamp him with an empty hand," Elliot said.

The robot smacked fist to palm with a clank. "I didn't specify what I would stamp him with, now did I?"

"No," Elliot admitted. "You did not."

The doors opened with an urgent rattle, and medical personnel rushed aboard to unfasten harnesses and lift people onto gurneys. Elliot was impressed with their speed.

"Man, this place must have a whole fleet of those wheelie-carts," Hubcap said as he undid his own harness.

Elliot nodded, doing the same. "They probably buy them in bulk."

"There must be a big room somewhere, with rows and rows of them just waiting to ferry about some poor fleshbag. Or maybe they stack them like those metal chairs." Hubcap started to stand up, then a gurney trundled past his face and he sat back down. "Maybe I'll just stay here for a little while."

"A fine idea," Elliot agreed, pulling his feet back from the walkway.

"So anyway, I want to find this room," Hubcap continued, leaning his head back. "I want to find it, and start a hallway jousting league. I will be grand champion."

"Sure you will," Elliot said with a smile, appreciating the robot's talent for lighthearted diversions. "And what do you plan on jousting with? Keep in mind, broomsticks would definitely hurt us fleshy types."

The robot waved a hand in dismissal. "I'll think of something. Maybe projectiles instead: water balloons and flourbombs and the like. The cleanest person wins."

"And the dirtiest cleans the hallway."

Hubcap pointed at him. "Yes."

At that point Tarja walked past behind one of the gurneys, carrying all four cameras hooked over both shoulders. The gurney held Dale, and Elliot could see Graham and Vic being loaded onto wheelie-tables of their own. Everyone was moving at a good clip, so the duo had to hurry to catch up. Elliot offered to carry two of the cameras while Hubcap made sure the rest of the camera crew was being properly cared for.

It was a long trip to the hospital wing, though more in terms of chaos than distance. The main medical facilities had thoughtfully been built next door to the parking garage. Everywhere Elliot passed, people were hurrying and scurrying and flat-out running from place to place. They all spoke at a yell. Official things were being decided somewhere he wasn't privy to, and for the moment, he was okay with that. He'd go find out later, when he was sure that the rest of his crew would be okay. There'd be quite the conversation with Ms. Kaleel, and Elliot wanted to make sure Vic was there for it.

"Hey, I think that was the room!" Hubcap said suddenly, pointing back at a door they had just hurried past.

"What room?" Elliot asked, craning his neck to look over the camera straps. He saw a closed door like any other. The air smelled of antiseptic.

"The one with the fleet of gurneys!" Hubcap said in delight.

"Did you see them in there?"

"I think so! If not them, then something else interesting in rows and rows." Hubcap rubbed his hands together maniacally as they hurried down the hall. "My hallway jousting will be a glorious sight to behold."

Elliot listened to his partner chatter on, and he wondered where the conversational habit came from. It was probably a holdover from lifting the spirits of anxious rescuees on the way to safety, though Elliot suspected it did double duty in keeping Hubcap's mind off the problems too.

"...And I will make a crown out of the winner's cleanest socks, and a scepter from writing implements and shiny wire..."

Elliot let him ramble. He hitched the cameras higher on his shoulders and hurried.

* * *

Hubcap didn't like waiting at the best of times. He'd done plenty over the years, and now that he could decide his own fate, he preferred to avoid it whenever possible. There were better things to do than stare into space and think.

Things like telling terrible jokes, and seeing how many of the people in line at the medcenter he could get to groan at the punchlines.

"Wait, you'll like this one," he said as the line shuffled forward. "What's brown and sticky?" He looked around expectantly while the various humans pretended to ignore him. After a silent moment, he declared "A stick!"

That was the best number of groans yet. Elliot was shaking his head, and Graham, still on a gurney, pretending to go back to sleep.

He fake-snored loudly.

Hubcap poked the elder human in the ribs. "You are fooling no one."

"Ow. Hey look at that, I'm awake! What'd I miss?"

"Some excellent jokes," Hubcap told him. "I can repeat them if you like."

Graham protested and sat up, exclaiming at how much better he felt. The other patients were in a similar state, none the worse for wear except for the odd bruise or scrape. They waited with varying levels of patience for a medical professional to bandage their SedEgg bites and grant permission to go back to work. As far as Hubcap was concerned, the group had gotten off almost suspiciously lightly after that kind of hullabaloo, but he wasn't about to complain about it.

Elliot and Tarja were unaffected by the frenzy. They and Hubcap stuck with the rest of the crew so they didn't have to find each other afterward. Someone had said the checkup would be fast. Hubcap was unimpressed so far, but when his group finally made it to the front of the line, the humans were indeed evaluated quickly. A woman with Indian ancestry and a crisply professional demeanor pronounced them good to go as long as they took it easy for the rest of the day.

"Try not to raise your heart rate, and report back if you notice anything out of the ordinary," she instructed them. Her name tag said "Dr. Chakraborty," and her expression said "Don't be as dumb as I expect you to be." Hubcap decided that he liked her. If this was the doctor that had seen to Mr. Lee, then no wonder the big boss had been kept successfully hospitalized for two days.

Vic nodded. "We will. Thank you." The doctor moved on to the next person, and they were free. Hubcap was the first to the door.

He was met in the doorway by a man both well-dressed and frazzled, with a message that the bosses wanted to see them and their cameras. Hubcap deferred to Vic, who told the man to lead the way. While they followed the quick tap of his footsteps, Vic quietly urged the crew to check over their equipment for damage. Everything came up intact before they reached the conference room.

Mr. Lee was waiting just inside, looking fully recovered from his frenzy two days earlier. "Welcome," he said. "Do come in!"

The room held a big table and several important-looking

people, who were all very interested in seeing the footage that had been filmed that day.

"Would you be willing to sell it to us?" Mr. Lee asked.

Hubcap knew what the answer would be even before Vic apologetically declined. The show's contract was clear, and no one here had the authority to override it. These people were more than welcome to make an offer to the showrunner back Earthside, but there was clearly little chance of it being accepted.

The footage was valuable to a degree that Hubcap was still coming to terms with. Everyone on Earth would want to see it.

"Would you be able to show it to us now?" Mr. Lee asked. "We promise there will be no illegal recording devices. We just want to have a better idea of what's happening on this planet."

Vic agreed to that. She had Tarja and Graham rig up a quick linkage to the screen in the room, and in moments the suit-clad individuals were on the edge of their seats watching Hubcap's first contact with an alien race.

This was the first time he had seen it from the camera's point of view. He had to admit the videographers were good; they'd managed to get the perfect angle of Rainbow's first appearance, and his subsequent reaction. One camera had stayed in close-up while the others panned out at the arrival of the other aliens. It was all very dramatic.

The executives oohed and ahhed over the scene, then made disappointed sounds when the frenzy started and the aliens fled. Tarja turned off the link. As the lights came back up, the executives erupted into a flurry of planning. People on Earth would need to be told. Officials would be notified, diplomats and xenoanthropologists would be brought in, they would need the best in translation technology and also would Vic mind if other people on-planet saw the footage?

After some negotiation that Hubcap happily kept out of, it was agreed that the TV crew would show their video in the auditorium after dinner. Anti-recording projectors from the bathrooms would be relocated to shield the screen from piracy attempts. The various employees would be doubly forbidden from bringing cameras into the room. Mr. Lee swore up and down that the show's copyright would not be breached; he would see to it himself. Vic said she would hold him to that. Hubcap silently promised to make *all* the Untrustworthi-Lee jokes if the man broke his word.

Dinnertime was fast approaching, and there was much to do.

The executives left with words of gratitude while Mr. Lee showed the TV crew to the auditorium. He called for various locals to meet them in the control booth.

Hubcap didn't have any duties while the camera jockeys worked to sync the machinery together, and neither did Elliot. The human checked his watch and muttered about dinner.

"Mr. Lee," Elliot asked, "Are we allowed to eat in here? Can I bring food back while all this gets set up?"

Mr. Lee gave permission. Elliot caught Hubcap's eye, and the robot happily joined him in the quest for human fuel.

Hubcap was privately glad to see that Elliot could find his way to the cafeteria from there without any help. Maybe the human was picking up his subtle hints about memorizing the layout of a new place. Good for him.

The kitchen workers were setting up for dinner when they arrived, and it didn't take much to convince them to allow a few early meals. This was the least they could do for the visiting TV stars who had discovered aliens.

"Word travels fast," Hubcap commented as one kitchen worker wheeled over a cart and another started loading food onto plates.

"With this kind of word, you bet it does!" said the pale guy with the cart, who seemed far too skinny to be a cook. Hubcap privately decided he must be a dishwasher. "How many meals do you need?"

"Five," Elliot said. "At least for us human folk." He turned to Hubcap. "For you?"

"Do you have any used fryer oil?" Hubcap asked the dishwasher. "It's a nice change from the algae-based biofuel the show sends with me." The man said he'd check. He left while the other employee, a stockier man, finished loading plates.

"I wasn't sure if you wanted to stick with the proven stuff," Elliot said.

Hubcap waved a hand. "A robot likes to smell like fried food sometimes, instead of pond water."

"Biofuel doesn't actually smell like pond water."

"But you can't say that fryer oil doesn't smell like food." Hubcap waggled his fingers. "Greasy, greasy food."

Elliot made a face. The kitchen worker finished with the plates and set a canned drink next to each. He asked if there was anything else they needed.

"No, thank you!" Elliot said. "We'll bring the cart and plates back as soon as we're done." The worker nodded and scurried off.

"You go on ahead," Hubcap waved Elliot toward the door. "I'll be right there. Hopefully with fryer oil."

Elliot agreed and wheeled the cart carefully out of the room. Hubcap stepped aside to wait while the other workers brought out food for the buffet.

A loudspeaker crackled to life with an announcement about the screening after dinner. Hubcap heard people in the kitchen speculating about what the aliens looked like. He was trying to decide whether to pop in and tell them when the man appeared with a plastic bottle full of amber-colored oil.

"Got it!" he said. "We set some aside for you, then somebody moved it. Enjoy!"

"I will, thank you," Hubcap said. "It even looks properly filtered. My compliments to the chef."

"I'll tell her you said so." The man said waved and headed back into the kitchen.

Knew he couldn't be a cook, Hubcap thought. After a moment's consideration, he decided to have his meal along with the humans instead of just drinking it now. He left the cafeteria and retraced his steps to the projector room.

He found it a busier place than the cafeteria. Apparently the equipment was being difficult. People walked back and forth carrying bits of technology in one hand and food in the other. Elliot sat in a chair out of the way. He waved at Hubcap and shrugged.

The cart had been pushed into the hallway. Hubcap pressed it against the far wall and made himself comfortable on top of it. The floor was flat enough that it didn't roll away, and he had a good view of the chaos.

"Hey there!" said a delighted voice. Sera approached from down the hall in regular work clothes instead of a biohazard suit. The rest of her hair was just as magnificent as Hubcap had expected: buzzed short on the sides with intricate patterns shaved deep. The top was braided, leaving only the bright blue tuft of bangs free. It reminded Hubcap of the paint jobs that one of his old rescue teammates had taken to in recent years. Creative.

"Greetings," Hubcap said with a salute of the oil bottle. "On your way to nourishment?"

"That and videos of *aliens!* I can't believe it!" She spread her arms. "How did that happen?"

"Well," Hubcap said, "One walked out of the woods, drawn

no doubt to my metallic splendor, followed by its friends. We were having quite the moment before a meathead had to go and frenzy on us."

"Oh no!" Sera said. "Did the aliens frenzy too?"

Hubcap waved a hand. "No, they ran off. We can only guess if they'll show up again."

"I hope so. I'm sure they will. Metallic splendor, right?" She grinned. "We just need to get you out there again."

"Yes." Hubcap opened the bottle. "Preferably without any frenzy to spoil the mood."

Sera watched him pour a careful stream down his throat. "Yes. Ideally."

Hubcap paused to talk. "I swear, it was bad enough when I just had to worry about the frenzy for humans' sake. Now I've got to watch out for a whole other species too. Very unfair."

"At least there's SedEggs. We can shut the frenzy down fast."

"Yes. Leaving unconscious meatbags to worry about instead." He resumed pouring.

Sera chose her words carefully. "Were you designed to care for our well-being?"

Hubcap finished the last of the oil. "Rescue." He screwed the cap back on. "And let me tell you, humans need a lot of rescuing. It's like a mission that never ends."

Sera leaned against the wall next to the cart. "How did missions usually end?"

Hubcap set the bottle aside and gazed across the hall at the ongoing chaos. "Maintenance and debriefing. Going into standby with the knowledge that the day was over and we didn't have to bother ourselves about it anymore."

"Can you just … tell yourself that each day is done now?" Sera suggested. "It's probably not the same, since you'll see the same people the next day, but maybe you can make a clean slate?"

"I don't think it's quite that easy."

The lighting in the control booth changed, and the little room erupted into cheers. Mr. Lee and several locals exited, all smiles. One woman greeted Sera, and they moved off to dinner together.

"Good luck!" Sera said to Hubcap as she was ushered away. "It's worth a try! Thanks for the aliens!"

Hubcap waved to her.

Elliot popped his head out of the room to usher Hubcap forward. The robot climbed down, leaving the bottle on the table.

Graham was already bringing plates out to join it.

The electronics had been wrangled into submission with plenty of time before the showing. Since the crew didn't want to leave their gear unattended, they stayed there chatting with the remaining technicians while the other employees ate. Apparently these folks had eaten at an earlier shift.

When the loudspeaker announced showtime, Hubcap was surprised by the polite stampede for the auditorium. The humans walked slowly enough, most of them, like the dignified professionals they no doubt fancied themselves. But the air buzzed with excitement as they filled every seat and then some.

"This auditorium is supposed to have enough space for everyone who works here," said the short woman with curly hair who was lead technician. "Looks like it's at least close." People were standing against the back walls and filling the doorways.

Mr. Lee made a brief introduction at the front of the room, then gave the command. Hubcap heard the humans around him sigh in relief when the correct images appeared on the big screen.

Elliot leaned toward Hubcap, eyes forward. "You are going to be so famous," he murmured. "I'm sure we'll all be in the history books somewhere, but you'll be on the cover."

"I have no problem with that," Hubcap said. "It does depend on whether we can find the aliens again, though."

"We'll make it happen. Mr. Lee says we can go to the same spot first thing in the morning."

"Glory hallelujah. Is it morning yet?"

Chapter 22

Elliot squinted through the glare of early-morning light as the aircar lowered into the clearing on its quiet hover engine. Once past the tree canopy, the sun was hidden and Elliot could better see the branches that the car had snapped the day before. There'd apparently been no rain overnight, since things looked dry. The aircar set down gently on the purple grass. Harnesses started unbuckling before the engines shut off. Elliot was one of the first people out, but Hubcap beat him to the tree line.

"Hang together now, folks," Owen called. "No straying ahead in alien territory."

Vic chimed in, reminding the robot that he knew better. Hubcap muttered and slouched back to wait.

Elliot got to pat him on the head for once. "Patience, young one," Elliot said in his best grandfatherly tone.

Hubcap scoffed. "I've spent plenty of time in my life being patient. When you've wasted an entire day sifting through beach sand looking for traces of jewelry or fillings that aren't there, then you can talk to me about patience." He pointed at Elliot. "And this was no fun-filled time with cheerful people either, mind you. This was townsfolk flipping out because someone was missing. I'd like to see you be patient through a day of that."

Elliot put his hands together and bobbed his head. "I bow to your superior experience and suffering."

Owen clapped his hands once for attention. "All right everybody, let's take it slow and try not to scare anything off. If you catch sight of something, let me know. Has everyone got their SedEgg in reach?"

Everyone did. The crowd moved out with Owen in the lead. There were about a dozen people here today, each biologist with their own low-quality camera and each with many coworkers back at base eager to go in their stead. The group had been kept small so they didn't startle the aliens. Only essential professionals made the cut. Dr. Rhodes had elected not to come, since his translator was useless and, according to muttered opinion, so was he. It was down to Owen's best and the TV crew.

Elliot was grateful to be part of this. Even so, he realized that he was markedly more stressed than he'd been the day before. The show's ratings were suddenly guaranteed to be good, and their sponsor would undoubtedly treat them like treasured favorites. But now they had to get the best footage possible so that it could be shared with news organizations and viewed by millions. As he had pointed out to Hubcap, they were literally writing the history books. Their writing had better be good.

The group walked quietly, scanning the area for all they were worth. Elliot was fascinated by the shapes of the trees, which ranged from the droopy things at the shore to the straight orange trunks near the clearing, to some that twisted into blue spirals with branches splitting off in every direction. He'd expected the plants in an alien forest to look different from their Earth counterparts, and he wasn't disappointed. Mostly he was glad that they were so eye-catching. Made for good television. And for an interesting walk. Even the scents were alien; he kept getting whiffs of spice and mud and fruity sweetness in odd combinations.

The muddy river sparkled through the underbrush. Owen led the group on a path parallel to it, likely for ease of navigation. Occasional chirps of what passed for birdsong filtered through the foliage, but no color-changing alien people appeared, despite Hubcap's echoing conversation with the birds.

As the group rounded a corner made up of boulders and fallen logs, snarling filled the air. Elliot saw a blur of motion.

He was already moving when Hubcap shoved him out of harm's way, giving Owen the same treatment with his other hand. Elliot tumbled to the ground while something bulldog-sized barreled past. Hubcap spun to avoid it while the humans scattered.

Elliot scrambled to his feet, slipping on leaves that smelled like curry. Owen was pulling him toward the bushes while Hubcap stared down an angry ball of black fur and snapping teeth. It circled around the robot back toward the cave it had charged from, snarling fiercely. The camera crew hid in the plantlife while the biologists stood with with stun guns out, waiting to see what it would do.

"It's territorial!" Owen shouted. "Give it space!" He pulled Elliot farther away, and Elliot went willingly. Hubcap held the creature's gaze while he took one measured step back, then another. The animal kept snarling, but it didn't charge again.

When the robot was level with the ring of humans, the toothy fluffball stepped into its cave to regard them from the shadows. It didn't stop snarling in one long uneven rumble.

Elliot looked around for more dangers as he followed Owen closely, giving the creature a wide berth. It might have been cute under other circumstances, but Elliot was more concerned with the teeth than the silky fur. Many dog breeders on Earth would have been jealous. He sought out the cameras while he and Owen joined the rest of the expedition. The crew regrouped on the far side of the area.

While Owen did a headcount, Elliot gave a rueful narration to Vic's camera, interspersed with Hubcap's usual opinions. "That was exciting!" Elliot said. "Nothing like walking too close to something's lair to get the blood moving."

"Your blood would have moved outside your body if it'd caught you," Hubcap said. "You're welcome."

Headcount done, Owen ushered the group forward. Elliot didn't object. He could still hear the thing growling faintly. But, he realized, no one had frenzied in the moment of heightened emotion, and that was a great sign. He tried to calm his heart rate as he walked. A quick sniff of his palms told him that the smell of the leaves would thankfully not be following him around all day, and that helped.

Things were much calmer after the scare. The group covered a lot of ground without anything jumping out at them, and with plenty of nonthreatening animals to see. Alien insects gathered in clouds while a variety of bat-winged creatures snapped them up; snakelike beasties with many legs twined around the tree trunks, and something that sounded like a foghorn hooted in the distance at uneven intervals. One woman spotted an indigo scale lying on the ground among the bushes, but for the longest time that was all they found.

Then suddenly, they found all too much.

Elliot was right behind Hubcap and Owen as they passed through a screen of bushes. Owen gasped and Hubcap cried out in anguish. It took Elliot a moment to see past them — he spotted trees, rocks, an overflowing pond — but then he saw what they'd seen, and he wanted to unsee it.

The ground was littered with alien bodies.

None of the still forms seemed to have been injured, but they were all a dull translucent white, like albino snakes, and they lay sprawled in every direction.

"No, Rainbow," Hubcap said, dropping to his knees beside one and touching it with more emotion than Elliot had ever seen him display.

"What happened?" he asked Owen, unsure how to deal with the robot's mourning.

Owen was examining another body, feeling for a pulse and looking for wounds. "It's too soon to say for certain," he said as the rest of the humans spilled into the clearing. "If I had to guess though, I'd say frenzy."

"Can you be sure?" Elliot asked, trying to keep his calm in front of the cameras.

Owen shook his head. "Not without a full examination. But I don't see any signs of violence."

Elliot nodded silently. He crouched next to Hubcap. "You okay?" he asked, too quietly for the cameras. Behind him he heard Graham tactfully turn away.

Hubcap shook his head. "We just met them," he said. "They were supposed to be different."

"Different how?" Elliot asked, confused.

The robot pointed skyward. "This is a new race of intelligent life, amazing and exotic; they were supposed to live forever, or at least a really long time!"

Elliot shook his head. "Who said that?"

Hubcap waved his hands. "*I* did, dammit!" He lapsed into silence, staring at the fallen alien on the ground before him.

Elliot said nothing. The fact that Hubcap had used a real swear word told him that this wasn't a casual conversation. He tried to think of something to say. "I'm sure we'll meet more of them," he tried. "This is just a freak frenzy accident—"

Hubcap was shaking his head. "And what if we can't protect the rest of them?" he asked bitterly. "What if they're immune to the sedatives like those seashore animals are? This will just happen again, and we'll have to watch them die."

Elliot had no response for that.

The biologists started unpacking foldable stretchers. For a crazy moment Elliot thought they must have found survivors, but then he realized they were collecting cadavers for autopsy.

Hubcap followed his stare, then turned away in disgust.

Elliot got up and went to talk with Owen quietly. He suggested that taking the alien dead might be robbing the survivors of closure and death rites. But his hypothetical concerns didn't make a dent in the biologist's scientific curiosity. Owen just replied that it was pure luck that they had discovered the bodies before any scavengers did, and that they should make the most of it.

Elliot returned to his partner in silence. The pair sat and watched as the crew worked, ferrying the aliens back through the trees, and they didn't offer to help. Elliot was grateful for Vic's discretion in directing the cameras elsewhere. She could get some face time from one of the co-hosts when Hubcap wasn't so uncharacteristically fragile.

The robot only deigned to get up when one of the younger workers began to freak out over touching the bodies. Elliot saw the signs of frenzy when Hubcap did, but he didn't move. Hubcap had it covered.

"Sit down," Hubcap ordered the man, who was rubbing his hands frantically on his pant legs. "Right now."

Not hearing him, the man kept babbling about alien germs until the robot stalked over and stamped his SedEgg square on the man's chest. Then he stuck a hand under each arm and lowered the slumping worker to the ground, laying him out next to the alien he'd been about to move.

"Medic," Hubcap said as three other workers came running up. He returned to sit next to Elliot while the rest of the aliens were carried away. Hubcap instructed the workers to be especially careful with the one he'd named Rainbow, and Elliot had to ask how he could tell them apart.

Apparently the robot had good enough vision and memory to recognize the subtle patterns of gray on its beak, which was the only part of the body that hadn't changed color. Elliot kept his amazement to himself. He should have known better by now.

"All right everyone, that's the lot of them," Owen was saying. "Let's get back to base to deliver the load, then come back for more exploring. The day is still young."

The TV crew followed the workers silently to the car.

Chapter 23

Hubcap didn't even get out of the aircar. He just waited in his seat until the scientists had ferried away their morbid cargo, and were ready to go out again. He knew that Elliot and the camera team were having interesting conversations, but he couldn't bring himself to care.

Finally the engines started up again, and they were off. The ride was just as long as it had been before.

They landed in a nearby clearing on the same mountaintop, avoiding the tree branches entirely this time and setting off on foot toward the meadow they had just left. Hubcap took the lead, and Owen didn't object. He reached the meadow and strode through without pause, avoiding the squishy terrain around the pond. Then he put his attention to looking and listening, and being as stealthy as possible.

Once again, the humans were holding him back.

"Just follow where I step," he whispered in exasperation as someone behind him trod on crunchy plantlife. "Let's try this single-file, shall we?" No one debated the point, for which he was grateful, and he set off again. There would be no delays this time.

Finally they found a clue: wet footprints of the right shape. Hubcap called a halt so he could inspect them. Heat vision showed a faint glow of yellow on the blue-black mud. Scent was useless, which was a new experience for him. He didn't have the individual's odor in his scent bank, and since it wasn't even human, its smell blended in with nature. But the tracks were fresh.

"All signs point to alien," he said, gesturing ahead like a detective. "This way!" He didn't wait for the others to follow. Elliot was in front, and could catch up fine.

This time he spotted the aliens first, and it filled him with joy to see them active and healthy. He peered through a screen of bushes, crouching low. There were six of them, all wearing scale armor on their torsos, and they were busy climbing on a gigantic mossy boulder, chasing something small that evaded them with ease.

"Are they chasing a squirrel?" Elliot asked, appearing next to him. "An alien squirrel?"

"Looks that way," Hubcap said. "Let's give them a minute."

The camera crew got right to work, taking positions in the bushes and zooming in, while the biologists did much the same thing with their pocket-sized cameras. There was a lot to film.

The squirrel-like whatsit made its escape, scuttling off like a shot, but the aliens kept chasing each other around on the rock. It looked like a lot of fun to Hubcap, and he wished he could understand their color-language better. It was obvious from the playful motions and the bright tones that this was a game, but he couldn't tell any more than that.

Finally, tired of waiting, Hubcap whispered, "I'm going to step out. Be ready." Without waiting for a reply, he slid into the open.

He was quiet, so they didn't notice him immediately. Then when one of the creatures paused on top of the rock to take off its helmet, it caught sight of him.

The Earthlings got a good view of the aliens' alarm system as that one made an unmistakable jerky motion, hopping in place to land with all four feet/hands flat on the rock, its scaly hide sprouting a riot of rippling yellows and blacks between the armor plates. All of the other creatures spotted the display and copied it, facing in the direction of the invaders in the bushes. A staring match ensued.

"Ahem," Hubcap said into the silence. "Hi there." No one moved. "How are you guys doing? Didn't mean to startle you. Did you know the critter got away?" He continued babbling, but the aliens didn't relax from their threat display.

"Why aren't they calming down?" Elliot whispered from behind him.

"Something's different," Owen replied. "These are all wearing armor, so maybe they're soldier types. Or maybe it's something on our end. What was he doing when the one approached him before?"

"Imitating the birds and things," Elliot said. "Hubcap! Copy the wildlife again!"

Hubcap admitted it was worth a try. He listened for the omnipresent chirps and clicks, then began repeating them back.

***

Pebblemoss was the first to see the strange animal, and he alerted the others; they joined him in observing it for danger. It didn't act like anything else they'd seen. Where most animals obviously had other things to do, this one was intent on only them. And it didn't seem to be hunting; that was the strange part. If it had been, it surely would have attacked by now, or it would have given up when it was spotted. Instead it just stood there, looking back at them and making weird noises. Its color was downright bizarre.

Pebblemoss saw from the colors of his companions that none of them knew any more than he did about the odd creature. He was trying to figure out what it was doing and whether they should leave, when the creature's noises suddenly changed.

=*That sounded like an air-swimmer,*= said Bigeyes in surprised circles. =*Did that thing make the noise?*=

=*I think it did,*= Pebblemoss agreed. =*Listen, it's doing it again.*= They listened closely as the strange animal made sounds that didn't belong to it, repeating back every call it heard.

=*Is it trying to communicate?*=

=*Yes.*=

=*With us?*=

=*It must be!*= Pebblemoss edged forward in amazement. =*Look at how it's staring at us. It's not looking back at the animals that it's answering*= A thought occurred to him. =*It can't talk in colors, the poor thing! But it's trying!*=

=*You think it's that smart?*= asked Quicktail with some skepticism. =*What if it's just echoing?*=

=*Then why is it watching us like that?*= Pebblemoss insisted, flowing forward off the rock. =*I think it wants to talk to us.*=

=*Your choice,*= Quicktail said, her disapproval obvious. Pebblemoss ignored her and took one cautious step after another.

The strange-colored thing stopped making noises and put all of its paws on the ground, appearing to imitate Pebblemoss himself.

Pebblemoss stopped, and the creature froze. He put one hand out in front of himself, holding it above the ground, and the creature matched him movement for movement. Pebblemoss felt delighted colors spread down his back. =*Look at this!*= he told the others, =*Look at what we have discovered! It's trying to talk to me!*=

Quiet footsteps sounded behind him as his companions pattered down off the rock to inspect the oddity up close.

=*That color is so strange.*=

=*I know! And its face — look at that; I swear there's something* wrong *with its eyes.*=

=*Do you think it'll let me touch it?*=

It did, and soon everyone was marveling at the feel of the strange creature's flesh, which was alarmingly hard and cold. It felt like a smooth rock from the coldest part of the stream, and yet it moved about on its own.

=*Yuck, its skin reminds me of a dead eel,*= Dustcloud exclaimed.

=*Be nice,*= Bigeyes admonished.

=*Why bother? It can't understand us,*= she pouted.

=*How do you know?*= Bigeyes countered. =*For all we can tell, it knows exactly what we're saying, and it just can't answer us.*=

Quicktail pressed in close, her snout inches from the creature. =*Can you understand us?*= she asked, =*If yes, then raise your tail. Or one of your paws,*= she amended, obviously realizing that the creature had no tail.

Everyone waited, but it did nothing, just looked from one to another of them.

=*Nope, it has no idea what we're saying,*= Quicktail decided, sitting back.

=*But it is trying,*= Pebblemoss said, =*It's a not-us.*=

=*Oh, I suppose so,*= Quicktail said, looking bored. =*But what good is a not-us that can't talk? It's not like it can tell us anything interesting.*=

Pebblemoss was about to reply when a different sound came from the bushes, and the creature answered it.

=*Are there more of them?*= Dustcloud wanted to know. There did seem to be something there.

Then suddenly there were many somethings, all creeping timidly out of the bushes and staring like the first one had. They were a similar shape, but these had more normal colors, and their flesh seemed loose like they were about to molt. Pebblemoss found it more disturbing than he let on.

Quicktail led the way over to these animals, inspecting them with a critical air. After just a moment, she turned her back on them dismissively. =*These ones don't even talk a little,*= she said scornfully, =*They must be juveniles.*=

=*Are you sure?*= Dustcloud asked.

=*Sure enough.*=

The juveniles started making noises again, and the adult answered them, then the juveniles began edging back into the bushes.

=*See, they're going home,*= Quicktail said.

Pebblemoss moved to follow them. =*I want to see what kind of home they live in.*= He was gratified to notice that the odd-colored adult was walking with him. =*Maybe this one will show us the way there.*=

It did. The adult moved slowly until everyone was following it, then it picked up the pace. Soon the group was frolicking through the forest, and not even Quicktail was pretending not to enjoy herself. The run ended at a clearing with a large *thing* in it. Pebblemoss thought it was a rock at first — a weird-shaped one with no lichen on it — but then part of the side opened in a startling way, and two more creatures got out.

The crowd slowed down, taking in the sight, and the strange adult thing led them to the opening. Pebblemoss inspected the not-rock in amazement. The others were talking in excited colors, and no one paid much attention when the group of juveniles entered the clearing. Pebblemoss was distantly aware that they were chattering away with the adult, but his attention was more captured by the fact that Dustcloud was venturing inside the creatures' den.

=*Bad idea!*= Quicktail said, snapping at Dustcloud's tail.

=*Ow! It is not!*= Dustcloud retorted, =*They invited us in, and I want to see it!*= The other female's objections couldn't sway her, and Dustcloud disappeared into the opening. Pebblemoss wanted to object, but Bigeyes was already moving to follow, and he smoothed his colors instead. He hurried to join them. The others were right behind him, with Quicktail reluctantly bringing up the rear.

Inside the den was a cramped space, and Pebblemoss couldn't figure out where the creatures slept. He supposed they must just curl up on the floor, though it was very firm there. Well, maybe the juveniles would molt soon and get hard flesh like the adult.

Quicktail had gotten over her objections and was now spearheading the investigation. She went all the way to the far end of the place, and was turning to come back when the wall there *opened* again. Pebblemoss still couldn't figure out how.

Dustcloud scrambled over things to be the first one in, and Quicktail followed. Pebblemoss was right behind.

Inside the opening, he found piles of things tied to the walls, in confusing shapes that smelled utterly unfamiliar. He nosed about, trying to figure what the objects were without damaging the creatures' den. He heard the others crowd in behind him.

Then something slammed, and the room was darker. Pebblemoss whirled, coloring in alarm, to see that the mysterious opening in the wall had closed again.

=*Nooo, let us out!*= Dustcloud cried, bounding over and patting at the door.

=*I told you this was a bad idea!*= Quicktail exclaimed, running up beside her and raking her claws over the surface. =*This is probably how they catch their food!*=

Pebblemoss searched for another way out while the others scampered back and forth in panic. His breath came too fast and he was getting lightheaded.

Then something began to roar, and it didn't stop.

The entire room started to move.

<h1 style="text-align:center">Chapter 24</h1>

"What are you doing?" Hubcap yelled over the sound of the engines. "Are you seriously going to fly back to base with aliens locked in the cargo hold?"

Owen looked at him with a grin that was more than a little wild. "Saddle up!" was all he said before darting off to his seat, shouting directions to the pilot.

Hubcap stared at Elliot, caught between amazement and anger. Elliot's tight-lipped expression said he didn't like it either. Hubcap gestured impotently toward the aircar. "He can't *do* that," he said over the engines.

Elliot shook his head. "He shouldn't. If these are intelligent natives, we could cause an incident by kidnapping them."

Hubcap waved his arms. "Even with regular animals, it's better to watch them in the wild. What kind of biologist is he?"

Elliot turned to watch the other humans piling onboard. "The kind who looks tempted to leave without us. We'd better hurry and sit down."

Hubcap sputtered some more, but followed Elliot into the car. The rest of the crew did the same. Hubcap strapped into his seat with a worried glance at the door to the cargo hold. He wondered what was happening on the other side. Glaring at the back of Owen's head did no good.

The ship took off gingerly, moving an inch at a time until they were well above the trees, then slowly gathering speed in the direction of the base. Owen was yelling for the driver to "floor it in a cautious manner," and the world sped by below. Hubcap dug his metal fingers into the straps of his harness and waited, hoping with all his might that the creatures in the other room would be unharmed.

The ride took an excruciatingly long time. When the aircar finally entered the hangar, Hubcap was out of his harness and waiting at the cargo hold door for the moment they touched down.

As soon as the engines shut off, he opened the door and

stepped in carefully, shutting it behind himself. He heard Elliot convincing Owen to give him a moment to calm the aliens down.

They were all curled into a communal ball of red and orange in the farthest corner, wedged between two packs of supplies. Raspy hyperventilating filled the air. Hubcap knelt on the floor and began talking gently. He babbled, saying words and phrases he had used on many a scared child over the years, then he switched back to birdsong in the hopes that they would find it familiar and soothing.

After a few moments, heads started to raise from the pile, with bright reds muting to yellows, and tense limbs relaxing. The breathing slowed, though it still sounded rough. Hubcap kept up his birdsong and his calm body language, and eventually the knot of sickly yellows dissolved into cool greens. The creatures began moving around the room, and Hubcap knew he had made progress.

Then the door opened with a bang.

The aliens scattered, darting from place to place in search of cover and finding none. One of the bigger ones flashed out the door in a streak of orange.

The humans exclaimed in surprise, and Hubcap gathered from the bang-scrape-thud that the outer door of the airship was still closed. Moments later the same alien rocketed back into the room and dove into the corner, where it was joined by others.

"Hey!" Hubcap snapped at the humans. "Hold still! You're scaring them!" The workers did so, looking sheepish except for Owen, who was talking about the speed that the creature could put out. He sounded impressed.

"That was amazing," Owen went on. "With legs that short, I would have expected them to be slower. Not great at stopping quickly, but—"

"And just what is your plan now?" Hubcap demanded. "We're here and they're terrified, and we still can't talk to them to explain what's happening." He steamrolled over Owen's words. "They had better not be in for hideously invasive science!"

Owen shook his head and made negating motions with his hands. "No, of course not. We want to learn from them, observe their behavior, and try to puzzle out this complex color language of theirs!" An incoming call beeped from the front of the car, and he left to answer it.

"You could have done that without the kidnapping!" Hubcap yelled after him. When he got no reply, he turned his back on the doorway. The aliens were all huddled in the corner again. Hubcap chirped more calming noises at them.

When Owen came back, it was with news that the other scientists who he had called from the air were waiting outside to meet the aliens. Hubcap inquired tersely about the plan, and learned that it had been thought through at least a little. There was a containment truck waiting at the door like an airlock, and a path was open to a room that had been prepared with all manner of things. The way Owen described it made the place sound like a playground with a viewport. It had been designed for scientific testing of some kind, but would now be the most important of guest accommodations.

"Guests who don't want to be here," Hubcap reminded Owen. "Prisoners. What are you going to do when the rest of them come after us for this?"

Owen waved a hand. "It'll be fine. This will be a brief visit, I'm sure, and when we get the communications straightened out we can apologize as much as necessary."

Hubcap angled his eyebrows into a stern frown. "You don't have any experience with interspecies diplomacy, do you?"

"Nope!" Owen said. "I'm looking forward to it. See if you can get them moving, won't you? Their luxury suite is ready and waiting."

Elliot stood behind Owen. He met Hubcap's eyes with a wince and a shrug, signaling that he didn't like this either. Cameras appeared over his shoulders.

Hubcap sighed. "All right, everybody go away. I'll see what I can do."

The humans obeyed, edging backward but not fully out of sight.

A multitude of wide eyes regarded him from the cuddle-puddle of sharp colors. The aliens relaxed as the humans retreated and nothing startling happened. Trying every bit of pantomime that he could think of, Hubcap urged them to follow him. They conferred with each other silently, in swirls and spots, then the bravest one took the first step.

The group made its way gingerly past the rows of seats to the front door that opened straight into the back of the promised truck. All the humans had edged outside when Hubcap was still at the other end of the aircar, and now there was nowhere to go but forward onto the layer of blankets on the floor. Tiny portholes near the ceiling let light filter in, just enough to see by.

It took some encouraging, but Hubcap managed to get the aliens into the truck. Then, given no other choice, he shut the gate and settled down next to them.

The truck's engine was thankfully quiet. The aliens crouched like cats hearing thunder, but they didn't run. The truck moved forward.

This airlock procedure was repeated several times, finally ending at a large white room with blankets, pillows, food, and toys. Once the aliens were safely in, Owen waved from the hallway for Hubcap to leave them there.

The aliens were sniffing around curiously. Hubcap stepped through the door. Owen slid it shut, then gave Hubcap the briefest of thanks before prancing away to join a dozen other humans crammed into a side room where they could watch through the two-way mirror. Someone tall and official-looking gestured for Hubcap to move in the other direction.

Moments later, Hubcap found himself standing in a hallway with instructions to go find something else to do. There was a door closed in his face. He wasn't quite sure how that had happened.

Elliot came jogging up with the camera team. "Hey," he said.

"Hey, meatbag," Hubcap said automatically, still in shock. "Apparently we're not needed."

"Yeah," Elliot said as he came to a stop. "They unearthed their own hi-def video equipment."

Vic strode past and tried to enter the room, but was brought up short by someone just inside. The two talked briefly and urgently before the door was shut on her too.

"Is that all we are in this?" Hubcap demanded, waving an arm. "Just here to document things and provide witty commentary?"

Elliot nodded. "And bait," he said.

Frowning, Vic moved to talk to Graham.

Hubcap turned away. "I want to know what's happening in there," he said. "And they don't seem willing to let us in." He heard muttering and shuffling behind him. "Any ideas?"

"Every room has air ducts," Vic said.

Hubcap perked up. "They do!" He turned to see her digging into a camera bag.

"Wait, won't we get in trouble for that?" Dale asked, shifting his weight uneasily.

Vic showed her teeth in a fierce grin. "I was just told in clear terms that we can film anything we want as long as it doesn't bother the new guests. And we can't use that door." She jerked her thumb over her shoulder.

Hubcap pointed upward. "To the ventilation shafts!"

"Do I have to be the one to climb in?" Dale asked uneasily. "I keep telling you, Tarja can get into tight spaces better than me."

Hubcap laughed heartily and put a hand on the young cameraman's shoulder. "Do you expect to climb into the plumbing too, when there's a problem in the pipes? These are way too small for a human."

"Oh," Dale said.

"No, they are built for something tiny, like…" Hubcap waved a hand in Vic's direction. The director took her time in producing the item in question, spoiling Hubcap's flourish. "Like … that!"

The clear case held a miniscule hovercam and its control pad. Vic handed it to Graham, who was the most experienced with the delicate controls.

"Right," Dale said. "Of course."

Hubcap clapped him on the back. "Let's go find an air vent!"

* * *

Some minutes later, Hubcap was up near the ceiling, complaining good-naturedly while he unscrewed a vent cover. "'Let the robot do it,'" he whispered from his position stretched across the narrow hallway. His feet were braced on a doorframe and his free hand pressed against the wall next to the vent. He knew full well that none of the humans were quite up to this, but that didn't stop him from mocking them in his most nasal tone. "'We are all weak, and we suck at climbing, despite our monkey ancestry,'" he continued. "'The robot is better at everything, so he should do all the work.'" Hubcap paused to point down at Elliot and the others. "You all stink."

"Nonsense," Elliot replied. "We've showered recently enough."

"So you say," Hubcap bantered back. "It may have been recent, but it was not recently enough. I can pick up your fleshy scents from here."

"Of course you can." Elliot was smiling.

"Oh, I can; don't you doubt me!" Hubcap waved his hand in front of his face as if to waft scents into his nostril sensors. "You used peppermint toothpaste this morning, and had overripe bananas for breakfast."

"That's the only kind of toothpaste I own, and you were there for breakfast," Elliot countered. "Back to work with you."

"Bah," Hubcap said, picking up where he'd left off. It didn't take long to remove the screws. Soon the cover was hanging from one corner with the screwdriver and other screws resting just inside. Hubcap gestured for silence and held out a hand for the hovercam. Elliot handed it up to him with an anxious glance along the hallway. Vic and Tarja were stationed at either end to watch for anyone coming. So far, so good. This hall was not a heavily traveled one, and it led right behind the room they wanted to see into. Thankfully, the chamber full of humans was on the far side. With luck and a little stealth, no one would hear them.

The rest of the camera placement went off without a hitch. Hubcap gingerly pushed the hovercam into the vent, then waited while Graham thumbed the on switch. The cameraman manipulated the controls to lift the tiny camera with an equally tiny hover engine. Elliot and Dale watched the viewscreen over Graham's shoulder as the machine edged its way forward.

Hubcap put the cover back in place, then jumped down to land silently on the linoleum floor. "How's it going?" he whispered.

"Good," Elliot told him. "Looks like we're almost there."

On the viewscreen, the shaft took a sharp turn before opening up. Everyone huddled close while Graham parked the hovercam against the grate, angled down so the whole room was in focus.

It was a good view. Hubcap was relieved to see that the aliens still appeared to be fine. They wandered about touching pillows, lifting blankets, poking food items, and inspecting the surprisingly large collection of toys. Narrow mirrors lined the far wall. Hubcap knew that the hovercam could focus to peek into that area too if they wanted, but they didn't. This main room was the one to watch.

"Let's get out of sight," Vic said. She opened the door across the hall that Hubcap had been standing over, which led to an unused conference room. Vic had scouted it out earlier, and now showed the wisdom of her choice by locking the door behind them.

"They've definitely calmed down," Graham said. He set down the viewscreen on the oval table. "Nice and relaxed."

Hubcap pushed forward to see for himself. The colorful aliens did seem to be settling in. Their patterns were less sharp, and their motions were calm.

"They haven't really touched the food," Elliot observed.

"Oh, they've touched it all right," Hubcap corrected him. "But more with their hands than with their mouths."

Elliot nodded. "That is some nice fingerpainting they've got going on there."

Hubcap put the screwdriver he was still holding back into Vic's camera bag. Then he made himself comfortable in a seat close to the viewscreen, and the humans pulled up chairs around him.

They filmed the screen for a bit, then simply watched the aliens for the rest of the evening. The only time anyone left was when Tarja went to bring back food, and Vic called to update the showrunner with Elliot tagging along.

They returned with the news that the bosses were pleased.

Vic grinned with all her teeth. "Ms. Kaleel said some very nice things about us. I don't think I've seen her as happy as when I told her we had live aliens under observation. She's a little concerned about the methods, but very pleased with the results."

Elliot laughed. "Apparently the news broke today to the world at large that there's been a new First Contact. And we just called her up with 'Hey boss, we've got some of those aliens you wanted.' This is the scoop of the century."

Hubcap punched a fist into the air. "Suck it, Space Fashion!"

"Yeah, our ratings will blow theirs out of the sky!" Elliot laughed, repeating the gesture. "Even if Owen does cause an incident, we'll be here to document it, and there's no way fashion models can beat that for ratings."

Hubcap was all in favor of keeping a close eye on the proceedings, ratings or no ratings. But it was a huge relief to not have to worry about losing the show anymore.

The TV crew celebrated quietly, aware of the thin door while they clapped each other on the backs and speculated about the future. They stayed up late in that little room, watching the aliens and talking. The humans eventually got tired and left for bed one by one. It was late indeed when Elliot left.

"See you in the morning," he said to Hubcap. "For a brand new day and some aliens to learn to talk to."

"Yes," Hubcap said. "I will teach them poetry and all the best swear words."

"I bet you will," Elliot said. "Goodnight." He shut the door, leaving Hubcap alone with the view screen.

The robot kept up a lonely vigil well into the wee hours of the morning, finally turning the screen off when the aliens had long been asleep on their many pillows and blankets. He retrieved the hovercam with no one the wiser. After stowing the equipment in an unremarkable camera case, he strolled off toward the sleeping quarters with thoughts of trying a manual mission debriefing like Sera had suggested.

His step was light. Things were finally looking up.

Chapter 25

The aliens were dead by morning.

When Hubcap heard the news, he set out to find Owen and yell at him, but he found the human in a state of dismayed guilt.

"It's our fault," Owen told him in the hallway. "I don't know how, or what we did, but this has to be our fault. There's nothing visibly wrong with them, and we had them under watch all night; there were no frenzies. They must have been allergic to the food we offered them, or to some chemical or germ here — or to us!" He looked heartsick. "What if the aliens are allergic to us?"

Hubcap didn't have anything good to say to that, so he said nothing. Other people hurried past, all of them looking studiously away from the head biologist's distress. Even Elliot and the camera crew weren't around yet.

"I was so careful not to let anything dangerous into the room with them," Owen went on, hanging his head. "It's like their hearts just gave out, or their lungs, or they weren't getting enough oxygen to their brains. What could I have missed? It's impossible to know!"

Hubcap looked at the human askance. This level of emotion seemed out of character.

Owen broke down. "It's not fair!" he wailed.

Hubcap frowned and got out his SedEgg. Owen didn't even see the smack on the arm, and moments later Hubcap was heading for the hospital wing with the unconscious biologist slung over his shoulder. He hissed to himself about being robbed of his opportunity to tear the man a new one — he could hardly take him to task when Owen was unconscious. Oh well. It could wait until he was awake. Maybe by then he'd have words to relay from Vic about just how much Owen's people had let down the show, and humanity in general. Not to mention Hubcap himself. Scenes of frolicking aliens replayed in his vision centers as he walked.

Hubcap reached the medcenter without so much as a twitch from Owen. As he entered, he was surprised to see a large number of frenzy victims laid out in the recovery room.

"Where did this happen?" he asked the attendant, nodding toward the rows of beds as he set Owen down on an empty one. He expected to hear of some distant expedition to an unexplored location, but he was surprised to learn that they had all happened around the base recently.

"It's getting worse," the attendant said tersely. "Keep an eye out, will you?"

Hubcap nodded and promised that he would, knowing full well that this request was more than the casual warning that the attendant gave everyone else.

Not for the first time, he missed being around other robots. *If the laws had changed sooner,* he thought as he left, *Or if this place had enough money for them to have bought a robot worker back when we were property, then I wouldn't be the only one here immune to the frenzy.* With this piled onto the other bad news, he felt unusually world-weary. *I'm used to being more durable than the fleshies, but this is a bit much.*

In a mood, he walked into the cafeteria to hear a healthy dose of paranoia served with breakfast.

"It's an alien epidemic," a heavy-set blonde man was saying. "And it's only a matter of time before it spreads to us!"

"But an alien disease shouldn't affect humans," said his over-muscled neighbor.

"What do you think the frenzy is?" Blondie retorted.

"It's not a disease; there aren't any germs involved," reasoned Muscles. "It's been tested many times over."

"So it's an alien kind of disease, with germ-things we can't detect!" Blondie exclaimed, spreading his arms.

"Or it's environmental, some kind of *allergy* that we can't detect," put in a small Asian woman at the same table.

"But that should show up on allergy tests," argued Muscles.

"I said, something alien that we can't detect."

"That's just a cop-out," Muscles said.

"I heard that there was evidence that the whole thing is psychological," a sunburned woman put in.

"What, you mean like mass hysteria?" Tiny asked, leaning on her elbow. "That's bull."

"No it's not; there have been tests—"

"Complete bull," she said. "I refuse to entertain the notion that we're all just freaking out because we think we should."

"It's more complicated than that—"

"No. I've had frenzy, and it came on with no reason." The

dinky woman pointed with a scowl. "Nobody else was freaking out about anything, but suddenly I was worrying about a tool I'd just dropped. It wasn't even broken! But I was mortified that I'd damaged the freakin' *solid steel* torque wrench! I've never had a panic attack in my life, but there it was! I'm telling you, there's something going on here, and it's not some stupid sheep-mentality group panic."

"Yes, well—" Sunburn tried.

"*You* shut up; you've never had frenzy," said a curly-haired man who had been silent until now.

"Neither have you!" she replied.

"Yes I have," he said. "I just don't like to talk about it, because it was horrible."

"Frenzy is always horrible."

"Well some times are worse than others," Curly insisted.

"Okay, now we have to hear it," said Blondie. "Spill."

"…I don't want to, all right? Just drop it."

"No way, we have to hear this," Blondie insisted.

"*No*, you don't," Curly said.

"Oh, come on; I told my story!" Tiny chimed in.

"*I said no!*" the man shouted, flinging his coffee cup at her. Hubcap saw coffee fly, one human go down, and others leap to their feet to pile on the one who was now raging about privacy and respect for other people's feelings.

There were plenty of SedEggs in evidence. Hubcap didn't step further into the room. Instead he spun on his heel, face blank, and walked back down the hallway toward the dormitories. Surely he could be useful there. Maybe something mechanical needed fixing.

Chapter 26

Elliot heard about the dead aliens moments after leaving the sleeping quarters. Two passing scientists told him what had happened, but not why. When he met Vic, he learned that everyone was wondering the same thing.

"I'm afraid it's something for the biologists to figure out," she said. "As much as I'd like to focus on that, our concern right now has to be filming. I've just heard that those other cameras they dug up are fine for indoors but useless out in the wind and glare, which means we're back on the team." She stepped aside while a cluster of workers carried an unconscious man past them. "We just have to get official confirmation."

Elliot gave them a wide berth, noticing the SedEgg punctures on one arm. "How do we do that?"

"I've been trying to find Owen, but no one's seen him. And not because he's out in the field either; I checked at the hangar. Why don't you get some breakfast while I ask around more? Tarja is already eating. Are Dale and Graham still asleep?"

"Yes." Elliot jerked a thumb toward the dormitories. "Want me to wake them?"

"Nah, I'll give the door a good knocking on my way past." Vic strode away. "Go eat. We'll meet you there."

Elliot gave her a nod and a wave, then entered the cafeteria's sea of noise. He spotted Tarja chatting with several scientists. After grabbing food he joined them, catching up over mouthfuls of eggs and toast.

Graham and Dale wandered in a few minutes later. Graham made a beeline for the coffee display with Dale drifted after him. When the pair had collected both coffee and food, Elliot managed to flag them down.

"G'morning," Graham said with a nod to various faces. "Where's Vic and Hubcap?" Dale sat down silently beside him.

"Vic's looking for Owen," Elliot said. "Heard the bad news?"

They had. Oddly enough, no one had seen Hubcap, though

the robot was known to wander off occasionally. Elliot planned to ask Vic when she returned.

When she finally did, it was after everyone had finished eating and were starting to worry.

"Welcome back!" Elliot said as she approached the table. "We have questions."

"I have answers." Vic sat down. "First of all, we are indeed on the team for the next trip out. That will be today, as soon as all the relevant parties get themselves together. Secondly, Owen is in the recovery room of the medical ward, very embarrassed about an 'unacceptable' lapse into frenzy, not to mention whatever happened to the aliens. He'll be out soon. Thirdly, Hubcap is tightening all the lightbulbs in the bathroom for some reason, and should join us here when he's done. Then we can grab our gear and wait in the hangar. Did I miss anything?"

Elliot said no. The others agreed. They spent the next few minutes planning the camerawork choreography: who would film closeups versus wide shots, and what would change when the aliens — hopefully — appeared.

When Hubcap showed up, he was quieter than usual, letting Vic finish her sentence rather than dominating the conversation as he often did.

Elliot wanted to ask him a question or two, but Vic was already whisking the group off to get their gear. Elliot decided not to ask about the lightbulbs. It wasn't the strangest thing that Hubcap had done. Instead Elliot put away his cafeteria tray and followed.

They arrived at the hangar to find Owen up and about, assembling his own people like he didn't have a freshly bandaged SedEgg mark under his longsleeved shirt.

"Which type of medical kit is that?" he was saying. "Good, stow it up front. Hello again!" Owen greeted the crew with a weak smile. "I'm glad to have you all aboard. Make yourselves comfortable. We'll be off soon." His expression darkened when he caught sight of Dr. Rhodes approaching in decidedly indoors-only office clothes. "Please excuse me," Owen said. Elliot stepped aside while the crew chief moved to have words with the diplomat.

Vic herded the group to wait near the aircar while various workers scurried around with supplies. Elliot asked if she knew how long they could expect to be part of the exploration team. Graham and Tarja were curious about the answer, though Dale and Hubcap watched the commotion around them.

"Not as long as I'd like," Vic said. "They're bringing in an official camera crew of their own. People they can boss around, and footage they can own. We'll just hope we can get more good material before we're replaced. And that means finding more live aliens, since the medical types don't want or need us around any autopsies."

Elliot let out a breath, glancing at Hubcap. "Hopefully they're not allergic to us, or sensitive to our germs."

Vic nodded. "I asked about that. As far as I've heard, there were no signs of anything recognizable as an immune response, to allergies or otherwise. It seems a lot to expect that our scientists could be that certain when looking at alien life they've never seen before, but that's what I was told."

"I hope they're right," Elliot said simply. "I don't suppose you know when that shuttle is expected?"

Vic shook her head. "Nothing definite. Sounds like soon though. It's possible that Owen might know."

Elliot followed her gaze to where Owen stood arguing with Dr. Rhodes. "I think it can wait," he said. Vic nodded in silent agreement. Someone called for their attention from the aircar, ushering them onboard. They hurried to get settled.

Owen entered and shut the door loudly behind himself, with no sign of Dr. Rhodes. Elliot deduced that the group would be venturing out without him. Not that that was likely to be a problem, since the aliens had responded so well to Hubcap before.

Hubcap, meanwhile, was being unusually silent as they buckled in. Elliot found himself unsure of how to approach him; the robot was always so upbeat, even in stressful moments.

"It's a good thing our new episodes come out with a delay," Elliot said as a conversation-starter. "The media team will want to play up the recent footage."

Hubcap nodded absently and grunted.

"So…" Elliot tensed. "Did you hear about the aliens?"

"It must have happened after I stopped watching," Hubcap said, staring at the empty seat in front of him. "Or maybe before. They supposedly died in their sleep, without any outward sign."

"That's what I heard too," Elliot said. "No frenzy, then."

Hubcap shook his head sharply. "Not that that stopped more humans from frenzying this morning. It's spreading."

"Maybe," Elliot allowed. "These are emotional times."

Hubcap held still, only his jaw moving. "Yes. Perfect for

frenzy." Then his mouth closed, but the robot continued talking. "Highly hazardous."

Elliot looked at him in alarm. The driver chose that moment to start up the engines, and talking became near impossible. Hubcap turned away from Elliot to look out the window. Elliot stared at his friend as the aircar lifted and edged out the door. Hubcap appeared to be watching the scenery with interest, showing no sign that the conversation had happened.

Elliot leaned back into his own seat and kept an eye on him. The ground flowed by underneath, as they flew toward an expedition that Elliot dearly hoped held live aliens and no tragedy.

* * *

The aliens were alive and dancing. Elliot crouched in damp leaves behind Owen and several other excited biologists, surrounded by yellow plantlife that probably wasn't poisonous, and he smiled. Cameras were watching his face for a reaction while others took in the colorful display beside the river. Elliot gave the nearest camera an exaggerated "Do you *see* that?" before turning back to look through the shrubbery.

The muddy floodwaters swirled into calm shallows, with none of the ambient roar of the faster water. The shallows were bordered by a flat rock surface that was artificially bare. Elliot wondered if the aliens had swept it. Several pairs now danced on top, with wild motions and flashing colors that had the biologists in a tizzy.

Even Hubcap showed interest, seemingly recovered from his moment in the car. "The dancing is all very nice," he said to Elliot, pointing at the river. "But are the ones in the water doing what I think they are? What's your opinion, as a professional fleshy person?"

Elliot nodded. He'd been waiting for Owen to say something about it. "Yup, that looks like mating behavior, in classic fleshy-person fashion."

"But in the water?" Hubcap pressed. "Is that why you people like hot tubs so much?"

Elliot started to reply, but he was interrupted by Owen's scientific enthusiasm.

"They're obviously amphibious," the biologist said, grinning back at them from his position in a muddy patch. "I wonder if they're laying eggs or if they have live births. Or even something else! See if you can zoom those cameras in, won't you?"

The camera crew obliged, while Vic edged to the side for a different angle and Hubcap persisted in making jokes about having to give the show an X rating.

"It's documentary footage," Elliot said with overdone dignity while Dale filmed his face again. "There's a difference."

"Oh sure, a difference in whether it's played in public or not," the robot said with a knowledgeable air. "But really, both types have been known to depict fleshy things doing their reproductive acts."

"How would you know?" spoke up a biologist from Hubcap's elbow. Tarja moved her camera to film a brown-haired woman with a cheeky grin.

Hubcap addressed the biologist with authority. "I have done research on the human brain," he said. "You might be surprised to learn how much of your normal behaviors stem from the urge to mate and rear offspring. I was certainly surprised. You organic types are all about this mating business."

"So, anyway," Elliot said, trying his best to redirect the conversation. "What should we do now, Owen? We probably don't want to interrupt."

"No, that would not do," Owen agreed, to Elliot's relief. "Let's document this mating dance, then see where to go from here. Perhaps we can interact with them a little farther from the mating grounds, so we don't alarm them."

The humans quieted and shuffled their position. The camera jockeys were allowed front row seats, while the biologists with their pocket cameras made do with looking over shoulders and heads.

The dancing was impressive from where Elliot was sitting. The actual motions consisted mostly of leaping about, rearing and posing, and twining together like snakes. But what made it truly remarkable were the colors.

It's like an orchestra in lights, Elliot thought with amazement, *the way the patterns move and shift, even going from one body to the other like they're thinking the same thoughts! And they change so fast!*

"They would put those human fan dancers to shame, yeah?" Hubcap said. "I wonder if each pattern is a word."

Then Owen went off again, yammering on about the various Earth creatures that used color to communicate. Elliot learned a lot more in those few minutes than he'd ever wanted to know.

"...But the cuttlefish is what they really remind me of," Owen said. "Now those animals are masters of communication. I've seen a male swim between a mated pair and show calm greeting colors to the male, while flirting brightly with the female on the other side. And the other male had no idea." He kept on talking, surely making an interesting soundtrack for the camera footage.

Elliot wondered how much of it the editors would keep, and how much of those visuals would be turned into a music montage. He hoped it would be done with some respect.

And then it really occurred to him that they were spying on what was likely the most private part of an alien race's society. "Owen, maybe this isn't something they'd want us watching?" he suggested. "It's kind of personal."

"Nonsense," Owen said with a wave of a hand. "This is out in public, with others of their species and any passing forest creature afforded an easy view. And this is too fascinating to miss without a *very* compelling reason!"

Elliot expected just such a reason to manifest any second now, in the form of some dominant alpha wanting to protect the mating grounds. He shifted his weight to make it easier to get up and run just in case.

Then the pair that had been dancing closest started doing something a little worrying. They started to dance faster, twitching and jerking with abandon, moving closer to the river and closer to each other. Elliot could see the creatures' eyes open wide as they spun together madly, the dance devolving into a lightspeed wrestling match, and their colors blinking off and on. Mating or not, this looked uncomfortably like frenzy.

The leaves rustled as others came to the same conclusion, starting to edge back in preparation for a run back to the car.

But Owen made them wait, and Vic didn't overrule him. Everyone stayed where they were, tense and waiting. Elliot held his breath. The cameras focused on the tumbling ball of color-changing flesh as it rolled into the water.

"I'm pretty sure they're laying eggs there," Owen said, pointing. "See, the male must be fertilizing the eggs right now. It's like frogs!" He went off on another ramble. Elliot didn't interrupt, preoccupied as he was with trying to calm his own nerves.

In a moment, the circumstances did the interrupting for him. The pair in the water spasmed, their colors flashing, then they collapsed to sink under the surface. Elliot tried to breathe evenly while the biologists all whispered and pointed.

"Crap, it got 'em!" said a deep-voiced man.

"Did it?" muttered a woman. "Is that really frenzy, or just how the alien things mate?"

"Oh come on, you know what frenzy looks like," the man said.

"Yeah, and I *don't* know what alien sex looks like."

"Shut up. It was frenzy and you know it."

"Hush, guys," Graham spoke up. "Pretty sure they're still breathing."

Everyone crowded closer, with the biologists looking from the river to Graham's viewscreen. Hubcap aimed Dale's camera at his own face to narrate. Elliot just watched, with a sidelong glance at his co-host.

The pair of aliens began to stir, then slowly crawl up onto the bank. There they sprawled again to breathe for a moment, then gave each other a cursory nuzzle and wandered into the bushes in opposite directions.

Owen bounced from camera to camera, trying to find out what was happening. "Where are they going?" he asked no one in particular. "We've got to split up. Two cameras and half of the crew after that one, and the rest after the other, okay? Is that all right?" That last was aimed at Vic, who agreed with a curt nod.

The group split quickly. Owen wasted no time in commando-crawling his way through the bushes with a gesture for Elliot to follow him. "Come on! This is important science in action. Anthropology, even. Let's hurry."

Elliot waved to Hubcap, then slid through the undergrowth after Owen, with Tarja and Graham in tow. He was amazed that all the noise they were making didn't draw any attention from the dancers, but their attention was admittedly elsewhere.

Once out of eyesight of the beach, Owen directed everyone onto their feet, then set off running pell-mell through the yellow bushes and blue corkscrew trees. Elliot was right behind him. A glance showed that the videographers had wisely holstered their cameras for the time being. They ran, and the handful of biologists ran with them. The air filled with the smell of salty plants and the sound of boots on leaves.

For a creature that had just left moments earlier, the alien was surprisingly hard to catch up with. Owen's handheld scanner kept them on track, but barely. When Elliot was certain that they were about to burst through the bushes to see the alien in plain view, they found only empty forest and more bushes. There weren't even footprints in the leaf layer.

Then something flickered across the trees ahead. Elliot looked closer to see a shadow. A large one.

"Doom bat!" someone shouted. "Get down!"

The humans scattered as an enormous shape whooshed overhead. Elliot slid under a growth of hand-sized purple leaves, peering upward to see a flying creature like the one that had tried to eat Hubcap on their first day of filming. It hadn't snatched anyone into the sky yet, but it appeared to be circling.

People were swearing. "What the hell is that doing this far south?" a man exclaimed. "We're hours away from their nesting grounds!"

"They have to feed their hatchlings somehow," Owen replied. "Hush up and maybe it won't pick us."

Elliot spotted Tarja and Xian the medic under the next bush over. The camerawoman was filming through the leaves while Xian shook his head.

"They really go after people?" Elliot hissed. "Anrik said they mostly eat jet pods."

"They eat meat too," Xian whispered back. "Whatever looks like it won't put up too much of a fight. And when they have young to feed, they're not choosy."

Elliot nodded and kept his head down, following the shadow and listening for the sound of wings. He remembered his other question. "You really call them 'doom bats'?" he asked.

"Yeah," the medic said with a grin. "It was either that or 'Oh-crap-run!'"

Elliot shook his head and watched the sky.

Soon the doom bat's flight spiral closed in on something, and the massive creature dove to the ground nearby. It landed with a thump. All of the humans held very still. Moments later, wingbeats filled the air as the predator took to the sky again.

Owen was the first out of cover to confirm that it had caught something nonhuman. Elliot joined the others in scrambling out for a look. He caught a glimpse through the trees of a large dark shape carrying something limp and white.

"What did it get?" he asked, shading his eyes. "It wasn't a person. Nobody is wearing white today."

"It almost looks like—" Owen checked his scanner, then swore. "I'll eat my shoe if that isn't the very alien we were following!"

"Are you sure?" Elliot asked.

"It was *an* alien, at least," Owen said. "And nothing's coming up on the scans." He heaved a sigh. "Well, let's keep looking in case there are more over here."

They searched, finding impressive black trees that looked like goth broccoli, but no aliens. Finally they doubled back towards where they had split from the other group, hoping to find good news when they met up.

Instead, they found frenzy.

Elliot heard human voices through the trees long before he saw anyone, and he knew what the strident tones meant. The others came to the same conclusion and ran with him toward the noise.

He burst through the trees to the bizarre sight of Hubcap hanging by his knees from a high orange branch, holding an unconscious man about the midsection while others fought below them. Hubcap freed a hand to stretch downward with a SedEgg, but he couldn't reach the fighters. Some were already unconscious on the ground.

Before Elliot or his group could take more than a step forward, Hubcap threw his SedEgg down at the knot of fighting men. Elliot couldn't see whether it hit anyone or not, but the fight did seem to be losing steam by the time Owen jumped in to break it up. Everyone involved got a dose of sedation for good measure, and soon the riot was reduced to a pile of unconscious and bruised biologists, some bleeding slightly from awkward SedEgg punctures. The attention of the intact humans turned to searching the bushes and taking a headcount. Many arms reached up to take the limp form from the robot in the tree.

"'Bout time," Hubcap grumbled. "This guy's straining my joints here."

"You liar," Elliot said. "You can carry much heavier weight than that."

The robot craned his neck to regard Elliot sideways. "Well, sure I can. Doesn't mean I want to."

"Of course." Elliot gave the men room to lay down their comrade and check his pulse. It was a good thing that Xian had been in the other group, since it meant the medic was unaffected now. Others were surely trained in at least the basics, but Elliot was glad they didn't have to rely on that.

Across the clearing, Vic and Dale pushed through a screen of bushes. Elliot was relieved to see them unhurt. He was about to ask if they'd run at the first sign of trouble, but he was distracted by Hubcap swinging down from the tree. The robot leapt clear of the people on the ground and landed smoothly, which always made Elliot's knees ache.

"So," Elliot addressed him. "What in the blue blazes just happened here? Honestly, I can't leave you alone for five minutes."

"You can go suck on a screwdriver," Hubcap said, pointing at the human. "This bit of over-the-top emotions came on like it always does: for no reason. We saw another mating dance moving through the trees, then Jim-Bob Whatshisname there started crowing about how amazing the whole thing was, and a second later somebody else freaked out that the aliens were going to find us spying on them and eat us." He pointed out workers as he spoke. "That one tried to calm him down, while she got him from behind with a SedEgg, and those guys took care of the first guy, then this nutcase started panicking too, and managed to climb up the flippin' tree before I could get to him."

"Fast climber," Elliot put in.

"I have learned that all of you monkey types can be fast when you're terrified, and this one was no exception." Hubcap gave a detailed play-by-play of the rest of the incident while Xian finished his examinations. The story included a heroic leap between tree branches to catch the climbing frenzier before he fell, some acrobatics once he was caught, and an attempt to end the fight on the ground by throwing the SedEgg.

"Nicely done," Elliot said.

Hubcap looked around for the SedEgg. "Thank you. Where is that thing? Ah." He bent down and scooped it up. "I'll tell you, these are very sturdy but not aerodynamic. The manufacturers should look into making some with a projectile attachment." He said that last into Tarja's camera. Elliot didn't know how much of the monologue she'd caught. "Anyway," Hubcap continued, "I assume we're heading back to base, and that I have to carry people."

He was right on both counts. Once the medic was satisfied that all of the crew were in stable condition, Owen organized a string of people carrying the many victims through the woods. Elliot checked with Vic. She and Dale were fine, if rattled. Dale in particular was grateful to be heading back to the car. Elliot didn't want to be the one to tell him that they'd probably just trade the injured workers for a fresh crew and fly out again.

The forest was now echoingly empty. Hubcap speculated that they wouldn't see a single alien on the way to the aircar.

"Another good guess," Elliot said, lifting the arms of another unconscious man. "Don't let it go to your head."

"Hah! Never!" the robot exclaimed. "I am a paragon of humility."

"Sure you are."

"It's true," Hubcap told him, walking past with a limp human over each shoulder. "People often tell me, 'Hubcap, I envy you. Not only do you have many impressive robotic attributes, but you are humble to an amazing extent.' And I tell them that their feelings are completely natural."

He went on like this. Elliot smiled and let him. It was the kind of self-involved ramble that he had been hearing for years, and it was comforting to listen to right now when the alternatives were tense mutterings and eerie silence. They walked the long, awkward trip to the aircar, then went back for more until the aircar was once again full of unconscious people strapped into their seats.

Elliot wondered if he was getting jaded to the danger that the frenzy represented, simply since no one near him had died of it lately. He had been other places that weren't as well-equipped as this, and the danger had felt much greater. One in particular had only had the most rudimentary sedatives available, and death had seemed to stalk the halls. People there had been afraid to show any emotion, which had led to quiet terror and a more hard-to-detect reaction to the frenzy. Hubcap had been on top of things, but Elliot suspected that if they'd been there longer, the robot would have had a hard time keeping up.

This place was different. The sedation was top-notch, and while people were worried that the affliction could spread to them, especially now that it was ramping up, they still weren't afraid to show normal healthy emotions.

That, and the hospital is good too, Elliot thought as he watched the last of the workers buckle up. *A clean record can lead to complacency, though.* He looked over at Hubcap, who was gazing out the window. *The people here aren't used to having someone completely immune to the frenzy, much less someone trained in rescue who can carry a few humans at once. I hope he doesn't add to a false sense of security. And I hope he realizes what kind of effect he has on them.*

Chapter 27

The ride to base was much too slow for Hubcap. He knew that it was important to get the sedated people to the medcenter for a checkup as soon as possible, but from what he'd seen, none of them had been frenzying long enough to have suffered any lasting damage. And the fistfight hadn't been all that dangerous. The people involved didn't know how to fight. Luckily for them.

"Andalé! Chop chop!" he urged the workers as they re-entered the car after handing off their teammates to the medical staff. Hubcap and the camera crew hadn't moved from their seats. "We've got aliens to find!"

The workers hurried into place, including the new people to replace the frenzy victims. In moments they were buckled in, and the aircar roared skyward.

This time, Owen directed the pilot to aim for the other side of the river, with hopes that there would be a better view from there. He speculated out loud about whether the alien captured by the doom bat had been killed by claws or frenzy, or whether the life forms on this planet simply reacted differently than humans did.

"At any rate, it wasn't our fault!" Owen concluded with a nervous laugh. Hubcap said nothing. It sounded like Owen was trying to convince himself more than anything.

Hubcap pressed his forehead to the window with a click of metal on glass, eyes scanning the ground for bright colors. Nothing yet. Just the flooded river winding through hilly areas like an indecisive snake. The flat patch of ground that the pilot aimed for looked much like the meadows they'd landed in before: the trees were the same mishmash of shapes, and the critters made similar birdlike noises. Hubcap didn't see anything new and exciting as they landed. It wasn't until everyone had disembarked and picked a walking direction that something surfaced.

That was when four of the biologists blundered past a nest of vicious little anklebiters that no one had seen yet.

"Ah! What the—" A tall woman with curly black hair swore

creatively, shaking one foot like she was trying to kick down a tree. Clinging to her ankle was a blur of gray fur that grunted angrily.

The older man beside her, previously stern-faced and serious, did a mad dance to shake loose the creatures on his own legs. Two other biologists behind them also stomped and kicked, one reaching for the attacker at his knee before thinking better of it and brushing the thing off with a fallen branch.

Hubcap laughed heartily.

"You know, you could offer to help," Elliot pointed out as Graham filmed them both.

"I could," Hubcap admitted. "The beasties do look unlikely to damage my superior metal skin. But they appear to have regular teeth, not drillbit heads like the supergophers, so I think the humans can handle it." He gave the scene an appraising glance. The little piranha-squirrels were successfully being shaken off. "I daresay they have the situation well in hand."

"Don't say—" Elliot began.

"…Or in foot!" Hubcap added, proud of himself.

Elliot just shook his head.

"All right, enough of that," Owen said to no one in particular. He strode forward, helping to shoo away the last of the creatures. "Does anyone need bandages or antiseptic? I'm sure you've all had your shots." He urged the group away from the bushes.

Xian already had his medkit open. He made the rounds swiftly while the critters grunted and chattered from their nest. This sounded pretty clearly to Hubcap like "And don't come back!" He chortled to the cameras about it.

When the various nips were tended to and the medkit was stowed away, Owen led the expedition onward. "This way!" he declared, blazing a trail through some dense yellow bushes, apparently following his scanner more than common sense.

Hubcap walked around the bushes while the humans obediently pushed through behind Owen. "Fancy meeting you here," he said on the other side. Vic filmed both his grin and Elliot's disapproving look. Hubcap smiled wider. He strolled ahead, glad to see that Owen had found the alien equivalent of a deer trail, which would make for easier going.

This route took them north of the cliffside that they had originally climbed, and past a small waterfall that Hubcap had thought he'd heard earlier. It was all new territory up here, but so far there were no color-changing aliens.

Hubcap peered over Owen's shoulder at the scanner. "Are we close?" he asked.

Owen shook his head. "It's hard to say. There's nothing coming up nearby, but this model doesn't have a very wide range. We know the water is that way, and the beach where we observed them this morning is farther along, so this is the way we will go."

"Good enough," Hubcap said. He moved back to walk with Elliot. Short minutes later, they saw the river from a safe distance. Nothing interesting happened there. They moved along the banks further north, sneaking through the scenery until a massive rocky bluff reared before them, blocking their way. Biologists grumbled about having to go all the way around and possibly lose the river.

Owen led the way out of the undergrowth to where they could get a better view. The mesa was roughly the size of a shopping mall. More grumbling sounded.

Hubcap spoke up. "Wait a sec. I'll scout," he announced, striding up to the near-vertical cliff face. "Higher elevation equals better view and all that." No one stopped him, so he began climbing. He knew he made it look easy. With silent skill, he clambered upward until he reached the distant top.

Bird poop painted the surface. He made a mental note to complain about it when he wasn't trying to be stealthy. Instead, he ran on quiet feet to the edge nearest the vast river, and looked down.

He stared in amazement.

It hadn't been visible from ground level, but the water in the center of the river was less muddy, like there was a barrier that he couldn't quite see straining out the silt. Under this clear water were buildings. Lots of them, looking like they were made of stone and decorated with those same bright shells. They went down a long way, farther than he could make out, and most of them were peppered with windows, even on the roofs. There were long-bodied shapes swimming to and fro throughout the underwater village.

Hubcap could almost hear the applause from the many awards ceremonies in his future.

Elliot's voice reached his ear sensors, in an attempt at a whispered shout. "Heyyyy. What do you see?"

Hubcap snapped out of his trance and hurried back to the other side, full of excitement. He poked his head over the side.

"Guys. Guys. You have to see this. Gimme a camera, one of the little ones. Go ahead and throw it, quick!"

Tarja did so without asking questions.

Owen was full of them. "What is it? What's there?" The biologist clamored for answers, sidling back and forth, looking for a handhold. "Is there a way up on the other side?"

Hubcap scooted back from the edge, fiddling with the camera. He needed a good zoom for this, with water-penetrating properties. *Ah, there we go,* he thought. *Now, let's film some historic footage!*

It was an amazing scene down there. Once he had the camera at the right setting, he could pick out the details. The stonework was very impressive for something that was apparently made underwater, and it all seemed designed to mimic the natural wear patterns of the river. There were no hard lines anywhere, only smooth curves and rounded doors. And the place was full of swimming armored creatures.

He'd assumed at first glance that they were the same aliens that he'd been seeing for the past few days, but he realized he was wrong. They did the same color-changing, and they had the same upper body shape and beaky face, but there were distinct differences. The biggest of which was the fact that the long torsos on these beings ended in fishy tails instead of hind feet. They looked a lot like eels with arms, and even those were shaped differently: longer, with webbed fingers. The crab-scale armor covered everything, fitting together amazingly well. Those pieces that the humans had found by the rocks appeared to have been the crudest of cast-off attempts. Many of these finished plates even had detailed pictures carved into them.

Not all of the aliens were wearing armor, Hubcap noticed — there seemed to be a distinct military caste, swimming with spears and alert posture. The civilians darted and swam at a leisurely pace, some carrying things, some tending to smaller ones that must be children. They certainly had the bigger eyes and rounded features of much Earth young. Most of the kids were clumsy in their swimming, though one older youth was moving with surprising speed, chasing after a large sharptoothed fish.

Hubcap filmed the progress of those two through the center of town, wondering why the other aliens were ignoring the dangerous-looking animal. It was obviously predatory, after all, and…

And a pet. He watched in amazement as the color-changing alien caught up to the fish and tackled it in a joyous hug. Moments later, the alien was throwing something out of the water, while the fish leapt to catch it.

Hubcap pulled back out of sight, even though the pair was

looking in a different direction. It was easy to forget, while looking through the camera, how far away they were. He waited for half a second, then moved back and spied shamelessly.

Wow. Hey, that building looks like a store, he thought, *I think they're selling plants. And ... is that a restaurant?* It certainly looked like one, with balconies set up against the side of the building for visitors to rest on. There was even a waiter, whose colors rippled in gentle pinks and greens, offering a basket full of something edible to one visitor after another. Hubcap couldn't make out what the things were — fruits, eggs, alien cheese — but he could appreciate the white spiral pattern woven into the green basket, which matched the single armor plate that the waiter wore. Dark blue with a carved white pattern, this shell plate was centered on the alien's chest with loops over its shoulders. Maybe it was a nametag, maybe the logo of the foodmakers, or the restaurant itself. For all Hubcap knew, it could be the sign of a criminal working off a sentence, or a traveling fungus salesman with free samples.

This is astounding, Hubcap thought. *It's all so civilized! And we couldn't see any of it from the shore.* He dialed back out of the water to look at the muddy beach. Movement caught his eye, turning out to be a mating pair of landwalkers doing their business in the shallows. After a cursory glance, he looked away, then paused when he noticed a number of the aquatic creatures swimming toward the landwalkers.

Well hello, Hubcap thought, zooming back in, *What's this, then? A territory dispute?* He expected the waterborne ones to attack, or at least gently usher away the preoccupied pair — the ones in the water wore armor, while the others didn't — but that wasn't the case.

To Hubcap's surprise, the small group of swimmers halted at a respectful distance, and waited while the pair shook and flickered themselves into a collapse.

That really does look like frenzy — now what? He watched the two still forms lying in the shallow water, with their own fertilized eggs floating in clouds around them. The water creatures were moving in. *Aha, now they eat the land creatures' young! Fiendish!*

But again he had guessed wrong. The aquatic aliens began gathering up the eggs with an air of extreme gentleness, ushering the floating things into woven baskets and taking pains to make sure they had collected every last one. They even went so far as to carefully move the two breeders. Hubcap was wondering if they were saving the eggs to eat later when the sleeping pair began to wake up.

Oh, now for a fight? But there were no hostilities. The pair's flesh lit up with lavender patterns that the others copied — a greeting of some sort — then they casually walked out of the water and strolled away without a backward glance.

The hell?

He zoomed back and forth between the departing land creatures and those in the water, who were swimming away with their covered baskets. Hubcap followed the swimmers until they entered a large building with guards posted outside. The two guards raised their spears and made more of the greeting-flares, then they floated aside to let the baskets past.

"Psst! Hey! Hubcap!" Distant human voices brought him back to himself. He took another quick look around the village, then shut off the camera and wriggled back along the rock.

"Oh, you guys are not gonna believe this!" he said, getting to his feet and hurrying to rejoin the humans. A conversation from several days earlier popped into his head. "Elliot! I told you there'd be mermaids!"

Chapter 28

The expressions of glee on the humans' faces were everything Hubcap could have wanted. They huddled around the tiny camera screen, then demanded to see the underwater city for themselves.

After some quiet searching, a section of rock around the corner was picked for climbing. The least clumsy humans went first. Hubcap stood below to hoist them up one at a time. It wasn't an ideal climbing path, but it would have to do. The videographers went up with their cameras safely in backpacks, though an extra camera had to be handed up to them. Everyone hurried.

Hubcap was the last to arrive at the top this time. He found the rest of the crew gathered at the drop-off, looking down at the water and whispering in excitement. Most had gathered around the cameras, watching the viewscreens for details that they couldn't make out themselves.

"This is amazing!" Owen breathed. "What a find!"

"Look at that arch over there!" whispered Elliot. "It looks like it's inlaid with gemstones!"

"Do you think they can throw those spears very far?" asked a woman. "What about out of water?" Hubcap recognized her as the Amazon warrior who'd fought off the anklebiters.

"We're pretty high up," said another woman with darker skin and a sharp nose. "If they live in the water all the time, maybe they only use them for stabbing. The water might slow down projectiles to where they're useless."

A pale guy with white-blonde hair spoke up from farther along the edge. "Ever seen anyone spear-fish? Projectiles go plenty fast."

Several people hushed him while the Amazon pointed out that human spear-fishers generally threw from outside the water.

Sir Sunscreen-A-Lot mumbled something about harpoons, but he kept quiet.

"Anyway," she said, "My question is whether they can huck those spears high enough to give us problems."

"Naw," said a man with more melanin.

"Probably not," agreed Lady Sharpnose.

Hubcap snorted an electronic snort. "What are you fleshies talking about? I could do it. Just because you tender things lack the strength, don't assume they can't."

There was a momentary silence. "The robot has a point," the Amazon said. "Let's make sure not to bother them, shall we?"

The others agreed and crouched lower against the rock, watching silently.

Tarja pointed past her camera. "Hey, look!"

Another mating pair had just danced out of the bushes, heading for the shallows. The humans with cameras aimed at the pair, occasionally straying to focus on the small welcoming party in the water.

Hubcap did his part by making sarcastic remarks about invasions of privacy. Someone had to do it.

"Don't be a hypocrite, metal head," Elliot replied. "You just filmed the whole thing a minute ago."

"That was different," Hubcap said. "I was documenting a rare find, so that I could share it with all of you. There's no need to document the same thing now, so let the poor things have their private happy time."

Owen gave him a look. "Which they are having in broad daylight, out in public, in view of those in the river," he said. "Stop arguing just to be contrary."

"Fine, take all the fun out of it." Hubcap subsided, resting his chin on his hands and watching the proceedings. Everything happened the same as before.

"So what do you make of the water-based ones?" Elliot asked Owen. "Are they a subspecies? Any idea what they're doing with the eggs?"

Hubcap piped up. "I think they're going to eat them, as you fleshy things tend to do." He pointed to the baskets. "See, they're storing them for later."

Elliot sighed. "Orrr…"

"Or," Owen said. "They could be taking them away to care for properly."

"That's a nice thing to do if they're a different species," Elliot said. "What do they get out of the deal? Do the land-based ones keep predators away or something?"

Owen was visibly thinking. "I suppose that's possible," he said. "But the more obvious — and interesting — answer is that these are all members of the same species. They are the same size, and largely similar. Either some are hatched to be aquatic while others are land-based — this would be like an ant colony, with drones, soldiers, and breeders — or they start out in the water, and it's only when they reach their adult forms that they move to land." He leaned back, pondering. "I think the second option might be more likely, since all of the eggs seem to be laid underwater, so it would make no sense to expect some of those eggs to hatch into air-breathers."

"That would be really cool," Hubcap said with exaggerated sincerity, while the other biologists burst into hushed conversation. "How do you expect they do this magical shape-changing from mermaids to dragons?"

"Oh, probably much like frogs," Owen said, unfazed by Hubcap's analogy. "A little bit at a time. Or maybe even in cocoons like the insects, though I haven't seen a sign of any. Still, that wouldn't mean much; if they're this civilized, then they would surely spend their vulnerable metamorphosis time indoors. They have the space, it looks like."

"Fascinating," Hubcap said.

While Owen nodded, Elliot agreed. "It really is."

Then Elliot slapped his hand toward the rock in sudden realization, stopping short of making a loud noise. "This is why the intelligence scanners didn't find them on the first go-round," he exclaimed in a loud whisper. "They were all underwater! Do we have the tech to detect brainwaves underwater?"

Owen's eyes were wide. "That must be it," he murmured. "How long do their life cycles last, to be missed so completely? I assumed it to be a yearly thing like most animals on Earth, but maybe it's more like cicadas, with their seventeen years underground!" He went off on a ramble.

Hubcap stared down at the underwater city. "We should ask them. Y'know, as soon as we figure out the whole communication business."

Elliot huffed a laugh. "Yeah, that minor detail. Somehow I doubt it'll be simple, more's the pity. I'd love to talk to them. And see those buildings up close!"

"I have always wanted to swim in a window," Hubcap agreed. "You know, one that's not attached to a sunken car."

"Of course," Elliot said.

"Is that floating thing a *garden*?" Owen asked no one in particular, squinting upstream. "It must be. That's incredible." The collective attention turned to this new marvel, cameras filming away and biologists muttering.

It was Dale who saw the fringe of knotted strings that one of the aliens was carrying. "Hey, look!" he said, pointing at his viewscreen. "Weren't people finding seaweed tied in knots, and they thought one of the scientists did it? I think it was these guys!"

Hubcap scrambled to peer over his shoulder. One of the warrior aliens in mostly-yellow armor had tucked their spear under one arm to hold the knotwork with both hands. An unarmored civilian treaded water nearby, long tail lashing and colors dancing in a purple-orange conversation that meant nothing to the robot. This one pointed to a knot, and the other alien said more color-words in response.

Hubcap patted the camerman on the shoulder. "That does look pretty clear. Good catch, Dale! We might just pay you after all."

"Gee, thanks," Dale muttered while everyone else searched for knotwork. They found it in several places: on a restaurant table, on a wall of the plant shop, and held by passers-by. One slender civilian rested atop a building with a basket of water weeds at the ready, weaving what looked like the world's longest beaded necklace.

Elliot beat Owen to the conclusion: "Guys, that might be a form of writing. It's something that won't wash off underwater, and it's portable."

Owen beamed at him. "I was just thinking that! There have been cultures on Earth that use knots to keep track of numerical things. I'm not sure if they ever decoded anything more abstract, though it's certainly possible."

"I wonder if we can find those pieces back at base?" Elliot said. "Not that we can read them yet." He gestured vaguely at the alien society below. "But give it time!"

Then something occurred to Lady Sharpnose. "Hey," she said with a smile. "What are we going to call them? Did anyone ever come up with something?"

Heads turned.

"No, they did not," Owen said in excitement, a bit louder than he should have.

It wasn't the first time Hubcap had seen the crew chief forget himself in favor of scientific interest. He would have bet someone else's money that it wouldn't be the last.

"So far it's been 'alien' this and 'native' that," Owen continued. "'Organism' if we're lucky. I'm sure these very foreign people have their own name for themselves, but it may be a while before we can communicate well enough to ask. What *should* we call them? Perhaps something scientific — based on the classification for cuttlefish, maybe. Cephalopeople?"

He was immediately voted down, and the other biologists weren't quiet either. Hubcap glanced at the surface of the river and decided that the aliens probably couldn't hear them. Probably.

"No, it should be something that regular people can say!" the Amazon exclaimed. "Like kaleidocritter."

"Oh, now that's just silly," Sharpnose said.

"You do better, then!"

"Skinspeakers," she suggested. "Or wordscales."

Dale jumped in eagerly. "What if we name them after the planet?"

The biologists weren't impressed. "You'd call them 'the natives of planet IGN-47'?" asked the Amazon.

"Oh," Dale said. "Right."

"That's not wholly bad," Hubcap said, taking pity on the cameraman. "Just a bit of a mouthful. What about something color-related, like spectrumspeakers?"

"That just sounds like a brand name for music equipment!" laughed Sunscreen-A-Lot.

"Guys, keep it down," Owen finally said. "Let's shelve the conversation for later, when we're not in earshot."

The humans quieted, agreeing to call the aliens "colortalkers" for the time being. They settled back to watching.

Hubcap broke the silence. "Owen," he said with false casualness. "Do you think the ones in the water have any influence over the ones on land? Can they summon air-breathing assistance?"

"I suppose it's possible," Owen said. "Why do you ask?"

Hubcap pointed at the armored aliens in the water below them. "Because it appears that we are no longer being stealthy," he said. They were gathering beneath the cliff, looking upwards and hefting spears.

"Annnnnd back we go," Vic announced, sliding out of sight. "Come, camera crew." They followed her while the biologists still clustered at the edge.

Owen shook his head. "Surely they're not going to throw — Ack!" He broke off as a spear flew past his face.

<h1 style="text-align:center">Chapter 29</h1>

The day had started out as a normal one for Rockcatcher. She made the obligatory pass around town before settling into watcher duty outside the main door of the Egg Home. Beaksharp was paired with her, and other trustworthy ninth-floods were stationed at the higher entrances. Rockcatcher approved. Now was not the time for few-floods to be at important posts.

The watcher's attention was caught by the flash of cheerful colors that was a second-flood chasing his large Biteless. Rockcatcher's scales prickled with disapproving colors around her armor, but she didn't berate the youngster. He hadn't scattered anyone's groceries yet, and appeared to be slowing down. She looked away when the chase stopped.

=*Good, he's going up to play catch at the surface,*= Beaksharp said in tart greens. =*There's less to bump into up there.*=

Rockcatcher agreed, and turned back to watching for alerts. Soon a squad of eggtenders were speeding her way in careful fashion, with bright colors and egg baskets marking them for all to see. Passersby got out of their way. The watchers came to attention. With a salute and a polite hello, Rockcatcher and Beaksharp let them past.

Another successful retrieval without any sign of predators. It was commendable, though any predator that would risk stealing eggs from an us-home this big was surely damaged in the head. But the warriors needed to keep watch anyway, in case there were other dangers.

=*Is that child playing too close to the Egg Home?*= Beaksharp asked, looking upwards. =*I don't like the direction his Biteless is going.*=

Rockcatcher followed her partner's pointed finger, and she agreed. =*He probably won't hurt anything, but it's not respectful or safe,*= she said. =*The team up top should be warning him off soon.*=

They did, with no-nonsense colors and gestures to swim back the other way. But to Rockcatcher's surprise, she watched the youngster approach the guards in colors of agitation. His Biteless swam in urgent circles beside him.

=*What's he saying?*= Rockcatcher asked, and her partner strained his eyes. It was a long way up.

=*I think the child saw something on the surface,*= Beaksharp said, unimpressed. =*Maybe a type of air-swimmer he's never seen before.*=

Rockcatcher observed the guards up top. One was swimming to the surface for a better look. He almost disappeared from view in the seasonal mud that plagued visibility here, then he darted back with alarming haste.

=*It looks important,*= Rockcatcher decided. =*You keep the post. I'm going up.*=

Beaksharp didn't argue, only suggesting that she hurry back. Rockcatcher wasted no time in powering upwards with her spear held close. When she passed other watchposts, she swam in colors of minor alert, and one watcher from each pair soon kicked up their tails after her. Each carried a spear and wore stunpods holstered in easy reach. Rockcatcher checked her own out of habit as she swam. Ready and fresh.

Halfway to the top, she met a guard coming down the other way, calling for backup. The growing crowd sped to the surface.

Once there, they found a cluster of warriors peering up into the air, looking at something atop the cliff. Rockcatcher joined the others in raising her face above the water to see.

=*What are those?*= she asked, and no one had a good answer. There were certainly lots of the creatures, all lined up along the edge and staring down at the us-home. Rockcatcher didn't like the view they were getting.

=*Are they holding weapons?*= someone asked. =*Those things they keep pointing at us?*=

=*I don't know, but we're going to warn them away,*= decided someone with rank. =*You, you, and you I've seen hunt air-swimmers with skill; come with me. Anyone else who thinks they can spear one, this way. The rest of you make sure no one wanders into the drop zone.*=

The guards scattered to do as the leader said, keeping the curious onlookers out of danger. Rockcatcher joined the spear squad. She was a fair shot at awkward angles. It was a pity that the interlopers were too far to reach with stunpods, but that was certainly also a good thing. They would pose a much greater danger if they were closer.

Once the area was clear, and it was confirmed that the spying creatures were still there, the spearthrowers lined up in ranks.

Rockcatcher held her spear at the ready just below the surface, and took a deep breath. She watched the leader.

=*On my mark,* = he said. =*Now ready, and … mark!*=

Warriors exploded out of the water, launching spears at the cliffside and the unwelcome creatures looking down on their home.

Chapter 30

The humans scrambled away from the cliff edge as more spears zipped through the air. Hubcap kept an eye out for any that might come arching back down on them. Most of the throws went back into the water or off to the side, but more than once he had to yell at people to be careful.

"You in the blue! Dodge right!"

The heavy-set man moved just in time, a spear clattering down where he'd been. "Gah!"

"Exactly!" Hubcap said, scrambling forward to grab the spear. "Watch the sky!" Moments later it happened again. This time he hit the oncoming spear out of the air with the first one, not bothering to yell at the human in the line of fire. Then the fleshlings were all out of range, and beginning to scramble down the rocky cliff. Hubcap hurried over to supervise.

"Put your foot there," he instructed. "No, lower — oh hell, let me." With that, he vaulted over the side to land with deep footprints on the ground far below, spear still in hand. He leaned the spear against the rock and climbed halfway up, then anchored himself in place and served as a stepstool for the humans.

Not a quiet one, though.

"That's right, step on my shoulder, lean your weight toward the rock like you love it in your strange fleshy way, try not to fall off and land on your head; I hear that hurts a lot — and you better not have stepped in anything gross. If my shoulder gets alien bird poop on it, I will be coming for your shirt to clean it off. Right, good job not plunging to your death. Next! Pass the camera down first! Why did we bring more cameras than backpacks, anyway? For shame."

The procession went smoothly, with the more agile climbers making their own way down without Hubcap's help, and only a few minor scrapes and bumps caused by haste or clumsiness.

That extra camera did turn out to be a hindrance, though, when a worker managed to bang it on the rock while passing it down. Everyone winced at the distinctive sound of something snapping off. The man apologized up and down, but it was indeed damaged and expensive.

"Did we bring the spare parts kit, or is it back at base?" Vic asked, inspecting the camera as everyone else climbed down.

"I have some parts, but not many," Tarja said.

"That's great. Let's keep moving," Hubcap said, picking up the spear. Owen would surely fawn over it when they reached a safer spot.

Owen didn't notice. "Yes, there could be terrestrial spear-throwers coming our way," he agreed, pointing in the general direction of the aircar. "Double time!" He took off running.

Hubcap made sure Elliot and the others were accounted for before jogging along. The spear didn't get in the way too much as long as he was careful. He was glad to see that none of the humans had been injured, so he could focus on watching for threats. That and listening to Owen chatter about First Contact.

"We'll come back as soon as possible," Owen was shouting as he ran through knee-high purple grass. "It's so frustrating that we can't talk to them! We don't know what they'll accept as a white flag! We're likely to get speared if we get too close!"

Elliot sped past Hubcap into conversation range. "They're probably just being paranoid because of the eggs," he said. "Should we look for a safer spot at a different part of the river?"

Hubcap saw Dale filming the conversation. He picked up his own pace to make sure the junior cameraman didn't plow into a tree. It would have been nice to get footage of himself running dramatically with an alien spear in hand, made of dark brown wood and red shell, but … priorities. And another camera would surely be online soon.

"That may be our best option," Owen agreed with Elliot. "And I hope the incoming VIPs bring us a better translator than the one Dr. Rhodes has."

"While they're at it," someone else piped up. "They should appoint a better diplomat. He has no idea what he's doing."

Owen pointed a stern finger and took the man to task about respect, while the camera crew tactfully filmed the scenery instead. There were plenty of those black broccoli trees making shadows on the purple grass. Hubcap made sure to position himself in front of Graham's camera as soon as Dale was past the biggest obstacles. Then he used the spear to hold back bushes for other people.

The rest of the jog passed in relative silence, aside from rustling bushes and muttering humans when they inevitably caught clothes or skin on sharp bits. Dale got his wits about himself and turned off his camera before pushing his way through the worst of the underbrush. Hubcap kept an eye on him anyway, but then he was watching everyone. Poking fun too, whenever it was remotely called for. That always made for fine television. And as far as Hubcap was concerned, a good roasting made the humans more aware of their surroundings. Less likely to do the dumb thing again next time.

"Oh, that was comedy physics 101!" he said when one woman let a branch snap back into another's face. "I hope someone got that on film. That was beautiful. And you should look out for stickyweed or something in retaliation; she would totally deserve it."

The two biologists glanced at the cameras and downplayed the incident, though Hubcap heard somebody snicker.

My work here is done, he thought.

The aircar finally came into view between the clumps of thorny brown shrubs that had held the anklebiters before. Hubcap was fully ready to watch the humans walk past the nest again, but Owen remembered and led them around it. A pity, really. Tiny teeth were grating in the bushes, too quiet for the humans to pick up, just ready to do battle against pant legs and shoes. Another day, perhaps.

The group reached the car with no sign of pursuit, and no injury worse than a thorn scratch. Hubcap did his own silent headcount, standing at attention with the spear, while Owen took stock of everyone. The various humans competed to appear least out of breath.

Hubcap was quietly superior about the whole breathing business. It did occur to him that a couple of his joints were probably due for a lubrication touchup though, something that he would never so much as mention in human company. He had a reputation of perfection to maintain.

Not that such a reputation was difficult when the meatlings were so fragile, of course. If today's ride back to base was free of the stink of fear, that would be delightful.

"And a million thank-yous to Hubcap, for catching one of the spears!" Owen said, turning to him with hands out. "May I see it?"

Hubcap handed the thing over with a flourish, as if presenting an ancient sword. Owen was gratifyingly pleased.

"Look at the craftsmanship," he enthused while three of the four cameras closed in. "This is polished to a shine, and likely coated with something to make it waterproof. And the carvings! Are these for grip, do you think, or do they have some other meaning?"

Elliot stepped forward to jabber away with him. Hubcap let them, adding his two cents about the patterns before slipping away into the background. Vic was searching pockets for something to fix her camera.

"So, what broke?" Hubcap asked.

Vic shook her head. "Just the clip that holds the directional microphone in place. Thought we'd lost the whole piece, but it's just the attachment. Can't really use it without a way of holding it on, though."

Hubcap held up a finger. "Allow me." He pressed a hand to the blank center of his chest, which had once lit up with a rescue halo. Now it slid back at his touch to display the duct tape dispenser that he hadn't needed to use in weeks. He tore off a piece and made grabby motions for the camera.

Vic surrendered it with a smirk that said she was humoring him. Hubcap deftly applied the silver tape, strapping the microphone down in a manner both secure and stylish, then handed it back.

"Ta-da. I have saved the day once again."

"Thank you," Vic said, pressing buttons to test it. "Good old duct tape."

"Indeed! It even substitutes for stitches, making it useful for fixing both machinery and messy organisms such as yourself."

"I'll keep that in mind," Vic said. "Let's see what our next move is."

Owen and Elliot were discussing just that. Owen favored setting out for a different part of the river on foot, while Elliot insisted that scouting from high above would be wiser. Hubcap settled the argument by stepping bodily between them and pointing at the bushes where he'd just seen a flash of color.

"Hey," he said. "Alien ahoy."

The humans clammed up and turned as one to regard the greenery with healthy suspicion. Owen even leveled the spear in that direction as if he knew how to use it. Silence fell. Cameras whirred and distant bird-things shrieked.

Hubcap's heat vision said that there were two patches of warmth holding very still. "They haven't thrown spears yet," Hubcap observed. "They may not be planning on it."

"Everyone slowly get into the car," Owen said. "Be ready. The door opening might scare them."

Xian was closest to the door. He slid it open gently, wincing at the rumble of metal wheels. Nothing moved in the bushes. Xian climbed in, followed by the other humans in single file. Hubcap hung back next to Owen. He kept one eye on the shrubbery and one on the camera crew. Vic made sure they all got onboard quickly enough, leaving Hubcap to watch for aliens. He heard Elliot narrating quietly from inside the car.

Owen was the last human to board, waving for Hubcap to join him. He did, closing the rolling door behind himself, his eyes glued on the bushes. They remained still. Eager humans gathered around him to watch through the windows.

For a long moment, everything was quiet. Wind made the purple grass wave while the green-brown shrubbery didn't budge. An airy clump of darkness drifted past, making Hubcap realize that the black trees were more akin to cattails than broccoli. If all that seed-fluff released at once, it would likely coat the area with a layer that would make the humans want face masks. Hubcap, of course, would frolic through it gleefully.

Something moved. Hubcap snapped to attention as a glimpse of pink slid into the open: a pair of four-legged colortalkers with no spears, no armor, and very cautious demeanor.

Elliot appeared next to him. "They don't look like they were sent to chase us away," he whispered. Cameras whirred over both shoulders.

Owen spoke up from Hubcap's other side. "Everyone be very quiet. We don't want to frighten them."

"Can they see us?" Hubcap wondered as the two creatures ventured nearer, moving in quick steps with their lizardy bodies held close to the ground.

"Probably?" Elliot guessed. "If they look up high enough?"

The two aliens scuttled around the aircar, inspecting it with growing curiosity but not seeming to notice the many faces at the windows. They touched the metal surface in what looked like awe, patting it and even scratching with significant vigor. If the car hadn't been designed to withstand tree branches and much worse, Hubcap would have expected someone to flinch about the paint job. Humans, he had learned, cared a lot about their vehicles' paint jobs.

"Stand back," Owen whispered. "I'm going to open the door."

Hubcap took a large step away, pulling Elliot by the sleeve and rearranging the camera crew. They were too busy filming to complain at him. The other humans in the car likewise made space, a few looking very nervous about it. One guy picked up the spear from where Owen had leaned it against a seat, but Xian convinced him to put it down.

Owen slid open the door.

The aliens were around the front of the car, their yellow-and-green tails visible from where Hubcap stood. He watched the tails slip out of sight as the creatures turned, then two beaky faces peered into the doorway.

It had to have been a shock, seeing a crowd of unfamiliar beings all staring back like that. Both of the aliens broke out in surprised colorbursts, one twitching in golden tones before settling down to greens, and the other doing far more.

It physically jumped into the air — the first time Hubcap had seen one of them do that — then stood there shivering with growing intensity. Its colors flared into bright ripples of red and orange, then those ripples started blinking on and off like the mating pairs' had done. By the squinting the other humans were doing, Hubcap could tell that they found it hard to look at.

"Is it frenzying?" someone asked in a loud whisper. The crowd edged back further from the open door.

Hubcap focused on the other alien. He would have expected it to tend to its friend, maybe do some arcane thing to banish the frenzy. But it didn't. Instead, it stared for a heartbeat, then jumped back, waving its hands through the air like it was brushing away parasitic flies.

"Wait, what's that one doing?" Elliot asked. Owen scrambled forward.

The second alien was jumping about the clearing, bucking and dodging, then it took off through the trees like a cat fleeing a vacuum cleaner.

The first alien had collapsed to the ground, still twitching and starting to foam at the mouth. Owen stood over it and dithered about, one hand going to his SedEgg before looking to Xian for help. The medic pushed past other humans to join him.

Hubcap held a hand in front of Elliot's face, commanding him silently to stay, then hopped out onto the purple grass where the alien was dying of frenzy.

"Should we sedate it?" Owen asked desperately. "That doesn't usually work on native life!"

"Worth a try," Xian said, crouching with his own SedEgg. The colortalker was curled into a ball, shaking like mad and staring blindly ahead. Hubcap could almost hear its organs shutting down. Xian pressed the many needles against its shoulderblade.

The sedative did nothing. In moments, the colortalker was still on the grass, its blinking colors faded to a dull white. There was silence from the aircar.

The humans knelt and stared at the alien. Hubcap stood behind them looking into the woods, in the direction of the one that had run off.

"Pretty sure that really wasn't our fault," he said. "Now what?"

Chapter 31

"Now," Owen said slowly, getting to his feet. "We go back to base. Is everyone feeling okay?" Everyone was. Hubcap scanned the group for wide eyes or hyperventilating and found none. Then Owen said that he wanted to take the dead alien back with them.

"What if it's contagious?" demanded a bald man from the doorway of the aircar. "It could infect us!"

"If you're not frenzied yet, I don't think there's much danger," Owen said with deliberate calm. "And we don't even know if that's what happened. The other one acted strangely, like there was something affecting it as well. We'll have to do some tests to find out what happened to this one."

The camera folk wisely started packing away their equipment as mutinous grumbles filled the air. Hubcap stood guard on the grass. Owen reminded the crowd that there had been alien frenzy victims in the car before, the first time they'd collected bodies.

"Yeah, but those weren't fresh!" Baldie insisted.

"And lots more attacks happened at the base after that!" a blonde woman added.

Owen pointed sternly. "The current increase of incidents began well before we brought those specimens back," he said. "Let's not be starting a panic here."

"Why not?" Baldie asked, clutching a railing next to Elliot, who scooted aside as the man continued. "The frenzy attacks are getting worse; we've seen them affect the native life forms, and you want to lock us in an enclosed car with the body of an alien that just died of it? This is the perfect time to panic!"

"Settle down or be sedated," Owen rapped out. "Now is the time to keep our wits about us. Here is a potential clue to what has been going on with the frenzy, and we need to get it back to the lab for inspection."

"We need to get the hell out of here!" Baldie exclaimed. "It isn't safe! It—" He shut up and collapsed as a large woman reached from inside the car to slap a SedEgg against his shoulder.

"Thank you, Rikki," Owen said. "Now let's get both of our victims into—"

"Yeah, the stupid, weak-willed idiots," Rikki said, letting the man fall at Elliot's feet without trying to catch him. "I am sick of this!" She went off on a rant about how many people had fallen to frenzy.

Hubcap was too far away to help. He stepped forward as everyone in the vicinity reached for their own SedEggs, Elliot and another worker dragging Baldie aside. A small nervous-looking man was sneaking up on Rikki when she whirled and swung a fist that the he barely dodged.

"How dare you!" she roared, winding back for another swing only to get dogpiled by several coworkers. SedEggs clicked as the scared-looking man continued to back away.

Owen was calling for order when the small man snapped and bolted from the car, wailing in terror. Owen swore and ran after him, followed by a few of the faster workers.

Hubcap outpaced all of them.

The little guy was quick, he'd give him that. By the time Hubcap passed the human runners, the frenzied man was beyond the treeline. Either the artificial terror was giving him immense amounts of adrenaline, or he was a natural sprinter — or both.

Why couldn't it be a slow guy who got the running frenzy? Hubcap thought. *It just had to be the fast one. In the rough terrain.* The robot leapt a fallen log and two bushes, hearing the humans crash through behind him. The man far ahead was barely visible through the dark trees. Then he disappeared.

Ah, human crap in a bucket, Hubcap thought, speeding up and jumping recklessly through a screen of plants.

Then he fell down the same slope the man had.

"Ow. Ow. Pain. Ow. Monkeys. Ow…" Hubcap defaulted to family-rated swearing patterns as his impact sensors overperformed. He held his arms tight about his head, rolling over gravely dirt. His spinning vision told him that there was a large rock approaching. Only one thing to do: he spread his arms in a sharp motion that launched him off the ground enough to clear the rock. Then he fell back to rolling. Kicking up a colossal dust cloud, he slid to a stop at the bottom of the hill.

Hubcap stood carefully, blinking his wiper panels. He tested all of his joints and sensors for damage. Everything came up intact, though he was sure there were a few new scratches.

If there was a human in this dust, he'd have a hard time breathing, Hubcap thought. Through the grit, he saw thorny brown bushes with a broken path down the center.

Hubcap looked back up the hill. "Hey Owen!" he yelled. "Watch out for the cliff!" The footsteps started to slow, which was good enough for him. He raced in the direction of the human-sized trail through the undergrowth.

He found the man a ways off, limping between black trees for all he was worth, covered in dirt and scratches. That limp made him stumble against one trunk. A snowdrift of black fluff floated downward. The guy limped away fast enough to avoid it, but no luck for Hubcap. The robot narrowed his eye sensors and plowed forward at full speed. The man was still running, despite the limp, and if Hubcap lost sight of him now, it would be more precious time before it was too late to sedate him.

The frenzier didn't turn at the footsteps behind him. Hubcap pulled out his SedEgg and executed a flying tackle. The man yelped as they went down, struggling like a landed trout. Hubcap tagged him solidly and held him in place against the forest moss while black seed fluff settled around them. But nothing happened. The man didn't calm down. If anything, he became more terrified. Hubcap spoke to him, but his eyes registered nothing. He hit him again with the SedEgg. Nothing.

Craaaaaap. Hubcap thought quickly. *Not good. Either my SedEgg is out of sed, or it stopped working for another reason. I really hope the humans aren't becoming resistant. That would suck an unbelievable amount.*

But now wasn't the time. The man's breathing and heart rate were at unhealthy levels, with no sign of slowing down. Hubcap freed a hand to search his own leg compartment for the backup sedatives.

Only they weren't there, because he'd left them out in the latest repacking. The SedEggs had seemed so superior that he'd decided he didn't need the older ones.

Stupid self, he thought. *Now what? I guess it's down to nonchemical means. Here's hoping he's healthy.*

Hubcap adjusted his hold on the panicky man, clamping both legs around his midsection and one arm around his neck. His other arm held the back of the man's head while he applied careful pressure to the arteries. The man squirmed, trying to get out of it, but the metal grip was strong.

Hubcap counted the seconds. After a few long moments, the

man slowly relaxed. Another couple of heartbeats to be sure, then Hubcap released his hold first on the man's neck, then on the man himself. He checked for pulse and other vitals. It looked like the guy would live, though his heart rate was still elevated. It would be a while before Hubcap could tell whether the frenzy was actually over. Common knowledge said that it ended when the victim fell unconscious, but right now he wasn't taking any chances.

And of course, there's always the possibility that he'll start a new frenzy when he wakes up, Hubcap reminded himself as he stood to peer back through the drifting treefluff. He brushed some of it away, glad that he'd landed out of the path of the worst of it. The ground was black halfway to the hillside. *I am not looking forward to carrying him up that hill. Maybe there's a way around.*

Hubcap heard the thunder of the other humans making their headlong way down the slope. He sighed, hoping that he wouldn't have to carry them too.

Luckily he didn't. Soon they had found him and the unconscious victim, and they worked together to carry the man back through the fluff and up the slope. It was difficult.

"You each take a hand and go up first," Owen suggested. "I've got his feet." A man and woman did as he suggested, while another man grabbed the unconscious fellow by the belt and lifted from there.

"Okay, ready."

"Wait, I'm slipping. Augh!" The man holding the right hand landed seat-first on the gravel.

"Got him," said the guy at the belt. "He's okay."

"Ow."

Hubcap said nothing, walking behind them with his hands out ready to catch anyone who completely lost it. He could have carried the limp human by himself, but the others were determined to handle things on their own. Who was he to interrupt?

The group stumbled their way up the hill, and at long last they all sprawled on the grass at the top to rest. Hubcap picked seed fluff from his seams and waited.

A moan said the guy was starting to come around. The woman smacked a SedEgg against his chest without getting up. Hubcap nodded in approval. He checked the man's vitals again, finding a healthier pulse than before. The other humans got up and took over the care of their comrade. One man had a pocket medical kit, which was useful for the many small injuries, not to mention several sets of SedEgg punctures.

While the unconscious fellow was getting decked out in the latest in antiseptic-and-gauze fashion, Hubcap confirmed with the woman that his SedEgg was indeed out of juice. She was impressed that he had managed to use it up so quickly, but there had been a lot of humans needing sedation in the last few days.

Owen joined the conversation. "I should have made sure you had refills," he said. "I am so sorry. Here. I have a spare." He handed it to Hubcap, who accepted it with gratitude. "We'll make sure back at the car that no one else is empty."

"Sounds good," Hubcap said, clicking open the new SedEgg to inspect the syringe field. "You have more spares in the cargo hold?"

Owen nodded firmly. "We do."

"Good."

The last bandage was taped into place. Once again, the humans took charge of carrying the unconscious man, and Hubcap did his part by scouting ahead and holding branches out of the way. No sounds of frenzy or other disasters reached his ears. Even so, he was a bit on edge until he heard footsteps coming their way. Several biologists appeared through the undergrowth, ready and willing to take over carrying the limp guy, who was probably getting heavy by now. That done, the group made their way to the aircar with its waiting medic.

"Sorry I didn't run after you," Xian said, checking the man's pupils. "I'm not that fast."

Owen shook his head. "No, you did right by staying. Any number of other emergencies could have cropped up. Good job, team! Way to keep level heads all around."

Hubcap raised metal eyebrows at Elliot, who paused his narration for the cameras to give Hubcap a thumbs-up. Apparently there really hadn't been any other frenzies while he'd been gone. Amazing.

Owen directed everyone into the aircar, and soon Hubcap was strapping in while the engines ramped up to high volume.

No more frenzy, he thought. *If we can keep this going, that will be a grand thing indeed.*

Elliot gave him a tired smile from the next seat. "Remember when the show's ratings were our biggest worry?"

Hubcap leaned his head back. "Long ago and far away."

Chapter 32

Elliot stared through the aircar window at the approaching base, first curious and then worried at the amount of activity there. People were hustling everywhere. Not running like there was frenzy afoot, but hurrying. When the hangar door came into view and the aircar was waved away toward the secondary hangar, Elliot saw why.

A large shuttle sat in the center of the room. Unlike the generic gray-and-white model that the TV crew had arrived in, this one was sunset orange, and reeked of money.

Elliot craned his neck as the aircar moved around the side of the building on its calm hover engine. He caught a glimpse of people in suits, surrounded by a mob of lesser peons. A glance forward showed Owen in urgent conversation over the radio.

Owen ended the call and swivelled to address the rest of the car. "Heads up! The overlords have arrived. Everything is up in the air now. I'm hoping against hope that we can get back to the colortalkers before everything gets taken away from us. The bosses aren't settled in yet." The car came to rest in the secondary hangar with a bump. "Let's have a bare skeleton crew to hand off our patients now. Everybody else stay onboard. Xian, you too."

Elliot saw the medic look surprised, then nod. There would be enough medical people on the ground.

The door slid open to show several of those medical people waiting. Owen snapped out instructions. The workers who he named moved quickly to get the unconscious humans onto gurneys, while Owen himself dragged the dead alien out from the back of the car. Elliot pulled his feet aside as the limp white form passed by, tail sliding along the floor. He realized that he was holding his breath. He didn't breathe again until the body was outside the car.

"It's probably not contagious," Hubcap told him as Elliot tried to be cool about letting out the air he'd been holding. "Probably."

"Thanks," Elliot said. He breathed deeply. The air smelled like fuel and cleaning chemicals.

Owen popped his head back into the car. "Everybody sit tight!

I'll be right back." He ducked out and jogged away. The gurneys were already wheeling toward the medical wing.

Elliot wondered if anyone there would have objections to the probably-not-contagious alien body, but things were likely too busy for anyone to care. Workers of all stripes ran past the aircar without so much as looking up at the windows.

The pilot shut off the engines. Quiet settled inside the car while chaos circled outside. Vic moved up to talk with the pilot, but everyone else stayed in their seats.

Elliot glanced at Hubcap. "Do you think he told the base about the underwater city?"

Hubcap flicked his eyebrows in a shrug. "Depends. If he found out that the overlords are here before he said something, he might have kept quiet."

"I'll bet they have their own cameras and biology experts," Elliot said. "Maybe even diplomats. I hope he held his tongue."

Hubcap used the belt harness to floss dirt out of a wrist seam. "If they don't have a translator that actually works, it won't do them much good."

They waited in silence while the local workers rushed past on a multitude of errands. Elliot thought he recognized Anrik in the distance, driving a cart of packaged jetpods, but it was too far and too crowded to be sure. Even the secondary hanger was jammed with people; some were ferrying objects around while others simply ran, and a few appeared to be cleaning. It didn't bode well for the new bosses' attitudes.

"Is that guy seriously washing the trash truck?" Hubcap asked. "Of all the vehicles in here, he picked that one?"

"Well, it is the dirtiest," Elliot said.

"The overlords must be neat freaks. What a horrible idea for them to come here." The robot shook his head, then craned his neck over the seat at the camera crew. "The first person to record one of the overlords getting filthy wins a prize. I don't know what yet; I'll think of something."

"Money?" Dale asked with a grin.

The robot made a static noise. "This gig doesn't pay well enough to be throwing that around. I was thinking more something like making pancakes for you."

"Somehow I doubt anyone here would want to eat anything you cook," Elliot said. "The lack of taste buds, and practice…"

"Nonsense, I've had plenty of practice!"

"…And regard for our intestinal health."

"Well, you may have a point there," Hubcap admitted. "It would be good fun to test out these 'laxatives' I keep hearing about."

"Like I said," Elliot told him. "Keep trying."

The conversation wandered in circles while the rest of the compound was a beehive of activity. Elliot was starting to think that Owen wouldn't come back when a door banged open and he came striding into the hangar, accompanied by a severe-looking woman and a handful of new crewmembers.

"Let's have introductions in the air," he said as he entered the car, ushering people aboard. The workers hurried to their seats, followed by the silent woman, who carried a mysterious gadget slung over her shoulder.

Owen muttered something to Vic, who hustled to her own seat while the click of many buckles filled the air. The pilot started the flight engines, not bothering to hover outside first out of courtesy. Workers skittered aside as the aircar backed out of the hangar. No one stopped it. Elliot waited for pursuit, but there was none. The car turned and shot into the sky.

Vic leaned forward. "Their camera crew is still getting set up," she said over the engines. "Let's make this trip count."

Owen called for attention. "Everybody, this is Ms. Acosta," he shouted. "She'll be spearheading the field operations from this point on." He named each of the TV crew to her, and she responded in a businesslike manner.

Well, she does seem more prepared than Dr. Rhodes, Elliot decided. The woman wore sturdy clothes that looked like they could take some dirt, her black hair was tied back in a short braid, and she had a no-nonsense posture.

Once the introductions were done with, she asked to review the footage of the underwater city. Vic passed over a small camera and Owen watched it with Ms. Acosta, pointing things out. She didn't betray any amazement at the groundbreaking discovery. When she was done, the rest of the ride passed in silence.

Once the aircar had crossed the mountain range and flown out over the flooded woods, this new leader directed the landing while listening to Owen's advice. The car aimed for a clearing to the south of the river, a short walk from the breeding grounds.

The landing was exceptionally smooth. Elliot wondered just how worried he and the TV crew should be about staying on this new authority figure's good side, if even the pilot seemed concerned.

Ms. Acosta ordered everyone forward with brisk efficiency. Owen silently waved for his workers to hurry. The TV crew did their best not to slow things down. Once out of the car, Elliot and Hubcap stood at attention with the biologists while Vic quietly directed the cameras to focus more on the surrounding environment than on the co-hosts. Aliens could appear at any time.

"Everyone silent," Ms. Acosta said. "Let's move out." She held up her compact mystery gadget and strode forward, eyeing the viewscreen like a compass. Elliot decided it must be a new intelligence scanner.

But despite the technological guidance, the forest proved to be empty of aliens. Native birdsong echoed through the orange trees and small things scuttled about, but there was no sign of the land-based colortalkers. Hubcap spoke up, suggesting that they head back towards the river, but he was ignored — no small feat. Elliot was quiertly impressed.

"Have the natives been growing more numerous or scarce in the time you've been here?" Ms. Acosta asked Owen, not looking up from her screen.

Owen thought about it while they walked over more of those slippery curry leaves. "Hard to say," he admitted. "We've hardly been able to do a census. And it's possible that our appearance at the breeding grounds scared them."

Ms. Acosta made a thoughtful noise and adjusted the direction she walked. Behind her, Hubcap made mocking gestures and imitated her posture. Vic gave him a sharp look. Elliot distracted the robot by pointing out an interesting cluster of blue corkscrew trees: the things had sprouted closely together and grown into a matted clump the size of a house. Brown thornbushes around the base were the only thing that kept Hubcap from instantly trying to climb the blue tangle; he reached and decided it was too far. Elliot could tell the robot was tempted to plow through anyway and risk a few new scratches to buff out later. Graham filmed this, stopping to hurry forward when the biologists appeared to be leaving them behind.

Elliot quick-stepped to catch up with the front of the pack. He was almost there when the group rounded a corner to the unwelcome sight of a doom bat crouched over a pile of dead aliens.

Earthlings scattered as the enormous creature spread its wings with a hissing snarl. Elliot dove for cover before he saw whether it was chasing them or not. He huddled behind an orange tree trunk and listened to his heart thump while people scrambled to hide around him. Hubcap stood in the open the longest, making sure all the humans were out of grabbing range before he dove into the thornbushes himself.

A long tense moment passed, while all that Elliot could hear was his own heartbeat, and everything smelled like spicy leaves. He was starting to hate that smell. So far he noticed it most while near ground level, worried about incoming predators.

When his heartbeat calmed slightly, he could make out the sound of wings flapping into the sky. He stayed where he was until Owen called the all-clear. Hubcap was already out of the thornbush and joining the group.

Elliot got to his feet, knees protesting, and hurried over to where Owen was explaining doom bats to Ms. Acosta. She looked more displeased than shaken. Apparently furry alien dragon things hadn't been in the briefing.

Most of the others seemed as shaken as Elliot felt, which made him feel slightly better. He made sure the camera crew was none the worse for wear before looking for Hubcap.

He found the robot staring at the dead aliens. They were slightly gnawed-upon. Hubcap turned away as Elliot approached, and wouldn't meet his eyes. The camera crew held back, but the biologists were soon on the scene. Elliot followed Hubcap back out of the way, and the pair stood quietly while Ms. Acosta asked Owen how this batch compared to his earlier findings.

"How many deceased natives have you discovered so far?" Ms. Acosta was asking. "Could they be dying out because of the frenzy?"

Owen admitted that it was possible. "All we've learned from testing is that they don't appear to be allergic to us," he added with a weak laugh. "We don't have all the answers yet."

When the biologists finished their inspection, someone asked if they would be taking the bodies back with them. Owen looked to Ms. Acosta.

"No," she said. "We're not here for the dead ones. We have some of those already, and we'll be sending them to experts on Earth posthaste." She gazed off through the trees. "The river is over there, so let's find that beach you told me about."

Owen opened his mouth, closed it, then led the way.

Minutes later at the water's edge, Elliot peered through bushes at an empty shore. There were no mating pairs on the sand, and no visible swimmers in the water. Vic stood next to him with her camera, trying to spot signs of underwater civilization from a distance. No luck.

Owen frowned. "There's no good way to get a look into the depths from here, not short of walking over and looking down," he said with a glance at Ms. Acosta. "And given the spear incident, that would be extremely unwise."

She nodded. "Agreed. Let's track down some natives on land." She pointed at the far end of the rock. "Can someone with a camera zoom in over there? Those look like footprints."

Tarja could and did. "Looks like one set, leading away from the river's edge," she reported.

"That way, then."

Elliot moved with the group, letting Mr. Acosta and Owen lead the way, but Hubcap stepped forward to take point.

"Superior robot senses," he said at Ms. Acosta's frown. She didn't press the matter.

Hubcap blazed a trail along the tree line, following the wet footprints until they petered out on the grass some distance away. By then Ms. Acosta had her techno-compass up and running again. Elliot walked close enough behind her that he could see the arrows and numbers on the screen. The biggest number was counting down. When it reached single digits, something rustled up ahead.

Hubcap raised a hand. Everyone stopped walking.

A curious, beaky face peered around a tree, with blue-green patterns skimming along its scales.

The humans froze, all except for Ms. Acosta. She stepped past Hubcap, holding up the viewscreen and rotating a part on the side toward the multicolored face. Elliot could see words forming on the screen. He held his breath, not wanting to scare it off.

Chapter 33

Sharpsand was getting close to the base of the Tallest Tree when he heard heavy footsteps in the leaves. He thought about continuing — he was almost there, after all this time — but if the creatures were dangerous, he might never get to see it. He'd spent most of his life wanting to see the root system that was rumored to be bigger than the town plaza. So he ran behind a smaller tree and held still, listening.

But whatever was making the noise had stopped. He waited a moment, then poked his snout around the trunk.

There were a lot of them, whatever they were, and they stood staring at him. He almost took off in fear, but they hadn't attacked yet. They weren't even spreading out to circle him, not acting like predators at all. And the shiny one in front looked downright weird.

Then a different one stepped forward, holding something up, and *words appeared in his head.*

"I greet you." The thought came out of nowhere, and Sharpsand twitched, shaking his head in reflex. What was happening?

"We will not hurt you," the un-voice said, and Sharpsand realized that the creature must be doing it. But how?

"Will you speak with me?"

Sharpsand stepped back, thinking quickly. This was frightening, but if he left now, he would regret it. He'd never heard of an air-breathing creature — or any creature! — that could speak directly into someone's head. It wasn't even sending him colors; each thought appeared as an idea that he instantly understood. It was amazing.

=*Yes, I will speak with you,*= he decided, stepping forward to plant all four feet in the way that he'd seen land creatures do. =*What do you want to discuss?*= He hoped that no fear-colors were creeping into his words, but he suspected that they were.

"We are curious about you," the un-voice said. Behind the lead creature, the others made mouth-noises to each other, and kept looking over the shoulder of the one holding the object. *"How long*

can you stay to talk?"

Sharpsand thought about it. This was beyond fascinating, but he didn't want to spend all of his time here. =*I can stay a little while longer,*= he said, =*But not long. I do have other things I want to do.*= He glanced up at the color of the sky. =*There is not much light left!*=

The other creatures made more mouth-noises, looking like they wanted to talk too, but couldn't. Sharpsand thought it was a pity they lacked proper voice-flesh. This conversation would be much easier if they could speak as well.

=*Will you have more time to discuss things tomorrow?*= the un-voice asked, =*When it is light again?*=

Sharpsand blinked, cocking his head at the creatures. =*No, I only get one day.*= How could they not know this?

"*One day for what?*"

=*For being in the air.*=

"*Then what?*"

=*Then I die,*= he said in exasperation. =*Like everyone does!*=

This seemed to throw them into confusion, and Sharpsand sighed, looking again at the darkening sky.

"*Do you live in the water for many days,*" the un-voice asked. "*Then move to the air for one?*"

=*Yes,*= Sharpsand said, losing interest in the conversation. =*Look, why don't you go talk to someone in the water? They have more time for this. There might even be a few adults who haven't emerged yet, though not many. And I need to be going.*=

"*One more question, please,*" the un-voice pleaded with him. "*What does it mean when someone — an air-breather — twitches a lot, then falls down? We've seen it happen to your people, and to ours as well.*"

Sharpsand was taken aback. =*You mean the stutter-sleep?*= he asked. =*That's part of mating. I don't know why it would happen to your people.*=

The creatures didn't know what to make of this. "*That is indeed strange. But what causes it, if someone is not mating?*"

=*Well, being in the air,*= he began, then looked up sharply.

As if the conversation had summoned them, a cluster of invisible blue clouds came drifting through the trees.

=*Those!*= he yelled in bright reds, pointing with his tail. =*Those cause it! Swim away!*= With that he took off, pushing on the ground in the awkward air-creature way, longing for the speed of water and hoping that he wouldn't be caught yet. He had already mated, and if the clouds caught him now, he would never get to see what the base of the Tallest Tree looked like.

He ran for all he was worth, leaving the strange creatures far behind.

Chapter 34

"What causes frenzy? What?" Elliot looked around madly, and the rest of the crew were doing the same. Except for Ms. Acosta.

"Shut your mouths and face front!" she bellowed, startling the workers into silence. "Are you children? Come on, march." She snapped the translator shut and stalked forward. The others followed, still nervous but much chastened.

The humans were, at any rate. Hubcap was quietly delighted. "You should have seen your faces just now!" the robot whispered. "Like a rabbit looking out for house cats, then hearing a lion! You just about wet yourselves!"

"Yeah, thanks," Elliot said. "That makes it all better."

"Oh, that was great!" the robot continued, audible to everyone. He turned to the videographers. "Tell me one of you got the expressions on film!"

The camera crew said nothing, still filming as they walked.

"Nobody? Were you all filming the air?"

"I might have been focusing on not wetting myself," Graham said, to which Hubcap guffawed.

The robot kept up his mockery all the way to the aircar. Elliot was a little surprised that Ms. Acosta didn't say to knock it off, then it occurred to him that Hubcap's teasing was doing more to keep people's minds off panic than a silent walk would have.

"Everybody in," Ms. Acosta said when they arrived at the aircar. "There's not enough daylight left to justify staying out today."

The crew obediently trooped onboard and buckled in. Soon the aircar was rising above the trees to turn toward the distant base.

"Wow, is this the first time we've left this place without at least one of you meatlings unconscious?" Hubcap asked with a gaping smile.

Elliot rapped his knuckles on the robot's temple. "Shut it; you'll jinx us."

Hubcap spent the rest of the trip making fun of his co-host for his superstitions, and Elliot saw the other people in the car cracking smiles. Even Vic smirked, and she was going to have to explain the day's adventures to her superiors back on Earth. It would be a long conversation.

* * *

The next morning Elliot went down to breakfast early in the hopes of finding out who was in charge now, and what that would mean for the TV crew. The cafeteria held only a few early risers. He spotted Hubcap satisfying his biodiesel needs with a jug of kitchen oil, courtesy of Ted the cook who was eating his own breakfast. Elliot gathered a selection from the buffet and joined them. "Morning," he said as he sat down.

Ted waved a hand in reply, his mouth full of food. Hubcap agreed that it was indeed morning. He didn't need to chew his own meal, only pausing in pouring the oil down his gullet. Elliot had found this offputting when they'd first met, but it was normal now. He was mildly surprised that Ted didn't mind watching someone chug skillet grease, though.

"Any word on the changes to the command structure around here?" Elliot asked, digging into a bowl of cereal.

Ted had plenty to say. "The CEOs are in charge now, not the folks who actually know how things work," he said over a mouthful of toast. "They're all about the big historical whoop-de-do that the aliens represent, and the little stuff can go hang. So they're not paying attention to the day to day operations, and those of us who know what's important here have to make sure that it all gets done. Either that or they're paying too much attention, like the group that's muscling in on Sera's science lab."

Elliot stared at a banana without seeing it. "That's … not great to hear."

Ted swallowed a mouthful. "True enough. But all we can do is complain about it." He gestured to a meat dish that Elliot hadn't tasted yet. "Try that; I killed it myself."

Hubcap set the jug aside. "Graduated from tubers to livestock, have you?" he said, beginning to stack coffee creamers. "Congratulations."

Elliot looked down at the orange-tinged slices of meat. "What is it?" he asked. "The buffet sign wasn't clear."

Ted forked a piece and stuffed it in his own mouth. "Gopher."

Whatever expression Elliot was wearing must have been a good one, since it sent the cook into gales of laughter.

"It isn't really, is it?" Elliot asked. "It's chicken and you're messing with me."

Ted shook his head, still laughing. "No, it's supergopher all right! We figured a way of cooking them that makes the meat taste pretty decent."

"The question is," Hubcap said, pointing with a straw. "Does it cause an unholy torrent of pooping?"

"Not so far!" Ted said. "Seriously, we've done tests and everything,. I's safe to eat. Tastes a little weird, but I've had worse."

"I'll take your word for it," Elliot decided, eating the banana and turning down repeated offers of exotic gopher flesh. "No thanks, I'm good. Ready to go figure out what we're expected to do today."

"Probably nothing, I'd guess," Ted said. "You can always help me in the kitchen again. I'll be washing some very exciting dishes."

"Really?" Elliot asked.

"No. Lordy, you're gullible today."

"Anyways," Elliot said with a glance skyward. "I'm going to try to find Owen and see how things stand."

"Oh, he went out early this morning," Ted said, standing and gathering plates. "With a carload of uppity types and fancy cameras. Sounds like he gets to play tour guide to the lot of 'em, and I don't envy him one bit."

"Well, dang," Elliot said, at a loss. "I got up before everybody just so I could talk to him. The rest of the crew is still sleeping."

"Yeah, sucks all around," Ted agreed. "But I've got to get to work. See you at lunch."

"Bye."

"Enjoy the exciting dishes," Hubcap put in.

"Oh, I will!" With a nod, Ted moved off towards the kitchen.

Elliot turned his attention toward Hubcap, who had constructed an elaborate structure out of cups, straws, and spare silverware. He was now adding a flag to the highest tower, made of a twist of napkin.

"Very nice," Elliot said.

"Thank you. I call it 'Chateau De Sporkworth the Third.'"

"And is it now going to suffer an attack by a gigantic sea monster?" Elliot asked. He'd seen Hubcap play with tableware before.

"No, I think I will leave this one standing, as a testament to the ages. And an entertainment for the kitchen crew." The robot leaned back in his chair. "At any rate, last time they made me clean it up."

"And that would *never* do," Elliot agreed, leaning on an elbow. He looked away, then back. "What are we going to do now?" he asked quietly. "I suppose we can find some random task to film around the base, but that's hardly the point."

"No," Hubcap agreed. "It is not."

"It's obvious that the aliens know something important about the frenzy. That one acted like it could see things coming after us! But—"

"But if we can't get out there to talk to them, we won't find out what it is," Hubcap responded in a flat tone. "And it's possible that these new idiots will unravel the mystery, but I doubt it."

"Well, they do have that new kind of translator," Elliot said. "They should be able to talk to the first alien they meet."

"That's assuming there will be an alien for them to find." Hubcap gave him a sharp look.

"You mean the air-breathers are dying out? That one did say they only live a day. And he doubted that many more would emerge." Elliot considered. "Well, there's the ones in the water. They should still be around."

"And of no use to us," Hubcap said fiercely.

Elliot looked up. "What? Why?"

The robot frowned back at him. "I checked up on those new translators while you were asleep. They're experimental things that work on brainwaves, but can only sense them through the air."

Elliot stared. "So if the air-breathers all die, there's no one we can talk to who'll tell us what's going on with the frenzy."

"Correct." The robot turned back to his creation. "And the frenzy seems to be getting worse." He lined up one metal finger with a fork at the bottom of the tower. "If we don't figure this out, it may kill all of you." His face showed no emotion. "Gods. Damn. It."

His finger snapped forward, sending the fork to ricochet off a wall with a piercing clang. People exclaimed and looked over as the architectural wonder collapsed into a mess of scattered cutlery.

The robot stood without a word and strode out of the room.

Elliot looked at his retreating back, then at the staring crowd. Whispering apologies into the silence, he hurried after his friend, tense with concern.

Chapter 35

Hubcap stalked down the empty hallway, cursing whatever programmers had thought it a good idea to give him human feelings. If they hadn't, today would have been a lot easier.

He'd tried having that part of his build deactivated once. It had been miserable. There was no way to pick and choose the emotions; it was either all or none. And Hubcap enjoyed laughing. And prank wars. And bad comedies. But the other half of the deal really stank.

"How do you cope with it?" he asked, turning at the familiar footsteps behind him. "Knowing you could die so easily?" He searched Elliot's face, hoping for an answer.

"We're used to it," Elliot said. "We try not to think about it. And, well, that's what the afterlife stories are for."

Hubcap scoffed with a static noise and looked away.

"There's no magical formula," Elliot told him. "Some people cope better than others. I met someone so paranoid about germs that he lived in a clean room, and wore a space suit whenever he left the house. Yeah, I know," he said at Hubcap's incredulous look. "But there's the other side of the spectrum too. People who do crazy fun things that could kill them with one mistake, and they love it. I suspect if you put someone like that in a super safe environment, they'd go mad."

Hubcap nodded. "I know this kind of human well. They are either an inspiration or a cautionary tale to all. The space rodeo was full of them."

"Were you really in a—" Elliot let the question go as Hubcap waved it away.

The pair stood in silence.

Elliot spoke up first. "I'll be careful, if that helps," he said. "I don't want anything bad to happen to me any more than you do."

Hubcap waved his hand again. "It's not even that," he said vaguely. "It's — hell, I know how your fleshy systems work, and what I can expect. With these new alien people, it's all mysterious, and they might drop dead mid-sentence for all I know." He crossed his arms and stared at the wall. "I almost don't want to meet any more of them," he said quietly. "But I know that we have to. Stopping the frenzy is too important to be put off by any humanlike weakness of mine."

"Emotions are not a weakness," Elliot began.

"Yeah, yeah, I've heard it," the robot interrupted. "There are good parts. But the sad-sack parts are a liability and you know it."

The human shrugged and didn't press the point. "Just let me know if there's anything I can do."

"Think of something worthwhile we can spend time on," Hubcap said. "While we wait to see if the bossy types find any aliens today."

Elliot thought about it. "Well, we could talk to the people in the lab and learn more about how the sedative works."

"Maybe," Hubcap said. "Assuming they don't flip out again."

"Or we could see if the jetpod harvesters need any more help."

"No point in filming that twice."

"How about we go to the hangar and find a mechanic or something, and look into a job we haven't tried yet?"

"Eh." Hubcap shrugged. "If we're in the hangar, we'll just be watching the sky all day."

"Orrr," the human said finally. "We could prank the camera guys before they wake up."

Hubcap's face lit up. "A fine idea! Now what to do — draw fancy mustaches on their faces, or get creative?"

The pair wandered down the hallway, plotting mayhem. Hubcap knew it wouldn't keep his mind off the problems completely, but he could pretend.

* * *

Dr. Rhodes was leaving his office when he overheard a conversation about something that had happened at breakfast.

"I'm surprised none of the dishes broke," a man in mechanic's clothes said to another as they approached. "It was loud. And I didn't see whether he smashed it all on purpose or not."

"I thought he just knocked out the bottom section," said the second man. "Either way, I've never seen a robot upset like that."

"Hell, I've never seen *that* robot upset, period," the first worker said. "The guy's always making with the jokes. Morning, Doc." He nodded in passing at Dr. Rhodes.

"Good morning," the psychologist said. "Sounds like I missed something. What happened?"

"Ah, well," the man said with the awkwardness that most employees showed when they felt they were tattling to him. "The robot knocked some stuff over in the cafeteria, then stormed off like an insulted date. No idea what it was about."

"I see." Dr. Rhodes raised an eyebrow. "Do you have any idea where he is now?"

"I heard the camera crew was on the top floor somewhere," the other worker put in. "He's probably with them."

"Thank you." Dr. Rhodes nodded them on their way, and the men hurried off with a wave. He ducked back inside his office for a pocket-size sketchpad and a handful of tiny conversation pieces that he used in therapy. Then he headed for the staircase, putting his errands off until later.

He may have been an abject failure in helping with First Contact, but this he could do.

As expected, he found people with cameras in one of the viewing rooms at the top of the building. The group of them were clustered at one of the large windows — the tall woman was scrubbing what looked like a drawn-on mustache off her face and chuckling while the others watched something outside, pointing at the distant ground. None of the cameras were filming. The robot wasn't there, but the human co-host was.

"Hello," Elliot said with some surprise, walking over. "What can we do for you?"

"I was hoping for a word with Hubcap," the doctor said. "Is he up here?"

"He went down the hall for a look out a different window," Elliot said, pointing in that direction. He lowered his voice, looking over his shoulder at the others. "He's not really in a talkative mood right now."

"I heard something about that on my way up here," Dr. Rhodes admitted.

"If you're hoping for a heart-to-heart, good luck. He's never been big on baring his soul."

The psychologist smiled. "Then he's in fine company. He's not the only person on this base who thinks that feelings are somehow unmanly."

"I believe it." Elliot smiled back. "That can't be fun to deal with every day."

"Well, I've learned a few ways to get past it. I'm hoping they work on a robot such as your friend."

"Good luck," Elliot said again, raising a hand in a wave.

Dr. Rhodes waved back and left the room. He walked with a measured stride, well aware that the robot would hear him coming. After a bit of a search, he found Hubcap sitting with his back to the door in a quiet room, staring at a fish tank full of tiny creatures and surrounded by empty chairs. He didn't turn.

Dr. Rhodes considered, feeling through the objects in his pocket. He came up with a refrigerator magnet of questionable taste. When he was certain that he correctly remembered the law that all robots were made with insulation against magnetic damage, he threw it gently.

It stuck with a tap against the robot's back.

Hubcap sat up with a start, turning to find the doctor regarding him with a calm smile. When Dr. Rhodes said nothing, Hubcap reached around to pull off the magnet.

He stared at it for a moment, then broke into a surprised guffaw. He flipped it over, searching for an explanation for the lewd poem. Then he looked up. "What the heck?"

"I figured you might appreciate it," the psychologist said, standing sideways with body language that said he was just passing through, and wouldn't be pressing for a conversation. "I heard you were a fan of poking fun at the human form."

"Well, of course," Hubcap said. "There's just so much fun to be poked!"

The doctor nodded. "Very true," he agreed. "And the wise person knows when not to take things too seriously. There has been far too much that's serious lately."

"No kidding," the robot said, slouching into a chair. "Serious and frustrating."

Dr. Rhodes turned to face him. "Are the workers getting in the way of your show?" he asked, deliberately misunderstanding. "I know some of them can obsess about being on TV..."

Hubcap waved a hand. "No, that's not it," he said. "We're being shut out of the whole alien situation, and the people in charge don't know what they're doing. At this rate, we're never going to figure out the frenzy before it overtakes all of you fleshy types." He spread his hands forlornly. "I can't protect everyone!" The robot lapsed into silence, staring down at the magnet.

Dr. Rhodes nodded to himself, considering for a moment. "It is very unfair for you to be burdened with the only invulnerability," he said. "I suppose you must resent us for our weaknesses."

Hubcap made a dismissive gesture, but said nothing.

"Considering seeking out a robots-only colony somewhere?"

Hubcap laughed. "I'll admit, sometimes it's damn tempting."

"To be somewhere you fit in?"

"To be somewhere I'm not the one everybody goes to when there's trouble." He slammed the magnet against the chair. "Dammit, that's why I left the rescue business! Humans break so easily, and now the new species is dying all over the place. I'm sick of this!"

Dr. Rhodes was silent for a moment. "I understand," he said. "I'm charged with the mental well-being of everyone on this base, and there are times when I want to slap some sense into them for having the same dramas month after month."

The robot looked up at him with new interest.

Dr. Rhodes continued. "There's only so many times you can tell someone that they're on the wrong path, only to see them persist in that same direction before you start to feel like you're wasting your time. And when a half dozen people in a row have relapsed or come up with some new insecurity, then it really starts to feel pointless."

"So what do you do?" the robot asked. "Take a vacation back to Earth for some counseling of your own?"

Dr. Rhodes laughed. "Sometimes, yes," he admitted. "Even I can do with a sympathetic ear now and then. It can can be terribly draining to feel like the only person everyone looks to for help."

Hubcap was nodding. "I'm just tired of not being able to do anything, you know? No matter how many frenzied meatbags I sedate in time, the problem's getting worse. And no matter how many wounds I've patched and prevented, they're all so *fragile!*" The robot crossed his arms and looked to the side. "That's the part I hate the most," he said. "Humans die so easily."

"Does it help to remember that they expect to be this fragile?" the doctor asked.

"Not really," Hubcap said. "I just feel sorry for them. I've seen so many friends die already!"

The psychologist pursed his lips in thought. "Here's a question for you. Are you concerned for their sake, or for your own?"

Hubcap looked up at him quizzically. "What do you mean?"

"Which is worse: seeing them suffer, or surviving the death of your friends?"

"Well, it's all part of the same thing…"

Dr. Rhodes shook his head. "I don't think so. It sounds to me like you're afraid of being lonely."

"No I'm—"

"You wouldn't be the only one," Dr. Rhodes said over him. "There is something called 'survivor's guilt' that is common among those who outlive their peers. Humans tend to question why *they* survived the accident, or why *they* didn't get the illness, and why the others did. I'm sure your subconscious was modeled off humanity, so it makes sense that you might be feeling, as they say, 'only human.' And all of this is beside the point."

"It is?"

"Of course," the doctor said with a smile. "You of all people don't need to worry about being lonely — you make friends *very* easily. You never need to be alone unless you want to be."

"Alone and lonely are two different things," Hubcap said, turning back toward the fish tank. "A conversation with a stranger isn't going to help when I've just lost a friend."

"But commiserating with a different friend will," the doctor said gently. He walked up to stand beside the robot, who rested his elbows on the table and stared moodily at the alien fish. "Take it from one who knows. Nothing helps a heartache like spending time with someone who *understands*."

Hubcap didn't reply. Dr. Rhodes dug into his pocket, coming up with a handful of plastic gemstones. They made for colorful and eye-catching metaphors. He set a bright blue one on the tabletop by the robot's elbow. Hubcap looked down at it, then up at the psychologist.

"Consider this a memory," Dr. Rhodes said. "You will likely be around for a long time to come." He placed another beside the first. "You'll probably have to say goodbye to many friends in your lifetime." Three more gems made a line after the others. "But you will get to enjoy the friendship of many more." He opened his fingers and poured a multicolored handful, covering the line of sorrows completely. "All those good times can easily outweigh the sadness of saying goodbye, especially when you are the only person who can dictate just how sad you feel."

Hubcap stared down at the pile of glittering symbolism, while Dr. Rhodes let silence fill the room. The robot picked up one of the gems, an iridescent purple one with many facets. He turned it over in his metal fingers, and finally replied. "Thanks."

Dr. Rhodes smiled. "You're welcome. If you ever want to talk or trade poems—" he gestured to the magnet in Hubcap's other hand "—I'm on the ground floor with a view of the silverbark trees."

He walked out into the hallway and toward the stairs, leaving trinkets and food for thought in his wake.

Chapter 36

The hover platform's quiet engines whirred louder as Hubcap leaned too far over the railing. Elliot was about to mention it when the maintenance man clonked the robot with a hose nozzle, telling him to quit rocking the boat.

"What boat?" Hubcap asked, pulling back and holding his pole-mounted squeegee at attention. "Use proper terminology, fleshbag!"

"Then use your brain, metal head!" Cecil shot back. "It's an expression!" He raised a wrinkled hand to catch the drips falling on him. "And mind your pole, fool machine!"

"Poor human," Hubcap lamented, moving the squeegee. "Can't take your water. Careful, you might rust." This sent Cecil into a lengthy comeback that had the robot snickering as he turned back to window washing.

Cecil was a cranky old man, so of course he and Hubcap got along swimmingly.

"Start at the top, y'idiot! Now you're going to drip down on the clean part!"

"I thought it prudent to do my scrubbing of the dirty parts first; otherwise there would be smears of whatever alien bug guts these are."

"Those ent bug guts! That's critter shit!"

"We'll have to censor that, you realize."

This just sent the man off into a storm of swearing, to which Hubcap provided an ongoing stream of censor beeps. Elliot leaned back and tried to keep out of the middle of it, wiping away at the windows from his end of the small platform. There wasn't much space with the camera people there too. They all had their attention trained on the entertaining banter between the robot and the window cleaner, which suited Elliot just fine. Whatever Dr. Rhodes had said to Hubcap had obviously helped. Elliot hadn't seen him in this lighthearted a mood in days.

Finally Cecil tugged off his cap, whapped the robot with it, then put it back on and considered the matter finished. "We'll need to move over to the last row now," he said. Hubcap brought his squeegee back to drip on the elder human, earning another whap with the hat. The robot just chuckled and was ignored.

Cecil manipulated the controls and sent the dirty platform jerking sideways to the last row of windows. Elliot looked down as they moved, watching the water drops fall a long ways, and he was grateful for the harnesses they wore. Slipping over the edge would be painful, but thankfully not fatal.

As the platform settled, Elliot gazed into the distance, seeing dark clouds creeping between the teeth of the mountain range, and he wondered again how bad the weather was there. The clouds had been darkening the last few times he'd checked, and now they seemed downright dangerous. A glint of light caught his eye.

"Hey Hubcap," he said, interrupting a debate about bacteria. "Can your mighty robot eyes see whether that's a returning aircar at the mountains?"

"Ah, such humility," the robot exclaimed, turning to look. "It gladdens my golden heart. And yes, that does appear to be an aircar fleeing the storms like a vulture from a volcano. At that rate, they should be here in minutes."

Cecil huffed. "Well, maybe we'll be done by then if you quit yer yappin' and get back to work!"

"Yes sir, taskmaster," Hubcap replied, hopping to it and scrubbing with vigor. "See how I go! Faster than an arrow from an archer's bow! That's how that line goes, right? Shakespeare or something? Anyways, these windows will be so clean, the critters will think they can fly in and poop inside!"

Cecil just snorted and went back to his own work, with Elliot doing the same and the camera crew pretending they weren't there.

The crew had loosened up since the morning's pranks, Elliot reflected. The shaving cream on Graham was long gone, as was the twirly mustache on Vic's face, though Dale had a lump on his forehead from where he'd hit the table when he sat up. It had been tricky to balance the coffee table over Dale's bunk, and the prank wouldn't have worked without an appropriate wake-up from Hubcap.

That was a pretty good airhorn sound, Elliot thought with a glance at the robot. *Somehow I'm not surprised he can make a noise like that.*

Tarja was the only one of the camera crew to have escaped the early-morning pranks, simply because she had already been awake by the time Hubcap and Elliot had arrived. She'd made up for it by helping find the pens and makeup. But the table idea had been all Hubcap's.

The rest of the cleaning went quickly now. There were no complications, or signs of the "bird nesty pests" that had taken a fondness to the roof. By the time the aircar came rocketing in toward the hangar, the window cleaners were already making their way down to ground level.

"Get ye going; I'll clean up the mess." Cecil waved them away when the platform touched down. "Go on, shoo."

"You don't require my able assistance in carrying these weighty buckets of suds?" Hubcap asked. "I will happily help, since you are feeble."

"Feeble this, you upstart kitchen appliance," the old man said with a rude gesture. "I'll suds you upside the head. Now get going."

"Thanks for your time, Cecil," Elliot said. The old man responded with a grumble and a wave, lifting the hover platform into the air again and skimming away.

The TV crew wasted no time in turning off their cameras for the jog toward the hangar. Elliot's mind raced, wondering what the explorers had seen, and why they had returned in such a hurry. He told himself that they could have solved everyone's problems already, but he couldn't bring himself to believe it.

When he reached the hangar door, he found a crowd of khaki-clad people arguing next to the aircar, and a visibly fuming Owen walking in their direction.

"Hey," Vic said in surprise. "What's—"

Owen shook his head. "Outside," he said.

The TV crew parted to let him pass, exchanging glances and following him around the side of the building. Elliot saw that not even Dale had switched on his camera. It was only once they were out of earshot of the people inside that Owen stopped and explained.

"These people are morons," he said with conviction. "They ruined every opportunity we had to talk with the natives. First there were none to be found in the woods, so we went to the water's edge, and they insisted on getting up close and personal with a pair in the middle of a mating dance!" He gestured wildly, stopping short of tearing at his hair. "Who interrupts something like that? And they knew damn well what was happening; I made sure! No, these 'expert diplomats' seem to expect any alien to drop everything in order to talk to us — the exotic outsiders that we are. Never mind what else they might have going on. Oh, and the screwups even got the ones in the water throwing spears at us again! Whatshisface with the stupid hair got grazed, and it's a miracle it wasn't worse. He'd better hope there are no contaminants on that spearblade." Owen stopped for breath.

"So I take it you didn't learn anything new about the frenzy?" Vic asked.

Owen laughed. "Not a thing. And you know what, even if the water-dwellers didn't want to kill us on sight, the translators only work in the air. Guess the manufacturors didn't plan on aquatic intelligence. We'd have to get one of the land-based adults to mediate if we wanted to talk to the swimmers, and they are vanishingly few."

"The breeding season is ending," Hubcap said.

Owen nodded. "And the rainy season is not. We had to leave early, or risk getting caught by the storms." He shook his head. "I'm just glad none of the fancypants took to frenzy. At any rate, they're planning to repeat today's disaster tomorrow with *more* people, and we are running out of time. There's no knowing how long it will be before the next breeding season. It might not be yearly. If we're honest, the frenzy is more common now than I can ever remember. We may not be here by the next season."

Elliot opened his mouth to say something optimistic, but came up with nothing.

Owen had already turned to fix Hubcap with a stern look. "The natives like you better than the rest of us," he said. "We need to get you back there again, so we can figure this out before it's too late." He let out another humorless laugh. "And there's just a few days left until the shuttle comes to whisk you off to your next assignment. We have to do this now."

"Will the overlords let us come along?" Hubcap asked. "They don't seem the type to change their minds."

"They're not," Owen said. "Be in the hangar an hour past dawn tomorrow. If anyone asks, you're helping Larry find something he dropped in the mud flats. Damn the overlords; we're fixing this ourselves."

Chapter 37

Hubcap opened the door an inch and peered into the hallway. Empty. No voices or footsteps. He waved the others forward and crept out in fine spy-drama fashion, alert for any signs of life. His feet made no sound, and he was ready to spring.

Elliot opened the door the rest of the way and walked right out, followed by the camera crew.

Hubcap scowled, crouching against the wall. "Shh, silent like ninja!" he urged. "The enemy will discover us!"

Elliot gave him a look. "Stand up. Let's go find Larry's lost equipment, then you can play around."

Hubcap stood. "Yes, his equipment." The humans were already walking toward the secondary hangar. "By all means, let's find that." He hurried to catch up, proclaiming loudly that the worker in question was foolish indeed for dropping something in so much mud. Elliot muttered something disparaging about Hubcap's acting skills, but Hubcap chose to ignore him.

They made it to the hangar without incident, skirting the cafeteria and anywhere else that the VIPs were likely to be, assuming they hadn't left for the day yet. The humans had planned ahead and eaten breakfast in the sleeping quarters.

Hubcap peered through the viewport in the hangar door, a handy little thing to keep people from wheeling carts into each other. No one was on the other side. The hangar held several parked aircars, but was mostly empty of humans. A couple of workers loaded boxes into the farthest car while early morning light filtered in from the wide open flight entrance. Satisfied, Hubcap turned the handle and stepped through with the humans right behind him.

"Larry?" Elliot called. "You in here?" The distant workers didn't look up.

Then a voice said "About time!" The door of the closest car rumbled open to show a familiar purple-haired human. "Come on, time's a-wasting! The airheads have a head start!" The short biologist windmilled an arm at them. "Owen's trying to direct 'em away from the breeding grounds!"

Hubcap led the charge. He hopped aboard with a salute for Larry. Xian was already seated near the front, while the rest of the car was empty. "Hello to both of you!" Hubcap said.

Elliot climbed aboard behind him. "Larry, good to see you. Xian, I'm glad you could join us."

"Oh, you know it!" the medic said with a grin. "It's only smart to have at least one bonesetter aboard. And I want to see the frenzy stopped! I'm sick of treating people for it!"

Hubcap placed a hand on his chest. "I feel you, brother."

"I bet you do," the medic chuckled while everyone found a seat and strapped in. "Can you imagine no more frenzy? No paranoia whenever someone yells or laughs too loud? Being able to just live without policing everyone's emotions?"

Hubcap nodded. "I can imagine it. Sounds like life back on good ol' Mother Earth. And even there, people are afraid of going into space. No more!"

"No more!" Xian agreed. He held up a hand, and Hubcap obliged with a high-five. He was even gentle about it.

"We ready?" Larry asked, hand on the ignition. At the unanimous nods, he started up the riotous flight engines and backed out into the sky.

Hubcap spent a few moments deep in thought about a frenzy-free life. It occurred to him that dealing with the hazard truly dominated his attention. *I work in space. In lots of locations. The frenzy is a danger in all of them. I can hardly imagine going to a new station and not having to ask where their sedatives are. …I really want to imagine that.*

And he did imagine it, until the flight leveled out and Xian caught his attention. The medic pulled a gadget from his bag that had a screen and a shoulder strap, and presented it to Hubcap, who accepted the pilfered translator with glee.

Vic looked over from her seat. "I have to ask," she said as Hubcap opened the thing and turned it on. "How did you get it?"

"Owen swiped it from the storage locker," Xian said. "There's plenty of the things, or at least there were last night. The rest of them are probably out in the other aircars now. D'you know they took three cars full of people? Those idiots are going to scare all the aliens away before they get close enough to translate anything."

Vic shook her head and discussed strategy with Xian while Hubcap played with the translator until he understood it.

"Oh look, it knows Yelliantian!" the robot said in delight.

"Perfect, another alien language to test. C'mon, somebody say something I can translate!"

"In Yelliantian?" Elliot said. "Good luck with that!"

"Surely you know something in hootspeak," Hubcap pressed with an impish smile. "Humans are supposed to be good at mimicry."

"I'd do a better whale song," Elliot said.

"I wonder if it knows that," Hubcap mused, typing away. He messed with the settings and options, finally looking up to find the aircar exiting the mountain pass. The vast floodgrounds had spread in the last two days.

"Crap, they're still circling," Larry said. He banked sharply and returned to the shadows, where he set the car to hover with its nose pointed toward the two silver shapes flitting about the treetops. Hubcap frowned out at them.

"You said they took three aircars," Elliot said to Xian. "Where's the third?"

The medic shrugged. "Landed somewhere," he said. "Impossible to tell. Hopefully it's not somewhere we want to be."

Everyone waited in silence. Finally one car picked a landing site and dove into the trees, with the other following it down. Several humans breathed a sigh of relief.

Larry gunned the engines and moved the car forward again. "I'm pretty sure they're at the central mating grounds," he said. "Owen said he'd have his hands full keeping them from disrupting things worse than before. Where should we set down?"

Hubcap wanted to find one of the meadows where they'd met aliens before, but he was overruled. Vic directed Larry to follow the river upstream in search of likely beaches. Xian agreed. Hubcap grumbled. Elliot reminded him that any remaining adults would probably be near the water's edge, for egg-laying purposes.

"Fine." Hubcap threw his hands in the air. "But if we're flying away from the only place around here that they'll actually be, I will take no pleasure in saying I told you so."

"That'd be a first," Elliot said.

Hubcap waggled a hand in front of his face, in his best thumb-to-nose taunting gesture. Not for the first time, he regretted passing on an aftermarket tongue that he could stick out at moments like this. Elliot ignored him.

Larry flew low over the treetops, checking the sensors for other aircars. He cut the flight engines early and coasted in on hover alone. Everyone peered out the windows, with and without cameras.

"How's that spot look?" Larry asked, pointing at an open space in the trees where water met grass. Vic agreed that it was as much a beach as anything else. Larry took the car in to land. Hubcap was out of his seat and waiting with the translator before they touched down.

"Hubcap," Vic admonished halfheartedly. "You need to follow the safety rules too."

"Yes, yes, of course, yes," Hubcap said, ready at the door. "But you know I won't get hurt if we stop suddenly."

Elliot spoke up. "Sure, but we might if you fall on us. Nobody wants to get an accidental robot to the face."

"That's the name of my next cover band," Hubcap quipped as the engine shut off. "Onward! Everybody listen for aliens and idiots!" He slid the door open and stepped out onto long purple grass.

The humans did as he suggested. Silently, they joined him in the meadow that sloped down into densely muddy water. Spiralling blue trees poked past the surface. Twittery things frolicked in the taller orange trees, chirping louder than the rushing water, but Hubcap wasn't here for them. He waved the translator about with the scanning function engaged, covering the area as thoroughly as possible. This just confirmed the obvious: there were no colortalking aliens close by.

"Off we go," he said, looping the travel strap around his neck. "Downstream toward the mating grounds, unless there's any objection?"

Vic agreed. Larry locked the aircar, and they set out along the water's edge.

It was slow going. The recent rainfalls had made the grass slippery, and there wasn't much flat ground between the trees.

"We should have gone back for the car," Dale grumbled, climbing over a rock. "This is taking forever."

"Hush up, you off-brand ape," Hubcap said mildly. "A little walking is good for you, and the engines would scare them off. Now quiet." He cocked his head in a pose that denoted listening over the river sounds, and the young human subsided.

"Anything?" Elliot asked. He stood on a different rock, craning his neck to look in all directions.

Hubcap dimmed his eyelights in scorn. "Nothing good. I hear the idiots that way." He pointed downstream.

By the sound of it, the official diplomatic party was at the mating grounds, and that they were Doing Diplomacy Wrong. There were far too many raised voices, argumentative tones, and occasional yelps of surprise. Hubcap was willing to bet money that there were spears involved.

He recounted this to the humans with inferior ears. Vic decided that they should press on in the stealthiest manner, and retreat at the first sign of other Earthlings.

"Agreed," Hubcap said. "All senses at maximum." He crept forward with the humans behind him.

Hubcap led his small group of rebellious heroes through the damp forest, following the edge of the floodwaters over dirt, sand, rocks and plantlife. The view finally opened up after they passed a dense grove of orange trees, and found what had once been rolling grasslands. Now it was just the edge of the river, with tiny islands popping up where the water hadn't risen quite high enough to cover everything.

Even now, there were no visible signs of civilization. The center of the floodwaters appeared less muddy to Hubcap's eyes, but he couldn't make out any details from this angle. And more importantly, the racket from downstream was getting louder. He could almost make out individual words. Moving along the shore, he approached a smattering of taller boulders that promised to be a good vantage point. He held his scanner up as he walked, expecting nothing, and was surprised when it flashed a positive sign.

Hubcap stopped in place, waving an arm and hissing for silence. Elliot looked over his shoulder at the screen, then glanced at the rocks. Hubcap nodded.

Vic got the cameras into action. The group crept forward, Hubcap in the lead, approaching the boulders with care. At first he didn't see anything. Then he rounded a corner and saw a splash of dark maroon perched on top of the highest rock.

He ducked back, gesturing wildly and not caring if the humans completely understood him. He reset the gadget to its translator function, and peeked around the corner.

It was one of them all right, laying on its stomach and resting its chin on its hands in a pose that looked part human and part jungle cat. Its transparent scales displayed a shifting pattern of reds and browns with streaks of green, except for its tail. Starting a few inches from the base, this was a dead white that did not change. The tail did move though, twitching idly as the alien watched the muddy river.

Then the colortalker shifted position on the rock, and caught sight of Hubcap.

246

Chapter 38

The air world was a fascinating place, with its clear views into the distance, and the unsettling way that everything was so *still*. Mudtail had felt almost sick the first time he noticed the way that the surface of the water flowed while all else was unmoving. It was very different up here, and when he had first emerged, he'd been captivated by it.

But now the novelty had worn off, and Mudtail was desperately homesick. He couldn't *swim* here; he could only get from one place to another by scrabbling along like a bottom-feeder. It took forever to get anywhere, it was tiring, and he was all alone.

He had been late to develop, leaving the water at the end of the season with the crowd of breeders all but gone. And those few remaining partners wanted nothing to do with someone with a speech impediment.

Mudtail curled up on the rock, tucking his tail against his side, reflexively trying to hide its lack of voice-flesh. That tail had made conversation difficult his whole life, with some words and ideas impossible to express properly. It was almost a mercy that the females had turned him down before he attempted a mating dance. He surely would have humiliated himself.

With a deep sigh, Mudtail watched the water swirl past. This was a quiet area upstream, with little to see but also few people to urge him onward. The emergence area had been full of helpful sorts. All of the near-adults were spending time at the surface, both in their duty to improve the air-breathing experience of the adults, and also in preparation for their own turn next breeding season. Mudtail had already had enough of their forced optimism in the preceding weeks. It was a relief when his gills finally closed, sending him into the air with his ears full of encouragement and his heart full of doubt.

It didn't take long for him to give up and sit staring aimlessly at the water. He knew that life was going on normally underneath without him — he caught a glimpse of a third-flood that he recognized, tending a garden in the clear shallows — and the thought that he would never swim there again made him shut his eyes tight and curl up closer.

I'm supposed to be brave, he thought miserably. *Air time is meant for exploring, and adventure, and experiences that no one back home could ever know. Not sitting on a rock wishing.* But he couldn't bring himself to get up. There was no point.

He heard an echo from downstream, and he flinched at the alien sound. The mating ground wasn't even safe now, whether or not there were females around. Not with those strange creatures harassing everyone. Before he had left home, there had been talk of the animals that the guards had seen, and now Mudtail had seen them too, from a safe distance. He had no desire to see them up close.

Not when the guards are warning everyone back, he thought. He was torn between wanting to leave for a safer area, and wanting to get closer in case there were any remaining females spying from the bushes. Hating himself, he did neither. He just sat on the rock and watched the third-flood harvest vegetables.

Then something caught his eye, and he turned to see a new animal looking back at him.

Mudtail leapt to his feet, ready to flee, but he stopped when it spoke to him. It talked in a double voice: one that he heard with his ears, and one that resonated in his head, meeting his thoughts at the source. Mudtail stared in confusion.

"Don't run," the creature said. *"I won't hurt you. Please, I need help."*

It was the last part that really caught his attention. Mudtail hesitated, taking in the sight of the tall animal colored like the reflection off a river. It wasn't moving to attack, and didn't seem threatening. But Mudtail had heard that one of the mysterious creatures harassing the town had coloration like this.

=*What do you want?*= Mudtail finally asked, not moving from the top of the rock.

"I need to know about the stutter-sleep," it said. *"How does it work?"*

=*Huh?*= Mudtail was nonplussed. =*Why do you want to know about that?*=

"It's hurting my people," the creature said. *"Can you tell me what causes it?"*

=*Well, sure, the invisible blue clouds do,*= Mudtail said, shifting uneasily. =*When a mating pair dances, the clouds cover them and help the eggs catch life.*= He made an awkward gesture. =*It's intended. Why?*=

The uncolor creature moved farther into the open, and Mudtail saw that it carried a mysterious object. *"What happens when the clouds cover someone who's not mating?"* it pressed.

=*They die early,*= Mudtail said. =*At the end of mating, people sleep and the clouds leave, but if they're caught again later, they don't sleep. The clouds eat their emotions until they don't have any left, and their time is done.*= It felt strange to be explaining this to someone now. He had passed on the wisdom to hatchlings before, but he'd never expected someone in the air to need it explained.

"That has been happening to my people," the creature said. *"How do we stop it? Is there a way to keep the clouds away from us?"*

Mudtail thought. =*They shouldn't like you in the first place,*= he said. =*They are intended only for us. They usually ignore other animals. And they stay in the air, where the breeding adults are.*=

"So we could swim to avoid them, but my people don't breathe water," the strange animal said. Then something seemed to occur to it. *"Wait, what makes them go after the adults? Will they pass over non-breeding adults to get a mating pair?"*

=*Yes, all the time,*= Mudtail said. =*They are meant for mating.*=

"Then there may be hope," the creature said with excitement. *"Do you know about pheromones?"*

Mudtail didn't, and the explanation that the animal gave was just this side of unbelievable, but these "pheromones" did sound like a logical way for the clouds to sense the breeders. Now that it was pointed out to him, the things did behave a lot like predators smelling blood in the water.

=*So how does this help you?*= Mudtail asked.

"Bait," the animal said. *"If we can collect some of the pheromones, we can make more, and use them to lure the clouds away from us."*

Mudtail realized that he wasn't scared anymore, caught up in the conversation. =*How do you collect them?*= he asked.

"From mating adults," was the answer. *"I don't suppose you can help with that?"*

Mudtail hung his head. =*No one will have me,*= he said. =*And there aren't any females around anyway. The creatures at the breeding ground scared away the last of them — are they your people?*=

"Not mine directly," the creature said with obvious disapproval. *"But I know them. Are they bothering everyone?"*

=*Yes. The guards called an alert, last I heard.*= Mudtail looked downstream. =*That was a while ago, though.*=

"We'll have to do something about that," the creature said. *"But do

you know where we might find any other breeders?"

=*They're probably all scattered, exploring the air like you're supposed to,*= Mudtail said. =*I don't expect to see any more emerge, either.*=

"Are there other mating grounds where they might gather?"

=*No. Well…*= Mudtail corrected himself. =*None close enough that we could get there in my lifetime.*=

"Really?" The creature sounded interested. *"Where are the others?"*

=*There's another village up the river.*= Mudtail pointed with his snout. =*But the distance is many days' swim, so I'll never see it.*= He lowered his head.

"Want to bet?"

Mudtail looked up at the creature's tone.

"Do you know what an aircar is?"

Chapter 39

Hubcap was nearly hopping with excitement, but he forced himself to appear calm. He didn't want to startle the alien. Belatedly, he introduced himself and brought out the humans, noting that while they made the colortalker uneasy, he did not run. Instead, "Mudtail" pulled himself together and greeted the half dozen offworlders from atop a rock that brought him to eye level.

The translator made conversation easier when put on the right setting. It already accepted Mudtail's mental words and beamed them to Hubcap in the same way, since he was the one holding the thing. After a few adjustments, it also repeated everything in spoken English. This ate into the translator's battery life though, so Hubcap set it back to one-on-one translating once the introductions were done.

Larry and Xian conferred with Vic, then took off to get the car, explaining that it would be easier to fly it back than to lead the timid native through the woods.

While they waited, Hubcap had more questions. The way Mudtail was describing it, there were creatures on this planet — "invisible blue clouds" — that fed on emotions. Hubcap was ready to wager a large amount of money that some of those creatures had drifted onto a human spaceship years ago. If they were really what caused the frenzy, then there were populations of very confused cloud-things all over human space now, searching for their symbiote race and finding other species instead.

It was too much to put into one question. "Why do you call them 'invisible blue clouds?'" Hubcap asked, letting the translator repeat it to Mudtail. "How can something be both invisible and blue?"

=*You don't see them with your eyes,*= Mudtail said in ripples of color, searching for words. =*They kind of smell blue — Oh, I can't say it right!*= His blank tail lashed, and the alien looked away. =*They just are,*= he said.

Hubcap left it at that. He made a note to check the settings of the translator to see if it could better pick up what the colortalker's speech impediment had gotten in the way of saying. The machine seemed to be catching only what was actually said, not what was intended. For the time being, Hubcap asked about the other village, and Mudtail told him everything he knew.

The alien was still talking when the aircar made its appearance around the bend. *=And they have a large herd of armormeat… What is that?=* Mudtail cut off to stare in speckled amazement as the vehicle from another world came in for a landing on the grassy shore, its hover engine whirring quietly.

Hubcap grinned widely. "That, my friend, is an aircar," he said. "With plenty of space for you with us. Ready to see the other mating grounds?"

Mudtail gaped, then visible excitement covered him in starbursts of gold. *=Yes!=* he said. *=Yes, I am very much ready!=*

Hubcap showed the alien over to the door, proud of his bravery, and he told himself not to get attached. Brave or not, Mudtail wouldn't live to see the sunrise. The alien's tendency to wheeze from excitement made Hubcap wonder if the air-breathing adults had defective lungs, or if their lifespan was more of a circulation problem. He focused on the task at hand, trying not to think about it.

Dale tripping over a loose floor panel made for a momentary distraction. Then as Elliot was helping him up, shouts from down the river reminded everyone of the unwelcome human presence at the mating grounds. Hubcap had a flash of inspiration.

He told everyone to wait before taking off, then had a quick conversation with Mudtail. A bit of prying with metal fingers was all it took to free the loose panel, then Hubcap began digging around for a waterproof pen.

"What are you doing?" Vic asked as Hubcap started to write. Mudtail sat and watched, looking from the panel to the rest of the exotic aircar.

"Helping the villagers send a very clear message," Hubcap replied. He wrote on the thin metal sheet in block letters: "Leave our mating grounds! We will only talk to the robot." Then he handed it to Mudtail, who tucked it against his chest and scrambled out to the water's edge. Vic nodded in silent approval.

Hubcap followed to see the alien splash into the water, heading for one of the little islands with a cluster of plantlife growing on it.

"What is he doing with that?" Elliot wanted to know.

Hubcap folded his arms with pride. "Giving it to one of the villagers. She'll give it to the guards, and they'll fling it at the humans on the beach." He looked over at his co-host. "I'm hoping it hits one of them."

Elliot shook his head. "Well, it'll certainly confuse them," he said. "Though there won't be any doubt of which robot it means. We should go before they start looking for us."

Hubcap nodded. "It'll take a few minutes to get the thing to the guards, and I figure that's plenty of time for us to be on our way. Who knows how quick the guards will be to whang it at someone's head."

Out in the river, Mudtail handed the sign to someone underwater, then came splashing back to shore. Hubcap lifted his translator to hear =*It's done! Let's go!*=

He welcomed the excited alien back onboard, and Larry started up the hover engine. Soon they were skimming the water on their way upstream. Mudtail ran from one window to another like a dog on the way to the park, and no one told him to sit down. Hubcap translated his stream of exclamations, delighted himself to be able to see into that clear part of the river beyond the mud barriers.

=*I can see the snapper pens!*= Mudtail enthused, =*And the play jungle! At the same time! Wow, they look so strange from up here! And I can see how many hatchlings are in the jungle, all at once! This is amazing!*= The alien scampered over to the other side of the car. =*Oh, I remember that spot, with the fallen tree that you can only swim over during flood! I haven't been there since I was little!*=

"It's a great view from up here, isn't it?" Hubcap asked.

Mudtail looked back at him =*This is incredible,*= he said in bright colors. =*No one from my town — no one anywhere! — has seen the world from this high before! I'm the first! Thank you!*= He went back to watching out the window.

Hubcap realized he was starting to care more than he wanted to. This was a friend he would lose in the next few hours. He started to pull back, but Mudtail continued.

=*I was sure that my life in the air was going to be miserable,*= the alien said. =*This is more than I could have imagined! Do you swim the air like this all the time?*=

"Often enough," Hubcap said. "What I don't do much of is swim through the trees. Your normal life is amazing to me."

=*Really? It's not that special.*=

"Sure, if you're used to it, but where I live we walk everywhere, and if we need to reach something high up, we have to climb to get it. You can swim straight there."

=*Well, I could,*= Mudtail said, and Hubcap regretted his words. But the alien cheered up again. =*And now I can swim through the air too! I will die happy tonight!*=

Hubcap found himself smiling. "I'm glad," he said.

Chapter 40

Mudtail's directions were good, pointing out which forks and tributaries of the river to follow. Navigation was still tricky due to the floodwaters obscuring landmarks, but the view was clear enough from this height to pick out other clues.

=*There should be one more turn at the three-trunked tree,*= Mudtail said to Hubcap, who sat in the copilot's seat. Mudtail peered through the windscreen, flicking his head from side to side and leaning over Larry's shoulder. The human piloted as if he didn't have an alien elbowing him in the head each time something interesting came into sight. The camera crew took turns filming their interactions. Mudtail didn't seem to notice. =*I think that's it?*= he said. =*Or is that just three trees growing close together?*= He pointed a hesitant claw at a cluster of trunks growing from muddy water.

"What about those—" Hubcap was interrupted.

=*Wait, it's that way! There's the sharp cliff that broke off last flood! There, there!*=

Hubcap translated the thought-words, still conserving battery, and Larry nodded. "I see it." He banked to the right in a gentle arc so as not to jostle Mudtail. No one had tried to make the alien wear a harness. Neither the belts nor the chairs would fit a passenger shaped more like a smooth-scaled crocodile than a human.

"What will we see first?" Hubcap asked. "How do we know when we're there?"

=*The Airwater that the city is named for,*= Mudtail said with pride. =*I've seen it once, and it's amazing. My home just has the Rockwall as a namesake, which isn't that special, no matter how many carvings are in it. We don't even have a very interesting history to carve. But the Airwater is useful!*=

Hubcap wanted to ask for clarification, thinking that the translator was missing something, but Mudtail perked up and pointed into the distance, bracing a scaly hand on Larry's shoulder in his excitement.

=*There, I can see it! This is so fast, I didn't think we'd be there yet! Look look look! Where the two tributaries meet!*=

Hubcap searched for a waterfall or geyser, but instead saw a tower sprouting from the river. At his noise of surprise, the humans behind him abandoned their harnesses and crowded close for a look. Hubcap could make out the glint of windows as the aircar approached.

"That is impressively tall," he said. "I didn't realize your people had mastered glass. It takes a lot of work with fire the way we make it, which I imagine is tricky underwater."

=*I don't know about all that,*= Mudtail said. =*I'm told the people of Airwater have a source of water-colored rocks that they carve into thin sheets. They won't tell the rest of us where the things come from.*=

"Probably underwater caves," Hubcap said. The details of the tower's stonework were coming into view, and they were intricate indeed. Cameras whirred behind Hubcap while he stared. The rocks fit together like puzzle pieces of different colors: gray and white and sandy yellow. The patterns that spiraled around the tower surely held some meaning to the inhabitants of the underwater city. Hubcap realized something.

"Is there water all the way to the top?" he asked, leaning forward in his seat.

=*Yes! That's why it's called the Airwater! Isn't it amazing?*=

"It sure is." Hubcap relayed this to the humans, who were equally impressed.

"No way," Elliot said. "Like one of those fish tunnels? Their caulking must be excellent! That's a lot of pressure to stand up to!"

The humans filmed away while discussing the logistics of building such a thing. They reasoned that there must have been a lot of breath-holding on the part of the stonelayers, and bailing out of the air trapped inside with buckets.

"But how would they even get that high if they don't have legs to climb with?" Dale asked as he adjusted his camera's focus.

"Scaffolding?" Xian suggested. "I want to know if they have reverse scuba suits."

"We can ask them later," Vic said. "Where do we land?"

"Keep an eye out for spears," Larry added. All eyes turned down at that, and searched the brown water for dangers. As the aircar crossed over the edges of the city center, the mud cleared dramatically. There was some sort of screen in place, like at Mudtail's home. Underwater buildings, gardens, and swimming citizens came into view. Thankfully, none of them held spears.

Hubcap asked Mudtail about that, and the alien said the aircar had flown right over the city's defenses. No throwing weapons were allowed in the city center for fear of hurting civilians. Hubcap would have asked more, but Mudtail was urging the aircar forward to hover next to the tower so he could talk through the windows, and Hubcap hurried to translate.

Larry glanced at Vic for approval, then moved the car closer. The water below was filling with curious onlookers in a multitude of colors. They poured out of stone buildings that were equally colorful, and they swam up from the depths. The water was surprisingly deep here.

Underwater skyscrapers, Hubcap thought. *Not what I expected to see today. I'm glad the camera monkeys are on top of all this.* He grinned to himself. *Suck it, Space Fashion.*

Three videographers took in the scenery, while Tarja studied the alien in their midst. As the aircar approached the tower, three cameras moved as one to film the architecture with a row of beaky faces gathering behind the wrap-around windows at the peak.

Larry brought the aircar to a cautious stop with its nose a few feet away from those windows. Still no one threatened them with spears. Hubcap was torn between scanning for danger and focusing on the amazing thing that they were doing. Amazement won out for once.

Mudtail waved through the windshield, flashing yellows and golds in excitement. Hubcap switched the English translation on, so the humans could hear Mudtail's words, though Hubcap still had to translate in the other direction. Mudtail hardly noticed, asking for the car to be moved so he could speak through the open door. Larry complied. Vic hauled the door open, and everyone gathered behind Mudtail as he made a formal greeting to the best of his ability. He hurried to explain that the cameras weren't weapons.

The translator couldn't penetrate the water inside the tower, so Hubcap kept it trained on Mudtail and figured out the rest of the conversation from there. He was picking up a lot of incredulity and surprise on the part of the officials, and eager entreaty from Mudtail.

=These are not-us,= he was saying. *=From a whole other world! They need our help in saving their own people from the invisible blue clouds, and I think we should give it.=*

The response was cautious, laced with more than a little suspicion, but the officials were willing to hear him out. Some, perhaps more educated than Mudtail, even understood pheromones when he explained what the offworlders wanted.

=*Invisible smells?*= Mudtail asked, struggling with the wording. =*It sounded like fertilizer for emotions the way they described it — Yes, that!*= He sparkled greens at hearing the proper name. =*That must be it! Can we get those?*=

But these officials didn't have the rank to make big decisions themselves. They certainly looked like they wanted to; Hubcap watched more colorful faces crowd into that room with every passing moment. A large one in front seemed to be doing most of the talking. According to Mudtail, this official said that the highest authorities were on the way, and would likely need convincing on stronger grounds than pity.

"What will they want?" Vic asked. Hubcap translated.

=*Well, relations with a new enclave are traditionally begun with goodwill gifts from both sides,*= Mudtail said. =*Assuming the advisors agree, they will arrange the gathering of pheromones as a gift to you. We need to present something of significant value.*=

There was a flurry of brainstorming on that front. People suggested offworld gadgets from inside the aircar, tools, medical supplies that may or may not be suited to colortalker physiology. Performances. Favors.

Elliot looked around. "Is there anything that they use from on land, but they have trouble getting?" he suggested. "Anything from those trees, or that mountain, or farther up the river?"

Mudtail talked with the officials, and came up with a short list of possibilities. One stood out.

"Jetpods!" Hubcap exclaimed. He cycled through memories of his first day here. "We know jetpods! Where are the nearest ones?"

According to Mudtail, the distance was many days' travel for swimmers, but only a short flight away for an aircar. The pods were valued as a delicacy, only rarely in reach when the floodwaters rose high enough, and only found when they had expended their seeds and fallen of their own accord. If these strangers from another world could provide fresh ones, the leaders would be most impressed.

=*They say that one jetpod should be enough to start ally negotiations,*= Mudtail said, turning away from the door.

Vic nodded. "So we'll get two. Leave the other in the car, just in case we need to up the ante at the last minute." She addressed Mudtail. "If you can ask them where we should bring their fresh jetpod — where we can land without sinking — we'll go get it now."

At Hubcap's translation, Mudtail nodded and moved to talk with the officials again. Vic suggested that he ask whether they wanted the jetpod with or without its jetting capability intact.

The answer was prompt: they wanted it as fresh and dangerous as possible. Mudtail didn't comment on the wisdom of this, but Hubcap suspected that he wanted to. Instead, he arranged a meeting location and bid the officials a polite goodbye.

When the door rolled closed and the aircar picked up speed away from the tower, Mudtail made a relieved sound and collapsed in roils of purple and green, exclaiming his disbelief at the situation he'd found himself in.

"You're great at mediating!" Hubcap told him. "Better than a number of human professionals I could name."

Elliot echoed the praise, offering a tentative pat on the shoulder that Hubcap confirmed for acceptable body language. The human also suggested food and drink, but Mudtail said he wasn't hungry. Hubcap did his absolute best not to dwell on why that might be, and on how many hours of daylight were left.

"So! Jetpods," he said instead, setting down the translator to rub his hands together in a series of clicks. "What's our battle plan?"

That took some discussion. The aircar full of rookies spent the flight figuring out how they were going to safely wrangle two jetpods without proper supplies. In the end they settled on using a stretcher as a net to catch the thing, and the biggest knife that Xian had with him to cut the stem. There was no arguing who would be the one to do it.

"Ah, this brings me back," Hubcap said as the jetpod trees grew closer. "Such memories. We were all fresh-faced youths back then. But we had a good crew chief to keep us in line, and we prevailed against the dangerous exploding plants." He sketched a salute in the air. "Anrik, wherever you are, I sincerely hope we don't mess this up terribly."

Graham laughed. "Amen."

Larry asked for advice on how to land on the side of a tree from someone who had actually done it before. This was a sobering realization that the TV crew were the most experienced people at hand. Vic picked out a spot and directed Larry toward it: a pair of large jetpods of approximately the same color as the ones they had harvested several days before. The pilot maneuvered the aircar into place underneath the things while everyone else gathered supplies.

Mudtail looked out the windows with delight, taking in the

long drop and the enormous trees with the same kind of amazement he'd shown when Hubcap demonstrated how the harness buckles worked. It was endearing as all hell. Hubcap wanted to pat him on the head. But duty called.

It wasn't the best plan, Hubcap reflected moments later.

He stood on top of the car in a safety harness, with Elliot and Dale crouched on either side holding the stretcher under a pod. They both wore their own harnesses and anxious expressions. Tarja stood in the open doorway below, peeking with a camera over the edge. Everything vibrated slightly from the hover engine. The ground was very far away.

Elliot gazed downward. "This is a terrible idea, you realize."

"Oh yes. Monumentally terrible."

"As long as we're on the same page about that." Elliot glanced at Dale. "You all right?"

"I'm ready." The junior cameraman shook himself and set his jaw. "Let's do this." Hubcap would personally have preferred to have Larry on the other end of the stretcher, but he was the only one certified to fly the aircar, so that was ruled out. And Xian wasn't visibly stronger than Dale, and Vic was a little too big to balance properly in the space available, and Hubcap realized he was stalling.

"Let's do this," he agreed. He grasped the tree bark with one hand and lined up the knife. "If I'm lost in an explosion of seeds and legend, make sure my remains are recycled into anything but hubcaps." He swung the knife.

Chapter 41

Owen was ready to start tearing his hair out. The executives who had taken over were doubling down on the failures of yesterday, running the same kind of disastrous expedition with more vigor. The aliens hadn't talked to them before, and no amount of yelling at the river would change that. There weren't even any real diplomats involved. Just a CEO and his various lackeys, none of whom were listening to reason.

"The colortalkers are going to keep threatening us," Owen said for the umpteenth time, stepping around the pair of official cameramen who kept getting in his way. "At this point all we can do is look through the forest for solitary adults."

Mr. Bhandari waved him into silence, watching the river. "Shut it," he said in clipped tones. "If I want your input, I will ask for it."

Owen threw his hands into the air and strode away through the grass. Ms. Acosta gave him a sympathetic look, but she didn't speak up. Dr. Rhodes didn't even meet his eyes — the psychologist stood forlornly at the edge of the crowd, despite having been relieved of his diplomat status. Mr. Bhandari had recruited everyone he considered to be useful now (which did not include Mr. Lee, who hadn't seen the aliens in person), and then proceeded to ignore them. He hadn't listened to Owen's advice earlier, when the pair of doom bats had been patrolling the shore. They had nearly flown off with a biologist before they were discouraged with stun guns. And the CEO wasn't listening now.

Mr. Bhandari was currently trying to convince some of the scientists wearing body armor to move closer to the shore, in the hopes that the natives would emerge from the water long enough to throw spears at them.

The men were reluctant to follow orders. "These aren't bulletproof," one worker pointed out. "We don't even have helmets. They could kill us with a good shot."

"And that last alien was carrying something that looked an awful lot like a gun," the other said. "I'm not sure we're even safe this far back."

Mr. Bhandari was trying to come up with a good answer to that, with his handful of subordinate executives either backing him up or keeping stonily out of it, when the aliens in the water suddenly flipped their tails and dove out of sight. The humans all turned to stare, with the cameramen stepping to the front.

Owen was uneasy. "Maybe we should move back," he cautioned. "In case they're readying something big."

"Get closer," Mr. Bhandari directed the armored workers. "See where they've gone." The men hesitated, looking from the scowling CEO to the head biologist who was taking his own advice and stepping away from the muddy water.

Then someone pointed out a single native swimming their way. It was moving fast, but it wasn't carrying a spear. It did seem to have something flat in its hands, but this was kept close to its chest and impossible to make out from the shore.

"Translators ready!" Mr. Bhandari said. "This could be our chance!"

Owen ducked behind a tree, peeking around the trunk. The native powered into the shallows, its finned tail working hard, and before it ran out of water, it reared up into the air. Then it threw the thing it carried.

"Talk to it! Talk — ack!" Mr. Bhandari cut off with a squawk as the flat gray item spun towards his head like a discus. The CEO barely dodged it, and the native disappeared back into the river. Mr. Bhandari swore. "What the hell was that? Did anyone talk to it?"

No one had. Owen left the shelter of his tree with a glance at the water, walking over to the flat thing that lay half-buried in the sand. He crouched, ignoring the storm of questions he couldn't answer, and he found it to be a square piece of metal with screw holes. He wondered with some concern where it had come from. When nothing happened as he touched it, he pulled the thing free of the wet sand and turned it over.

Then he broke into a grin and stood up.

"The natives have spoken," Owen said, brushing sand off the message and holding it up. He had no idea how Hubcap had gotten it to them, but this was a good sign.

Mr. Bhandari disagreed, launching into a hearty round of swearing in which he cursed the robot, his camera crew, their families, their pets, and anyone who had helped them get in the way of progress. He ignored his own camera crew, who were filming his every word.

"Are you quite done?" Owen asked when Mr. Bhandari showed signs of winding down.

"No!" he shouted, pointing a finger at the biologist. "That clanker has ruined any chance we had of establishing relations with this settlement! He's out here somewhere, putting a wrench in the works!" Mr. Bhandari turned to the assistant with the radio and had her contact the third aircar, which was currently scanning the woods to the south. That carload of employees was directed to look for the offending robot and anyone else he might have with him.

Owen sighed and wished the fugitives luck, deciding there was no point in trying to change Mr. Bhandari's mind. He just hoped that something good would come of all this.

The radio crackled with a brief sighting of what had to be another aircar flying far upriver. Mr. Bhandari ordered everyone back into their own two cars.

Owen followed the crowd, crossing his fingers as the aircars roared upstream with flocks of startled alien birds in their wake.

Chapter 42

Hubcap hadn't realized earlier, when they'd left one jetpod in a clearing before zipping over to the river's edge, just how much inhospitable terrain there was between the two. What had started out as a triumphant march back with the allegiance settled had turned into a single-file climb up a devilishly slippery hill. Even though the ground was dry, it was coated in leaves and near vertical. Elliot went first, mapping out trees to hold onto. Cameras were stowed for safety. Hubcap was in the middle of the group, carrying the precious jar of pheromone-soaked gauze.

The alien ambassadors had arranged things while they were at the jetpod tree. They'd gathered the remaining few adults at the mating grounds and explaining what was at stake. By the time the aircar full of offworlders had touched down on the flat rock shelf, several pairs were ready to tolerate a minor indignity for the greater good.

There had even been a mate for Mudtail — more than one willing, after what he'd done. The colortalker society as a whole certainly thought well of Mudtail now, despite his "deficiency." He had been crucial in a world-altering alliance. There was almost a fight over who got the honor of doing egg business with him.

And now Mudtail was off exploring the woods with the other adults, his own pheromones in the mix and his reputation cemented for generations to come. He'd been the first to allow gauze pads to be taped on in strategic locations. The waterbound medical professionals who'd poked their heads into the air had suggested where. And the swarm of important underwater people had been extremely interested in the proceedings.

They'd also been interested in the jetpod. That had been the first order of business, rolling it carefully from the aircar into the water, then moving the car to make space for the mating dances. Larry had flown back to where they'd left the spare pod, with the others planning to join him when the hurried ceremony was complete.

It was done now, with liberal use of the translator. Hubcap and his "designated allies/assistants" were now trade partners with the town of Airwater. Hubcap would have been more excited about that, and about Owen's likely reaction to the news, if not for the urgent need to get the pheromones into the hands of the right scientists before anything happened to them.

An alarming sound reached Hubcap. "Hey, shush," he said, interrupting a debate over whether or not to drop off the second jetpod as a gesture of goodwill. "I hear engines."

The humans froze. The distinct sound of aircars was loud enough for even them to hear, and approaching fast.

"Hurry!" Vic barked, lunging up the hill. The others followed, scrambling toward the car that waited at the top.

They had barely made it past the trees when a car full of armored humans landed in front of them. Two men jumped out, yelling orders to stand still, and aiming stun guns that could stop a heart.

"Hands where we can see them!"

"Do not move!"

The TV crew stumbled to a halt, breathing heavily. Hubcap studied the pair with the stun guns. They looked like mercenary/ bodyguard types, dressed in dark blue battle gear with threatening body language. One was saltine-white and the other was middle brown, like mismatched bookends of Hired Goon. The other people following them out of the car were local critter-wranglers, dressed for work and looking none too pleased at being roped into all this. But they followed orders and surrounded the camera crew to make sure nobody tried anything funny.

Hubcap held the jar of pheromones close, trying to stand unobtrusively behind Vic. The humans kept their hands where they could be seen. Across the field he saw Larry, seated in the aircar, keeping his own hands away from the controls. Three locals that he probably knew on a first name basis approached with weapons made for capturing human-sized aliens.

Hubcap was thinking over the logistics of firing a net launcher inside an aircar when he heard more engines on the way. Goon One and Goon Two herded the rebellious group to the side, telling them in no uncertain terms that they had better behave.

"The boss is coming," said the darker one.

"Do not anger him more than you already have," added the one with skin the color of sunscreen, his eyes flicking skyward.

As these new aircars approached at unsafe speeds, Hubcap wondered what they thought of the jetpod resting on a dense shrub some distance away. Larry had insisted that if he was the one to stay with the vehicle, that he not have to worry about the jetpod going off behind him if he sneezed. No one had thought it worth arguing about.

Now there appeared to be a different argument in the offing.

The two other cars landed, making the meadow distinctly crowded, and people rushed out. One man was shouting as soon as the door opened.

"Where are they? You! How dare you!" He was well-dressed, with skin that was naturally tan but unnaturally reddened with anger. And he was prepared to vent all of that anger now. He stomped up to the group and yelled at them, focusing first on Hubcap, but shifting his attention to Vic when she replied with calm authority.

She explained that they had found the solution to the frenzy. The man yelled right over her, not even letting her get to the part about starting diplomatic relations with the alien city.

Everyone that the man had brought with him was keeping quiet. The row of suit-clad executives looked displeased about the dampness of their pant cuffs, but that was it. A pair of offworld camera jockeys had started filming from a distance, but one of the Goons was quietly convincing them to turn the cameras off. Hubcap spotted Ms. Acosta staring stonily ahead, Dr. Rhodes glancing about like a prey animal, and Owen standing at the edge of the crowd watching the proceedings with disbelief. Hubcap knew the scientist had heard Vic's revelation. He would want desperately to find out what the camera crew had uncovered.

But Shouty McYellington wasn't interested.

"…Then despite direct orders to stay out of it, you stole a company aircar and ruined the entire operation!" the man exclaimed, striding back and forth.

Hubcap raised his hand. "Point of order," he said. "We didn't steal anything; we had full permission. Not to mention, *we just saved your butts*. You should be thanking us."

Shoutyface stopped pacing. "Thanking you? For ruining our diplomatic relations with the native village? And who gave you permission to take the car?"

The robot put a fist on his hip and frowned, still holding the jar. "I see no reason to tell you," he said. "Not if you're going to be irrational about it."

"Irrational?" the man seethed.

Vic tried to interject calming words, but Hubcap kept talking. "Yes, irrational! We just solved the mystery of frenzy — which has been killing meatbags such as yourself for years — and we have provided the beginnings of a cure! You should *not* be yelling at us!"

The executive pointed. "You disobeyed orders and ruined a company operation!"

Hubcap tapped metal fingers against the side of his head. "You might not know this, but we don't actually work for you. And again," he said, flinging his arm upward, "We just did a Very Good Thing."

An unexpected voice spoke up. "Your pardon sir, but if this is true," said Dr. Rhodes, "They've done us a great service by disobeying." Rageface whirled to stare him down, but the psychologist held his ground. "They have."

"Is that so?" the man said, turning his ire toward the new target. "By hamstringing our relations with the new species of alien?"

Dr. Rhodes shook his head. "With all due respect, the frenzy is a far more important issue. The alien city will still be here later, but the frenzy is killing people every day. I think we should hear what they have to say."

"You have the temerity to reevaluate my priorities?" demanded Anger Management Man. "On what grounds?"

Ms. Acosta stepped forward. "Sir, the frenzy is one of the fastest-growing hazards of space travel today," she said, stopping beside Dr. Rhodes. "You have read the reports. You were briefed before coming here—"

He cut her off. "I won't have some weak-minded imbecile's fainting fit get in the way of business!"

Dr. Rhodes cocked his head. "You haven't been off-world before, have you, Mr. Bhandari?" he asked. "I can assure you, reading a report is very different from watching the people around you go violently mad."

"A cure for the frenzy would be invaluable," Ms. Acosta persisted. "Taking these people to task for going behind your back is like shooting the person who gives you a winning lottery code." She spread her hands in exasperation. "You hired advisors, and it would be wise to listen to our advice."

"How dare you!" said Bhandari the Blatherskite. "I should—"

He went on at length about what he should do, while several people tried to wrestle the conversation back in a useful direction.

Hubcap looked around for ideas. When Owen threw his hands in the air and strode away toward the aircars, a thought started to form. Hubcap assessed the scene. Yelling man. Lackeys. Locals there for show. Goons there to be reckoned with. Aircar nearby. A jetpod in a bush.

He edged backward, putting the others between himself and Apoplexy McGee, then set the jar on the ground. This freed both hands to use the translator in a way it wasn't intended.

Owen twitched like a startled cat when words popped into his head. *"Hey. Can you hear me? Think really hard."*

"Who is this?" Owen's thoughts came back to Hubcap.

"This is your conscience speaking. No, not really. It's the robot with the brainwave translator. Heyo." Hubcap waggled his eyebrows across the crowd.

Owen didn't question it. *"What did you find??"*

"Our alien friends tell me that the frenzy is caused by airborne creatures that we can't see," Hubcap said, *"They're attracted to mating pairs, but will settle for anything with emotions. We've deduced that pheromones are what the things really go for, and have — at great risk to life and limb — collected a sample of the pheromones for duplication at the lab. Oh, and we're officially trade partners with the big city up the river now."*

Yellingman Spittlefountain moved on to taking Xian's head off for trying to convince him to listen.

Owen edged back closer. *"What now? Can you sneak me the samples?"*

Hubcap eyed the various enforcers and armored locals. *"Not without a distraction."* His gaze slid sideways to the jetpod. *"Get ready."*

"What are you going to do?"

"Something stupid. Tell Larry to start the engines." Hubcap turned off the translator, removed the loop from around his neck, and crouched to set it next to the jar. He paused for a moment, calculating trajectories, then opened his leg compartment and straightened back up. He palmed the knife as he did.

It is a curious thing, for a robot to defy its programming.

It makes for a kind of terrifying euphoria, much like that of a human at the peak of a roller coaster that is much steeper than anticipated.

Hubcap had always held a certain degree of disdain for the former cleaning robots who sought out paint and food to make giddy messes, and the medical bots who took up sharpshooting in their spare time. He'd never seen the appeal.

Now, as he took aim at something that he was *mostly* sure wouldn't kill anyone — in order to save everyone — he felt that he finally understood roller coasters.

He flung the knife, grabbed the jar, and ran. The explosion was deafening.

Chapter 43

Elliot had been looking at Mr. Bhandari when something flashed across his vision, followed by a thunderous boom that shook the ground. He flinched as shrapnel blew past him. People cried out, some knocked off their feet.

Mr. Bhandari shouted louder than before. "What the hellscape dancers was that?"

Someone else was yelling a command to hold position: one of the armed enforcers. Elliot realized as the man raised his blaster that he was aiming at Hubcap.

"Don't!" Elliot yelled. Hubcap was at the door of the aircar, boosting Owen in while the engines roared to life. The bolt of energy hit him square in the back.

Elliot stumbled into a run as the robot seized up and pitched forward against the side of the aircar. Owen and Larry exclaimed next to him while the closest armored locals looked visibly conflicted about who to aim their net launchers at.

A scream of panic was all the warning Elliot got before he was bodyslammed off his feet. Disoriented, he tried to roll away only to nearly get trampled by heavy boots. He made it to his hands and knees. Chaos was unfolding around him.

An armored man dove into a bush, wailing in fear. A woman climbed a tree. Another man dragged one of the first two out by his feet, shouting about unseemly weakness. And in the center of the clearing, Mr. Bhandari was a towering inferno of rage.

It was only when Ms. Acosta stamped the CEO with a SedEgg — using more force than was necessary — that Elliot belatedly realized what was going on.

We're near the mating grounds, he thought as he struggled to stand. *The invisible cloud creatures are everywhere.* He pulled out his own SedEgg only to nearly drop it when an angry shove sent him sprawling.

This time he rolled back onto his feet, ready and waiting for his attacker, who turned out to be one of the two enforcers. Elliot's heart rate hitched.

But someone else got the man from behind: a local who nodded at Elliot and darted away as the enforcer fell. Scuffles were breaking out everywhere. Elliot turned back toward the car and saw Hubcap getting up.

Of course. He's built to withstand lightning strikes.

Elliot's relief was eclipsed by a burst of maniacal laughter behind him. He whirled to see Ms. Acosta moving in a devastating display of empty-handed strikes at the workers around her, with the SedEgg forgotten in the grass.

"You bastards want to fight?" she asked with a brutal kick to a man's knee. "You can't even — uck." An arm around her neck earned her attacker an elbow to the teeth, but he held on just long enough for someone else to tag her arm with a SedEgg. The pile of people fell. More were fighting behind them.

Stay calm, stay calm, Elliot chanted, taking deep breaths and telling himself that everything about the situation was still salvageable. With another glance to be sure Hubcap was okay — he was stepping away from the aircar and waving it into the sky — Elliot dashed back into the fray with his SedEgg at the ready, looking for the rest of the camera crew.

Vic had kept her cool. She had her own SedEgg and someone else's as well, and she stood protecting a pile of camera equipment. Tarja was on the ground beside it. No sign of Graham or Dale.

Elliot dodged past a knot of wrestling workers, tagging an arm and two legs that might have belonged to different people. He kept moving. He heard Hubcap exclaim in exasperation and do the same. It was an encouraging sound.

Dale turned out to be hiding ostrich-style between two mossy boulders, and he went limp when Elliot stamped his backside. Elliot left him there for the moment. It seemed safer.

There we go. One down. He looked back up at the riot. *Leaving only … everyone.*

The scene was pandemonium. People fought, hid, ran, and collapsed over each other. A couple workers had retained enough presence of mind to sedate the others through their armor, but they appeared to be fighting a losing battle. Even Hubcap was getting bogged down by a cluster of angry men.

Elliot felt a splash of true fear.

We're all going to go down, he thought in wide-eyed shock. *The frenzy is going to take everyone, and we're all going to die out here!* His heartbeat exploded in his ears, and the world turned into bright flashes of sight.

People fighting — two men with their hands around each other's throats and their faces set in blind grimaces. A woman ramming a fist into another man's gut. A graybeard with a camera who he should have recognized running into a tree, and the two human shapes up in the branches retreating from the impact.

Then the trees were moving past him, faster and faster with every flash, and bushes jumped up out of nowhere for him to trip over. Every time he fell, he rolled and clawed his way back up onto his feet; the world was a spinning reel of grass and dirt and bushes and sky, with trees blinking in and out of existence where they should not have been.

All he could hear was his pulse and a faint raspy sound that he distractedly realized was his own breathing. It didn't matter. Nothing mattered, not the branch that swept close to his head, not the colorful flapping animals that filled the air, not the way the ground beneath him turned uneven and made his vision even more jerky. The world tipped sideways and gave him a view of the grass. Somehow he got back up and kept moving.

The way his vision kept dipping to the left after every other step didn't matter. All that mattered was running, getting away from the danger. He no longer remembered what it was. He only knew that he needed to run.

The sound of his pulse was getting quieter. The images that he saw of the trees and bushes and dirt were getting smaller, being eaten away at the edges by a speckled darkness that seemed oddly comforting. He kept pushing himself forward, unsure of how fast he was moving, but knowing that he had to keep going. He had to get away—

Then his vision jerked again, more than before, and he was looking at dirt. Something else was there, reflecting in front of his eyes while that speckled darkness chewed away at the image until nothing was left. It looked like a metal hand. Then it was gone.

Chapter 44

"…And stay down!" Hubcap yelled at the prone form of his partner. "You daft running bastard! You were so sure that you'd never get the frenzy, then when you finally do, you take off like a rabbit on rocket fuel! You batty meatwad!"

He sat down with a thump, watching the unconscious human's lungs heave. The pulse beating visibly at his neck was already starting to return to normal.

Hubcap looked back toward the distant mess of humanity. They had come a long way. Broccoli-shaped trees and other weirdness was all he saw.

"And now I have to carry your fleshy self back there. No gratitude at all." He stood up and put the new SedEgg back in its compartment, making a note to get it refilled as soon as he reached base.

Well, right after seeing this maniac safely to the medcenter. He crouched and gathered the limp human in his arms, tucking his head in close, then set off at a brisk trot.

"You could have frenzied a different kind of fear, you know," Hubcap said in a conversational tone. "You could have decided to climb a tree, or stick your head in a bush. Heck, you could have gotten angry at the rest of the idiots and taken a swing at someone. I'm sure you can hold your own in a fight. I'd bet money on you." He chattered away as he ran, picking up speed now that Elliot was balanced securely.

The run took much longer this time. And yet, as he approached the battered clearing, he saw that a number of fighting humans still lurching around.

"You sleep well, like a good human larva," Hubcap said, setting Elliot down under a tree. "Daddy has to go knock some heads together for the good of all humanity. Or at least the humanity in this forest."

With that, he was up and running with his SedEgg at the ready.

"Sit down, dammit!" he shouted. "I have a medical fist! Don't make me use it on you!"

In the end, there were a half dozen stubborn humans who needed the tender ministrations of his medical fist, all tough worker types who hadn't managed to fall down on their own. The people in suits were mostly at the bottom of various piles. Once the remaining belligerents were down and snoring, Hubcap began checking the still forms on the ground. And those in the branches and shrubbery. And the heaps of humanity under the trees.

"Good shot, Vic," he said to the director who had fallen from a tree squarely onto the only bush big enough to break her fall. "You probably could have landed on one of those guys too, if you had a choice. They look like they would make fine cushions." The camera pile was intact. Good.

The men in question were sprawled on top of each other, bruised and bloodied but still breathing. Hubcap pulled the humans into more comfortable positions and moved on, still talking to no one and everyone.

"And they wondered why I keep pushing the employers to look for more robot workers," he said. "Look at this! What a mess! None of you meatbags would be getting out of here alive if not for me. You're welcome. And you're welcome, and you're welcome..." He found more bodies in the bushes, and carted them back to the clearing for a head count.

"Eight, nine ... How many of you idiots were there?" Hubcap said to the unconscious forms. "I'd never hear the end of it if I missed somebody, and let one of you fleshies shiver himself to death in a shrub somewhere. Especially when I have my nice fresh MEDICAL FIST!" He held the SedEgg up, looking around for replies. "It's sterilized!" No new faces popped up, and he resumed counting. "You lot had better be grateful, is all I'm saying."

He uncovered Xian in the middle of the biggest pile of fighters, looking like he may have been knocked out by an actual fist instead of a sedative. At any rate, he was breathing fine but had a lump on his forehead that would make an impressive bruise the next day. The other medics back at base could handle any concussion damage.

"No more headbanging for you, young man," Hubcap quipped as he laid Xian out on the grass instead of on another human. "Or you either! Goodness, you all look a fright. I told your father that mush pot was a bad idea, but did he listen? Heavens, no! The man never does." Hubcap paused and thought, with a limp arm still held in his hand. "Is it mush pot or mosh pit? I always get those confused. Oh well, it's some form of human stupidity. Always trying to hurt yourselves, and I get to pick up the pieces. Pieces of you!" He pointed to an unconscious man who was missing teeth. "Keep track of your pieces, blast you!" He muttered away, lifting and pulling and checking vital signs. All of the idiot meatbags appeared tenderized but still functional.

"Thanks to me," he repeated.

"Heeey," called a faint human voice. "Anybody still alive back there?"

"Yeees," Hubcap replied. "Do you require assistance?"

"Yes please," said the voice, sounding relieved and female. Hubcap left the field strewn with sleeping meatheads and followed the voice, which turned out to be coming from a human he hadn't talked to before. She was quite some distance away, at the bottom of a muddy ravine, with two unconscious men at her feet.

"What ho," Hubcap said with a wave, looking down. "Are the gonads breathing?"

"If you mean these guys, yes," she said with a strained smile. Her brown hair was coming out of its ponytail, and she brushed it aside tiredly. "I don't think they even broke anything. Wanna help me get them back up there?"

"I would love to," Hubcap said, picking his way down the slope. "I would like nothing better than to lug two more humans across the landscape. This terrain will be a nice change of pace."

He slipped a little at the bottom, managing to turn it into an intentional slide. "Ta da!" he said, raising his arms at the dismount. "Which one first?"

"Doesn't matter," said the woman. She and the men wore the armor of conscripted locals rather than imported kneebreakers. "How about this one. Do you want me to get his feet, or would that not help at all?"

"Bah, I am robot; I am mighty! You just focus on getting your fleshy self up the hill without falling and breaking that neck you all prize so dearly."

"Yes sir," she said. "I'll be up there, then."

"Come, meathead," Hubcap addressed the first sleeping man. "We're going up the hill."

His feet sank much farther into the mud with the human in his arms, making his progress undignified and slow, but he managed. He didn't even topple forward and drop the guy.

"So what happened?" the woman asked from atop the slope as he approached, covered in mud. "Is everybody okay?"

"Everybody is breathing," he told her. "And that's the best that can be said. I think you three are the last to join the happy circle of snoring, which makes you the only fleshling to retain consciousness throughout this frenzy attack. I am most impressed."

She chuckled as he set down the man and went back for the other. "Thanks. I figure it's 'cause I got far enough away when the mess started."

"Ah, the tactical coward's retreat, then?" Hubcap asked from downslope. "A wise gambit for protecting your squishy self."

"It was not a retreat," she said with a stern smile. "I was chasing these guys. Fred here got the mad frenzy and took off after Vince, who was running like the wind. Somebody had to track them down before they ran off and died. Or killed each other."

Hubcap nodded as he lugged the man upward. "Ah, I see. A glorious victory then. Well done. You have won yourself bragging rights over every other meatbag in this lot. You should get your selection of mates."

"My what?" she laughed.

"Your pick of the herd," Hubcap said, dumping the second man next to the first. "Individuals who are heroic and impressive get to select any mate they choose, since all are in awe of their skills and virtues." He nodded. "That is how it works. I have done studies."

"…There's a little more to it than that," the human said. "Let's get these guys back to the others, and I'll see if I can explain it on the way."

Hubcap bent down to pick up the man again. "Nonsense, there is nothing more to explain. I have seen it many times, with your firefighters and other such heroic specimens. You will do well. Tell me, did you tackle them both at once, or one at a time?"

"I tagged Fred when he was trying to get — What *are* you doing? Do you want help?"

Hubcap draped the limp man across his shoulders. "Nonsense. I am robot."

"You are mighty. Right. And this is a creative way of — ah, carrying both. All right, then."

Hubcap got to his feet, balancing one human across his shoulders and one in his arms. He could barely reach the arms and ankles of the one on top.

"Yes. I am mighty. Onward!"

"Right this way." The woman went first, holding branches back for him, and he followed, leaving a trail of extra-deep footprints. "Here's hoping the radio signal is strong enough to reach base from here," she said. "I'd rather not have to hike all the way back."

"I can fly an aircar!" Hubcap said.

"Really."

"Probably. Given a moment of study."

"Uh huh. The real question is, do you want to lug all of these people carefully back to the cars, and get them strapped in, making sure any injuries don't get worse and no one wakes up screaming, with just the two of us to do it all?"

Hubcap regarded the human. "You make a fine point. Rescue vehicles it is."

"Good. Cuz I don't want to lug them around either."

"Yes, unconscious humans do get awkwardly floppy when they are lifted," Hubcap said, stepping around a fallen corkscrew tree. "It can be annoying. Someone else should definitely do it for us. We have handled the difficult part, and deserve to relax. After all of the meatbags are safely in the recovery pose. And arranged into conga lines for our amusement."

She laughed at that. "The CEO should be at the front."

"My thoughts exactly."

The woman shook her head as she walked. "I'll have quite the stories to tell when I get back to Earth. I'm glad I made it out of that one! Granted, I would have had good stories to tell in the afterlife, but even so. Here's to living for more!" She raised an arm in tired victory.

His own arms occupied, Hubcap could only look at her. He privately decided that there was a conversation he needed to have. Then he changed the subject.

"That is an admirable outlook," he told her. "You should indeed have your pick of mates. Might I recommend the eccentric redhead who is always followed adoringly by the camera people? He is prime breeding stock."

She made an awkward smile. "Sorry, but I like girls."

"Ah. That is unfortunate. Elliot has many girlish qualities, but he does not officially qualify. Perhaps one of our lovely camera ladies." He freed a hand to pat her on the head. "We'll set you up with a nice girl."

The human laughed. "Thanks, Dad."

"You are welcome," Hubcap said with dignity. "Then we will plan a lavish wedding… with pink and purple bows on everything… and human foods with frosting… and a conga line with people who are actually awake!" He rambled on in this vein as they navigated the forest, making the human laugh and the time pass much faster.

Chapter 45

Elliot woke to bright lights and a headache, lying on a stiff mattress in a very white room. He was at a loss about what had happened until he gingerly turned his head to the side, and found Hubcap sitting there with his hands full of yarn.

"Guh?" Elliot managed.

The robot beamed at him. "You live! Marvelous. I will make this into a stylish sling instead of a fancy tie. You will love it."

Elliot blinked, trying to focus on the mass of color. "It's pink."

Hubcap leveled a knitting needle at his face. "You will love it, I said."

"All right, fine, I'll love it." Elliot let his head roll back to center. "So, I remember some frenzy happening earlier," he said with false casualness. "How did the others do, then?"

"Oh, in typical foolish human fashion," Hubcap said, knitting away. "There were bruises aplenty, and meatheads in the plantlife, and running rabbits like you making life difficult."

"But did anyone *die*?" Elliot clarified. "Are they okay?"

"Okay enough, thanks to me," the robot said. "And one other unflappable human female. She was quite heroic, and should be getting her choice of mates now." He gazed down at Elliot with a grandmotherly expression. "I tried to set her up with you, but she is wired different and wouldn't have it. So we'll just have to find you a nice mate from somewhere else."

"Wait, what?" Elliot started to shake his head but thought better of it. "Why are we suddenly trying to find me a mate?"

Hubcap waved a hand. "So you can settle down, live the quiet life, and follow your biological urge to procreate. Or just spend time with a like-minded female for mutual squishy biological urges."

"Um. Thanks," Elliot said slowly. "No hurry there. I have plenty of other things to occupy my time right now. Speaking of which, do you know how long I'm supposed to be here?"

The robot raised a bedpan. "As long as it takes," he intoned. "I have been instructed to assist you with all manner of embarrassing fleshy things."

"Oh great," Elliot said. "I feel better already. In fact, I think I can go home right now. Thanks anyway!"

Hubcap set down the bedpan, unimpressed. "Touch your toes," he instructed, going back to his knitting.

Elliot tried. He lifted his head from the pillow, reached for his feet — one foot was in a cast and one in a sock — then everything hurt and he found himself curled on his side, never wanting to move again. "Ah!"

"Oh darn, I was hoping you would do some projectile vomiting," the robot said mildly. "That's always entertaining when I don't have to clean it up."

"Your bedside manner sucks," Elliot gasped, trying to straighten out.

"Yes, I know," Hubcap said. "I traded that bit of programming for a better knowledge of dirty limericks." He set down his knitting and began to recite. "There once was a man named Enis—"

"Stop that."

"Killjoy." Hubcap said, knitting needles clicking away.

"Where did you learn to do that, anyway?" Elliot asked, feeling like he had missed a substantial chunk of time.

"Here."

"When?"

"Half an hour ago."

"Why?"

"Because boredom is boring, and the lady in the next room felt like teaching me," Hubcap replied, still knitting. "Also, I think the nurses were getting tired of my artistic endeavors."

"Do I even want to know?"

"Probably not," Hubcap said. "At any rate, they took away the interesting stuff. And you just can't make a proper voodoo doll out of strained peas."

"I bet you can't," Elliot said. "So, how long have I been here?"

"Overnight," the robot told him. "You slept through the fun times of rescue car and long journey. But you did not poop yourself, so I am grateful for that."

"What? Why would I do that?"

"I don't know; you'll have to ask the smelly individuals who did," Hubcap said. "My guess is some fleshy mammal defense mechanism. If you are afraid, and there is a predator about to eat you, then you will be less appetizing if you smell like poo. Also, pooping makes you lighter, and thus better suited to running away at great rates of speed."

"I can tell you've put a lot of thought into this."

"Such things do go through your mind when you are busy scrubbing human stench from your pristine robot self."

A nurse poked his head through the door and told Hubcap that the communication lines were open for the call he'd requested.

The robot thanked him. "I'm on my way."

Elliot lifted his head again. "What call?" he asked. "Is it about the show?"

"No, unrelated," Hubcap assured him. "Don't worry your dented little head about it. The show is the most popular thing on the screens right now, and we're guaranteed many seasons of adventures. Space Fashion will be jealous forever. I will return soon, and tell you about everything you missed. Like my Pied Piper run through the compound."

"Your what? Don't leave me with that!" Elliot protested.

Hubcap just waved and left the room.

The nurse was lingering in the doorway, and thankfully he had some sort of answer for Elliot's questions. "Yeah, the scientists came up with something to clear the air of whatever causes the frenzy," he said. "Your pal there was running around everywhere with it earlier. I'm not sure how it works, but there haven't been any frenzy attacks indoors today."

Elliot bombarded the man with questions while Hubcap's footsteps tapped away down the hall.

* * *

Hubcap grinned to himself at Elliot's consternation, then turned his thoughts toward the conversation to come. It hadn't been simple to arrange, and he would be paying a chunk of salary to cover the transmission costs, but it seemed worth it. No one on this planet would have the answers he wanted.

In the same small room that Vic had used to call headquarters, Hubcap sat down in front of a screen and keyed in the connection number. The call took a few seconds to go through while the signal bounced between satellites and space stations. But it had been prearranged, and someone picked up on the other side. A face he hadn't seen in years appeared on the screen.

"Hubcap, old chum, it's been ages! How goes the excitement?"

The butler model looked unchanged, with perhaps a touch-up to his caucasian paint job. His black metal hair was as slick and stylish as ever. There was a splash of what might have been applesauce on his ear. The room behind him was full of sunlit walls and ritzy paintings.

Hubcap smiled. "Hey, Fishkicker. The excitement is mostly settled, though I shouldn't give anything away until those next episodes air."

"Oh, of course," Fishkicker said. "I've arranged a viewing party for the big one. The teaser segments are quite something! I must say, we're all very proud."

"Thank you," Hubcap said, without his usual bluster. "I try."

"Well, you most certainly succeed!" Fishkicker laughed. "A new alien race! And by the looks of it, you played a big part in their discovery!"

Hubcap nodded. "And in the frenzy solution. Has that hit the news yet? Never mind, I shouldn't tell."

"The what? Oh my. That is monumental! You'll have to tell me everything once the official channels have had their go at it."

"I'll make sure to call you," Hubcap promised.

Fishkicker wiped the applesauce off his ear with a handkerchief. "So why the call? I assume not to talk about world-shaking discoveries."

Hubcap gathered his thoughts. "I wanted your perspective on something," he said. "How many humans have you buried?"

The butler robot blinked. "Three generations," he said. "All good people, and all in their time. Why do you ask?"

Hubcap paused before answering. "How do you deal with it? Knowing that they'll keep dying while you continue on unchanged?"

A look of pity appeared on the butler's metal face. "My dear boy," he said gently. "Your programming didn't plan for this, did it? You were supposed to rescue strangers and never see them again. I was made to shepherd a specific set of humans through their entire lives, as long as they'd have me, with the knowledge that their lives would end but my service would not. There's always another generation."

Hubcap looked away. "I'm not serving a family," he said. "I have friends who can't be replaced. And I just met some new ones who I know I'll never see again. But I think I'm starting to get it. The new ones seem more at peace with the idea than most humans

I've known."

Fishkicker nodded. "Some people certainly are. They've done what they set out to do, in regard to career, or family, or experiences, and they can move on with a clear conscience."

Hubcap thought of the new clutches of eggs in the river. "That sounds about right."

"I've actually had a child express sympathy for me, if that makes it better."

Hubcap looked back. "What? Why?"

"Because I won't have children of my own, and I won't grow old in the company of a spouse." Hubcap made a static snort, and the butler laughed. "I know, that's not something that I'm hardwired to desire like most humans do. But that child did feel acutely sorry for me, and I imagine she would for you as well." Hubcap was silent while Fishkicker continued. "You asked for perspective; I give you Kabira-Marie, age nine. It's worth considering who's truly the fortunate one."

Hubcap breathed an electronic sigh. "Thanks," he said. "That does help. Now what's new back on good ol' Earth? What's everybody doing these days?"

They talked for a long time about the other robots who Fishkicker had mentored into human society, including many of Hubcap's fellow rescue bots. Some had pursued careers in off-planet exploration, while others had gone into construction. One was a metalworker. Three were animal control specialists. Five had stayed in search-and-rescue, though as contracted employees rather than tools. Only Hubcap had gone into television, though two others were making names for themselves in robotic sports.

There was much to talk about. It was only when Fishkicker's human family (including the thrower of applesauce) returned from their outing that they had to wrap up the call. Hubcap signed off in a better mood than he'd been in for some time. He walked back to the small hospital room on light feet.

Elliot was still waiting for more of an explanation. Hubcap obliged and went into detail about the faux-pheromones that the scientists had come up with overnight, and the swarm of invisible creatures that had gathered when he ran around the compound waving the sample like a torch.

"Then I threw it into the test chamber," he concluded. "And shut the door on that mess. I can't promise there's not a stray beastie hiding somewhere, but no sign of one yet."

"Fantastic." Elliot let his head drop back to the pillow, wincing and visibly regretting it. "So how do we keep more from getting in?"

Hubcap waved a hand. "The engineers are working with the science types to build better airlocks. They're hoping to make some sort of detection system so they can see the buggers, but that could take a while. I think they're doing autopsies on the dead aliens to figure out how they can sense them." He paused, fighting disapproval. "But, being dead, they shouldn't mind," he finally said.

"This will help a lot of people," Elliot said gently.

"Yes yes, we are grand saviors of humankind," Hubcap said, shaking it off. "Frenzy traps will be sold to all and sundry, and we will be hailed as conquering heroes. Especially once the government people finish all their scanning and interviewing, and agree that we did good by making friends with the aliens without disrupting their way of life."

Elliot gave him a sharp look. "Are they here now?"

Hubcap waved a hand. "Arrived last night. Even with the high-end scanning ships, they probably would have missed the underwater cities if we hadn't told them where to look." He shook his head, unimpressed.

A knock on the door preceded Vic into the room. She wore a concerned expression, and also a green floral-print shirt that was a striking amount of color compared to her usual work clothes. Today was a day for schmoozing instead of filming.

"How do you feel?" she asked Elliot.

"Could be worse," Elliot said with a weak smile. "Glad to be here, really."

The director nodded. "And we're glad you're here too. That was a dramatic end to your never-caught-frenzy streak." She rolled her eyes ever so slightly, to Hubcap's approval.

Elliot chuckled at himself. "Yeah, so that's what it's like. Can't say I recommend the experience."

"Just wait 'til the painkillers fade," Vic said with a wide grin. "The SedEgg marks itch." She reached up to tap over her own shoulder.

"Great." Elliot sank down on the bed. "That's something to look forward to."

Vic leaned against the doorframe, still smiling. "Well, the good news is that you may never catch frenzy again. We're getting it figured out, and it's pretty much agreed that the whole thing originated here."

"Really?" Elliot moved like he wanted to sit up. "For certain?"

Hubcap gave Vic his full attention.

"Yup!" she said. "This planet was settled ten years ago. How long has the mystery plague been ravaging ships and stations?"

"About ten years," Elliot beat Hubcap to it, voice soft with amazement. "So I guess some of the air creatures left the planet with the first ships?"

"Looks that way," Vic said. "They never made it to Earth because the quarantine filters there are legendary. Instead they've been surviving off humans in space, rather than their intended symbiotes."

"Wow," Elliot said, settling back. "We're going to be part of history in a big way."

Hubcap nodded. "Yes, and it's good that we got our footage before the overlords took over. It will be in high demand. We should be getting more money."

"Meaning we will?" Elliot said with a glance at Vic. "Or we just should?"

Vic waggled a hand. "Jury's still out. I'm working on it."

Hubcap inclined his head to its most arrogant angle. "They'll come around. We're worth a raise or five."

"I won't argue that," Elliot said.

"Now we just have to find you a nice mate," Hubcap replied.

"Not right now we don't," Elliot said. "What about you? Looking for a nice girl robot?"

Hubcap snorted. "You know better than that."

The human grinned. "Yeah I do. It's still a funny idea."

"Not as funny as your face," Hubcap said. "Hey, we should find nice mates for the camera crew too." He turned to Vic. "Do you think we could get good dowry money if we married Dale off? We could use it to hire a proper robotic camera handler."

Vic just shook her head.

Elliot groaned. "This conversation has gone in an absurd direction, and I hereby petition for a new one."

"All right," Vic said. "What's your opinion on the best name for the colortalkers? We haven't had a chance to ask them what they'd prefer, and the name that's getting a surprising amount of traction now is 'Mayfolk.'" She made disdainful finger quotes.

"What? May? Like merfolk of the spring?"

"No, like mayflies," Vic clarified. "Because they only live a day in their adult form, just like mayflies on Earth."

"I see," Elliot said. "I think I like 'colortalkers' better."

"I think they should be named after me," Hubcap suggested.

"That reminds me," Vic said, ignoring him completely. "I heard that there will be a crew of robots on the next shuttle, to help with whatever this station turns into — maybe just a jetpod harvesting operation, for trading with the colortalkers. There will also be swarms of human professionals, of course: diplomats, biochemists, ecologists. Even some linguistic specialists to study that color language and knot-tying writing. But there will definitely be a good number of robots."

"As it should be!" Hubcap exclaimed, hands in the air.

"Oh good!" Elliot said at the same time. "That's been a long time in coming."

"Yes, and it is all thanks to me," Hubcap said with a hand to his chest. "None of you human types died of frenzy while I've been here. Or of anything else that I could prevent."

"Well done, you," Elliot told him.

"Yes, well done me. You helped, of course. As did the others."

Vic smiled. "How gracious of you."

Elliot waved a hand like a conductor. "I'm sure there will be parades in your honor. What would we do without you?"

"Probably die foaming at the mouth," Hubcap said. "Up a tree, head stuck in a knothole. Pooping your pants in terror."

"You paint quite the picture," Elliot said with a tolerant smile.

"Don't I though?" Hubcap asked. "I am an impressive weaver of words. I should be a storyteller on the rooftops, with my dulcet tones echoing out over the landscape for all to hear and appreciate. It would be glorious."

"I'm sure it would," Elliot said. "What else could you ever want to do with your new status as Robot Beloved By All?"

"Pssh, that's not new," Hubcap said.

Someone called for Vic from the hallway, and she left with a promise to return with updates.

The door closed. Hubcap picked up his knitting. "What I do want to do," he told Elliot, "Is get my trustworthy hands on a translation device of my own, to go out and socialize with the natives some more." He broke into a grin. "And I get to, since the swimmers won't raise their heads above water for anyone but me."

Elliot shook his head. "Try not to abuse your power," he said as Hubcap let out a maniacal cackle.

"Oh, I'll set them up with Owen soon enough," Hubcap said,

relaxing in his chair. "I don't want to be stuck here forever, and he'll make a fine spokesperson, along with ProudLee and whatever alien experts get posted here. They can set up trade agreements with all the towns, in properly respectful fashion."

"Respectful, yes. Unlike other people we could name."

"Oh, guess what!" Hubcap told him. "Scuttlebutt says Bhandari the Blowhard is getting fired! Or, y'know, forcibly retired."

Elliot nodded in approval. "Exciting developments all around."

"Oh yes. This is quite the place to be! I'm sure we'll be hustled off sooner than we'd like, but as long as I get to swim through the underwater town first, I'll call it a win."

"That does sound like fun," Elliot said.

Hubcap patted the convalescing human on the arm. "I will bring you along as soon as you are done being broken."

"Thanks," Elliot said, gazing at the cast. "It'll be a while."

"Oh, not all that long. I'm sure the aliens will find a wheelchair fascinating."

Elliot looked at Hubcap in surprise. "What, you're not going to insist I stay in bed until all my fleshy injuries are healed?"

"Why waste time?" Hubcap said. "If someone who lives only a day above water can enjoy life, so can you. It's just a broken ankle and a concussion. And various cuts. And spectacular bruises. You know, nothing serious."

Elliot cocked his head at his friend. "Does this mean you'll be harping at me less to be careful I don't break my fragile self?"

"Oh no, I'll still do that," Hubcap said. "You are sadly frail, lacking all the benefits of a wonderful robot body like my own. But I see no reason for that to ruin the fun."

"Well, all right then," Elliot said with a slow smile. "I can live with that."

"Yes, we will go out and see the sights in your wheelchair," Hubcap said. "I will try not to push you across too many rocks on the way to the underwater city. We will explore this exciting alien world, and I will protect you from the dangers of the now less-mysterious space frenzy."

"And I'll protect you from the dangers of modesty."

"Darn right," Hubcap said. "That stuff's to be avoided at all costs."

Acknowledgements

I'll be forever grateful to my husband for his support, encouragement, and late nights sharing story ideas.

Big thanks to the members of my online writers' circle, who are an endless source of knowledge, commiseration, and positivity. There are far more friendly and helpful people around than I could ever name, though I'm particularly grateful to Ark Horton, Katherine Shaw, Jayme Bean, Astrid Knight, and Chapel Orahamm.

While I'm at it, thanks also to David M. Simon, C. J. Henderson, Debbie Iancu-Haddad, Emily Ansell, Craig Rathbone, D.S. Levey, Pan D. MacCauley, S. L. Parker, Jesse Lynton, Dewi Hargreaves, Peter Linton, and Alfred Smith. Thank you to Stephanie Stone for some excellent constructive criticism. And thanks to everybody else who's been even tangentially helpful in getting this off the ground.

Mara Lynn Johnstone grew up in a house on a hill, of which the top floor was built first. She split her time between climbing trees, drawing fantastical things, reading books, and writing her own. Always interested in fiction, she went on to get a Master's Degree in creative writing, and to acquire a husband, son, and three cats. She has published three books and many short stories. She still writes, draws, reads, and enjoys climbing things. She can be found up trees, in bookstores, lost in thought, and at:

Website: MaraLynnJohnstone.com
Twitter: @MarlynnOfMany
Tumblr: @MarlynnOfMany
Facebook: facebook.com/AuthorMara